MAFIOSO
PART 7: And Then There Were None.

NISA SANTIAGO

This is a work of fiction. The characters, organizations, and events portrayed in this novel are either the author's imagination or used fictitiously.

Mafioso 7: And Then There Were None. Copyright © **2022** by Melodrama Publishing. All rights reserved. No part of this book may be used or reproduced in any manner whatsoever without written permission except for brief quotations embodied in critical articles or reviews. For information, address info@melodramabooks.com

ISBN: **978-1620781296**
LCCN: **2022916590**

First Edition: **April 2023**

MAFIOSO – And Then There Were None!

One MAFIOSO
Who's about that life
Went roaming through his hood
Looking for his wife

But low and behold
Scott found three
Ignited a lifelong beef
A tangled web he weaved

Four MAFIOSOS
All seemingly in love
Three with the same man
So, push came to shove

Four MAFIOSOS
And things get loud
They slap and punch
Because four's a crowd

Four MAFIOSOS
And Sandy got knocked up
Layla murders Sandy
But Maxine got locked up

Four MAFIOSOS
Now we're down to two
Sandy is buried
And trial Maxine blew

Two MAFIOSOS
Dem babies make eight
Maxine is now Max
Controlling her enemy's fate

Eight MAFIOSOS
Until there were five
Max is seeking revenge
She wants no one alive

Five MAFIOSOS
Now here comes the feds
Franklin shows no mercy
Lucky's presumed dead

Two MAFIOSOS
Maybe two shall survive
Scott, Layla, Bugsy, Meyer
Or is no one left alive?

CHAPTER 1

Layla tossed and turned before sitting up in bed. She removed her face mask and stared down at her husband. Scott slept face-up, a position she hated because it reminded her of a dead body in a casket. He was a sound sleeper, didn't snore, and always got his full eight hours. As her eyes adjusted in the dark, she wondered why she couldn't sleep. Something was off—she could feel it. An eerie, ominous feeling had seeped into her psyche, and her heart was beating irregularly.

Was she having a stroke? Whatever this was—she didn't like it. Layla didn't bother putting slippers on her bare feet as she walked through her home. Her mother's intuition was pulling her to her children's rooms. Of course, her first stop was Meyer. Without knocking, she opened his door and was shocked to see a female's ass crack. The unknown woman was naked, body draped over her sons, and both were asleep.

Layla made a mental note to curse his ass out in the morning for bringing one of his hood rats to her home. That's what hotels were used for. In this game, you never let outsiders know where you rest your head. Meyer knew better. Something was going on with her son that was fucking up his brain cells, and since she's only caught him smoking weed, with no signs of cocaine or intravenous drug use—she was stumped.

Bugsy's room was next to Meyer's. She went to push it open, but the lil' nigga had it locked like he paid bills around this bitch. It took a few minutes to retrieve the key, and she walked in. He, too, slept face-up like his father. His hand gripped a 9mm, clearly implying he still didn't trust his parents. Layla smiled. *He was the smart one.* She and her husband were capable of anything—but now all she wanted was peace.

The last room was Lucky's. Layla twisted the doorknob, and it was unlocked. So why hadn't she walked in? Layla's whole body was involuntarily shaking, and a cold chill washed over her. *What was she afraid of?* Was she not Layla West? Killer. Queenpin. A street legend in her own right. Her name had been circulating for decades; she's put in work. Layla inhaled the air and held it briefly before taking a long breath. She called "Lucky" in a low whisper before pushing the solid wood door open. And there it was—a perfectly made bed and nothing more.

Lucky was gone.

She repeated, "Oh my god! Oh my god! Oh my god!!" The chant started as a whisper and escalated to full-blown hysteria. Martha looked at the crimson-colored blood pooling around Lucky's head and lost it.

"My god! What have you done?!" she shrieked, her face awash with tears. "You killed her!"

Her accusations were directed at her thirteen-year-old son, Junior. The smoking pistol still gripped tightly in his teenaged hand. Neither father nor son could take their eyes off the dead female lying face-up on the kitchen floor; her face was frozen. The copper smell of blood permeated their nostrils and lungs before Martha yelped again— "Do something!"—and snapped Franklin out of his daze.

"Both of you, take all your clothes off and leave them in a pile. And then go and take a shower. Don't come back downstairs until I say so. Understand?"

"What do you mean?" she asked. "You're not going to call this in?"

Franklin stood to his feet to look his wife squarely in her eyes. She was always cunning, thinking six moves ahead. Martha knew what this was, and, more telling, what he had done to Lucky. The only person who completely walks is her, and she was ready to sacrifice her son. Martha would gamble with their son's future if it exposed her husband. Her calculating brain had probably deduced that Junior wouldn't be charged as this was a clear case of self-defense. The trending tagline was, *I felt threatened.*

Franklin—on the other hand—wouldn't be as lucky. Since the early nineties, he had been robbing drug dealers and stashing his ill-gotten gains in a shed at his in-laws. And his wife knew all about it. *And* his numerous affairs.

With Lucky West murdered on their floor, his hands' prints painted around her throat, the sex tape and baby would open an investigation. The bureau wouldn't protect him. And if she gave testimony against him, he would lose everything. Martha had that *Beautiful Mind* brain; the only caveat was that her husband knew this.

Eye to eye, he said, "Let's focus on Junior. When he's squared away, we'll discuss calling authorities—you and I, together. This should fall on the parent, not the child. It's not his fault. Do you agree?"

She nodded.

Franklin, careful not to step in Lucky's blood, walked to the sink and grabbed a dish towel. He then took the smoking gun from his son's grip and wiped his fingerprints. He said, "Junior. Take off all your clothes where you stand."

"Right here, dad?"

Franklin nodded.

"But mom's here."

"Don't worry about mom. She won't look."

Martha and Franklin's eyes met again as their son began removing articles of clothing. *What was he thinking?* She wanted to know. What did *this should fall on the parent* mean? Was he really going to call the cops and confess to murder? That would be interesting.

When Junior was entirely naked, he hurriedly exited the kitchen to his room to shower.

"We have to get our stories straight," Franklin coached as soon as they were alone. "Junior's not getting wrapped up in our mess."

"Our mess?" she spat. "As long as I've known you, you've never taken full responsibility for your actions. It's always someone else's fault for why you do things. If criminals didn't sell drugs, then you wouldn't rob them. You're the good guy, right Franklin?"

Franklin was calm. He said, "Look. It's been a traumatic afternoon. Emotions are high right now—"

"Ya think?" Her voice dripped with sarcasm. "Your pregnant, drug-dealing mistress is dead on my kitchen floor, and it's *your* fault! Not *our* goddamn fault. Yours! Am I making myself clear?!"

His head moved in agreement.

She continued, "And I never asked you to steal any of that money over the years or anything else. That was all you!"

Again, Franklin nodded. Martha continued her rant, and mid-sentence, her husband said, "Hold this for a second."

Instinctively, Martha reached for the pistol he held with the rag; but paused. A huge grin swept across her thinly shaped lips. She was nobody's fool. Their eyes locked aggressively.

"You tried it," she accused. "You may get away with your antics when going up against the underworld but remember who used to cheat off whom in university. My mother taught me that if I can't marry rich and established, then I should marry less intelligent than me but ambitious. I did the latter."

The smug look on this bitch's face had pressed all Franklin's buttons. Martha continued, "What? You thought I was the only one being used? That I was your token white woman to help you get into social circles and climb the success ladder. I used your Black ass too!" She boasted. Her words felt like Lingchi. It's Chinese torture, a slow death, where you're sliced with a thousand cuts until you bleed out.

"Look at me, Franklin!" Martha laughed like she was at a dinner party and heard something funny. "I'm a solid three, possibly a four in everybody's eyes except a Black man. You made me feel like a ten. Do you think I could get a rich white man going against the Gisele's of the world? I had to get what I could, and that was you!"

If Martha felt like she was venturing into dangerous territory, she didn't show it. She just kept digging the hole that was sinking their marriage.

"You're an eight unilaterally. That crossover, Barack Obama eight, and you settled for a three. You snatched up the first white girl you could and never looked back. And I went along for the ride for more than half my life. I have a beautiful home, two luxury vehicles, half your pension, and let's not forget that blood money is also half mine. I want you out, Franklin! Pack your shit tonight." Martha's eyes quickly scanned the rooms, taking inventory of the home she'd finally have for herself. She would even be willing to have Junior live with Franklin once he was settled. A boy needs a man, and father and son are practically twins. Apparently, Franklin had strong African American genes—she saw very little of herself in her son.

Martha's eyes swept over her open-concept kitchen and landed on Lucky. "And get this bitch off my kitchen floor!"

After hearing all that, Franklin had to quiet the rage that was bubbling inside. She hadn't said anything he didn't already know. Yet hearing the truth spoken so casually had raised his blood pressure.

"You want me to leave now...shortly after our son murdered someone. Do you know how selfish and irrational you sound? And let's not forget while you're up on your culpability tour— you were screaming, *'kill her!'* And our son did. So, like I said, *our* mess."

"I wanted *you* to kill her. And since you couldn't do that, you just killed our marriage. I'm done!"

Franklin lunged at his wife, and she shrieked in horror before she turned to run. But he was too quick, tackling her to the ground. His knee pressed firmly into her back—an arrest maneuver, while he bent her wrists behind her. His total body weight controlled her, and she felt fucked.

"Please don't hurt me," she began. "We can work something out. I'm your wife, Franklin! And the mother of your *only* child."

He said nothing.

Martha began to whimper. She could no longer separate the man she married from the man he'd become—sadistic, greedy, merciless. Martha could see her husband's dead mistress from her peripheral and wondered if she was moments away from the same fate.

"Please, no, Franklin. I'm sorry! I'm so-o-o sorry, honey. You know how much I love you. I would never speak of this to anyone, ever. I was jealous of...*her!* And acting emotionally."

Franklin was on a mission, which didn't include listening to her bullshit. He took her fingers and wrapped them around the gun handle and trigger. Once he had enough of her prints on the murder weapon, he stood up, releasing her. Martha gasped for air in an overly dramatic way, flipping on her back, clutching her throat.

Franklin placed the gun in a Ziploc and spat, "We got shit to do."

The Four Seasons luxury hotel on E. Delaware Place with the doorman, concierge, and valet was an upgrade she could get used to. The three-hour flight—in first class—was just the beginning of what he promised would be an exceptional trip. Elliot, her new beat, had shown her more love in the brief moment they were together than the whole time she'd spent with Meyer.

They'd met when he and his friends drunkenly stumbled into Chaos, where she was dancing, and when she finished her set on stage, he'd instantly sobered up. Their eyes locked, and Lollipop sauntered over and asked if he wanted a private dance in the Champagne room.

"How much for your time?" he asked.

Her eyes rolled — "Goodbye!"— and she spun around.

Elliot stepped forward and gripped her forearm. The nasty look she shot over her shoulder told him that was a bad idea. Releasing his grip, he explained, "I meant to talk. I know you're working...and this is a strip club." He smiled sheepishly. "By the way, I'm Elliot. Elliot McDonald."

Lollipop's night was almost over, having worked an eight-hour stretch, but she charged the stranger $700 for a two-hour cap. He impressed her when he pulled out ten large and said, "Let's go."

The two walked the city, stopping in eateries for tapas or drinks, window shopping on 5th avenue, and then strolling through Central Park. That was four months ago, and they were seemingly inseparable.

Now they were here. Elliot had flown her into The Windy City to meet his parents; she was sure he would propose this weekend.

Riley, her government, was the only name she now answered to. With Elliot's encouragement, she quit stripping and was opening a shoe boutique. He helped her with all the paperwork, branding, and incorporation while covering all her bills for the past couple of months. His entrance into her life had prompted Meyer's exit. Riley sent Meyer to voicemail, didn't return his missed calls, and deleted countless messages. Yes, she missed her dude, but Elliot had made offers she couldn't refuse.

Truth be told, Riley wasn't in love with Elliot. She could have easily changed her cell number, but that would make things final. Her heart still belonged to Meyer, but she'd say yes if Elliot proposed this weekend. She had to. Riley needed to move on, and Meyer made it clear that she wasn't good enough for him. He wanted classy when she was sassy; he wanted a good girl, and she was a bad *gal*; Meyer wanted a fling, which she wanted forever.

"So. How do I look?" she asked. Riley had squeezed into a lemonade-colored Marchesa dress with black Manolo Blahniks and a matching clutch. She had a shape women nowadays bought—that homegrown cornbread and collard green curves. Of course, she got it from her mama, but she maintained it in the gym four times a week.

Elliot's grin was broad. He whistled, then said, "You lookin' too cute, Riley. I don't know if I should let you meet the homies."

"You so silly," she grinned.

Elliot slapped her on her phat ass before enveloping her from behind. He inhaled her perfume and then planted a couple of wet kisses on her neck.

He said, "You ready?"

Riley glanced into the mirror and replied, "I am."

The weekend was planned. Tonight, Riley would meet his childhood friends for dinner. Elliot would take her to his parent's home tomorrow for brunch and sightseeing. And finally, dinner at the Four Seasons with friends and family on Sunday, where she suspected he would propose.

The two slid into the back seat of the car service the concierge had called for them, and Elliot gave the address to Momma Luigi's. Riley rambled on about her new business, her excitement over meeting his peoples, and how nervous she was to meet his parents.

All he kept repeating was that they would love her. After nearly half an hour on the highway, she asked, "Where are we going? West Bublefuck?"

"No. It's not that much farther."

"They should have just come to us. There are a million places to eat by the hotel."

Elliot nodded. "I know. But I wanted this trip to be special. The place we're going is where my friends and I always went after each football game we played in high school, and the food is so good."

Riley shrugged.

The Italian restaurant didn't look like much and wasn't in the greatest part of town. It looked mom-and-pop-ish, but Riley tried not to judge. She was a little miffed that she'd wasted this dress and heels just to come here when jeans and a sexy shirt would have worked.

When they walked in, his friends were already seated; both stood to greet Riley.

"Hi, I'm Malcolm."

She nodded. "Riley."

Malcolm looked to be in his late fifties but said he was thirty-two. To Riley, he had that *older man trying to hold onto their youth* vibe. Malcolm wore an Adidas sweat suit with matching sneakers, an expensive watch, and a chain. She would bet her life that his hair was dyed a store-bought black, and he had the man-weave fade you could now get at any local barbershop—dyed mustache and beard completed his look. Malcolm looked old enough to be her daddy's daddy. Perhaps he had a hard childhood, most likely harder than most if it aged him. Malcolm's features were straight from the Motherland and not in a good way. His eyes and smile felt disconnected, as if the windows to his soul had betrayed what he was trying to convey.

Another hand extended, and she heard, "Nice to meet you, Riley. I'm Steve."

"Nice to meet you as well."

Steve said he was Elliot's age, thirty. He had reddish-brown skin, fiery red hair, freckles, broad nose, full pink lips, and shifty eyes. His mustache connected to his goatee, and his soft, coily hair was in the beginning stage of a low afro. He wore a cream-colored tailored suit, alligator shoes that worked best in the '90s, and cufflinks.

At first, it was a little awkward that she was the only female. She'd assumed this would be date night, but both friends quickly claimed they had no attachments when asked.

Elliot was right—the food was delicious. Riley ordered jumbo shrimp and linguini with garlic, basil sauce, buttered garlic bread, and Merlot. She gave no fucks about her breath. This food was good. And the way the owners treated Elliot and his friends like they were important people was impressive. She understood why he'd taken her there.

After dinner, Malcolm tossed the keys to his Maserati to Elliot. "I'ma ride back with Steve. I'll pick it up on Sunday. You and your lady enjoy your weekend."

Riley's eyes scanned the sleek vehicle, and she nodded her approval. *Meyer has one of these,* she thought. And as soon as she thought of him, her cell rang. She looked down at the number, glanced at Elliot and his friends mid-conversation, and answered.

"What?" she snapped. She hadn't picked up for him in months. And she wasn't sure why she did now. Perhaps it was because she was feeling herself, maybe it was because she had a new nigga, or because she thought in less than forty-eight, she'd have a massive rock on her finger.

"Yo…shit fucked up. Lucky's missing."

Her eyes rolled. This family kept the melodrama going. "Why are you calling me Meyer?"

"I'm scared, Lollipop. My fuckin' sister…is gone."

There was something in his voice that made her heart hitch. She expected to hear him cursing her out for ghosting him for so long. Promises and threats, or a mixture of many lies with a grain of truth—anything to get her back in his bed for a night or two. Instead, Riley heard *fear,* and Meyer didn't fear shit.

Lollipop was ready to cut this muthafuckin' trip short and run to her man. Her eyes cut to Elliot, his friends, and then Momma Luigi's. Her future was twenty feet away. All she had to do was stay the course, pivot away from her past.

Meyer didn't love her. His actions said what words could not. Riley finally spoke.

"Meyer, don't call me anymore. I'm engaged, and my new beat ain't here for it."

She exhaled a long-winded release. Riley wanted to burst into tears and cry, but she couldn't. She disconnected her call and powered down her phone. Her energy shifted as she stood in five-inch heels waiting for Elliot to wrap up his conversation.

Riley was now in a foul mood and could only blame her corny, hard-working, not *Meyer West* boyfriend.

Why am I with him? She thought. He had no swag, could barely fuck, and bored her to tears.

Finally, Elliot ambled over, none the wiser of the emotional turmoil she was experiencing.

"You ready?"

She snapped. "I been ready!"

He looked down at her feet and assumed he knew where her discomfort stemmed from.

"All right," he said, shoving the key fob in her hand.

"What's this?"

"I'm fucked up. I need you to drive us back."

"I was drinking too," she protested. "And I don't know where the fuck we are...take this key, Elliot. I don't want to drive!"

Riley had never been this assertive with him, but it is what it is. Her eyes were wild, and she had to swallow the vile taste in her mouth that had crept up. Meyer was gone. It was over. She'd just told him so. She wanted to throw up these past four months and return to ground zero.

Elliot stuffed his hands in his suit pants pockets. "What's up? What's going on with you?"

"What do you mean?"

"Who were you on the phone with?"

"What?" she repeated, stalling for time. And then shouted, "My mother!"

"And she got you behaving like this?"

"Look, I'm just ready to go."

He nodded. "I'll program the hotel in the navigation."

CHAPTER 2

The twins' walked in on their parents, having an epic argument. Their loud voices could be heard outside their apartment, reaching penthouse tenants exiting the elevators. Numerous noise complaints were made to the building's concierge and security. Still, no one on the building's staff wanted to knock on the door of the building's most notorious tenants.

Layla looked a hot mess. The sun had risen and set twice, and she was still in her pajamas, hair uncombed, body uncleaned—no sleep. It had been two days since Layla walked into Lucky's empty room and went into full panic mode. Every few hours, she would call each borough's morgues, hospitals, precincts, and courts, looking for her daughter—an exhaustive and worrisome task.

"Why are you working yourself up?" Scott wanted to know.

"Are you dumb?" Layla hollered. "Our fuckin' daughter is gone, Scott. She's been missing for days, and I'm telling you that Red Negro did something to her!"

Calmly, Scott replied, "Let's agree to disagree."

There was a pregnant pause before Layla asked, "What do you know? If you know something nigga spit it out!"

Scott had just come from his cardio workout at the gym and grabbed a Gatorade Zero from the refrigerator. He, too, was concerned about Lucky's absence but for different reasons. Scott took several gulps of his beverage, quenching his thirst before addressing the issue.

"I agree that she's with that fed, Ragnar...or whatever his government is. But I also believe she left of her own volition."

"Meaning?"

"Meaning she's snitching."

Layla roared, her voice a husky baritone that traveled from her core. She spewed, "There's no fuckin' way that girl is a snitch! Why? For what reason, Scott?"

"She's pregnant, bitch! For Lucky, that's enough!"

"You're one stupid muthafucka if you think that! Lucky didn't want that baby any more than she wanted a cold. She's attracted to conflict, controversy, and melodrama—the *idea* of being a mother. No way is she sneaking out of her home with nothing into the arms of a fed over a baby, Scott!"

"That's exactly what she did!" Scott admonished. He and Mason had already discussed Lucky's disappearance, and both arrived at the same conclusion. In fact, Mason had predicted this would happen months ago when they were in Dubai when he called Scott with intel on Uriel and Jacqueline.

"Scott, you better find that red nigga and kill him—"

"That's still a priority!" Scott barked. "And don't tell me how to run my business—"

"Our business nigga! You built this business off work I put in."

Scott gave an amused chuckle that infuriated his wife. He took another sip of his drink. He didn't want to go off on a different tangent, so he ignored her statement and focused on

Lucky. Scott said, "We need to ruminate about impending indictments, our front door being kicked open, and wiretaps. Because I feel in my gut that our daughter ain't missing!"

Before Layla could erupt again, Meyer and Bugsy, who up until now stood watching their parents like a Netflix series, spoke up.

Meyer said, "Pops, I gotta ride with Ma on this. I think something happened to Lucky. She's missing."

Scott glared at his son. "Meyer speaking to you is like talking to your mother. Y'all act alike and think with one brain."

"What about me, though?" Bugsy asked calmly. "I don't think my sister left on her own accord. I'll admit that we do strange things for love, but what Lucky and Ragnar had going on wasn't that; she knew it. You gotta remember, Pops...this the same dude that posted a porn video to the gram. You think Lucky ran into his arms and betrayed us over him? No fucking way. She thought she had a plan to save us *from* him. What changed?"

Hearing Bugsy break it down gave Scott pause, but he didn't want to fold so easily. "So, if she isn't cooperating with the feds over love and a baby, there's self-preservation. We all know the methods the feds used to get convictions against us. They locked you up, Bugsy. You got an active case right now. They sent two undercover agents after me and your mother, who followed us worldwide. They froze all y'all assets, leaving you without adequate counsel. Am I missing anything?"

"But this is Lucky, Scott. Your daughter who grew up in this life," Layla remarked, her voice softening. "Would she really flip?"

"If any one of us is capable of being flipped," Scott snorted. "It's Lucky."

Scott's assessment was enough to reignite the argument, prompting Bugsy to head back out the front door. Meyer grabbed a can of grape soda, cough syrup, and Jolly Ranchers. He needed an escape.

Body disposal and cover-up were two main reasons people got caught when they murdered someone they had a history with. Martha grabbed house towels to soak up the blood that had coagulated, but Franklin stopped her.

"Paper towels, bleach, and use plastic gloves and bags. I'll have to burn it all once we're done."

"Burn it? Where?"

"Don't worry about that. I'll find a place."

"What will you do with her?"

He shrugged. Franklin didn't have a clue. The question had him stumped. They were genuinely fucked if he didn't figure this out. As his mind searched for solutions, Lucky's phone began vibrating, and that's when he panicked. He fell to his knees and dug her burner from her jeans. It was a local New York area code, and the person called back-to-back but didn't leave a message. When the phone finally stopped buzzing, Franklin pulled out the sim card and tried to slow his heart rate.

He ran to the window and looked out. His eyes darted frantically up and down his block. *Who was out there? Was someone waiting for her? How did she get there?*

"Franklin, what's wrong? Is someone coming? Are we in danger?"

"Martha be quiet!" he snapped. "Let me think."

Franklin took the carpeted stairs up to his bedroom two at a time to retrieve his weapon. Without thought, his fingers punched the code to his gun safe with muscle memory. The Glock was tucked securely into his waistband, and he made his way downstairs and circled back to the kitchen. Once again, he rifled through Lucky's pockets and retrieved a rental car key.

Lucky had transitioned into a corpse that had now become an object, like a bowling ball or golf clubs—they could move her about without feeling repulsed or remorse.

"I'm going to clear the block to ensure she arrived alone. And I'll have to move her car from around here. It'll trace back to us."

Martha cringed each time he said *us, we,* or *our,* but she knew that she, too, had a lot to lose with her husband's fingerprint stunt. It was a smart play. With her fingerprints on the weapon, she'd never convince anyone her federal agent husband set her up to take the fall for his mistress's murder.

"How long will you be?"

"I'm going to drive her vehicle to the south side of the roundabout near the park. There aren't any cameras back there, and then I'll cut through and make my way to Bradley's house and pick up Junior's game. So, if there's ever a question of why I'm over there, I'll have one. It shouldn't be more than forty minutes. Close all the blinds, keep the doors locked, and keep Junior in his room." He paused with an afterthought. "Don't fuck me on this, Martha, or you'll regret it."

The red and blue lights lit up in her rear and side-view mirrors. Without thought, her eyes scanned her speedometer. She was doing the speed limit.

"Elliot, wake up," she said. "Elliot!"

"I'm up," he replied, trying to focus. "What's up?"

"I'm being pulled over."

"For what?"

She shrugged. "I don't know. I wasn't speeding." Riley hit

her right blinker as she spoke and slowed to a complete stop on the highway's shoulder.

"Pass me the registration," she said, and it didn't escape him that her voice trembled.

"Relax, Riley. You good. You didn't have as much to drink as me—"

"But I *was* drinking," she snapped. "That's why I said I didn't want to drive."

"You could have said no."

"I did!"

Riley could see both officers exiting their vehicle and proceeding with a slow yet cautious walk toward them. The officer on the passenger's side unclipped a flashlight on his hip and illuminated the front seats, nearly blinding them.

Riley rolled down her window and waited for instruction.

In a sour voice, she heard, "Do you know how fast you were going?"

She nodded. "Yes, sir. About sixty?"

"No, ma'am. You were going over seventy in a fifty-five."

Riley's head shook rapidly. She read his nametag. "Officer Peterson, I wasn't going that fast. I kept checking my speedometer, so I know…that's…not right!"

Her voice's octave was higher than necessary, but the fact that she didn't want to drive in a strange car and an unknown city had her irked.

The officer ignored her remark. "License and registration."

Begrudgingly she opened her clutch and retrieved her wallet. At the same time, Elliot fiddled around in the glove compartment and flipped down each visor. His voice was low, and he whispered, "It's not here. The registration…I don't have it."

Their eyes locked. Shit was about to go left.

Her voice lightened, "Here's my license. And if you'll allow my boyfriend to call his friend and ask where's the registration that would be great because we can't find it."

"Step out of the car, please," was her instruction.

"Me?" she shrieked. "For what?"

Guns were drawn, and a seemingly routine stop quickly escalated.

The officer forcefully repeated his command. "Both of you! Out of the car! Now!"

"Do as he said," Elliot whispered while holding his hands in surrender. His posture was stiff, rigid as he eyed the officer, not wanting to as much as blink, thinking that movement would ignite a flurry of bullets.

The officer on Elliot's passenger's door opened it and took several steps back. At the same time, his police-issued firearm was locked onto Elliot's chest cavity.

Both were subsequently frisked, handcuffed, and sat on the ground a few feet from an active highway. Not many cars were passing for now, but it was still dangerous.

Riley watched as Officer Peterson retrieved the key fob and was about to pop the trunk.

"You can't open my trunk," she said. "Not without probable cause." She didn't know what prompted her to go there, but she knew it was what Meyer would have said. Only Elliot wasn't her last man, nor did he do shady things as her last man did. Riley needed to relax. But she couldn't. She was hunched over on the nasty pavement, wrists cuffed behind her back, and her new Manolos' had gotten scuffed.

Her statement paused Peterson's movement. "Are you a lawyer?"

"Nope!"

"Good. Because I would have said that your alma mater owes you a refund." He walked aggressively toward her and continued, "Your back brake light is out, you were swerving between lanes, *and* I smell marijuana inside your car."

"That ain't my car!" she retorted.

"But you just said it was."

Before she could spew her rebuttal, Elliot spoke. "Riley, just be quiet and let them search so we can get out of here. Whatever ticket you get, you know I'll handle it. This is race related and petty."

Her eyes rolled, and then she reluctantly nodded.

While this exchange was happening, the second officer found a firearm under the passenger's seat.

"What do we have here," he sang. "I call this probable cause."

But when Officer Peterson popped the trunk, pulled out a black nylon duffel, and revealed the contents—her life flashed before her eyes.

Peterson whistled and then said, "Gotcha!"

The walkie-talkie crackling cut through the night's quiet aggressively. The assailant on the other end spoke in a rushed whisper, relaying his current situation. "All good on my end. No movement."

"Yo, nigga. Only hit me if something pops off!" he barked.

Whistler was finally putting the arsenal of stolen weaponry to use. He was back in Delaware, lying in the cut for some broad to come through. At least that was the intel he had received from the lil' young nigga up the block. A-God, twenty-seven, was the uncle of the unsuspecting thirty-one-year-old dealer, Isaiah.

Isaiah had just graduated from hand-to-hand and was now moving bricks, making a name for himself. He had several baby mamas—too many to count and treated them like disposable razors. Isaiah was a pretty boy with good dick, a lethal combination for the ladies. His uncle, A-God, was the quintessential jealous-hearted nigga who hated to see his nephew rise to the top if he wasn't along for the free ride.

A-God was one of the dudes who couldn't look Whistler in his face when he walked the blocks out of fear, but soon he began nodding when Whistler passed by. That gesture morphed into salutations and a lengthy conversation about robbing Isaiah.

"He should have at least a couple ki's," A-God enthusiastically offered up. "And some bread. You go in there, clean. He won't resist, and we split shit."

Home invasion was in Whistler's wheelhouse and just what he needed. Streets say you don't go to war unless your money's right, and he needed more than anger and rage to go up against Scott.

Isaiah and A-God had spoken less than an hour ago. Isaiah told his uncle he was waiting for a sex worker he ordered from Craigslist. Isaiah had his pick of women but was finding it harder to get no-attachment sex. They all wanted more.

The Camry's speed decreased after the driver made the righthand turn onto Linden Place before pulling into an open spot. The woman inside paid the Uber driver before exiting. Whistler was hiding in plain sight with nothing more than a Chestnut Oak tree to camouflage. Dressed in all black, he watched the female pull down her short dress that barely covered her ass. She then fluffed up the hair on her lace front wig, exhaled, and strolled toward the front door of the rental home.

Isaiah opened the door before the girl could knock, which threw off Whistler's timing. He had to bolt up the steps, ramming his body weight into the woman's back, which sent her flying forward. Isaiah's brain tried to process what was happening while his gut pushed him into fight or flight mode. Pivoting, Isaiah tried to flee but was viciously hit on the back of his head with the butt of Whistler's .45—his knees buckled, and he was down.

Whistler kicked the front door closed, grabbed the dazed and confused female by her wig, and pulled her to her feet. Astonishingly no one screamed as if this happened to them each week. All they wanted to do was comply so they could live another day.

On his knees, in a most vulnerable position, Isaiah stared straight ahead even as he felt the barrel of Whistler's gun to his temple. He knew the blurry figure that rushed in didn't have a mask on and didn't want to give the assailant any reason to kill him.

"You!" said Whistler. "Up, nigga. Stand to your muthafuckin' feet."

Isaiah complied.

"You got any weapons on your person?" he asked. Whistler had been in law enforcement's custody for so long that he began sounding like them.

Isaiah's head shook.

"Shorty, pat him down."

The female thoroughly searched Isaiah, checking his waistband and ankles, hoping this scored her some points with the gunman.

Isaiah was clean.

"Walk to your bedroom, and if you try some gangsta shit, I'ma 1-8-7, you nigga."

Isaiah finally spoke.

"You won't have a problem with me," and then added for sympathy. "On my kids, we're good."

His eyes were facing the floor, unsettling thoughts bouncing threw his mind. Isaiah assumed the prostitute had set him up.

"Look at me," said Whistler. "Both y'all."

At that moment, the woman lost it. She wailed, "Please don't kill me. I have a daughter…I have a child."

"Bitch, I said, look at me!"

Reluctantly, their eyes met his, and uncontrollable fear coursed through their bodies as they stared at the one-eyed monster.

Isaiah wanted to cry too. He was torn. Does he continue to comply, hoping for a good outcome? Or should he fight for his life?

Whistler saw the negligible change in Isaiah's body language and snickered, "Try it, nigga. I fuckin' dare you!"

Isaiah's eyes dropped to the ground again as he spoke. "I said you won't have a problem with me." His hands went up in surrender. "My room's this way."

Isaiah led everyone to his bedroom, where Whistler dropped his duffel and told the woman to duct tape Isaiah's wrists and ankles. Isaiah, lying face down on his carpeted floor, said nothing. When she was done, the same was done to her.

"Locations. All of them. Now, nigga."

Isaiah spewed the locations of three ki's and $17,000 in cash. While Whistler went to retrieve the stash, Isaiah realized that the girl didn't set him up. He went over the possibilities and settled on his baby mamas. *Who else?* He thought. It could be any one of them. His heart rate now slowed to an average pace. Even though his relationship with his children's mothers was tumultuous, he had convinced himself that neither would want to see him dead. He was the bread and the butter.

As if reading his mind, Whistler came back. His duffel had fattened up like a turkey after adding stuffing.

"You figured it out yet?"

"Nah. I don't know what you're talking 'bout."

"Who set you up?" Whistler placed duct tape around the woman's mouth as he spoke. "That shit gotta be fuckin' with you."

That dreadful feeling came gushing back to Isaiah. His voice quivered as he said, "It don't matter…we good. No retaliation on my end. I just wanna see my kids again."

The tape now went around Isaiah's mouth. Whistler reached for his walkie-talkie and, in a calm voice, said, "We still good, nigga? Five-oh ain't come through, right?"

A-God whispered his reply, "We good. You almost done?"

"Yeah. Meet me in the whip."

Whistler didn't need to say it, but it was said. "That was your uncle A-God. He's a greedy, lil' nigga. He wants half of whatever I score, yet he ain't put in no work."

A pillow was placed over the woman's head. In shock, she didn't wiggle, wail through the tape, or move her head incessantly. Janine was her name. And her last thought before Whistler put two bullets in the back of her head was of her daughter, Reign.

Bak! Bak!

Whistler kept talking. "It's always the ones you love and trust that will do this type of shit to you."

He walked back over to the bed and grabbed the last pillow. "Same thing happened to me, playah. I trusted Shorty and lost my eye." Whistler kneeled low and hovered over Isaiah, who was sobbing. His body was convulsing in almost hysteria. He couldn't believe this was how his life would end.

"Baby-girl made a mistake...I lived." The barrel pressed firmly against the goose-down pillow. "You won't."

Bak! Bak!

After walking out on their parents' argument, Bugsy went off to clear his mind, and Meyer didn't want to worry about him. What he needed was not to feel; anything. And the elation he felt from the Lean drifted him to a place where nothing mattered. When the euphoria swept over his body, the tingling morphed into a numbing sensation, making his issues bearable. His consciousness shifted from woke to dazed and confused, from reality to unbothered, unaware, unfazed. In his inebriated state, he could just chill.

Meyer poured the remaining cough syrup and grape soda into an expensive crystal glass. He dropped a couple of Jolly Ranchers inside. Coincidentally, his television was on Euphoria, the HBO show. Meyer glanced at the middle-aged man and underaged girl engaging in sexual activities, but that couldn't hold his attention. Soon he was coasting on Cloud Nine as he kicked off his Balenciaga's, reclined into plush pillows, and leaned into his addiction.

Hours later, he awoke to troubling thoughts about Lollipop. It had been twenty-four hours—a long twenty-four hours since he'd spoken to her. Usually, he wouldn't give a fuck about her, but something had changed. Knowing some other man was interested in her, had put a ring on it, made him jealous. He remembered the same jealous feelings long ago when Sergeant Douglas McAuliffe was messing around with Lollipop. His temper and emotions made him pistol-whip the cop publicly, creating backlash from other cops in Delaware. Scott and Whistler had to fix it to prevent future troubles from law enforcement.

And then his thoughts circled back to Lucky. He actually hoped she was snitching because the alternative was something he felt he couldn't live with. Visions of his sister in a casket was fucking with his sanity. He hadn't eaten a full meal since Layla burst into his room, hollering and screaming about her missing daughter. The situation felt heavy. His body was weighted down with grief as he struggled to process it.

Just coming out of his high, Meyer yearned to return to his oblivious state. It was late when he walked to the bodega to buy some more codeine. He scurried inside; of course, he wasn't alone. Snuggly tucked into his waistband was a 9mm, and another pistol in his ankle holster. With his parents back in their corner and the team of high-priced lawyers on deck—that combination had emboldened him and his brother to begin carrying again.

At the register, out of the blue, Meyer decided. He would kill the nigga who snatched up his bitch.

Franklin returned in under an hour, and as asked, his wife had lowered all blinds, fed her son in his room, and continued to clean up the blood. There was a full trash bag of bloody paper towels, and the house smelled of bleach. Lucky's head was wrapped in plastic and sealed with duct tape. The only thing left was to get rid of the body. While he was out, Martha took the liberty of retrieving the pink diamond earrings from Lucky's pocket. She adorned her ears with them, which Franklin first noticed when he returned home. But he said nothing. She had earned them.

Franklin could tell his wife was in a better mood than less than an hour ago. And he had to admit she'd done a great job in such little time.

"Plan?" she asked.

He nodded. "I do. I'm going to leave her body in the trunk of the rental, park it in a shady area of the Bronx, and the story writes itself."

"No, you're not!" Martha challenged. She now had just as much to lose as anyone. "Her body surfaces dead, and there's an investigation that eventually leads back to us, thanks to your affair. Now I can handle myself under questioning, but I worry about you and Junior."

Franklin was amused even under the circumstance. "Oh, I see you got jokes."

"I don't know how you'll do it, but you'll have to Jimmy Hoffa her."

"Hoffa, huh?"

"Exactly!"

Franklin balanced the weight of her words. He hated Lucky, felt nothing but disdain and disgust for her and her kind. But to make sure she's never found, to deny her a burial, and to leave her family and friends in limbo until they crossed over was intentionally cruel—even for him.

A-God was sitting two blocks up in the black stolen Accord's driver seat. The engine was idle, and he kept his head on a swivel waiting on Whistler. Whistler slid into the passenger's seat and faced his partner.

A-God said, "It went smooth, right? He didn't resist?"

"Not at all. All good."

"He don't know I dropped dime...that I'm behind this shit, right? You left him clueless?"

Whistler blew out air. "I left that nigga dead!" He squeezed his trigger finger, and one round entered A-God's temple— "Just like you."

Whistler exited the car and made his way up the boulevard, where he could disappear into the night.

CHAPTER 3

Markeeta was sweaty, sticky, and more than irritable as she banged on her mother's apartment door. She could hear lots of chatter, loud voices, and movement, which heightened her anger to the tenth degree. She and her son had traveled far on the New York City subway system dragging trash bags ripping at the seams. She had to curse out panhandlers, wrestle for seats, and kick the shit out of a pervert who rubbed his dick across her backside as she fought through a crowded train.

The last thing she wanted was an audience to her misery. And that's precisely what she'd get from the sound of things. Finally, after minutes of banging and yelling out her mother's name, the door opened. The teenage girl was wide-eyed and unknown to Markeeta, who pushed past her, Ralph not far behind.

Leaving her bags up front, Markeeta entered the living room and saw a sea of cousins, neighbors, and old acquaintances. She heard her name being called numerous times as her eyes searched for her mother. A couple of women glad to see her came barreling her way, but she curtailed any chitchat.

"Not now!" she barked, stopping the pair mid-stride.

Markeeta looked at the dark-colored outfits and tin foil pans of food and knew someone was dead.

Finally, her mother came out of her bedroom and noticed her daughter.

Markeeta said, "Who died?"

"What are you doing here?" Delores was not too pleased to see her daughter because it only meant Markeeta needed a handout.

Markeeta repeated, "Who died?"

"Your cousin, Suge."

"Oh," she said dismissively. "When your company leaving?"

"When they leave," Delores barked. "Markeeta, don't come up in here starting no shit! You can turn your ass right back around and go home to your big ole fancy apartment!"

The two rooms—kitchen and living—volumes lowered to whispers as everyone began to ear hustle. Delores and Markeeta were legendary in their neighborhood and throughout the family for their arguments and fistfights. It was like watching two Pitbulls fight over a steak when they started.

Under any other circumstance, Markeeta would have leaned into this argument. But she knew enough that you don't bite the hand that feeds you, and she was starving.

"Ralph, say hello to your grandmother," she ordered as she made her way into the kitchen to fix herself a plate. Her lips were prominently poked out, and the recognizable scowl told folks to keep their distance—most now afraid to give her eye contact.

Markeeta piled her plate high with baked macaroni and cheese, collard greens, barbeque spare ribs, potato salad, and fried chicken. She grabbed a Heineken beer and made her way to her room.

Her queen size bed, dresser, and nightstands were replaced with two twin beds, a bunk bed, and a tween shade of pink on the walls. Matching comforters and decorative pillows adorned each bed, and a desk and chair anchored the room. She saw a few laptops, iPhones, and large flatscreen television. There was a shelf with a row of African American dolls with curly and kinky hairstyles and a vintage Cabbage Patch Kids doll. *Where was all this luxury when she was a kid,* Markeeta thought.

Although she hadn't lived with her mother in a few years, she had no idea that the apartment was at full capacity.

Choosing the closest twin bed, Markeeta made herself comfortable when Ralph came in.

"I'm hungry," he whined.

"Then go fix yourself something to eat!"

"Grandma told me to ask you to do it."

"Boy, if you don't get outta my face and find someone to help your big ass fix a plate...so help me, I'ma fuck you up in here!"

Ralph slammed the door and didn't come back in.

Markeeta barely remembered being shaken awake, pulled out of the twin bed, and led to the sofa. The trauma of Lucky and Meyer at her front door and the stunts that Tannery and Brown had perpetrated against her had sucked all her energy. After she ate, she fell asleep late in the afternoon and woke up 24 hours later to her mother's husky voice.

Markeeta's eyes adjusted to an apartment she hardly recognized. She was sleeping on a new, expensive leather living room set, and a massive flat-screen television, area rug, and paintings were also new. To the right, she could see a six-seat dining room set, hutch, and portraits of four girls and a teenage boy. All smiles—the pictures were of Suge's kids; Patricia, Pamela, Piper, Patrice, and Paton.

Delores had done well for herself after her crack addiction. Early on, she got a city job with Transit. Two years in, she had gathered enough medical records from a psychiatrist to go out on Social Security Disability. That was nearly thirty years ago. Back in her day, disability was the latest hustle.

A lot of people who were intravenous drug users were the first to get up on the scam. If you were addicted to heroin in the eighties and applied for a rehabilitation program or were ordered by the court to one, you were put on Methadone. Which was supposed to ween addicts off the powerful narcotic. Heroin, like Methadone, produces a *'nodding'* motion, slurred speech. What people in the hood call the *Methadone Lean* and Jadakiss rapped about. With the crack epidemic leveling neighborhoods and wiping out lineages, a new virus called AIDS sent millions to an early grave. And heroin addicts contaminating the population using dirty needles, congress had to do something.

Crack sellers *and* users were incarcerated under the Rockefeller Drug Laws. AIDS patients were ostracized and stigmatized. And heroin addicts got what crack addicts felt was a winning lottery ticket. Not only did doctors give them a prescription each month to get high—Methadone is also an opioid, but the state also financed their lifestyle. Opioid-addicted adults couldn't work on Methadone—leaning and slurring, so most got a monthly social security disability check. And for the hardcore user who had no intentions of rehabilitating, they sold their Methadone and used the money to buy heroin. *And therein lies the problem,* said every republican.

Delores's quick stint as a crackhead had overseen all of this, and she seethed. She watched neighborhood junkies get their dope for free while she had to scheme, lie, and steal for crack. These heroin addicts were treated like royalty: free drugs, free money, *and* free needles. Delores caught on quickly. She used different means but got the same result. She pimped the system for all it had. Her favorite words were—*I retired*—like she had given the city a solid forty. Section 8 housing, a guaranteed monthly check, and a few side hustles throughout the years helped her raise her kids and keep a roof over their heads.

Delores wasn't above running numbers, selling candy to the kids after school, or hot plates of food at card games. She did all this while her brother's rise to the top was documented. Scott rode around Brooklyn in expensive cars, flashy jewels with different women. He didn't even have the decency to hit her off with some money, even after seeing her get her life together. Apparently, he was still salty about this little misunderstanding with her taking the stand against him.

Delores spent no time looking back at the past. You couldn't change it, so why bother?

Those disability checks were great for sitting around and watching soap operas all day. But if she wanted to live her best life, Delores knew she had to supplement her income.

She knew exactly what to do when she heard that her cousin, Sugar, was sick with terminal ovarian cancer. Delores accompanied her to doctor's appointments. Convinced her to drink apple cider vinegar with the 'mother' because it had healing properties and brought in a woman Delores claimed was anointed. All she had to do was lay hands on Sugar; if Sugar believed, she would beat cancer.

Delores realized that her con was working too well. She had given Sugar hope, and evidently, the universe was responding. The color began to come back into her cheeks. Sugar got around without much assistance, and her appetite had returned somewhat.

The goal of befriending a distant cousin to trust Delores enough with her five children wasn't easy. But it was done. With Sugar's permission, Delores had started the paperwork for the Kinship Foster Care Program through New York State. Sugar's four girls and one boy now resided with her. This was a long, arduous process but came with many perks for Delores.

Delores got an extra four grand a month, tax-free for the kids, and a huge check for furniture and school clothes. Sugar also had a $100,000 life insurance policy and named her new BFF as the beneficiary to help support her children. The whole family warned Sugar not to trust Delores, but no one gave her an alternative. The children's father was murdered when her youngest was just six months, and Delores was the only one who knew about Kinship Foster Care. If other family members knew they'd get a check for Sugar's kids each month, cousins would have lined up.

As far as Delores was concerned, these children had done more for her than her own. She wanted no parts of Markeeta or her grandchild, Ralph. Unless Markeeta was going to sign him over through Kinship Foster Care—he was getting kicked out too.

Delores spoke. "Look, Ralph done explained what went on over at your palatial estate, and I saw all those bags by my front door. This ain't no flop house!"

Markeeta glared at her son for telling their business and wondered why her mother was yelling unprovoked.

She continued with, "I ain't who I used to be, so I ain't gonna be arguing with you in my house! These kids got a routine, and you and whatever mess you got yourself into ain't gonna mess that up for me. You can stay for two weeks—"

"Two weeks, Ma?!" Markeeta spat. "Where are we supposed to go? I don't got no money!"

"Yous a grown-ass woman with a child! Figure it out like I had to do!" Delores took several steps toward the kitchen and left one parting message. "And tonight, take a couple of blankets and sleep on the floor. I don't want ya big ass making dents in my new sofa."

Markeeta seethed. She observed her mother fawn over those five children like they were gold nuggets—treatment Markeeta had never received growing up under Delores's roof. Delores had done a one-eighty. And all it took was three decades, a monthly stipend, and a life insurance policy.

The contained crime scene was quickly taken over from local Detroit police by the Federal Bureau of Investigation as soon as the victim's name was entered into the national database. It flagged Agent Dough, and a call was placed. Agent James Dough was an alias—one of many he had used throughout his illustrious career. Sometimes he was Odell, Donovan, Jayson, George, Malcolm, Lamont—a host of hoaxes he had mastered, but his last name remained the same.

The 37-year-old female was shot once in the head and left slumped in the driver's seat of her Tesla in the red zone, a shady part of town terrorized by the Bloods gang. Her government was Karen Williams, and he had recruited her using the alias George.

Karen was from Brooklyn and had made a name for herself by being one of the top boosters in the borough. She took risks, and sometimes those risks landed her in jail. Agent Dough watched Karen and her crew for a few years and noticed that she was a drama queen. She had a flair for theatrics which kicked in the moment the undercover detectives were coming to detain her for shoplifting.

Karen didn't know this, but Agent Dough would always place a call to the store's Loss Prevention Unit, and she'd be released. Karen hung out with two other females, but she was who he wanted. Watching her from fifteen to nineteen, he knew her most intimate details. He knew who and how she fucked, when she was on her monthly menstrual, and how many abortions she had on her jacket. Agent Dough found himself attracted to the teenager, but his introduction to her was supposedly strictly business.

There was a major player in the drug distribution food chain in Atlanta that he needed her to infiltrate. The guy's name was Dexter, and he went by Big Dee.

Big Dee cleared hundreds of millions a year, and Agent Dough wanted in. He met with Karen for months, schooling her on the type of women Big Dee liked, how to catch his attention and the perks of working with him.

"You'll never work a day job," he promised. "You'll live in the best apartments, drive top-of-the-line cars, and be ranked higher than local PD in all fifty states. If you wanted, you could spit in the face of a police officer, and I'll have you released within an hour of your incarceration. Trust me, baby, it gets no better."

Karen not only helped Agent Dough apprehend and convict Dexter, but she did what she was recruited to do: find Dexter's cash. That was two decades ago. Karen played an intricate part in many dealers getting life sentences and tens of millions usurped by Agent Dough.

Karen helped him, but he helped her too. Whenever she wanted, she would add a frenemy to a list of people he could fuck with. Ruining lives was in his wheelhouse, and you didn't have to sell drugs to earn a coveted spot. Karen, drunk off her newfound power, wasn't above exacting revenge for the slightest infraction.

She was twenty-one when she gave the order for George to have a fourteen-year-old girl robbed at gunpoint because they had words. Karen would argue with the teen like the young girl was her peer. When she called George for the request, he took it further. The teenager was working twelve-hour shifts at a bodega in the Bronx bagging groceries and wouldn't get home until two in the morning. She'd then have to walk a mile and a half alone to get home once she got off the subway.

George waited for payday. And the unsuspecting teen walked right into the ambush. After being robbed, the girl called the

41

police. The blue and whites showed up just as George had requested, taking the teenager on a ride she'd never forget. They told the girl they would drive her the mile and a half home, but instead, they locked her in the back of the police car under the guise of cruising around to look for the suspect.

"I just want to go home," she said meekly, traumatized by the night's event, after riding around for an hour.

"You stupid, fucking bitch!" one officer admonished. "We're trying to help you get this fucking perp off the street!"

Stunned, the girl shrunk in the back of the patrol car and remained silent. Thirty minutes later, she was in another borough, parked across from an unknown housing project, while the cops got out and left her there. With a security screen separating the front and back seats, lock levers removed from the passenger doors, she felt like a caged animal, claustrophobic. And with the doors locked, engine off, she nearly suffocated in the summer's heat. They left the young Black female locked in the back of the cop car for six hours before ultimately driving her home. Five years later, Karen ordered another robbery of said girl, and George used the same assailant just for kicks. They traumatized the woman for decades and would, as Karen exclaimed, "crack up," laughing over this young woman's pain.

But here she was. Karen. With a bullet in her head. Agent Dough refused to blame himself. As it unfolded, he watched the live footage of Karen's assassination in real-time. Still, there wasn't anything he could do. Her car was wired with audio and video; her latest mark was a Detroit rapper, Bo Jangles. He was younger than Karen, at 29, but Agent Dough did what he does best; he created a situation where Bo Jangles wouldn't have a choice but to fall for the sexy vixen.

Bo Jangles made millions in the music industry from downloads, streams, and concerts. Still, he also couldn't stop pushing them ki's. Daily, he wore nearly two million in diamonds draped around his neck, and with Karen's help, he was promptly robbed at gunpoint by James's goons. Bo Jangles went out the next day and bought all the same jewels, and he was quickly robbed again. James now figured that the second robbery exposed Karen's hand to Bo Jangles.

Agent Dough was juggling a lot and shouldn't have made such an error, but it is what it is. Not that he wasn't saddened. Karen wasn't just his informant; he had been sleeping with her on and off for years, but he couldn't marry her. All he could do was make the promise that she'd never want for anything in this life. And as far as he was concerned, he had fulfilled that.

It was a quick flight from Illinois to Michigan, where he would retrieve Karen's body. He made a quick call as he stood under a white canopy, watching her body being loaded into the coroners' van.

The person picked up.

"Tannery here."

"Tannery, this is Agent James Dough from the Chicago bureau."

"What can I do for you?"

"I heard about the assistance you got from Markeeta West on your Manny Machiavelli case."

"Yeah? And?"

"I also heard y'all parted ways, and I have a job in Detroit she would be perfect for."

Tannery didn't like the, *I heard* bullshit. As far as he was concerned, he hadn't left a paper trail with Markeeta, which meant someone in his office was spilling secrets. He thought about his response and said, "I cut her loose, but I ain't *done* with her."

James knew exactly what that meant. Tannery was going to punish Markeeta for his reasons and his reasons alone. It was an unspoken pastime for agents.

"I get it. And I won't get in the way of that just as long as you won't block Detroit."

"Sure. Fuck it," Tannery replied. Anything to help out a fellow law enforcement brother.

CHAPTER 4

Delores's apartment was what Markeeta called Spic and Span clean. You could practically eat off the floor. Her mother spent her days maintaining her apartment, not a thing out of place—except her and Ralph. Delores took pride in her place, her replacement kids, and new lot in life. Her bank account had over six figures, her rent for three large bedrooms, a large living and dining room, a spacious bathroom, and a huge kitchen was a paltry two hundred a month. And her neighborhood had undergone gentrification. Her community had gone from a crime-infested, murder-riddled dungeon to top-rated charter schools, an influx of retail stores, a farmers' market, and a few supermarkets. It was no longer a food desert with newly renovated parks, a Magic Johnson movie theatre, and an ice-skating rink in the winter.

Usually, she woke up in a great mood. The children were bright, well-behaved, and had manners—that *yes and no* ma'am stuff Delores didn't teach her children. When her eyes opened for the past four days, she remembered Markeeta and Ralph were in her home, and her mood quickly soured.

Delores did what most did when they didn't want you around—they made you feel uncomfortable and unwanted. She hollered all day about how much food Ralph was eating, for Markeeta to pick up after them and to turn the lights off when they left a room. Markeeta hollered back; it was just like old times. And then her cell phone rang.

"What!" she snapped.

"Markeeta?"

"Who's this!"

"FBI Agent James Dough."

"I'm listening."

"If you're available, I have a job for you."

Markeeta didn't hesitate. She answered with, "I'm down. What I gotta do?"

James didn't know that she was this amenable. He wondered why Tannery had cut her loose.

"The jobs in Detroit—"

"Detroit?!" her heart sank. "Ain't no fucking way, yo. Y'all gonna get my ass killed. Where's Tannery? His bitch ass."

"This doesn't involve him. If you accept the assignment, you'll deal with me and *only* me. And I can promise you I've never lost an informant," he lied.

Markeeta didn't know a soul in Detroit; all she knew of the place was that it resembled Brooklyn in the '80s, and it's 2020.

"That's a hard pass for me," she replied. "You don't got someone in New York? I told Tannery that I got mad peoples I could set up."

He now knew why she was a throwaway. She didn't listen.

Dough repeated, voice stern, bass deeper. "I said, this doesn't involve Tannery. Tell me your concerns, and we'll work them out."

"First off, I don't know Detroit, their peoples, or any friends there. I'd need to feel safe cause it's just me and my son. How you gonna make that worth my time?"

Her cell phone dinged several times, alerting her that she had texts.

"That's me. Take a look at those pictures, and let's discuss."

Markeeta took a few minutes to go through pictures of a luxury building, a vehicle, and a private school—all slightly above the status Tannery had given her. But this was no New York. This was Detroit. And she gave no fucks about it being the birthplace of Motown. But what gave her pause and reconsideration were the pictures of Bo Jangles. A well-known rapper that she followed on Instagram and TikTok.

"Bo Jangles? You want me to befriend his girl or something?"

"I want you to *be* his girl."

"You want me to fuck him?"

Most of his recruits usually wanted to be coaxed into this, like he had to do a lot of arm twisting, but her voice was a matter of fact, like she was a straight shooter. He took a chance.

"Yes. I'd work with you to get Bo Jangles's attention, and we'd go from there. You'd also have a confidant there; his stylist works for me. I got her placed in his employ a year back."

Markeeta knew his stylist too from Instagram. She had mad followers. "Are you talkin' about Chanel Dior?"

"Absolutely."

Markeeta couldn't believe it. She had no money. Had just been humiliated by that ugly fuck, Tannery, a few days ago. And now she was being offered the job of a lifetime. But could she trust him?

"I don't know..." she stalled. "Things didn't end well with my last gig. I was fuckin' used! That fat bitch tossed me out on the street with nothing, not giving a fuck that I got a child!" Markeeta was about to go off on a long rant, but she checked herself. He wasn't Tannery. She said, "I'm gonna need reassurances."

"I'll tell you what. Get me what I want from Bo Jangles, and I can promise you a monetary gain."

"You can do that?"

"I can do whatever the fuck I want."

She felt a presence standing over her body, willing her eyes to open. Her lids slowly widened as her pupils adjusted to view a shadowy figure. Startled, her breath hitched before she asked, "Paton?"

As the streetlights illuminated the room, Delores knew it wasn't Paton. It was a face she quickly recognized but hadn't seen in decades. An aged face, hardened from time, grief, and loss. This man's heart had broken so many times that it could no longer be stitched together. Any love he had once felt for his sister had dissipated long ago.

"Scott…is that you?" Her voice unmistakably quaked. "What are you doing here?"

He didn't answer. Delores watched as he pulled out a pistol and began a twisting motion, slow and steady.

Is he gonna shoot my ass, she thought. Why? This can't be real. She sat up in bed. One part thought she was dreaming; the other *hoped* she was. Delores tried to click on the lamp at her bedside, but the bulb was removed. Fear is an emotion that you only wish on your worst enemy. It sweeps through your body so thoroughly, not leaving one inch of you unaffected. Delores's body quivered uncontrollably down to her toes, her heart pounding through her eardrums.

Visions of her taking the stand, hand raised in the air, oath taken upon a Bible flashed before her. Her betrayal was not so cavalier, dismissive. Her action now had a consequence.

She now saw that he was twisting a silencer onto his gun.

Delores pleaded, "Scott, on mama, what are you doing?"

Scott said nothing. He rather enjoyed watching her squirm.

"If this is about your trial, that was fucked up on my end, and I should have apologized once I got my mind right, but I swear, Scott, I've changed."

No words.

More excuses from Delores. "I was in a drug-induced haze, but I'm doing right by people now. I have five beautiful children who need me, Scott. They're your cousin Sugar's kids. She died a few months back, Scott. There's nobody else to take care of them but me."

Delores didn't know if she had gotten to her brother's softer side. She couldn't see his eyes, but she would have seen only darkness if she had. Hollowed out and devoid of any light. Scott was a broken man drowning in the pain that only a parent who had lost several children could feel.

He finally spoke.

"Where's Markeeta?"

As a mother, Delores knew she shouldn't feel relief thinking that her brother's wrath wasn't directed toward her but toward her daughter. However, relieved she felt. She sighed a visible exhale, her shoulders relaxing from their stiffened state.

"Markeeta? She left last week and took her son with her. Why? What'd she do?"

"Where does she live?"

Delores shrugged. "Hell, if I know. I told her she couldn't stay here. All that girl is to me is trouble. From the day I pushed —"

Poot!

The bullet lodged into Delores's torso. It would take her several minutes to bleed out. Time Scott had carved out. He sat catacorner on the edge of her bed, half his body facing her, the other facing the door.

"Scott...please...get help," she squeezed out. Her hands clutched her open wound, crimson red oozing through aging fingers. Of course, Scott saw fear in his sister's eyes, but he also saw hope. Delores *hoped* he would see her in this vulnerable state, call for an ambulance and save her ass. She still couldn't reconcile that he was holding on to a thirty-year-old beef. It wasn't that serious to her.

"I've tried to put myself in your shoes, but I can't. Men like me will never understand how one from our era, our pedigree, our history cooperates with the government under any circumstance."

"Scott, please...I won't make it if you...don't help me live."

He continued. "You were an addict, and that's an illness. But even addicts have moments of clarity. You took that stand and tried to get me *life* in prison." Scott bent down as close as one could come to another's face and keep it platonic, and repeated, "Life!"

Scott's face tightened into a ball of fury. He wanted to beat his sister to death with his bare hands, pound her skull open with the butt of his gun until it cracked like a walnut.

Tears began streaming down Delores's face. She wanted her mother, right here, in this room, in this bizarre moment.

"I loved you," Scott said. "I took care of you! Anything you needed, I'd do for you—even kill."

Delores nodded. She had broken his heart so long ago. Yet she had always been so arrogant about the incident. As if she had stepped on his toe and not the stand.

"Had I murdered you back then, you wouldn't have given birth to Markeeta, and my daughter wouldn't be missing!"

"What...did Markeeta do?" She wanted to know.

"What you taught her!"

With that, Scott emptied his clip into his sister's face. She would have a closed casket funeral—only he wouldn't attend.

Scott then grabbed her cell phone from the nightstand, took her thumb, unlocked the phone, and reprogrammed a new security code. He'd give the phone to Mason to see if he could find Markeeta's whereabouts.

Scott left half a ki of cocaine under her mattress, tossed a few things in her home, and grabbed some valuables meant to make her death look drug-related. He exited his sister's place without a second glance.

Scott had buttoned up a thirty-year beef in a matter of minutes.

Riley was placed in a holding cell and handcuffed to a wall where she had to stand. After a couple hours in her heels, she kicked them off and stood barefoot on the dirty cement floor. No longer concerned about her expensive shoes, or designer dress, she repeatedly called out to be taken to the bathroom.

"I've got to pee!" she bellowed, her voice laced with urgency. "Take me to a bathroom!"

Nine hours in, and she couldn't hold it in any longer. A warm urine stream slid down her leg and splashed on her perfect gel pedicure. Humiliated, Riley sobbed and then screamed more until her voice was hoarse.

"I wanna see a judge!" she hollered. "This shit is illegal."

Twenty hours later and her legs trembled incessantly. Every inch of her body ached, her feet were swollen—two giant balloons and her throat burned.

When two suits came to her cell with a uniformed cop, she knew they weren't detectives. These were the boys that were called when you had a trunk full of kilos and an out-of-state license.

"You fuckin' pissed yourself," the officer asked as he neared Riley, smelled the familiar stench, and saw the puddle.

She began crying again. No one cared.

The handcuff was removed, and a recognizable voice spoke to the uniform, "I'll take it from here."

Riley's eyes were puffy and unfocused, but as he got closer, she saw that this man was Steve, Elliot's friend from last night.

"Steve?" she asked. "How is this even possible?" And then anger resurfaced. "You set us the fuck up!"

"Let's clean you up, and then I'll explain."

She noticed that he had on a different suit, had probably gone home, got a solid eight hours of sleep, had breakfast, coffee, and time to spare as she wasted away in a holding cell.

Riley was given used clothes from the Lost and Found bin— a sweatshirt, pants, and oversized off-brand sneakers. Riley was led to the woman's restroom. She used recycled paper towels to wash between her legs and generic hand soap to clean everything else. She pulled her hair into a top knot bun and tried to streamline her thoughts.

Her dress and shoes were tossed in the trash, feeling she wouldn't need them for a while, perhaps twenty to life. Besides, keeping the clothes you were arrested in was bad luck. Everyone in the hood knew that.

Riley was led to the obligatory interrogation room where she sat in a metal chair—table, video camera, and one-way mirrored window also present. The oversized sweatshirt, bare face, and bun decreased her outward appearance from an adult to a young teen. The curvy, outspoken woman from last night was reduced to a frightened female.

"I'm Agent Garrett," he said. "You met me last night as Steve." He waited a beat for Riley to respond. She didn't.

"Did you know that your boyfriend is one of the biggest cocaine distributors in the Midwest?"

"Elliott? Moves cocaine?" Riley snorted. "Lies!"

Agent Garrett's eyes didn't warm up to her indifference toward his statement. He continued, "Were you not arrested with four duffel bags of uncut, pure white last night?"

Her head shook. "Y'all planted that shit. I know how this goes. I want a lawyer."

Under all interrogations in the United States, the interview should have ended. But that rule only applies to those that follow the rules. These men did not.

"Sure. You can go the traditional route and get a lawyer, one phone call, and even an arraignment before a judge. But you won't make bail because none will be given. We will allow you to use the phone, but every call you make will go to the person's voicemail. We'll place you in a cell with federal informants who will swear under oath at your trial that you admitted to being in business with your boyfriend and muling his drugs."

"This is all illegal. I have rights!" Riley was regaining her strength.

"But you don't, though. You *think* you do…but you actually do not." Garrett walked over to Riley and leaned down, invading her personal space. She locked eyes with him to show her strength—she wasn't afraid but quickly looked away. He continued, "I owned you when you thought you could push kilos through my city. The moment you flew here with your drug dealer. In fact, I own you if you did none of the above or all of it, just because I fucking said so. You got me, bitch?"

Riley looked past Agent Garrett to the silent one and spoke. "If y'all gonna do all he just said, then just fuckin' do it!"

"Hear me out first," the silent one responded. "Let me show you something."

The agent placed several pictures in front of Riley of Elliott McDonald and Steven, aka Agent Garrett doing numerous drug transactions. She saw warehouses full of drugs, triggermen, weaponry, and stacks of cash. She couldn't believe what her eyes were witnessing. Elliott? Her cornball? Pushes weight?

"I bet he asked you to drive, didn't he?" the agent continued. "He does this to all his mules. Last night was just a test run. Today, he would have asked you to take the vehicle with even more drugs to an address he would have programmed in the navigational system. And Sunday, it would have been unloaded and repeated."

Tears flowed freely from her eyes—humiliation and grief swelled in her throat; she couldn't speak if she tried to.

Agent Garrett rejoined the conversation. "He told you we were good friends from our youth. That was a lie."

Finally, she asked, "If y'all know I had nothing to do with this shit, why am I still here? Send me home so I can get on with my life. Y'all got who y'all want. What do y'all need? For me to testify against that piece of shit because I will!"

Bingo!

Garrett finally took a seat. He softened his voice, his stern demeanor dissipated, and it was his pleasure to discuss business.

"Actually, we won't be needing you to prosecute Elliott. The case against him is airtight."

Riley wanted to exhale but knew there would be a *but* in her future.

"But, if you could assist in the apprehension of your ex-boyfriend, Meyer West, we would show our gratitude by dropping the case against you."

"Meyer?" she wailed, holding her head and sobbing. "I can't do it."

Garrett chuckled. "Sure, you can."

Scott had thought of many ways he would murder those responsible for what he was now convinced was his daughter's disappearance. Each one's pain would be so excruciating that they would beg for death, but they would live another day to endure more pain. He had it all figured out. Delores was on his torture list. She was supposed to lose several fingers and toes, have her eyes removed with a spoon, and a drill bit would saw into her cranium until she was a drooling fool. And then she'd ultimately be put down.

But she was his sister, so he'd shown her mercy. One's mercy is relative, so Scott knew Delores would have objected to his method of mercy, but it had to be done. Scott was on a warpath; no one would be spared.

Depending on the day, Lucky's status went from missing to murdered. Layla begged Scott to have hope.

"Until she surfaces dead, then she's alive, Scott. I don't want to hear otherwise, or I'ma fuck you up," she threatened her husband.

Scott understood.

Layla was unstable. She was chain-smoking and numbing her pain with expensive champagne. Her eyes rarely closed for more than a couple hours, and the rest of the day was now spent hovering over her two remaining sons. With three children murdered *and* one missing, the scale was equally balanced, but it wasn't equally yoked.

A meeting was called.

After having his home swept for listening devices, Scott, Layla, the twins, and Mason sat at the kitchen's breakfast bar and discussed revenge.

"Where are you with Delores's phone? Any beat on Markeeta?" Scott asked.

Mason's head shook rapidly. "Nah. My guy was able to go back two years, and Markeeta had limited interaction with her mother. Besides Markeeta sending her mother a gloating text with several pictures of the high-rise apartment in the Regency Heights building a few months back, we got nothing."

"Well, get something!" Layla snapped. And then recovered with, "I'm sorry, Mason. I know you're doing all you can."

"No need to apologize. You have every right to want results."

Layla continued, "And no word on Ray Negro?"

Again, Mason delivered terrible news. "We got our hands dirty on a few niggas, tortured them until we were up to our knees in blood—but they weren't feds. Just had the unfortunate luck of being born with red hair and working in lower Manhattan."

Meyer spoke. "What about Larry? I know he's working with those peoples. Let me torture and lullaby his snitching ass!"

"In due time, son," Scott said.

"Why all this waiting and planning shit, Pops! I say we go in and lay all them niggas down! Feds too!" Meyer simulated mowing down people with an assault rifle. "Show 'em who the fuck we are!"

Scott stuffed his hands in his suit pants pockets and directed his attention toward his hotheaded son. He never expected Meyer to make it past his twenty-first birthday—not with his temper. But here Meyer was, a nickel away from turning thirty, and had outlived three of his siblings, possibly four. At this moment, Scott felt he needed to sow into Meyer, as he had with Bugsy, or he'd be burying another child.

"I'm a nickel away from living half a century, and I've already lived three lifetimes for a man on my level. You don't make it this long in the drug game on luck and bullets. You make it to my age with planning, patience, and infrastructure. Angel took out your whole organization seemingly in one night. But realize that it took planning, patience, and infrastructure. You and Bugsy are only alive because he allowed it. Don't think otherwise."

"Fuck, Angel," Meyer growled.

"Shut the fuck up!" Layla snapped. "And learn something. Your father is trying to teach you how to avoid being carried by six, dummy."

Meyer's nostrils flared, but he curtailed any rebuttals.

Bugsy spoke. "Pops, what about agents Randall and Devonsky? They gotta be the ones who put Ragnar on Lucky. I know you want us to focus on Markeeta, Larry, and Ragnar, but what about them?"

"And that fuckin' cracker Fitzgerald," added Meyer. "He gets it too!"

Scott would kill the world for his daughter, but his sons didn't know and were about to find out that he also had his wife to think about. Layla's life was still in danger; Javier Garcia had said as much. And then there were the two sicarios. Scott didn't cower away from shit, and his enemies didn't stop until you were dead or until you negotiated a way to live in estrangement.

Scott had a lot on his plate. As the head of the household, he needed to kill his enemies *and* keep his family alive. He said, "We can't kill any fed we want when we want."

"Why we can't? It was easy enough for me to get at Understanding and Jackie." Layla purposely called her nemesis by her abbreviated name and hoped she heard it in hell.

Scott was stunned. He had no idea his wife was behind the double homicide in Dubai. She hadn't said a word until now. Not even when the feds stormed the plane, not when they were dragged off to jail, or several weeks later.

"I assume you had help?" Scott finally asked.

Mason nodded and then answered. "She did. Layla called me with her concerns. She explained that she was your third eye since day one and wouldn't allow you to walk into something you can't see coming. I flew in and out on a fake passport, and we handled the situation using locals."

"Handled, huh? They locked my Black ass up." Scott feigned anger for a few seconds. He looked at his wife, gave her a sly wink, and grinned. They were definitely fucking tonight. At that moment, his eyes swept over his two single sons. No one special in their lives. Just as Layla had explained to Mason, he realized she was his third eye. Layla always had his back under *all* circumstances. You couldn't buy that kind of loyalty and love.

Murdering the two agents who had pursued them for a few years was risky. But Lucky was worth it. She was and will always be his baby girl.

Scott spoke. "Mason and I will get at Randall and Devonsky to give up Ragnar. The right torture technique will get us what we want. Meyer, I want you on Larry. He might have been working on the same team as Markeeta. Meet with him, drop a few breadcrumbs, and Bugsy will tail him to wherever he meets with his handlers. Hopefully, he'll lead us to whoever he works for and with."

Layla smiled, "I guess that leaves Fitz's bitch ass to me!"

Scott nodded.

"Now. We need to discuss the Garcia cartel."

CHAPTER 5

Markeeta and Ralph were flown first class from JFK to DTW in Detroit. They were met by a man dressed in a two-piece dark-colored suit and white shirt, holding a sign that read: M. WEST in the transportation area of the airport.

"I'm Markeeta West. Are you Agent Dough?" she asked.

"I'm your driver and will take you to your new residence. Do you have any luggage?"

Markeeta copped an attitude. "I told Agent Dough that I wasn't bringing shit!"

The only thing of value she brought with her was the ostrich, peach-colored Hermès Birkin bag that Lucky had gifted her. It was the most expensive item she owned.

Calmly he nodded. "Very well. My name is Carlos; please follow me."

The home was a four-story brick townhouse on a treelined block in an affluent neighborhood of Detroit. These were million-dollar homes, and one was hers. It was just past eleven a.m., and the weather was cold with a brisk wind. The driver pulled into an empty park in front of a tan-colored, well-appointed brick home with two cars parked in the private driveway—a Bentley Phantom and a Porsche.

Carlos got out and opened her door, Markeeta got out, and Ralph followed next. She was handed a heavy manilla envelope that had weight and girth.

"Everything you need is inside. I hope you enjoy your stay in Michigan."

"Where's Agent Dough?"

"As I said, everything you need is in the envelope. Good day, ma'am."

The driver got into the vehicle and peeled out.

Markeeta stood there for a second or two, stuck on stupid. She expected the agent to come out from inside one of the residences to get them. Just as her pressure began to rise, Ralph spoke up.

"I think the house keys might be inside that package."

Markeeta opened the envelope, and several keys were inside, along with bundles of cash and paperwork with instructions. Markeeta's head was on a swivel as she clutched the package stuffed with money and dug inside for keys. She pulled out the keys for the Porsche, house, and Bentley. The house keys were labeled with a sticker that read: 1227, the home she was standing in front of.

They made their way up the first landing of steps to the wood and glass double doors. Two keys let them into the vestibule, and a second set allowed them into their new home. This wasn't the home she had received pictures of. This home was some celebrity shit.

She and Ralph's mouths dropped as they stood in the massive foyer. This house was new *and* smelled new. To her right was an alarm system with the alarm code on a post-it note. As they walked through the home, there were notes for

Markeeta throughout. The Viking refrigerator was filled with gourmet foods—caviar, expensive cheeses, pricey shellfish, and healthier selections like almond milk, vegan cheese, and plant-based *meats*. The post-it read: *This is your new diet. Get used to it.*

The walk-in pantry held bottled spring and sparkling water, whole grain and chickpea pasta, Larabar's, and many supplements.

There was a fully stocked bar in the living room. One-thousand-dollar bottles of the finest champagnes and wines, scotch, and gin. She didn't see Hennessey, beer, Absolut, Malibu, or anything she liked to drink to get fucked up.

The main level had a large kitchen, formal dining room, home office, guest bedroom, ensuite bathroom, and full-service home gym. Toward the back was the floor to the lower basement level. The post-it read: *Ralph*.

Markeeta and Ralph walked down the carpeted steps to the street-level walk-out basement, her son's apartment. Ralph had a large bedroom, ensuite bathroom, huge game room, kitchen, smaller gym, and a home theater with leather theater seats and a popcorn machine.

He lost his mind.

"This all mine?!" he hollered. "I love it here already!"

Ralph's refrigerator was stocked with more kid-friendly foods. Still, she did see that a few items were substituted with healthier choices. Ralph and Markeeta began to feel what was expected of them if they wanted to stay. Even though Markeeta never sat down and explained what she was into to her son, he had pieced it together. His mother was doing shady things to give him this lifestyle.

Markeeta left Ralph to go finish touring her new home. The three upper floors were hers. And she wasn't sure how she felt about Ralph sleeping so far away from her each night, but she understood the optics. Living here was work, and as far away her son was from her job, the better.

The upper levels had three bedrooms, including the primary, and four bathrooms. The walk-in closet was stuffed with designer clothing and shoes that would rival her cousin, Lucky's. Designer handbags, luggage, belts, and scarfs were neatly arranged and color coordinated.

Markeeta didn't know who Agent Dough was but knew she wanted to please him. No fucking way was she messing this up. She then remembered a stack of papers in the envelope with instructions. Markeeta climbed onto the bed with her sneakers on, dirtying the silk comforter with scuff marks. Her jeans, which sat throughout the airport and plane, now sat on her pillow.

She began reading what would be required of her, from losing twenty pounds, tightening her stomach to ideally six-pack abs, and firming her gluts. There was a laundry list of reading material, ten meals she would need to learn how to cook and master, and a booklet of meals she was allowed and forbidden to eat. Markeeta could no longer eat processed foods or dairy. She could only eat a small portion of lean meat—the finest cuts, seafood, low carbs, and low sodium.

The last requirement seemed odd. A bundle of religious material, articles, books, and pamphlets was on her side table. Markeeta immediately recognized the Bible—NIV and King James versions. Books on Buddhism, Kabala, Catholicism, Judaism, Christianity, Taoism, the Hebrew Bible, and The Holy Quran. The post-it read: *Pick one and master.*

Her phone rang.

"Are you settled in?" the voice said.

"Yeah."

Agent Dough snapped, "Not yeah, but yes!"

Markeeta swallowed hard. He was more like Brown than Tannery, but it was all good in her hood because James Dough was paying the cost to be her boss.

"Yes, I am."

"What are your thoughts on your new diet, food restrictions, and recipes. Can you handle it?"

"I'm used to eatin' four chicken wings and shrimp fried rice from the local Chinese restaurant. But working with Tannery, I now understand that I have a part to play, and I need to look the part."

Dough avoided lashing out and again scolding his new protégé on removing Tannery's name from her conversation. Instead, he said, "Good. And religion. What shall it be?"

Markeeta chuckled. "Now, on that, I ain't down. I mean, ain't no purpose. I ain't tryin' to be reading these thick boring books about things and peoples that don't affect me."

There were so many grammatical atrocities Markeeta committed in three sentences; Dough wanted to implode. He hardly ever questioned his judgment, but now he wondered if he had made a knee-jerk decision calling her to replace one of the best that's ever done it. Markeeta was nearly a decade older than he liked to recruit. She wasn't rough around the edges—she was simply rough.

James needed to handle Markeeta like she was a teenager, which meant his approach to this subject would be practical. Dough thought about what was trending and said, "If I gave you a test tonight on religion and the outcome of you and your son staying in that townhome and you getting to drive those luxurious cars, which subject would you choose? The Bible, the Tanakh, or The Holy Quran. If you had to pick one? Humor me."

Markeeta's stomach churned. She didn't like this man. At all. After a moment of silence, she replied, "I'd have to say the Bible would be easiest to master."

"Good. Start with Genesis, and don't stop until you've finished Revelation."

Markeeta sucked her teeth. "Okay."

"I'll be there at six to meet with you," he instructed. "Just you. Don't have Ralph around. Keep him downstairs. Understand?"

She nodded and then verbally replied, "Yeah...I mean, yes. No problem."

The music blared throughout the nightclub in midtown Manhattan, and Fitz and his lady friend, Eloise, were dancing the night away. Both looked bubbly as they glided and slid across the dance floor in perfect harmony. The young woman, at nineteen, was nearly half his age. She was tall and slender, with dark hair, brooding eyes, and full, arched eyebrows. Scarlet red lipstick gave her thin lips a fuller appearance, which she used to pout whenever she wanted to get her way.

Fitzgerald was a big spender, her sugar daddy paying her rent and sending her thousands a month through Cash App. Eloise knew she wouldn't marry him. He was already showing signs of hair loss. It wasn't glaring, barely noticeable, but the process had begun—receding around his temples, dime size spot at his crown. Fitz was successful, but rich, powerful white men weren't a scarcity for her. Fitzgerald was Mr. Right Now for her; she knew he felt the same about her. He didn't try to possess, control, or own her.

They danced through several songs, and Fitz even got a little touchy, touchy with her, fondling her booty and thighs with a naughty smile. Eloise didn't mind, allowing his mischievous touch to continue against her body. After the club, he wanted to spend the night with her. Fitz wanted sex; usually, he got what he wanted from women. They'd been friends with benefits for so long that it was an unspoken rule that she'd be available when he called.

"You look beautiful tonight," he told her.

Eloise smiled. She took the compliment nonchalantly. Eloise wanted to free her mind inside the dance club—only for tonight because she would transition into the bait she was paid to be after the last song played.

Fitz grabbed her from behind and twirled her around, grinding his groin into her backside. They did a couple spins and rapid movements, both dancing offbeat.

Fitzgerald left the club after three in the morning with his arm wrapped around Eloise's tiny waist, feeling great. He had a good time and was ready to have a magnificent one. He was ready to return to her place, or his, and continue their intimate dance.

They strolled arm-in-arm toward the parking garage, chatting and laughing like lovers and friends. They walked approximately a block from the nightclub and quickly approached his luxury sedan. It was dark on the side street with the late hour, but this was New York; he could see and hear taxi cabs roaming the roads looking to pick up a fare.

"So, you want me to stay the night?" Fitz asked.

Eloise chuckled. "Aren't you presumptuous," she said.

"I am...I want you, and I miss it."

"You do, Mr. Spencer? You're not getting any from the other women in your life?" she taunted.

"You know there's no one else."

"What about your secretary," Eloise replied dryly. "I know she wants you."

"Julia?" he asked, sensing sudden tension in her tone. "It's not like that at all with us."

"You don't have to lie, Fitz. We're not exclusive."

Fitz wasn't lying. He wasn't cliché with his personal life and fuck secretaries. A man of his caliber didn't fuck the help, and that's what Julia was in his eyes. Now had Eloise mentioned one of the associate attorneys, he'd be guilty as charged.

Coming closer to his vehicle, he reached into his jacket

pocket. He removed his key fob. Fitzgerald deactivated the alarm. The moment he did so, he was instantly caught off-guard and confronted. From the shadows, they hurriedly attacked him with a taser to his neck, and 50,000 volts were shot into his body, quickly immobilizing him. Fitz went down like he got hit by Mike Tyson. He was fucked up, but he was still aware, and his attacker hit him again with 50,000 volts. His body went slack, his mouth duct taped, and he was thrown into the trunk of his own vehicle.

Layla glared at him and uttered, "I think it's time you and I have that talk about the feds...don't you agree?"

They closed the hatch on him, and Bugsy and Meyer got into Fitz's sedan and drove away with his muffled screams crying out in vain.

Layla and Eloise followed behind them in Meyer's vehicle.

Franklin and Martha sat dumbfounded, mouths agape, eyes bulging wide in disbelief. They were called to the principal's office of Junior's high-priced private school in midtown Manhattan. Most children were chauffeured to school in Bentley's, had nannies, butlers, and substantial trust funds.

The graduates of Windsor Academy usually had Warton, Harvard, or Columbia University in their futures—all on the trajectory to success.

Principal Cummings continued, "He's told several students, really, anyone who would listen, that his father's ghetto mistress came to his home and held his family at gunpoint because his father had robbed the woman of her diamonds. And forced her to do sexual things that his father videotaped. Franklin said he

66

then wrestled the woman's gun away from her and shot her in the face, saving the day. Your son said he was ordered to his room while his parents chopped the body up into tiny pieces so they could 'Jimmy Hoffa' her."

"Mrs. Cummings—" Franklin tried to address the situation before being rudely interrupted.

"Mrs. Garrett, you know this behavior is unacceptable at Windsor." Principal Cummings directed her eye contact toward Martha, whom she felt was more suitable to hear what she had to say. Principal Cummings knew Franklin worked for the government and somehow could pay his son's hefty tuition, yet she saw through him. His son's kinky hair was cut so low he was almost bald. More than half of the school's students wore sneakers with their uniforms, yet Junior came to school in Penny Loafers. Penny Loafers? Despite the school having other African American and biracial students—all of whom were actually wealthy; Junior had no friends of color.

Yolanda Cummings was a privileged biracial woman who presented as Black, whose father made his fortune in real estate. Her African American father forbade her to have Black friends. All her acquaintances had blonde hair and blue eyes for the first fifteen years of her life. She went through an identity crisis in her teens, wanting to have straight, blonde hair and wearing hazel or blue contact lenses. She was a hot mess until she met her husband, Tyrone. He encouraged her to remove her weave, remove the contacts, and self-identify with her inner self. Now approaching her sixtieth birthday, she recognized her father in Franklin Garrett. Especially when a new Black student came to the school, Yolanda personally asked Junior to show the student around. Junior came to school the next day and announced that his father told him to tell Mrs. Cummings to find someone else.

"Mrs. Cummings, I can assure you those are yawns spun from a boy with an active imagination," Martha explained. "Junior has aspirations of becoming a writer."

"Sounds like lies from a child reaching out for help or with psychological issues," Yolanda replied bluntly.

Franklin spoke up. "Please don't disrespect my son or me, undermining his mental health. Now my wife said he was using his writer's imagination."

"That she did," Yolanda replied. "And I'm calling bullshit. Frankly, should his behavior continue, I'll have to contact authorities."

"Don't fuck with me," Franklin exploded. "I *am* authorities!"

"You are," Yolanda nodded. "But you're not *my* authority. In fact, you've left me no choice but to suspend Junior for a week, contact the board and report this incident and place it up for review, and contact our local precinct. And finally, my husband's uncle is the police commissioner. I have three aunts who are senators in three states, my first cousin is the Secretary of State, and my husband has your boss on speed dial. Excuse my French, but don't fuck with *me*. I fuck back!"

Bugsy and Meyer beat Fitz with their fists, making Fitz's face look like ground beef. He was tied to a chair and bleeding—dazed and traumatized. He had no idea what was happening. One moment he was having a good time with Eloise, and the next, he was beaten and tortured by his former client and her thug sons.

This was *only* personal. Fitz had chosen to fuck Bugsy and Meyer over while their parents were away, and now he would have to pay for his decision.

Bugsy struck him with a powerful right hook, making it feel like the man had removed his jaw. Fitz moaned as blood spewed from his mouth. He was slumped in the chair; his restraints were tight around his wrists and ankles. For however long, he would be their victim—their punching bag, as they wanted him to sing like he was Pavarotti.

"Tell us about the feds, cracker!" Meyer spat; his face crumbled in a frightening scowl.

"What?" Fitz was clueless. "Feds? I don't know anything about the federal government!"

Layla stood before him. She was every bit the heartless, sneaky, conniving cunt Fitzgerald despised. She said, "Sure you do. You were working with them pigs to keep my son incarcerated on a weapons charge!" She pulled out a pack of Newports and lit one up. Layla took a long drag and casually blew out a circle of smoke. The smoke billowed conspicuously in front of the hostage. For Fitz, the action was a sweet refuge from the pain—a tiny pocket of peace. He wanted her to smoke the whole pack if it meant no more torture. Layla's anger returned, and she barked, "A fuckin' gun!"

Bugsy took a baseball bat and attacked his kneecaps with it. The pain was unbearable, and Fitz's howling echoed throughout the bricked and secluded area.

"Layla, please listen...please." He was drooling large globs of saliva down his chin as he searched for words. His head felt too heavy to hold steady as it rolled back and forth, side to side. "The only thing...I'm guilty of...is...getting greedy...I swear...I only tried to extort them...nothing more."

"Only?" Meyer spat. He took an ice pick and attacked Fitz's hands, puncturing his flesh and bones.

"Ahhh!" Fitz screamed an ear-piercing pitch that cut through the room, sending a chill cascading down Eloise's back. She was still there, front and center, watching her lover tortured. The rumbling in her stomach quickly surfaced, and Eloise took a couple steps before regurgitating her last meal. Sweating freely, she wiped her forehead with the palm of her hand. After witnessing this depravity, the money they had promised her wouldn't even cover the therapy bills she was sure she'd need. The hoodlums had said they wanted to smack him around a little. *I guess little is relative,* she thought.

"Get ya shit together, snowflake," Layla hollered. "Or you can join your lil' boyfriend!"

Eloise slid her hands over her dress, straightening out imaginary wrinkles. Clearing her throat, she swallowed a vile taste before responding, "He's not my boyfriend!"

Fitz couldn't concern himself with Eloise or what role she played in his abduction. He wanted the pain to stop but not in conjunction with his life.

They continued to beat him something awful. He was a bloody, ugly mess. While they were torturing him, Layla stood right there and watched it happen with an unsmiling expression.

"I've been nothing...but loyal to you," he painfully cried out. "I saved your life from imprisonment...got you acquitted. What more do you want?"

"Keep fuckin' him up. I want him to talk," Layla uttered unsympathetically. "Feds, nigga! Tell us what the fuck you know!"

She was heartless—never had one.

Bugsy continued his sadistic action with the baseball bat— *"Pop!"*—the noise akin to hitting a ball out of the park; you could hear his bones breaking. Fitzgerald's blood-curdling screaming was almost deafening. But they were someplace where Fitz could scream his lungs away, and no one would hear him.

"Pop!" another hit, and Fitz's leg seemed to dangle—all bones fractured, splintered, or broken.

"Didn't I tell you to not fuck with me and mine?" Layla asked. She walked over and grabbed a handful of his tussled mane. His hair was damp, stringy, unruly, and sweaty. The pretty boy with the golden locks and playboy looks was no more. She leaned down, face to face, spittle spewed on his cheeks. In a low menacing voice, she said, "My daughter is missing, and so help me God, if you don't tell me who put you on to my sons...to fuck up their shit...play fuckin' ring around the rosy games with Meyer! Got him selling damn near his ass to get his brother outta jail—"

Layla's rant was interrupted when Bugsy and Meyer broke out into laughter.

"Ma, not selling my ass...." Meyer cracked up at the thought. "Yo, you wildin' right now."

Layla got the joke and began laughing too. Her shoulders lifted up and down as she released some much-needed joy.

Bugsy took over the interrogation.

"Just tell us about Ragnar. Who is he, and where can he be found?" Bugsy's voice was tempered, soothing as if he didn't just participate in beating the shit out of Fitzgerald.

Fitz was so confused. If he knew his history, Ragnar was a Viking warrior; he was never contacted by the feds and was clueless about a missing daughter. Finally, he resigned himself to die.

The hotshot lawyer, successful, brilliant, and held in high regard by his peers, had squandered his career and made the ultimate sacrifice—his life over greed and ego. He wanted to rewind to the day Meyer had called about his brother, the confiscated money, and frozen assets.

Fitz would have done what he does best—make fools of the government while getting his name in the papers, garnering more high-paying clients. He would have been in this infamous family's debt, not on their kill list. Now it was too late. He sobbed heavily and pleaded once again.

"You don't kill lawyers like me," he said. "The feds didn't contact me to go against you or your family. Allow me to live so that I can defend you!"

His face was so sweaty and distorted that Layla couldn't see his tears, but she knew they were there. She walked over and folded the broken man into her arm. His head fell into her breasts, trembling, and Layla felt the shudders from a dead man. He sobbed against her as she gently rubbed his back and whispered that he would be all right.

"Fitz, we go way back," she exclaimed. "I don't want to hurt you."

"We do," he agreed. "And I care and treasure the relationship we have."

Layla found his remark amusing. "Care...?" she scoffed. "You stole from me! Left my son to rot in jail! And railroaded the other one. How the fuck does that equate to anything less than hate?"

Fitzgerald whimpered some more. When she outlined his actions, it sounded really fucking harsh.

Meyer screamed. "Where is he? All you have to do is give us a fuckin' location, and we can end this, Fitz!"

"I don't know who *he* is!" Fitz bellowed, tired of being beaten, bullied, and brainwashed into believing he knew something about something.

"Where is that bitch, Ragnar, Fitz?" Layla heatedly demanded.

Fitz huffed and puffed. Layla simply shot a look at Meyer, and he already knew what to do. He took the ice pick and went to work brutally amputating two of his fingers from his right hand. The pain was excruciating, and Fitz intensely fidgeted in his restraints. He wanted to pass out, but Bugsy dowsed him with cold water and yelled, "Stay awake muthafucka!"

"Say something, nigga!" Layla shouted.

Still, nothing. Fitzgerald had nothing to give up.

"I'll admit, he is a tough and stubborn sonofabitch," Meyer uttered.

He wasn't. He just didn't have any information to trade for his life.

"Yous a dumb cracker!" Meyer barked. "You gonna go out

like this for a fed?" he asked.

Fitz was barely conscious now. They brutalized him in ways that no one could imagine. His legs and nose, and jaw were broken; he looked unrecognizable. He was in such bad shape that he wanted to die. The pain was great, but what hurt the most was that he hadn't settled down, had children, no one to carry on his name for his legacy.

"This nigga ain't talkin', Ma. He ain't sayin' shit," Meyer uttered. "Maybe he really don't know anything."

"He knows something," Layla replied to them.

"Well, he ready to die than talk," said Meyer. "Let's see if I'm right!"

Meyer reached into his waistband, hand tightly gripped on his Glock. As he extended his arm, the gun went off.

Bak...bak, bak!

A bullet whizzed past his mother's head, causing her to duck. The other two lodged randomly into a wall.

Layla frowned and seethed.

She asked, "What the fuck was that nigga?"

Meyer was stumped. He had momentarily lost control of his weapon and could have killed his mother. Meyer knew he hadn't felt like himself lately, but this was next-level incompetence.

All he could say was, "Shit, crazy."

The room fell quiet as everyone processed what had just taken place. Bugsy knew that this wasn't his twin. It was an inferior version of his brother, and he didn't like it. But now wasn't the time for a family intervention.

Layla broke the silence and snapped, "Fuck it, just get rid of him. And this snitch bitch too!"

CHAPTER 6

On the other side of the looking glass stood Special Agent James Dough, aka Malcolm, and Agent Terrence Barnes, aka Elliott McDonald. Both agents were located in the Chicago field office, the same office where their colleague, Laurence Warren, reported to. When Laurence was murdered on location, his superiors called in Dough to help bring about a resolution. James's assignment was Scott and Layla West, but he felt the children were more vulnerable. And so did others.

His initial interest in the case was money; the young Wests' had lots of it. But further investigating, he found that not only did the young Wests get wiped out of their illegal gains in one night. But someone had also hit their residences, stolen millions, and destroyed the rest. James saw the numerous photographs of destroyed paintings, vermin infestation, and an empty safe.

James had already sent Agent Barnes after Lollipop, and Terrence was gaining traction as Elliott. And then a gaggle of high-priced lawyers filed paperwork on behalf of the Wests'. A

John Doe agent had allegedly had an affair with Lucky. The agent videotaped a sexual encounter, uploaded it to the worldwide web, and was behind the home burglaries where five million was stolen. An internal memo went out with the agent's name redacted. Only those with high enough clearance were privy to who this agent was.

It was easy for James to get his hands on an unredacted copy, and Franklin Garrett's name appeared throughout. But Franklin wasn't done with his bullshit. New accusations were filed; this time, it alleged that Lucky West was missing and presumed dead. James knew the drug queenpin wasn't missing. He didn't have to see a body or witness the murder firsthand to know Garrett had put his murder game down.

A couple of conversations and Agent Dough negotiated a transfer for Franklin to the Chicago office. He arrived with his family a few weeks ago and was settled in. Garrett thought the seasoned Special Agent Dough had offered him a handout, a new beginning. The chance to get away from the accusatory eyes and judgment his colleagues were doling out. But James wasn't a giver. He took what he wanted when he wanted; as far as James was concerned, Franklin had stolen from *him*. That five million was his to take—and then some.

James looked at the pretty red nigga and felt nothing but disdain. He hated niggas like him growing up, getting all the women, using his looks as a weapon. Men like Franklin would clown men who looked like James until James would pick up a brick and bash in their faces.

One year away from his sixtieth birthday, James had been in the military for years before joining the bureau. Growing up, kids teased him because he resembled the former President of Uganda, Idi Amin. James wasn't unattractive; he was ugly—by everyone's standards. If he wasn't being teased, he was overlooked or blatantly ignored. So, his powerful, pronounced looks shaped his outlook on women, morals, relationships, ethics, politics, and religion.

Everybody needed to suffer was his mantra. And as a Special Agent, he had the tools to do so. If Franklin had a god complex, James felt he *was* God. And being omnipotent, he demanded complete control. The women informants that worked under his tutelage had three things in common, which made them easy to spot. Whether they wanted to or not, his snitches had to work out in the gym. He needed their bodies tight to fuck whom he wanted them to fuck. The women had to be well-read. He had them read nonfiction and self-help books; he needed conversationalists. He preferred them to have a bachelor's or master's degree. If not, he would send his stable of minions to online accredited schools. They'd go one day a week in accelerated programs. His informants would get a four-year bachelor's degree in eighteen months, and a master's an additional eleven. They didn't have to *actually* do the assignments; the teachers were under James's umbrella and would get these F students straight As.

And his final requirement was religion. All his women began talking about God and atonement, praising Jesus constantly. For James, it didn't matter what faith: Christianity, Catholicism, Islam, Buddhist, Mormonism, Judaism, Taoism, or Hinduism because he, himself, didn't believe. He wasn't agnostic; he was an atheist.

James Dough was the Picasso of reinvention. He would watch these hood females, whom he employed to set up drug dealers to be murdered, robbed, and incarcerated, speak about Jesus, atonement, and karma and revel in the transformation. He was operating a cult, and they all drank his Jesus Juice.

To James, Franklin was a fool. You don't kill women like Lucky West. You leave them alive so you can repeatedly rob them. Why kill the engine that's supplying you with the gravy train? And you certainly don't do petty shit like fuck the subject and post it to social media. Those actions were flagrant. But Franklin was now on his turf, and he would school this youngin.

James would get his five million from Franklin. Whatever stash Franklin had accumulated throughout the years before ultimately bumping him off. And along the way, he was going to pit Lollipop against Meyer and close a drug case against the Wests that none of his peers are seemingly able to close. James would have a full meal off this case. He would have his cake and eat it, too, leaving no crumbs left on the table.

"Yo, what's good?" Meyer asked when Larry picked up on the first ring.

Larry was shocked that he was receiving this call without provocation. "You tell me, playah."

"Your peoples…make that happen."

In a rushed tone, Larry replied with, "We could meet today. Just give me a place and time, and I'll make it happen."

"How about now."

"Now? No doubt. Let me hit you back—"

Meyer chuckled. "I'm fuckin' with you nigga. Ain't no connect of their caliber dropping everything to meet anyone. Not even me."

Larry realized that he sounded thirsty, a little too eager. He needed to calm down. Larry said, "You right. You right. But they my peoples, so I figured they'd come through on the strength of me."

"Word?"

"Word."

There was a pregnant pause, and then, "Listen, Bugsy's home, and he wants to meet with just you first. If he's on board, you set up the meet with your connect...run some numbers...see what they're all about."

With Bugsy fresh out of jail on bail, the DEA warned Larry that the twins would cautiously ask plenty of questions about his connect. Larry had to answer these questions convincingly at the drop of a dime. One stammer, a moment of hesitation or uncertainty, and the meeting would fall apart.

Two weeks later, Larry had his meet. But he had to jump through hoops to have a sit down with them. The twins had removed themselves from the day-to-day operations and insulated themselves from the streets. As Larry was making his rounds in the hood, it was evident that few had put eyes on Bugsy, Meyer, or Lucky. That information was relayed to Tannery and Brown, who dismissed it.

"Not important," Tannery said. "We focus on getting the brothers in a room with Pablo and Diablo and purchasing tons of cocaine. That's the assignment!"

Tannery knew the FBI was fucking with the family, so their behavior was normal. And as long as they trusted Larry, little else concerned him.

Larry took a nervous pull from the cigarette in his hand. He felt tension inside his chest as his eyes darted around his head like two balls in a pinball machine. Becoming a snitch—a government informant made him extremely paranoid. He felt like a blind man wandering around an active minefield; one wrong step—*boom*, no more Larry.

The car idling on the Harlem block he was parked on wasn't too far from where he ran, hollering, shooting blanks at the two block huggers Meyer had beef with. Tannery chose that location to trigger trust and remind Meyer that Larry had his back.

Meyer was running damn near an hour late, and the feds

kept blowing up Larry's phone.

"Why isn't he here yet?" Brown bellowed.

"How the fuck should I know? You tell me? Y'all the intel niggas."

"Don't get cute," Brown warned. "All I'm saying is that he better show up! Or your little stint as kingpin is over!"

Larry was over the threats. He started chain smoking by lighting a new cigarette from the butt of his last cigarette. The outside of his car was piling up with Newport butts. His head was on a constant swivel; he kept his eyes on every approaching vehicle. Every sound startled him.

"C'mon nigga, get your nerves right, don't blow this shit," he said to himself.

Behind him, headlights loomed closer. Larry fixed his eyes on the vehicle from his side-view mirror. From the silhouette of the approaching truck, he could see that it was an SUV. It moved closer and stopped parallel to where he was parked. The passenger window rolled down, and Meyer hollered, "Get in."

Larry took a deep breath and removed himself from his driver's seat, gun in hand out of habit. Meyer said, "Yo, you ain't gonna need that."

"You sure? You know we stay at war," Larry replied dubiously.

"This a fuckin' tank we rolling in, bulletproof." Meyer was pushing Scott's Tahoe. One of two his father had bought after the sicarios kidnapped him and Layla. "Besides, this is just a meeting, right?"

"Yeah," replied Larry halfheartedly. "But are you strapped?"

Meyer barked, "Nigga, don't worry about me."

Reluctantly, Larry left his useless gun behind in the car and climbed into the passenger seat of the Tahoe. It drove off. Larry sat back and tried to keep his nerves calm.

Within a minute, Meyer asked, "Let me see ya phone."

"My jack? Why?"

Meyer was silent, and Larry took that to mean there wouldn't be an explanation. He handed his DEA-issued cell phone to his former boss and hoped Meyer didn't have some device that proved it was a federal-issued recording and tracking tool.

The driver's window slid down, and the phone was tossed out. Larry swallowed hard and expected an automatic pistol to be placed at his head. He waited a beat and nothing.

Larry barked, "Yo, what you doin', Meyer? How you gonna just toss my shit?"

"You ballin', right? Buy a new one."

"But that ain't the point!" Larry was still trying to remain in character.

"Oh, yeah…," Meyer asked. "What's the point?"

"Nothing," Larry mumbled. "You actin' real extra right now."

"It is what it is," Meyer casually replied. "Yo, look in the glove compartment and put on that blindfold. And I don't want to hear you complaining like a lil' bitch, or I can turn this truck around now and drop you the fuck off!"

Reluctantly, Larry placed the black bandana around his eyes, trusting the feds' ability to successfully tail them without his phone and hopefully without being spotted.

Larry made small talk. "Yo, I been flooding the streets…thinking 'bout expanding my territory just like y'all did. You and Bugsy. Whatchu think about that?"

Meyer ignored the question.

Larry said, "You saw my whip when you pulled up? That's my new ho…she cost a nigga $200,000…cash. I went to ya man, over in midtown. I remember when you took me there back in the day and dropped half a milli cash on two whips and crashed one joint that same day. You remember that?"

Casually, Meyer asked, "You wired nigga?"

The question had Larry stumped. How was he supposed to answer? What did Meyer know? Plump, round sweat beads traveled down the outskirts of his face, outlining his lying mug. He managed to play offended. "Don't even say no disrespectful shit like that! I would never turn snitch. That's on my mama's soul...may she drop dead now!"

"I'm just fuckin' with you nigga. My bad."

Larry chuckled nervously.

Meyer gave him the side eye. "You alright? You seem different?"

Larry's rebuttal was the most used scapegoat. "Tired. You know how it is."

Meyer nodded, navigated the SUV toward the Major Deegan Expressway, and they traveled north toward the Bronx.

Half-hour later, Meyer guided Larry into the bleachers of Yankee Stadium. The property was closed and secluded, with no staff or pedestrians. It felt like he was being led to his death. He took a deep breath, and time felt like it was moving slowly. All this to meet with Bugsy?

The blindfold was removed, and Larry had to adjust his eyes to his surroundings. He was thoroughly patted down by Meyer for a wire but knew not to voice any objection.

Bugsy was chatting on his cell phone in the vast stadium, busy with a quick conversation. It wasn't Larry's business whom he was talking to, but he couldn't help but eavesdrop, maybe get a name for Tannery. But when Larry set foot in Bugsy's personal space, he curtailed the call.

Larry had Bugsy's undivided attention.

He intently looked at Larry and said, "Meyer tells me you got some peoples you want me to meet."

Realizing he had only one shot at making this work, Larry thought about how eager he sounded with Meyer. He decided to switch it up. Mainly because there was something about Bugsy. Meyer invoked fear, but Bugsy's aura demanded respect.

"Nah. That ain't how it went down," Larry started slowly, wanting Bugsy to pull the information from him—but not forcefully.

"Okay," Bugsy replied. "Then tell me how it went down."

"Yeah, tell me too," Meyer chimed in, amused.

"Meyer mentioned he was shopping for a new connect. I told him I got y'all...and on the strength of how we're practically fam...I'd give y'all a low number." Larry lifted up his upper lip, revealing a missing tooth. "You see how that conversation went."

Bugsy feigned disappointment.

"You know, sometimes my brother uses his fists as full sentences. But this is a business meeting, and you're dealing with me now. We're looking for new distro, and it seems you got one."

"Yeah. They broke off from the Los Pepes cartel and got quality pure white. Their powder is grade A...so good, I'm about to expand my territory."

Meyer asked, "Who these niggas you talkin' about? What're their names?"

"Diablo and Pablo. Colombians."

"I never heard of these niggas." Meyer's voice was gruff, and he moved a few inches closer to Larry, making him visibly uncomfortable.

"They like to keep a low profile, Meyer."

"And you sayin' their legit peoples?"

"Yeah, Meyer...I vouch for these niggas."

"Like you vouching for these niggas mean anything to me," Meyer rebuked.

"You can meet them and feel 'em out yourself. I'm sayin', just ask around about them."

Meyer kept his skeptical eyes on Larry, sizing him up from head to toe. Larry stood tall and tried his best not to look nervous, but he was shook. The conversation had to flow like running water, and Larry was doing well so far. He kept regular eye contact with the brothers and kept his nerves together.

"Yo, how a nigga like you connect with these bosses?" asked Meyer.

"You remember my cousin Malik that did a bid upstate a few years ago?"

"Nah, who?"

Meyer was dragging him, making Larry work hard to sell his story.

"Anyway," Larry said, ignoring the disrespect. "Malik's cellmate was Gino, Pablo's first cousin. We all became cool; you know what I'm sayin'? I reached out to Gino knowing he was connected, and things been all love ever since."

"A'ight. We'll meet with these niggas, see what they talkin' about. But if these niggas ain't legit Larry...you already know! Ain't no second chances," Meyer warned him.

"Hell, naw! I can only be accountable for myself. Y'all grown men. I said I can setup a meet...the rest is on you. Y'all meet with them and talk...vet these niggas on the spot. If you don't like what these niggas got to say...fuck 'em," Larry said heatedly. "These niggas seem shady, then lullaby these spicks. I don't give a fuck! I'll find a new connect."

Larry hoped that his performance had passed the smell test. He could have approached this meeting in many ways, but the best way was to cover his ass. Larry realized mid-meeting as Bugsy's eyes bore holes into him. If the DEA agents mess up in the meeting and the twins get wind that they're federal, he's the first person getting murked. But and however, his words, the ones he just uttered, would undoubtedly ring true that he was not involved.

"You just vouched for these niggas!" Meyer barked.

Larry shrugged. "Shit done changed."

Inwardly, Larry breathed a sigh of relief. But he kept a deadpan expression. The hard part was over, Larry felt. Once the brothers met with Diablo and Pablo, he was sure they would be convinced they were the real deal—Colombian drug traffickers.

Because Larry was easily fooled by them. There was no way they would smell law enforcement from these two men.

Bugsy said, "Set up the meeting with your connect,"— and walked off.

Larry was happy to leave his presence.

He climbed into the passenger seat of the Tahoe, blindfolded, and was driven back to his sedan. The ride was silent. He and Meyer spoke no words to each other. Arriving at his parked car, Meyer finally told him before Larry could leave, "Nigga, they better be who you said they are." And then simulated a gun with his hand, pointed it at Larry's temple, and pulled the trigger.

Larry didn't reply. He climbed out of the vehicle, and Meyer peeled out. With the SUV gone in the wind, Larry took two steps to his car, quickly bent over, and threw up chunks of vomit onto the pavement. It was all that nervousness spilling out of him.

He thought, *how is this all gonna play out?*

The incident at the principal's office left Franklin no choice. He signed his son out of Windsor Academy that day, noting that he would be home-schooled moving forward. Franklin and Martha knew that they were taking a considerable gamble. Believing that their numerous talks with their son about keeping what happened in the privacy of their home between them was foolish.

Junior had been kept home for a week after he murdered Lucky, and several times a day, his parents would have a talk with him.

"What happened here was an unfortunate incident," Martha would say. "But I want you to know you saved our lives, Junior. And I know you might feel sad or have difficulty processing the situation. Is that true? Do you feel sad about the woman who came to hurt us?"

"No, mom. I know she was a bad lady, and I had no choice."

Franklin spoke. "You might want to discuss this with someone, perhaps your friends. And under any other circumstance, we would let you speak with a therapist so you could explain things that you don't feel comfortable talking about with us. But you know that daddy has an important job, and if you told anyone about what happened here, I would get in trouble. Do you want me to get in trouble?"

"No, dad. I understand, and I won't say a word. It's our secret, right? I won't tell anyone. Ever." He crossed his heart with his right hand—his trigger finger hand and said, "I swear."

For a week, Junior said all the right words. And then went to school and spilled family secrets. When the Chicago bureau called and asked if he could transfer to help on a case, he didn't even consult with his wife before accepting.

Martha wasn't too pleased about leaving her parents and certainly wasn't partial to moving to The Windy City, but she knew her ass was on the line too. She and Junior flew out ahead of Franklin. He stayed behind to continue covering their tracks and place his home on the market. Luminol pinpointed precisely what needed to be done, and his kitchen floor was ripped up and replaced.

In Chicago, he settled into a beautiful rental, and Martha homeschooled Junior right before he joined in on the tail end of an investigation. And there he was, interrogating Riley Baker, having a full circle moment.

He said, "I know you love this man, but the feeling isn't mutual."

"You don't know shit about us!" she bellowed.

"I know you've been with Meyer for years and never graduated to his main woman. His *wifey*, as your generation calls it."

Her eyes rolled.

"Meyer has bought women cars and condos throughout the years. What has he done for you?"

"I said I ain't gonna snitch, so lock me the fuck up and throw away the key! I'm done talking."

Riley was delirious. Not only was she sleep-deprived, but the realization that she was tricked into coming to Chicago to mule drugs had her drained. She was facing life in prison for something she didn't do and was now asked to play an important role in sending the man she loved to jail for the rest of his natural life. All her fight, energy, witty remarks, and comebacks were zapped out of her. At this moment, a jail cot and baloney sandwich were equivalent to The Four Seasons and a steak dinner.

A hand tapped on the glass, and both agents walked out without excusing themselves.

Inside the adjacent room, James said, "Give her one phone call and send it to voicemail and then have her arraigned, held without bail, and put our team of COs on her. Under those conditions, she'll contact us for cooperation in a few weeks."

Franklin shrugged. "You sure? She seems like a tough nut to crack. That ride or die hood love can be strong."

"Would you rather I had Agent Barnes fuck her and post it to the web?" James spat. "Is that the remedy to make women fold under pressure?"

Franklin fumbled for words. "I...not exactly...I was just—"

"I know what you were doing. You were trying to undermine me in front of my team. Perhaps trying to salvage whatever dignity you have in your pathetic core to still call yourself an agent. Make a mental note," James's eyes were onyx black. "This is Chicago. And I run shit."

CHAPTER 7

Meyer was full nod in the privacy of his room when his family invaded his personal space. He looked up to see his mother, father, and brother with scowls on their faces.

Not now, he thought. *Please don't fuck up my high.*

Meyer wasn't in the mood to go on a killing spree, thinking that was what they were there for.

"What the fuck are you on?" Scott asked, getting straight to the point. "You getting high on your own supply?"

It took longer for him to answer questions when he was fucked up because the words filtered slower when he drank Lean.

Finally, he said, "Y'all...know...I smoke weed."

Meyer attempted to reach for his blunt in the ashtray. Everyone watched in sheer horror as his arm moved as if they were watching a video clip on *Slo-Mo* setting.

Scott was about to do it, but Layla's reflex was quicker. Her open hand swiftly and harshly landed across her son's face, and he toppled over on his floor. Meyer tried to get up but was too faded. He settled face up, lying on his back, drifting in and out of consciousness.

Finally, Bugsy understood what was happening.

"You drinking Lean, aren't you?" he asked. "You on that dope fiend shit?"

Scott and Layla hadn't heard of Lean; it wasn't their generation.

Scott said, "Lean? What's that?"

"Cough syrup. You drink enough of it, and niggas end up overdosing. Dead, Meyer! Is that what you want?"

Bugsy thought about rappers Juice WRLD, Big Moe, and Pimp C, who had allegedly OD'd on the sweet, potent drink and refused to let his brother go down that path.

"You drinking codeine like a fucking junkie!" Scott roared, yanking his son by the collar like a ragdoll and tossing him on the bed. The jolt woke Meyer up. He sat up in bed, and a hard right to his jaw leveled him back down. Scott reigned punches down on his son, giving him a litany of body shots. At the same time, Meyer folded into the fetal position and covered his head. "You see what the fuck happened with my sister!"

Bugsy hated seeing his brother violated like this, but the addiction was worse.

Scott continued, "You could have killed my wife! My *wife*, nigga...you hear me!"

Meyer didn't mumble a fucking word as his body drank in all those hits. He could hear the disappointment in his father's voice even through the haze. Meyer thought about his sister, Lucky, and then Lollipop. Shit was fucked up, and he needed an escape. What part didn't they understand?

Bugsy finally pulled his father off his brother before he broke something, and then Meyer would be prescribed opioids. And it would be a full circle moment.

Layla jumped in to get her hits off when Scott dialed it back. She slapped Meyer several times across his face and then burst into tears. Emotional Layla was so foreign that Scott and Bugsy were both at a loss for words.

Layla sat beside her favorite son and cradled his head in her lap.

"No child of mine will be a junkie," she said tearfully. "You're better than addiction. You hear me, Meyer?"

Layla was massaging her son's back as her tears dripped on his sleeve. She continued, "You're Meyer West! These streets will remember your name decades after you're gone, and it won't be because you fell off, were murdered, or were incarcerated. They'll remember you and Bugsy for the long reign y'all will have on these streets. For men under twenty-five who took an illegal operation and turned it into a legal corporation. The streets will praise your business acumen and wish they were you…not mention you as the blueprint of what not to do. You hear me, Meyer?"

Meyer gave a weak head nod, but it was all the acknowledgment that his mother needed.

"You're going to the best rehabilitation center our money can afford."

Scott said, "No, he's not."

Layla looked up and smirked.

"He's going to detox here and suffer through it like the gangsta he is. Because if we make this addiction public—if our enemies get a whiff of this; FBI, DEA, or hooligans, his addiction will be weaponized. And we can't have that…not with everything we've been through and still have to go through."

"It's settled then. I'll call Mason," Layla said, understanding her husband's position.

Riley was given one phone call to call the only person she knew with enough clout, money, and attorneys on speed dial: Meyer. Her heart sank when the call went to his voicemail, but in a panicky plea, she gushed, "Meyer, first, let me apologize for the other night. I'm not engaged to be married, but in Chicago arrested for the distribution of drugs. The feds are tryin' to railroad me, and I need your help. Please get me out of here...please get me a lawyer and post bail. I hope you know this, but my government is Riley Baker. Meyer, I need you. More than ever...and you already know that I love you. You'd never want this for me, even if you don't feel the same. We have history, Meyer—"

"Your phone call is up!" the officer announced and disconnected the line. "Let's go."

Maxine sat outside the Chase bank on most days, panhandling for coins. One or two times a week, Gregory would come through. After her barking incident, she didn't expect to see him again, and for a while, she didn't. But after a few absences, he returned. At first, he would walk by quickly and drop a crisp $20 bill in her cup twice a week. That transitioned into money *and* a Starbucks coffee. Finally, Gregory summoned the courage to sit beside her—smelly, ravaged, broken Maxine, and eat his meal with her on his lunch break.

He would remove his jacket, roll up his sleeves, and sit next to Maxine on her cardboard in his two-piece suit and smart shoes. They'd share various meals from Chipotle to Subway before he'd head back to his office. He noticed Maxine would always only eat half her meal and wrap up the rest.

"Are you saving that for dinner?" He asked one day.

"No. I'm saving this for my housemate, Wendy. We look out for each other, and meals this good and fresh are hard to come by out here."

Each time after that that he came with lunch, he had an extra meal for Wendy. Maxine's eyes welled up with tears from his generosity and compassion.

Gregory didn't ask what Maxine had asked Wendy, which was how she ended up homeless, and he rarely mentioned the past.

Instead, he remained present. He would tell Maxine funny stories of what happened at work that morning and how he looked forward to seeing her that day. Or something as minute as what they thought were the ingredients in the meal he had bought. The bottom line was nothing heavy was discussed. Gregory felt heavy things had broken her; all he wanted to do was piece her back together, one meal at a time.

Maxine found herself looking forward to his visits. She'd search the used clothing bins for nicer outfits and get as many free showers as possible at the women's shelter. Wendy noticed the change in her but said nothing. She watched her roommate getting all dolled up and gave her her space. Maxine was a private person, and if she wanted to share her business—she would.

As summer transitioned to fall, Gregory came as usual with lunch. Before he departed, he reached into his briefcase and pulled out a Gap bag.

"Here," he said. "Just something I thought you'd need on those chilly nights."

Maxine opened the gift and saw an orange wool hat, scarf, and gloves. Her eyes instantly welled up until round, warm tears slid down her hot chocolate-colored skin. Her heart swelled with gratitude, and she gave him a spontaneous hug. Maxine's arms wrapped around Gregory's neck, and when she tried to release him, he gripped her tighter, lingering in her embrace. Gregory inhaled a mixture of stale scents, body odor, and layers of filth and grime and didn't cringe. He had loved this woman since the beginning.

Obviously, this wasn't her first gift. And she had trash bags full of raggedy hats and scarves. It didn't escape Maxine that despite her circumstance, he treated her with dignity and respect. Most exes in his shoes would gloat. The, *look how your life turned out* would be on repeat. Maxine had upgraded to Scott over Gregory and still ended up here. Most would say her fall from grace was karma, payback for all the shit she'd done in her life. But it was more nuanced than that. Complicated and complex yet simple and senseless.

Her fate was sandwiched between two facts; She loved the wrong men and trusted the wrong friend.

On the ground, sitting cross-legged on a cardboard box, mid-embracing, Gregory and Maxine were interrupted by one of his colleagues.

"Greg?" she asked. "What's going on?"

Gregory looked up to see Felicia. They had been working together for the past four years, and in the first two, he had asked her out on several dates, and she'd repeatedly turned him down. He wasn't the only one. Almost every man in that office building wanted her. Felicia was a natural beauty; she favored an older version of Megan Thee Stallion. With her moisturized skin, olive-shaped eyes, long, natural hair, and a shape he dreamed of caressing on many nights.

Felicia didn't date nine-to-fivers. Since he's known her, she's dated a record producer, R & B singer, and an actor with bit roles on *Law & Order, Scandal,* and *How to Get Away with Murder.*

Gregory stood up, so Maxine did too.

"Hey, Felicia. I want you to meet Maxine. She and I went to school together, and she broke my heart." He smiled. "I guess I don't have much luck with the ladies."

Felicia was aghast. Her eyes traveled from Maxine's dirty boots to her wild, matted, funky dreads. She couldn't believe it. Nor could she believe he had the gall to make an introduction. She felt he should have avoided eye contact with her and held his head down in shame at being caught fraternizing with the homeless. Mostly, not have the inflection of pride in his voice when introducing this lowly specimen to someone on her level.

The thought that Felicia had even considered fucking Gregory once upon a time ago had instantly angered her. Was this how he saw her? Equivalent to this degenerate parasite?

"You meant you never had luck with *this* lady," she spat and took a couple steps back to not catch anything they obviously both had.

The slight went over Gregory's head but not Maxine's. She said, "Lady? Bitch, please!"

"Are you speaking to me?" Felicia looked to Greg to answer her. "Is she speaking to me? Let your friend know that I don't fraternize with common folk!"

Max took a couple steps closer to her prey. "You just got your walking privilege revoked. You see, this common folk bitch is the mayor of midtown. Now, you can't walk, stroll, or strut your bougie ass from 34th street all the way up to 59th ...or else!"

Felicia let out an amused chuckle. And said, "You sound crazy!"

Max put her thumb and index fingers in the corners of her mouth and whistled—a distinctive, high-pitched assistance call. The sound brought forth several panhandling vagrants barreling her way. The whistle had been enacted after several homeless men were murdered, being plucked off one by one by an unknown assailant.

The men and women came to Maxine's aide, surrounding her, waiting for further instruction.

"Y'all see this woman," Max announced. "She's no longer allowed to walk our streets. Spread the word!"

The group all studied Felicia, who was now clutching imaginary pearls. Her eyes were wide with fear and confusion, anxiety quickly taking over.

All she could do was pivot on her heels, walk quickly—then run away.

"Bye, Felicia!" Maxine shouted.

Larry felt like he was about to have a panic attack. His heart was racing, and he had chest pains. His hands were clammy, and Larry seemed to be having breathing difficulties. How could he relax when he felt himself being pulled in a tug-of-war? At one end of the rope were the Wests', whom he had to deceive and lie to, and on the other, the DEA, who he had to appease to stay out of jail. He met Tannery on the outskirts of New York.

Albany, New York, was a long drive, but it was a cautious one. Every mile he drove, Larry felt that he was being followed. He constantly looked in his rearview mirror and took unnecessary turns to throw anyone off who might be trailing him. But Larry didn't see anything. He soon arrived at Tannery's chosen location: a storefront parking lot. It was out of the way and quiet, nestled in a small town with provincial customers. Larry had little to fear being seen by anyone he knew.

He climbed out of his McLaren and approached the dark blue Dodge Charger that sat idling. He climbed into the backseat to give his update. The first thing Tannery said to him was, "Why the fuck did you toss your phone?"

"I told you it wasn't me; it was Meyer," he said. "He just took it and tossed it out his window."

"What the fuck you mean he took it? I told you I wanted you mic'd up whenever you meet with them. You meet with Bugsy and come to us with only hearsay." Tannery was annoyed, relying on Larry's version of the meeting. "I think we need to take additional precautions, go old school, and have you wear a wire."

"Meyer fuckin' searched me before I even got to meet Bugsy. If I was wearing it, I would be dead. This is my life on the line, not yours," he rebuked.

"Next time, I want you wired up, no excuses," Tannery warned him.

"This is some bullshit!"

"You do the crime; you become mine. You're my fucking puppet, Larry. Do you understand that? I control you. You do what the fuck I say, and you fuck me over, I'll fuck you over. Capiche?"

Larry frowned. And he dragged out, "Yeahhh...I understand."

"Now, your meet with Bugsy; he's onboard?"

"He's interested in meeting your guys."

"That's great news."

"Yeah, it sounds like it, but I don't trust it. It felt too easy with Bugsy, and I heard Bugsy is never that easy to deal with. Now, Meyer. He was acting like himself...." Larry's mind went over the meeting. He said, "Again, something with Bugsy was off. I think he knows."

"Bugsy's desperate, that's all. He's warring with the cartel, got this gun case in his rearview, and needs a new connect to keep his cash flowing."

"Meyer asked a lot of questions."

"And how did you hold up?"

"I did good. I remembered everything y'all told me, but still, it's the way Meyer keeps coming at me." Larry was angered at continually being played and disrespected. "Even seeing me at this level, pushing the hottest whips, fuckin' the hottest broads! I'm moving tons of weight, and he's treating me like I sell hand to hand. A corner boy!"

Tannery didn't know if he should remind Larry this was all make-believe. But then he realized he should be grateful that the less-than-smart criminal remained in character. He said, "It's his world. He was just trying to throw you off your game. As long as you hold up and stay strong, this entire thing will go over smoothly for you. Easy," said Tannery.

Larry sighed. *There's nothing easy about snitching,* he said to himself.

"We get Bugsy and Meyer on a big buy like this, and it's going to open the door for more convictions, possibly the cartel," Tannery added.

Larry nodded.

Tannery looked at him and said, "Don't worry; you have nothing to worry about. Once we get what we want, your cooperation will be noted to the United States Attorney, and you do your little bit of time, and after that, you can have a life again."

"Yeah, about that," Larry began. He wanted to renegotiate his deal. "I'm takin' all the risk here with the most infamous family on the east coast. If this shit was easy, y'all would already have locked them up. So, I ask myself. Why am I passing go and heading off to jail when I'm done? I need a *get-out-of-jail-free* card, Tannery, and I think you're the man to make that happen."

Tannery's jaw tightened. First, he was threatened by Markeeta, and now this motherfucker. Did they think he was a clown? A fucking joke. A man to be trifled with. He wondered if Larry would have approached Brown, Pablo, or Diablo with this shit.

Tannery bellowed, "Get the fuck out of my car!"

And Larry did.

Riley was denied bail at her arraignment as her court-appointed lawyer was dismissive and condescending when she tried to ask questions. The sitting judge also had harsh words for her. "In Illinois, we don't take kindly to New Yorkers coming to our cities to distribute narcotics, Ms. Baker. We're going to have to make an example out of you...show you that you should have stayed north with your criminal intent." Judge Alexander's eyes were small, beady pebbles of anger and rage. He had already convicted her, yet she had pled *not guilty* because she wasn't.

He continued, "You're remanded to the Metropolitan Correctional Center without bail until your trial date. Next on the docket."

That was it. Riley's wrists and ankles were shackled, and she was led back to a holding cell until she was transported on a bus to MCC. The group of women, Riley counted eighteen, were led to the showers by four women correction officers.

"Shower from head to toe," one yelled. "Including your hair. If you have a weave, that shit's coming out! And don't start fuckin' complaining about how much your weave cost. We don't give a fuck. Point blank. Period!"

Another chimed in with, "Braids too. To be crystal clear, all hair extensions are banned here. Hair extensions can be used as a weapon or to hide weapons. Those are the rules."

Riley listened to a few women with hair extensions mumble incoherent words, but no one wanted to challenge the guards.

After she showered, she heard — "You" — she was singled out. "Follow me!"

The Black female guard, CO Katz, led her into a room where two male guards were.

She said, "Remove your towel. Bend over, spread your ass cheeks, and cough."

The guard began putting on latex gloves. When Riley didn't move, she barked, "Did you fucking hear me, inmate? Or are you fucking retarded? A mute?"

She then began moving her hands as if using American Sign Language. And in a disrespectful, mocking voice, with fake hand movements and gestures, repeated, "Remove your towel. Bend the fuck over. Spread your ass cheeks. Cough, bitch!"

It wasn't a stretch for Riley to deduce that this was precisely what Agent Garrett said would happen. From her phone call to Meyer, the lawyer, judge, and COs, they all operated outside the law. And although she wanted to cry her eyes out, boo-hoo, until she couldn't shed another tear, she refused.

Her towel dropped, and she endured every humiliating cough, probe, grope, and cavity search, all while the men gawked at her nakedness.

At the tail end of processing, she was given prison garb— orange khakis pants and shirt, a white t-shirt, bra and underwear, tube socks, shower shoes, and a pair of canvas slip- ons.

Riley said, "These are a six. I wear a woman's seven."

The guard looked past her. "Next!"

Riley didn't move. She repeated, "These aren't my size. They're too small."

The correction officer repeated, "Next! And call the Sergeant. This one wants to go to the hole on her first day!"

The girl behind Riley whispered, "I wear a six. I'll get a size seven, and we can switch."

Riley stared at the young woman who didn't look one day over eighteen and nodded. She mouthed, "Thank you," and kept the line moving.

CHAPTER 8

The decision-makers of the Garcia cartel were all present to discuss murder. Two sicarios—Félix and Pedro—also attended to discuss their fallen comrades. A windowless room contained the billowing smoke from several lit Cuban cigars that clashed against the wood-paneled walls. A large, Mahagony round table with sturdy high-back chairs held men of importance. Crystal glasses filled with expensive cognac were placed throughout. This was a grown man's meeting to plot grown men's things.

"That bastardo...that insect...that little cockroach dies!" Javier bellowed and slammed his fist on the table. "He thinks he can disrespect me and live?! He's crazy!"

"Calm down, Javier," said Gustave. "We need you focused."

Javier gave his underling the side eye and continued his rant.

"If I say, kill. That little monkey better say how many! If I say, fuck your mother...Scott is supposed to ask how many times! He is a nobody! I made him and will break everything and everyone associated with him."

The room nodded.

That display of anger had raised Javier's blood pressure, and he found himself winded, his breathing sparse, shallow. As his chest heaved up and down, he tried to regain control of his airwaves. Stalling in his seat, he adjusted his suit jacket, examined his cufflinks, and smoothed his already-slicked hair back. Javier was handsome, with salt and pepper straight hair, a clean-shaven face, and brooding eyes. In his sixties, his jowls began to broaden, and his tan skin began to crease. He was showing age in more ways than one. For Javier, sixty wasn't the new forty. Too many plates of rice and beans and tequila shots.

Félix spoke. "Send us to America and let us kill the putas, Scott and his whore! Make an example of them for what they did to Arturo and Raffa."

"Their bodies were never found?" Gustave asked the obvious.

"I personally went to Australia with a couple top men in my militia, and the bodies were never recovered. We last tracked them to Scott's villa, and the trail went cold."

"They were murdered, Gustave. Why are you beating a dead horse? Let's move on and remain present." Javier cleared his throat, indicative that he needed everyone's attention. "I hear he has a grandchild living on this side of the border."

Everyone's ears perked up.

"A grandchild living in México?" one man asked. His name was Ignacio, and he ran the Durango section of México for the cartel. "Why?"

"Because Angel Morales is the father, and the puta's mother is Scott's daughter, Lucky. The bitch that murdered my nephew!"

The men were all aghast that Angel had fathered a half-Black child considering his position and the rule of law for Méxican cartel members.

Pedro asked, "Is this information trusted?"

"It is," Javier retorted. "I understand that Angel has stepped down from the head of the Juárez cartel, and his cousin, Louis, now runs it. The source also said that Angel dotes upon this child night and day, and she is expected to have a very good life here in México."

The room was silent. No one knew where Javier was going with this information.

Félix asked, "What is it you want us to do? Kill the baby?"

Javier slumped back in his seat and bridged his hands together in the prayer position. "You're too eager, my good friend, Félix. The baby will die, yes...but in due time. I am a man of my word, so as I promised the uppity negro, Scott. His wife will die in front of him. A long, excruciating death—"

"She forfeited a good death!" Gustave chimed in.

"Exactly, Gustave. Layla will die in utter pain, and her husband will follow. But not before we explain our plans for his children, Bugsy, Meyer, and Lucky. And right before his execution, we will explain what will be done to his only living grandchild, Lucchese. Scott West will have no legacy. No one will remember him. His lineage will not live on!"

"If we go after Lucchese, that will ignite a war with Juárez, and we've recently called a truce," Gustave warned.

"Angel is no longer Juárez, so there is no threat."

"But his men might still hold allegiance to him or his father. He's only newly retired," Gustave deduced.

"The murder of Lucchese West Morales will be dealt with under *The Genocídio War Rule*. We will do our ancestors proud."

The Genocídio War Rule dates back to the early 20th century when their predecessors used strategic war tactics to destroy their enemies. That approach had gotten watered down and then disregarded in the mid-eighties. Cartels were popping up like toast to get in the drug game, and strategy and tactics were replaced with Uzis and assault rifles. It was far more economical and efficient to kill your enemy quick for total annihilation and domination than to outwit your opponent.

What Javier just noted would happen with Lucchese is controlling her life's trajectory, dictating her every move. These men would shadow the unsuspecting child throughout her life, ensuring she met with heartache, heartbreak, and despair at every turn. *The Genocídio War Rule,* also called *A Living Death,* would ensure that Lucchese lips would never hold a smile, her eyes would never sparkle. And her heart would never be filled with love.

And when she yearned for death by her own hand, it would be at that point she would be tortured and then murdered.

Javier asked, "Have your men ever met the walking dead?"

The room shifted in their chairs and shrugged, already bored with today's agenda.

"You will," Javier boasted. "You will see it with your own eyes!"

Every culture has its traditions. Sicilians believe the best way to destroy their enemy is to kill them and kill off the male heirs—quickly. If not, the remaining boys can seek revenge as men. The Méxican cartel felt that *La Cosa Nostra* was too merciful in not killing women or girls. They couldn't subscribe to this level of compassion, not when México bred fierce women like Sandra Ávila Beltrán, Enedina Arellano Félix, and Claudia Ochoa Félix.

Javier smiled. "Lucchese West Morales is marked for an extended death."

Angel had settled into his fortress by the sea with his four children. He was the first to admit that he missed his former life, including his wife, Dahlia. She had repeatedly called for forgiveness, noting that she could accept Lulu as her own if

Angel took her back. Angel knew his wife had only fallen on her sword after going to Juárez. After she had spoken to Louis and other cartel members, exposing that her husband was harboring a half-Black child.

"La Negra," she kept repeating, tears streaming down her exquisite face. "That little baby is Angel's! They must be dealt with."

"Sure, Dahlia," Louis had said. "We understand."

Dahlia didn't know that Angel was also present at the meeting. Louis had Angel on speakerphone, and he heard his wife pleading for his and Lulu's executions. Angel didn't realize that you can't break a broken woman; that was Dahlia. He brought his love child into his home and treated her like gold and glass—priceless, precious—regal, and rare. It ate Dahlia up inside, watching them interact, her stomach somersaulting, swirling uncontrollably like a tornado. And then she was beaten and discarded.

Her calls came next. "I want to come home, husband," she had said. "My niños need me, including your niña. I will love her, Angel, as I love Mary, mother of Christ Jesus…may you let me raise her as my own."

"You may," Angel finally agreed.

The chauffeured-driven Maybach picked Dahlia up at her parents' home in Chihuahua. The shack had running water and an indoor bathroom—more than most, but it was still a lifetime away from what she was used to. Dahlia had to wear shoes all day because of the dirt floors, and her windows were kept open to allow air to circulate.

She wore her best dress to see her family. Sat back in the luxury vehicle's plush seat and marveled at how grateful she was to feel the air conditioning against her pasty skin.

Dahlia arrived at her home's massive iron and stone gate a long ride later. The car sat idling as her driver buzzed the intercom for entry. Soon she saw Angel carrying his cockroach daughter in his arms, and she swallowed her disgust. And then she saw Marbella—the traitor, and Louis. Why were they there?

As they approached, Dahlia didn't know why she was nervous. Maybe it was because she was reading something in their eyes; evil.

The driver exited the car, opened her door, and escorted her out. At that point, she knew what this was—her execution.

Dahlia refused to run, cry, or beg for mercy. She saw an opening and took it. Dahlia had underestimated Louis's loyalty to his cousin and overestimated the significance of Méxican law to men who broke the rules every day.

She was led to the front gate, which was still closed, and stood there. Her eyes scanned how close her sister was standing next to her husband, a victorious, gloating look in her eyes.

"You'll never be me, Marbella," Dahlia spat. "You may be keeping my side of the bed warm, but he'll never *love* you!"

"You sound bitter, Dahlia," Marbella returned. "It doesn't look good on you."

That response boiled Dahlia's blood. She wanted to rewind to the day she even allowed Marbella under her roof to share in her newfound wealth, to enjoy the amenities of the rich and infamous. And this was how she was repaid.

Angel said, "Lulu, look at Papi." He then gave a head nod to his driver.

Dahlia yelled, "You're a coward, Angel. You couldn't do this yourself! A fuckin'—"

The bullet pierced through her temple and exited out the other side leaving a large exit wound. Dahlia's body toppled over and collapsed on the imported cobblestone pavers.

The spectacle was over.

Whistler spent countless hours in Manhattan surveilling the West family. And it was enough time to see that he wasn't the only one. That family was hot like fire; feds were all over them. Feds didn't have eyes on them around the clock, but they popped up every few days.

It appeared that the twins were living with their parents. But no matter how many locales he frequented that the Wests were partial to, he couldn't find Lucky. The last time he saw her was at her residence, akin to a war zone.

The 1996 Corolla had a rebuilt transmission, new tires, and a hundred thousand miles on it. Whistler bought it, cash, to creep in. It was legit, inconspicuous—no broken lights, dents, or tints. No reason for the cops to pull him over.

Whistler was playing an ole skool Nas CD. The older model car didn't have Bluetooth, nor did he have a smartphone. Technology was a blessing and a curse. They lull you in with convenience and ease and then use those same conveniences to stalk you.

Whistler's head bopped to the beat. He was half a block away from Scott's home. He could have killed the whole family a million times—they were that clueless that he was out there. This fact irked him somewhat. That he was so easily disregarded as a threat. Scott and Layla should have been scouring the world looking for him, looking to finish what they had started. Yet here they were. Handling their day-to-day operations, unaffected that he was still alive. Unbothered that he was their enemy.

His binoculars were placed on the passenger's seat as he reached for an empty water bottle. Whistler unzipped his jeans, and the tip of his penis filled the opening, and he relieved himself. Three other bottles had been topped off with his piss, things that had to be done when stalking.

Whistler picked up his binoculars just in time to see a low rider circle the block for a second time. He could see a few heads, so they were riding deep. It was late, murdering hours, and he knew something was about to jump off. And then the knucklehead came bebopping out of his luxury building, oblivious he was about to be ambushed.

Today would be Meyer West's date of death.

Strapped, Whistler had a .44 in his waist, double nines in his arm holster, and a .380 in his ankle holster. He watched the car slow to a rolling stop and heard, "Meyer! Where the fuck is our money, nigga?!"

Meyer spun around toward the voice and reached for his Ninas only to realize he wasn't strapped. He was fresh out of his detox and still wasn't fully woke. But Meyer was aware enough to determine who had come to murder him. He saw Rakim and other relatives of the men who lost their lives the night Angel's men attacked the warehouses. The family members who felt they were due hefty payouts.

Meyer's eyes scanned the street for an escape route, and just before he took flight, he heard a barrage of bullets. And the four men standing were standing no more. Meyer frantically checked his person for blood, wounds, and holes, but he was fine. He could hear pedestrians screaming; from his peripheral, he saw people running for their lives. And when he looked up, he saw him. Whistler Hussain was standing before him, smoking guns in his hands. The killers eyed each other, neither one making a move. Meyer gritted his teeth. Ready to die without fear.

But his foe didn't kill him. Instead, he smiled—sinister and mockingly. Through deuces in the air and backpedaled away.

The young girl that Riley met at intake was named, Lineeka. She was arrested for trafficking women and assault with a deadly weapon and given a bail she couldn't make. After the shoe exchange, Riley was taken aback when Lineeka was assigned as her cellmate. *She's a snitch*, Riley thought. Just as the agent said, they would plant.

Lineeka spent her days ruminating about the boyfriend she had fought over, the man who didn't appear at her arraignment, and the lover who didn't post her bail. Lineeka spent so much time spewing details of her life that Riley began to doubt that she was the informant—she didn't ask Riley any questions.

They were on the line at chow time when Riley asked, "You love him?"

"Absolutely," she replied. "I know how things look, but the only reason he's ghost is that he doesn't want to get wrapped up in my case. If he comes to visit, well, you know how it is. Feds don't play fair."

Riley nodded. She hardly was in a position to judge this girl about her man when Meyer wasn't shit.

The line always moved progressively quickly until it was Riley's turn. She placed her tray up for her serving of what looked like Salisbury steak, artificial mashed potatoes, canned string beans, and cornbread. Yet, the servers didn't move.

Riley whispered to Lineeka, "Every day they fuckin' do this." And then she said to the kitchen staff, glaring at the two women glaring at her. "What's the holdup? I'm hungry. I would like to eat."

Both women said nothing.

Within minutes another inmate came into the chow hall in janitorial garb. Her jumper was damp. A direct result of the splashed backwash while she cleaned urine and feces from the bathroom toilets. Her long, unpolished fingernails were caked with dirt, and her face held a condescending grin. The woman did not have on a hairnet or gloves, nor did she wash her hands as she reached for Riley's plate.

"I don't want you to serve me," Riley demanded, finally speaking up after a week of these shenanigans. "You don't work in the kitchen!"

"You can eat or not," the inmate stated. "But how long do you think you can refuse food? 'Cause I'm your server. You don't have to like it!"

"I want to speak to someone."

"Sure. How about we just run and get the President of the United States?"

The trio of women burst out into laughter.

"A CO will do because I'm not moving!"

The women inmates behind Riley began to protest, spewing threats of violence if she didn't keep the line moving. Riley didn't budge.

Eventually, the prisoners, including Lineeka, went around Riley and were served by the kitchen staff. Finally, CO Katz came to address the ruckus.

"What's the holdup, Baker?"

Riley said, "I don't want her fixing my food. She doesn't work in the kitchen!"

Katz stared at the janitorial staff inmate and nodded. "You can leave." And then she addressed Riley. "I'll make your plate tonight, but whoever MCC chooses to make plates will do so whether you approve. It's your prerogative to not eat."

"But she's filthy!" Riley protested.

"And this is jail," Katz mocked.

To Riley's surprise, CO Katz walked to the back and came out with a tray already prepared with her dinner. Riley looked at the food warming in the trays before her and had to ask. "Why didn't you just fix my plate in front of me?"

"I did you a favor," Katz spat. "This is untouched. Now get the fuck off my line."

Riley looked at the clock, and ten minutes were left for chow. She grabbed her tray and quickly found Lineeka waving her over to her table.

Lineeka said, "I guess you like being a troublemaker, huh?"

"How so?" Riley asked as she stuffed a large chunk of minced hamburger ground in her mouth, the gravy sliding down her chin. "You mean to tell me you don't see the shit they're pulling?"

"Who's they?"

Riley had to weigh her words. She couldn't say that she was being targeted by federal agents because the implication would be they had her lined up to snitch. She replied, "The COs. They've had it against me since intake."

"And you think challenging them over your food will garner you favor?"

"Are you kidding me?" Riley snapped. "How about every day you and I switch trays, and you eat the food handled by those nasty contaminated fingers."

"Why would I do that? I haven't angered the correctional staff," Lineeka bluntly replied. "And who said your food is contaminated. So what, there's a different person to serve you? You're eating from the same tin pans as the rest of us."

Riley's eyes rolled. She stuffed a large fork full of steak and mashed potatoes into her mouth, leaving the lukewarm string beans alone. She took her cornbread and sopped up the gravy, clearing most of her plate before it was time to go. Her mood had shifted. Her anger transitioned from the kitchen staff to Lineeka.

A sharp pain jolted Riley to attention less than an hour after chow. Her eyes widened as she braced herself for what she knew was coming. Her stomach rumbled loudly as she clutched her abdomen, trying to lessen the excruciating pain. Each step quickened as she headed toward the bathroom. Riley's mouth watered with a vile taste as a bug surged through her body.

She almost cried out as her stomach cramped into painful knots, perspiration dampening her back and forehead. Riley crashed landed on the toilet, and expelled watery diarrhea that splattered throughout the bowl. Each time she thought she had emptied her stomach's contents, she'd have another episodic shit fest, each bout shorter than the last.

Riley remained on the toilet for the better half of three hours. Finally, on wobbly knees, she felt confident enough to return to her cell. There, Lineeka was already tucked neatly onto her bunk—and old Jackie Collin's novel in her hand.

"Where've you been?"

Riley didn't have the strength to reply. She kicked off her slip-ons, climbed onto her bunk, and within minutes she was asleep.

A vagrant, who everyone called Slick Willy Pete, didn't want to wait his turn and decided that jacking Wendy was in his best interest.

Aggressively his bony, weathered fingers grabbed a stronghold on Wendy's bag, and he pulled, scratching her hand with his long fingernails. His bloodshot eyes and rotten tooth snarl said he meant business. He was hungry, and no female would stop him from taking what he wanted.

Wendy flipped open her straight-edged razor as one would open a Japanese pleated hand fan and swung. The sharp stainless-steel blade sliced open his leathery cheek, opening his face to the white meat. However, Slick Willy Pete was liquored up and felt nothing. He continued to charge at her while exchanging words.

Pete said, "Give me this food bitch 'fore I beat ya silly ass to death out here!"

Wendy said, "What business you in, Pete? 'Cause I'm in the knife business!" She quoted her imaginary husband, Delroy Lindo, in *The Cider House Rules*. And Wendy meant those words. She would kill this man dead if he tried to take what belonged to her. Wendy swung again. This time the blade nearly severed the tip of Willy's nose, that cut he felt. Slick Willy Pete's hands went to his face, and he realized he was gushing blood. He hollered for help, but everyone just scattered, including Wendy.

Back at home, Maxine laughed uncontrollably as Wendy rehashed the story while gobbling up her meal. And then she became resolute.

"Things get serious around this time of the year," Wendy warned her protégé. "The weather changes, and the city goes on lockdown, rounding up the homeless trying to get us off the streets, fearing we'll freeze to death." Wendy was sucking the last remnants of meat off the steak bone. The seasoning exploded in her mouth, and she didn't want the meal to end. She continued with, "Fewer people throw food away in the winter than in the warmer months because they spend longer time indoors and simply reheat their leftovers."

"I've noticed that they're less charitable too."

Wendy nodded. "Exactly. The colder months usually provoke depression in some folks, the gloomy days, less sunlight, and such. And then its holiday season…a tough time for many people."

"So, you're telling me to watch my back out here?"

"I'm telling you to rethink your whole situation." Wendy stopped smacking and stared at her roommate. "You're not that far gone, Maxine. This means you can still return to your previous life and acclimate to society without the transition being too rough."

"I told you, I can't go back!" Maxine snapped, showing a glimpse of her former self.

"Then go forward," Wendy said, still challenging her. "It seems you've met someone...who has good taste in meals. Maybe you can start a life with him?"

"Why don't you look in your mirror before cleaning mine?" Maxine reached for a few layers of clothing. "If you don't want me here, just say that!"

CHAPTER 9

The conditions for Riley at MCC didn't normalize for her. At chow time, when it was her turn to get served, as usual, one of the females from janitorial duties would come out to make her plate. The same hands, just elbow-deep scrubbing shit out of a toilet, were now handling her eggs. Sticking hands with dirty fingernails into her soup and dipping those fingers in her juice cup.

Every couple of days, Riley would go on a hunger strike. She would skip all three meals until her mouth was pasty chalk—white and sticky. Her energy and strength were depleted. She'd hold out as long as she could, her body on the brink of shutting down before she'd fold. The lack of nourishment and nutrition caused migraine headaches for her, and she spent most of the days trying to sleep through hunger and hunger pains.

Reluctantly, she'd return to chow. And within a half hour of eating, Riley would get violently ill. She'd rush to the bathroom and spend hours on the toilet with cramps and watery diarrhea, and what didn't come out of her rear end was then regurgitated. Chunks of vomit would spew out into the toilet like she'd turned on a water hose.

"I can't take this," she cried to her bunkmate. "How long is this torture supposed to go on?"

"With your food?"

"What else?!" Riley snapped.

Lineeka was sitting on her bunk penning a letter to her man and wasn't here for the drama. She said, "Well, you haven't ever seen anyone do anything to your food. Have you?"

Riley didn't like the implication—blaming the victim. "What's your point?"

Lineeka puckered her lips, kissed the bottom of her letter with scarlet red lipstick, and blew out air. "My point is until you see the kitchen staff fuck with your food, you would do well to focus on more pressing matters like beating your case—whatever that entails. Because you could very well be allergic to something. That white girl shit...what's it called? Gluten?"

Maybe she's right, Riley thought. What if her body was having an allergic reaction to something.

Riley thought the jail's infirmary was a refuge for her. The female doctor and two staff nurses were all so warm and friendly. They spoke in soft tones and promised they would get her well. A couple tests were done, and she was told she had H. Pylori—a bacterial parasite that is transferred when food is prepared in unsanitary conditions. Hearing the diagnosis, Riley complained to the doctor.

"I knew it! They're doing this to me on purpose," she admonished. "Every day at chow, my food is handled with no gloves. And they always call some random girl from the janitorial staff who's always filthy, sweaty, and unclean."

"This is a jail, Riley," Doctor Middleton said. "A lot of things may not meet code in the kitchen."

"No, it's not like that," she continued. "They make a show of it. A production. The whole line stops when I approach, and they call for someone to *only* serve me. And then I get sick!"

"Oh, I see," Doctor Middleton retorted. "That doesn't sound right."

Riley nodded.

"I can file a complaint and speak with the Director on your behalf."

Riley thought for a beat. She had repeatedly complained to the guards and was told she could eat or starve—there wasn't a gray area.

"I don't want to cause any trouble," she said.

"Then why complain?" snapped one nurse, and the veil had dissipated. The medical staff was always so friendly to her that she stupidly thought she had allies. But the stone-cold look in this nurse's eyes told her otherwise.

"You're right," Riley folded. "I shouldn't complain about something so petty. I have bigger things to consider."

The doctor shot the nurse a dirty look. She said, "Well, if you change your mind. I'm always here to help."

Doctor Middleton began naming what procedures she was about to do. "I'm going to give you two shots in each arm which are antibiotics." Middleton removed two needles from the drawer and a small bottle with liquid. "And then I'll puncture each arm with a small prick." She then smiled wide and warmly. "And then I'll write you a prescription for a liquid antibiotic. Are you allergic to anything?"

"No."

"Sulfur?"

"Sulfur? What medicine has that?"

"It's just questions, Riley. Do you have any tattoos?"

Riley was incredulous. "Doc, you can't be serious with these questions."

Doctor Middleton looked up and scowled. "I am. It's your medical history. Abortions?"

Riley shrugged. "No for all questions."

"Good. The prescription is for Amoxicillin. You'll need to drink two tablespoons each night until the bottle is gone."

Riley asked, "Liquid? I'm used to antibiotics in tablet form."

"Liquids are more cost-effective for the county and preferred because they are not time released and work rapidly to fight the infection."

Riley nodded.

The shots were given, one in each arm, and Riley left.

That night, she drank the two tablespoons of antibiotics and quickly felt nauseous. She began to sweat profusely, and her heart rate increased. She was sure she would end up on the toilet or throwing up over the sink, but that didn't happen. Riley finally fell asleep and woke up to excruciating back pain the following day. She couldn't move without bolts of pain shooting throughout her backside.

"Are you okay?" Lineeka asked when she saw the pitiful look on Riley's face.

"I'm not sure," she replied. "My back is hurting."

Lineeka's eyes rolled. "Join the club. These cots will do it to you. You probably slept wrong last night. Does your neck hurt?"

Riley shook her head.

"It's probably the cot."

She hoped that was all it was. However, a week later, a painful, blistering rash appeared from her shoulder bone down her backside. She reported back to the infirmary.

"Riley, you're back," Doctor Middleton acknowledged. "I hope the H. Pylori isn't actively upsetting your stomach."

"It's not that," Riley blurted out. The pain felt like it had seeped into her brain cells. Every muscle in her body ached; she could hardly focus and could barely think. "I think I'm allergic to something. Maybe that prescription you gave me. I stopped drinking it."

Doctor Middleton ushered Riley into a room where two other inmates were being treated. Riley climbed on the exam table and lifted her shirt. Hundreds of red, blistering bumps cascaded down her back like a Nike swoosh logo.

The doctor looked at the rash and instantly assessed the situation. Quickly, she said, "Oh, you have shingles."

"Shingles?"

"Yes. It's just a rash that will clear up in two weeks with meds."

"How did I get it?"

"You must have had chickenpox when you were a kid. The shingles virus lays dormant until triggered by either stress, age, a reaction to a prescription, or other unknown factors."

Riley's head shook.

"I never had chickenpox."

"You must have," the doctor said knowingly. "And you triggered the zoster virus that causes shingles. I think it's due to stress. I can imagine that things aren't too positive in here."

On cue, Riley heard from one of the patients. "Oh, my fuckin' god, this bitch got herpes! She got the zoster! Get me the fuck outta here before I catch that shit!"

The other chimed in. "Doctor Middleton, you can't allow her back in gen pop...not with herpes!"

Riley roared, "Bitch, I don't got fucking herpes! Say it again, and I'ma fuck y'all both up!"

The COs on staff quickly pulled the two inmates from the room and allowed the doctor to finish treating Riley, who was damn near in tears.

Doctor Middleton administered two more shots in Riley's arms and sent her to the pharmacy with another prescription.

"Do you drink lots of water?" the doctor asked.

"No. Not really."

"You should. It'll help flush your system. You have to start taking care of yourself, Riley. Maybe go to the gym room, dance, get your body moving."

Riley shrugged dismissively. She had entered MCC in excellent health, worked out several times a week, and watched what she put into her body. Now, seemingly overnight, her health was failing. It didn't add up. And she didn't like that dance comment. Was the doctor taking a shot at her past? The fact that she stripped for a living. She quickly dismissed that theory. How would the doctor know?

Riley refused to believe that the feds had a doctor on payroll. Would Doctor Middleton really violate Riley's HIPAA rights for what...? Money? Clout? Fringe benefits?

She didn't know the answer, but she would figure it out.

As the weeks turned into a solid month, Riley finally began to feel better. Her stomach had settled, her energy returned, and all signs of bacterial infection were gone. She believed it was because the janitorial staff had stopped coming to serve her. She didn't know why, and she wouldn't question it. Riley did feel that Doctor Middleton must have stepped in on her behalf and spoken with the Director even though she had asked her not to. Not that she was complaining.

By month two, she hated to admit it, but she had settled into a routine. She and Lineeka bonded over their niggas, and in jail, that was enough to solidify a friendship.

"I see you don't have any visitors," Lineeka remarked. They were playing Blackjack in the Rec Room to pass the time. "Your man, Meyer. He's just gonna leave you in here to rot?"

Riley snapped, "You should worry about what your man is doing on those streets before worrying about mine."

"I've already admitted my man ain't shit. It took me a minute, but I've arrived."

Riley stared at the woman sitting across from her. What was the point of this conversation?

Lineeka continued, "When I first got knocked, I gave him every excuse for why he didn't have my back. But if he can't visit, then why not send his sister? Why not bless my commissary if he can't make my bail?"

Riley saw that her cellmate was about to get emotional before she pulled it together. Lineeka fought back her tears, but it took all her strength to not cry a river.

"I love that man," Lineeka replied bluntly. "From the ground up, I nearly worshiped him. Fuck it. It takes a real bitch to admit that he used me."

Riley's eyes widened. "How?"

"I'm sitting here, and he's enjoying his freedom!" she replied dryly. "Trafficking women was his idea, but he convinced me to be the face of his organization. He knew young girls would trust another young girl, so I recruited them. When one female got away, who do you think she fingered?" Lineeka pounded on her chest. "Me!"

Riley found it hard to feel her pain. "You know that's fucked up, right?"

"I know. I just said he's a fucked up individual."

"No. I meant you," Riley clarified. "Recruiting your peoples, young girls, young women to be trafficked. That shit's evil."

Lineeka was stunned silent; momentarily. Wise beyond her years, she took a moment to process the allegation before lashing out defensively.

"I know it was, but I had to eat! Wasn't nobody taking care of me or paying my bills."

"Still fucked up."

"You're right," Lineeka finally agreed. "It's why my family won't visit. They can't get behind what I've done."

Riley nodded.

"And you? Meyer? Are you also a fucked up person, Riley. Is that why no visits?"

"I've tried reaching out to my family, but I can't get through. If I were in New York, things would be different."

"And your man?"

Riley thought honestly. "To keep it one hundred, Meyer isn't my man. He's an ex. In fact, I'm not sure he was *ever* my man. And whatever we had, I had broken it off a while ago, moved on to a new dude who wasn't worth my time."

Saying those words out loud had put things in perspective for her. All these weeks crying herself to sleep at night for Meyer's alleged betrayal when there were so many loose ends. And truth be told, he didn't owe her anything. She had refused his calls. She had told him to leave her alone. It was her voice that announced she was engaged. How many times could she push him away before he finally left?

"Oh," Lineeka said. "Was it *the grass is always greener* type of romance?"

"Is there any other kind?"

"How was the sex?"

"Eh?" Riley replied, making a fifty/fifty movement with her hand.

"You mean to tell me that you left the love of your life for an inferior version of him with *weak* dick?"

"He treated me respectfully."

"That's it?" Lineeka's eyes widened and then rolled. "Shit, *respect* is just another hustle."

The inmates finished their last hand of Blackjack before heading to the gym. Riley had begun to put on weight, especially around the upper quadrant of her body—waist, stomach, and arms. Her upper arms ballooned, her waist widened, and her abdomen swelled to an unpleasing sight. Riley always assumed she had that snap-back body that would act accordingly if she did enough reps due to muscle memory.

However, her sweat equity seemed in vain because everything now wiggled and jiggled, and not in a good way.

The weekly call came on time. Dough picked up, "Lineeka, how's our prisoner doing?"

Lineeka chuckled. "She's losing her mind."

"Good. I listened to the recordings and didn't like how Riley judged you."

Lineeka had been working for Dough for a few years now. She was one of the few females under his umbrella that wasn't afraid to enter county jail on assignment. Lineeka was a tough, young broad and had made a decent living out of informing. She asked, "Judged me? When?"

"When she told you you were fucked up for trafficking women."

"Well, it kinda is, isn't it?"

"My point is she's in no position to be passing judgment against anyone. She's a stripper who fucks dealers. She needs to be punished."

"Punished?"

"That's what I said."

"You're right," Lineeka now agreed. "What do you have planned for her?"

James whistled. "Let me handle the details."

"Well, what you've done so far is working. Riley's spending hours, and I mean hours, in the gym trying to get her shape to snap back. You should see her, Dough," Lineeka laughed hysterically, reliving the moments. "She looks so pitiful doing hundreds of reps, sweat pouring down her face. And I'll ask,

'Riley, you ready to leave here yet?'" Lineeka imitated her cellmate's voice and replied, "No, not yet."

Dough laughed too.

"That poor girl doesn't realize who she's up against."

Riley's private musings, intimate conversations, opinions, or angry outbursts were all scrutinized by Dough. It didn't matter that these conversations weren't meant for his ears and were hardly punishable offenses—free speech and all. He still felt he had a duty to check her. Keep her in line.

Next, he called Doctor Middleton.

"Our lab rat's truce is up. I'll have the kitchen staff resume contaminating Riley's food. When she comes to your office, I want you to triple the dosages."

"On everything? The steroid shots, spiked water, and shingles?"

"That's what I said," he snapped. "But let's add another red herring to the equation. She won't know what's happening. I think now is as good as any to taint her water bottles with tasteless sodium. High blood pressure runs in African American communities, and Riley will accept the diagnosis."

It was the simplest of plans but no less effective. The antibiotic shots were steroids which caused fat deposits and began showing up on Riley as unsightly cellulite. Stubborn belly fat joined the party. No squats, treadmills, burpees, or lunges would make it disappear.

And that liquid antibiotic for H. Pylori was a placebo. It was really Aloe Vera juice with a healthy serving of the zoster virus that caused shingles. In addition, her water was tainted with arsenic.

At the height of her medical trauma, he gave Riley a reprieve. He told Elane to fall back on the shots, tainted water, and food for a couple of weeks so Riley would think she was getting better, calm her nerves, and give her hope. Maybe say a prayer or two of thanks for the spiritual healing.

"You've been praying to the wrong God, Riley," Dough said and snickered.

This was too easy.

Psychological and emotional warfare could do more damage in a battle against your enemies than a knife or a gun. Even if your nemesis knows all your moves and knows exactly what's coming next, all you must do is pause—just fall back. Allow a pocket of normalcy to return. Your prey will begin to relax, hoping that the tide of the battle has turned. Their breathing will normalize, smiles will return, and just when they're about to fully embrace that the situation is behind them—you go nuclear.

The short version is akin to pulling the rug out from under them.

Tannery was vexed that Pablo and Diablo hadn't made any inroads inside the West organization. Especially since they were supposed to be some big-shot undercover agents. It had been months, and they were nowhere.

He called a meeting. Brown was there too. They met at the warehouse in Williamsburg, Brooklyn, now a temporary federal building. Tannery spoke, taking charge of things like he always did. Tannery had gotten word from customs, confirming that Scott and Layla were back in the states.

"Why the fuck are we so late to find this out?" Tannery barked.

"We don't know," Pablo said, puzzled.

"What the fuck you mean you don't know? These two have been back for weeks, and we don't know shit! What the fuck is going on out there!" he yelled.

"Look, me and Diablo are busting our asses out there,

circulating with the underworld, but this shit isn't an open-and-shut investigation! Most times, we go deep cover for years...fully immersed, you know this," Pablo explained.

Diablo added, "Your snitch struggled to plug us in."

"You two are supposed to be the best!" Tannery ranted in rare form. "You're supposed to be bringing information to me. Aren't you supposed to have your own informants?"

Diablo exploded. "Listen, fat boy!" Spittle flew in Tannery's face. "I know what we can do and what we've done rubbing elbows with the underworld. You see these hands?" Diablo held his large, weathered fingers like a duck's webbed toes. "These hands have been drenched in human blood up to my elbows on behalf of the DEA! So don't ever question my commitment while you sit behind a fucking desk and move papers! I don't work for you!"

Calmly, Diablo added, "If we're ever disrespected...this much"—he held out his index and thumb a quarter of an inch apart. "I will bash your fucking skull in with my boot."

The two DEA goons left, leaving Tannery and Brown; speechless.

To avoid getting sick, Riley began eating what she felt couldn't be contaminated, like grabbing a banana or an orange, cold cereal with unopened milk. Or bartering with other inmates for their ramen noodles. Her weight dropped drastically. Yet her arms began to balloon and jiggle as her grandmothers did. She had Popeye the Sailor Man's arms—two meaty drumsticks protruded from her shoulders. Her booty now had dimpled cheeks, her toned thighs and knees had fat deposits, and her six-pack abs now had a pouch. Riley looked and felt terrible. She was a shell of her former self, and it had only been a few months.

Each morning she would awaken to her throat burning like she had the onset of a cold or strep throat, but additional tests said she had none of the above. Her once healthy pink tongue had turned white, and the mucous membrane lining was peeling. The lining of her cheeks was peeling off like when she was a child, and she put Elmer's Glue on her palm, let it dry, and then pulled it off. The scaley skin peeled without provocation.

The headaches came next. Riley was weak, lethargic, and thirsty no matter how much water she drank. Per the doctor's orders, the sicker she became, the more water she drank. One day, her roommate gave her a chamomile tea bag.

"This may help settle your stomach and help you sleep tonight," Lineeka said.

"Thank you so much," Riley admonished.

Riley boiled the water, poured it into a glass, and then noticed it was cloudy.

"What the fuck?" she said, puzzled. She then took a sip from the bottle, and it was tasteless.

I'm bugging, she thought. *They can't be fucking with my water.* She called Lineeka back to their cell.

"I don't get commissary, so I have nothing to barter other than labor, so if you give me one of your waters, I can do your chores for you for a week."

Lineeka gave Riley a quizzical look because she had her own water. The jail gave all inmates two bottles a day.

Lineeka shrugged.

"Okay, cool. No problem."

Once alone, Riley did another test run. She boiled Lineeka's water, which was clear; she then took her last bottle for the day, and her water was cloudy once again. Whatever substance was in her water was clear and tasteless until she boiled it. It left a white residue.

"They're fucking poisoning me," she concluded. And the tears fell like autumn leaves after a gust of wind.

CHAPTER 10

Marbella had spent most of her life in the shade of her sister's shadow. Dahlia was the youngest, prettiest, and most revered by their parents. Although they grew up poor in Chihuahua, it didn't stop her parents from skimping and saving for years to throw Dahlia a lavish quinceañera. For Marbella, no such celebration was given.

A quinceañera is held on a girl's 15th birthday to punctuate the moment she turns from a girl to a woman. Marbella still remembers how sick she felt watching her sister dance with their father in her blood-red frilly dress and satin heels. Dahlia looked like a Latin version of Cinderella, her jet-black hair pulled tightly into a bun to highlight her Swarovski crystal tiara. During the daddy-daughter dance, their father, Pacho, cried real tears as he looked lovingly into Dahlia's eyes, a look Marbella hadn't ever seen.

At that party, Pacho introduced Dahlia to Angel Morales, whose father was the head of the Juárez cartel. Marbella would attend another grand celebration three years later—Dahlia's wedding. Carlos Morales spared no expense for the heir to the throne for his son and daughter-in-law. Dahlia chose not to have bridesmaids or maid of honor because she refused to share the limelight.

She and Angel were driven into the courtyard of his home, a palace, on white horses and a carriage. Her Swarovski crystal tiara was replaced with a million-dollar diamond crown, her wedding dress, a custom Vera Wang, and her ring designed by Neil Lane. After the ceremony, Angel gifted his new bride a custom bulletproof blood-red Lamborghini, Dahlia's favorite color.

Although all the wealth and opulence Dahlia had married into, Marbella and her parents went home to a dirty, roach, rat-infested shack. Dahlia never came around or sent money to help them out. When the grandchildren were born, Pacho and his wife, Sofía, received birth announcements with a picture. The slight from their youngest daughter didn't stop them from bragging, though. The whole town of Chihuahua knew that Dahlia had married Angel Morales, and that alone was enough for them.

There wasn't a day that went by that their parents didn't mention or compare Dahlia to Marbella. Five years ago, coming home from church service, Pacho's faulty brakes on the old family car gave out, and they crashed, instantly killing him and his wife. Although Dahlia hadn't seen her parents, cousins, sister, or former friends she grew up with since her eighteenth birthday, her hometown welcomed her openly.

Dahlia threw herself over her parents' caskets, hollering and screaming while people fought to console her despite her absence. Inside, Marbella seethed. So, it was quite a shock when Dahlia invited Marbella to live with her and Angel, which she accepted. Marbella was thirty years old, never married, had no children, and now her parents were dead.

Over the years, Dahlia never missed an opportunity to degrade and humiliate her older sister—sometimes in private, most times amongst friends and staff. To her face, Dahlia would call Marbella 'the ugly one' and get a laugh from whoever was in earshot. Marbella bided her time until the right moment, and that moment was now.

Marbella realized that Dahlia kept her around because she trusted her. She was always there, yet no one noticed her as if she were wallpaper. People spoke freely around her, and Marbella found ways to eavesdrop when they didn't suspect another set of ears had joined the conversation. Dahlia knew her sister's skills could come in handy should anyone plan an attack against her or her children or any other misdeeds that took place. But Marbella had her own agenda, and Dahlia's trust in her would be her last mistake.

"What do we do with Dahlia," Marbella heard Louis ask Angel after the meeting.

"She's harmless, Louis."

"Harmless?" Louis chuckled. "Dahlia is like radiation…silent and deadly."

"She's strong-willed, yes," Angel admitted. "That Latina blood attracted me to her, but she could never want the father of her children murdered."

Yet, that was exactly what she had asked Louis to do. But Louis couldn't concern himself with his cousin's marriage drama. He was a newly minted cartel leader with enemies to kill, drugs to distribute.

"Adios, Angel."

"Adios."

A few hours later, Angel walked in on Marbella sobbing uncontrollably. She was in their primary suite, only recently working her way into his bed. His first instinct was to turn around and rest in another wing of the estate, but her wails were loud and drama-filled that he had to ask, "What's happened?"

Her head shook as she dabbed at her eyes with a handkerchief. In a soft voice, she said, "I...sometimes...I just can't believe the tenacity of my sister."

"Dahlia? What's she done?"

"She's so cruel and vengeful. I just can't do what she's asked...not to such a beautiful baby. Oh, Angel, I can't...and now she will kill me too!"

Marbella collapsed on the floor, hollering and writhing around until Angel came barreling her way. His hand reached down and clutched her neck in a death grip, squeezing her airwaves until her eyes bulged. She was lifted to her feet, where an open hand slapped her back to the ground.

"What does she want you to do!" he bellowed, and his men came swarming toward the home's west wing to assist their boss by any means necessary.

Marbella hadn't anticipated an audience, but the additional set of ears would help punctuate her message.

"She...," Marbella began, lip trembling for dramatic effect. "Wants me to drown the baby...sweet Lulu in a bath and blame the nanny. When I told her that I could never do it, that I love Lucchese like she's my own...the child I never had...she threatened to have our cousin, Cayetano, to kill me."

Angel came and embraced Marbella. "Don't worry about Dahlia or Cayetano. They'll be dealt with."

Marbella thought about this exchange as she sat at her sister's funeral in Chihuahua. Dahlia was buried in her blood-red quinceañera dress, which still fit with the Swarovski crystal tiara. Meanwhile, Marbella sat at Angel's side in a blood-red Marchesa dress, and her sister's diamond tiara crowned her head. Lucchese sat on Marbella's lap, grinning and waving to everyone.

The whole town came out to show Dahlia respect. They were puzzled but not truly surprised to see Marbella standing in proxy for her sister as Angel's new woman. Everyone took turns kissing the ass of *'the ugly one'* they used to ignore.

The hearse and funeral procession did one last lap around Dahlia's family shack before driving through the town on their way home. As they moved toward the highway, there, dangling from an overpass bridge, a rope twisted around his neck was Cayetano, Marbella's innocent cousin. A sign posted around his neck read: *Don't Fuck with Juárez.*

James, Terrence, and Franklin sat at their headquarters, meeting about Riley Baker and the status of their investigation.

Terrence said, "We got Meyer calling Lollipop several times a day. The kids going crazy over her absence and his missing sister. He sounds unhinged."

"I'm sure you meant to say his *dead* sister. Isn't that right, Agent Garrett?" James eyed his nemesis with unbridled hatred, but Franklin broke the stare, which was a big mistake for a man like Agent Dough. Franklin showed he was the weaker species and was prey in James's arena. Prey got devoured.

"I wouldn't know anything about that," Garrett curtly replied. "Whether she's missing or otherwise. We should focus on intel, not supposition and rumor."

"Let's," Terrence agreed. "What do we know about our subjects. The last official reports we got from the New York office after our colleague was murdered was the string of robberies at three residences belonging to the Wests'. Where a large sum of money was stolen."

James jumped in, "Five million if I read the report correctly. Is that the information you have, Terrence?"

"Yes, five million."

"What about you, Franklin. What does your report say?"

Franklin observed the cosplay and felt a jolt of anger ping pong throughout his body. He thought he was brought to Chicago to redeem himself and help close a case he helped build. But it was clear their actions were strictly monetary. Dough and Barnes wanted what Franklin called his *take-home* pay. All conversations always led back to Lucky and the missing money.

Franklin hated a jealous negro. In fact, he hated working with men of color. And James and Terrence were both *blue-black,* as his mother would say. Two ugly, hating ass niggers who obviously didn't know whom they were fucking with.

If they kept it up, he'd call in his team from New York and dole out Jimmy Hoffa verdicts all around, starting with James.

Franklin finally responded after a pregnant pause, "It says five, but an informant told me it was double that. Someone walked away with ten million dollars, and there isn't anything anyone can do about that."

Franklin grinned, broad and gloatingly. You could cut the tension in the room with a hacksaw.

"Oh, you'd be surprised," James said.

"Surprise me," Franklin quipped back.

Terrence cleared his throat. "So, Elane Middleton is on schedule with the doses given to Riley; the COs and inmates are all playing their parts. Should we bring her before a judge again? Maybe have the court-appointed lawyer scare her about her case?"

Franklin added his two cents. "What I know about these ghetto girls is that threats don't scare most of them. *Might* is too broad. Saying to Riley she *might* do life in her eyes is like spinning the bottle. There's always a chance she *might* not. We must operate on absolutes; she absolutely has a virus she never had. She absolutely will not have proper nourishment. And she absolutely will be a former shell of herself—those things that will keep her up at night."

James nodded. He listened to his men's input but decided, "We have two inmates jump her. Call ahead and make sure guards not on our payroll are around. And then we'll do a little gaslighting. Franklin explained that Meyer didn't care for her and would convince her that she was crazy to think otherwise. Call the studio and have Icon Hollywood record a two-minute segment saying Meyer is engaged. We'll run the story while she's recuperating in the infirmary. If that doesn't tickle the wire and have her reaching out to bury his ass, I don't have much more leniency and patience for her."

Icon Hollywood? Call the studio? What was going on, Franklin thought. Icon Hollywood was nationally syndicated, and what studio worked with the feds to plant fake news? He asked, "Why would Icon Hollywood help us with a drug case by planting fake news? Also," Franklin smirked. "Wouldn't Meyer see the story or be told about it?"

While robbing drug dealers and stashing his gains somewhere safe away from Uncle Sam, Franklin didn't know that James had monetized his side hustle. In the eighties, through the mid-nineties, robbing dealers was lucrative. And then those Rockefeller Drug Laws had dried up his food chain, and he realized that the new side hustle was the movie industry.

James started small, getting his girls—his informants under his umbrella into music videos. He believed that if he could find one female, use his federal resources to make her a star, he'd eat off her career for life. But and however, finding a natural-born actress wasn't an easy feat. James thought looks, confidence, and sassiness equated to an A-list actor. It did not.

His stint managing his girls in the music industry wasn't a failure. He met rap video directors in awe of the illusive man who seemingly came out of nowhere draped in expensive jewels pushing exotic whips. The man who seemed to know everything about anything. These video directors morphed into low-budget movie directors, and who did they come to for seed money?

James Dough. Who went by several other first names, but his last name spoke volumes.

By 2000, James had made an independent film, getting his feet wet. It was terrible because he cast one of his informants in the lead role. Not making that mistake again, he realized many talented Black actors were underpaid and out of work. These gifted actors would do a movie for five large. Peanuts to him. And the rest is history.

Now, two decades later, when he wasn't prosecuting criminals or shaking down rappers, James was rubbing noses with top celebrities who were none the wiser. His name—any of them was never credited on anything; he refused to take photos at these A-list events. And he certainly didn't let the right hand know what the left was doing.

James's company executive produced Icon Hollywood. And he would have them do a quick segment about Meyer that would only run on Riley's television at the jail, in the infirmary. If he was anything, he was creative with it.

Terrence added, "We should have them say he's engaged to one of them young movie actresses."

"Not engaged," Franklin corrected. "That will be the first thing Riley would bring up when she saw Meyer. Too easy to verify it isn't true. Have the clip say he's rumored to be dating. That way, if she does mention it, it could be summed up and explained away as gossip."

"Not some random hot chick." James sat back in his chair and bridged together his hands in the prayer position. "How about we promote Riley's enemy."

Promoting one's enemies is a familiar play the feds used in their wheelhouse; one of the more common tactics but no less effective.

"You exalted me above my foes. Psalm 18:48," Franklin commented.

"You prepared a plate before me in the presence of my enemies. Psalm 23:5. Old school psyche shit," James remarked.

"I thought you were an atheist." Franklin was incredulous.

"I am," James confirmed, noting that he'd never discussed his religious affiliation with this man.

"But you find time to read the Bible? Why? I mean, what's the point? I only ask because I take my religion seriously and don't like people who use it as a tool."

"I read a lot of things, a good portion on religion. You think you're the only educated brother in this office?" James chuckled. "And I got news for you, Catholic. Everyone uses religion as a weapon. Even the preachers who preach it."

"But again. The Holy Bible?!"

James leaned forward and stared Franklin squarely in his eyes so there'd be no ambiguity and said, "You and I kneel before the same altar, and it's not before God."

Franklin's reddish-brownish skin deepened to a blood-red hue. He was motherfucking livid. No one challenges his love of God. And he was rivers away from being anything like this barbarian.

He shot back, "How do you find the time to read Psalms between railroading your perps?"

"Oh, you should know," James smirked. "Satan never sleeps."

"That nigga was in front of my home!" Scott bellowed. "He hasn't gotten enough of being on the losing end of us?"

"We should have gone after his ass and finished what I started," Layla remarked. "He could have killed Meyer!"

"He had me to…dead to rights."

"Shouldn't he be in Wit-Sec?" Layla thought out loud. "They probably dropped his ass after our acquittals."

"This isn't me," Scott said. "Leaving loose ends. That's why Meyer is still breathing. Whistler is pissed that I don't think enough of him as a formidable enemy, to get at him. He needed Meyer to let us know he's still out there, sitting at our fucking doorstep. He knows where we are and wants us to come find him."

Layla said, "He's one ignorant man. If he wants to be murdered, just say that. Nobody was even thinking about the one-eyed monster! Now we gotta add him back on the list of enemies."

"He shouldn't have been taken off," Scott assessed.

"True," Bugsy affirmed. "Whistler's disrespected our family more than most. He needs to die."

That night Scott sat in his home office playing chess against himself. He used times like this to think. His enemies were expanding, Meyer wasn't who he used to be, and he was sure he was still under an active federal investigation. Shit was thick. Before he went to bed, he concluded that he needed to hire reinforcement.

The weather was crazy. Meteorologists were announcing a lot of firsts would be happening and using an almanac to help compare temperatures from 1882 to 2020. A terrible blizzard would hit the east coast, and neighborhoods would be buried in snow.

Gregory put on his parka, snow boots and hopped in his Pathfinder to find Maxine. From their talks, he felt like he had an inkling of the vicinity of where she would be. His first stop, he parked near the Brooklyn Bridge and got out. There were rows and rows of tents, cardboard boxes, shopping carts, and metal bins that some used to start fires for warmth.

The frigid night air was biting at his face, pushing him forward as he searched for her from station to station. About a third of the way in, he peered into a tent with a cooler, kitchen utensils, and solar lantern. Attached to the tent were large boxes constructed with duct tape and staples. He didn't know if anyone was in there. He called out, "Maxine?" Gregory waited a beat and called again.

Maxine was hunched over as she came from the boxes to the tent. When she saw Gregory, she had a puzzled look on her face. She tossed up a hand gesture that meant, *wait a moment*, and then returned fully dressed in a ski jacket and her gifted hat, scarf, and gloves. Maxine stepped outside, about ten degrees colder than her home, and shivered.

"What are you doing here," she asked. "How did you find me?"

"It was easy," he noted and smiled. "It wasn't hard at all. But, um, I came because there's going to be a storm. A big one."

She was still perplexed.

He continued, "And I wanted to invite you to ride it out in my home." Before she could object, he blurted, "I have a spare bedroom and will give you your space. And you can leave when you're ready."

He touched her heart. She said, "Gregory, I'm fine. I'll be fine here."

"I'm sure you can take care of yourself," he explained. "But folks can't win against mother nature. This could be another natural disaster like Katrina or Hurricane Sandy. I won't be able to function knowing you're out here. Come until the storm blows over."

Maxine exhaled. "I can't leave Wendy. She's my roommate and was kind enough to put a roof over my head when I had none."

"Bring her too," he hurriedly said. "Y'all can share the guestroom."

Maxine grinned and then nodded. "Okay, give us a moment to gather a few things."

Maxine went inside and explained the situation to Wendy.

"Maxine, you go. You need to remember I chose to be out here; you didn't. I've survived storms out here, including Sandy."

"It's only for a couple days," Maxine said. "Don't you want a hot shower and warm bed if only for a couple nights?"

"The fact that you even asked that question shows that this lifestyle isn't for you, sweetheart. You're a good person. A good woman...don't let anyone tell you otherwise. And take it from me, you can't always bring everyone along for the ride. I don't know that man, but he seems like a good one. Even if it's only platonic. If I were you, I'd keep him around."

"You're speaking like you won't see me again."

"I hope not." She grinned. "Now give me a hug and get! That man is probably a popsicle by now."

CHAPTER 11

For self-serving reasons, Markeeta wanted to dress up for her introduction to her new handler, James. She wanted to impress him and also revisit something he had said over the phone about getting paid for putting in work. The house and cars were more than she'd ever had, but as Tannery had shown her, those things were on loan—not even on lease. Because with a lease, you had an expiration date, time to restructure. What Tannery did was pull the rug out from under her.

Snitching had opened her eyes to new possibilities. That's what Tannery had exposed her to, and she was hooked.

The walk-in closet held designers she could hardly pronounce, and the tags had astronomical figures. Shirts cost five thousand or more, dresses were ten large, and furs were more than a fully loaded car. Everything she tried on was her size down to the footwear.

Markeeta settled on a one-piece Valentino jumper and YSL pumps and flat ironed her hair that fell past her shoulders. She took scissors and evened out her bang to accentuate her eyes and high-arched eyebrows. Markeeta looked more like Lucky than herself and loved every second of the upgrade. There was a buffet of high-end perfumes; without reading the bottles, she sprayed one.

James had thought of everything, including makeup which the bathroom was fully stocked. Nude lipstick, eye shadow, and blush brightened up her face giving her cinnamon-colored skin a glow.

"Okay, bitch," she said in the mirror. "Do you!"

James was punctual. He arrived at precisely six and let himself in at Markeeta's annoyance. When she heard the front door open and slap shut, she ran downstairs with the scissors gripped tightly.

Without introduction, she deduced, "Dough, you can't just be walkin' up in here whenever you like! I could have been undressed!"

"Markeeta West," James calmly said. "If you ever speak to me in tones louder than this, I will send your ignorant, unemployable ghetto ass on the next flight out to New York. Do we understand each other?"

The threat was straight, no chaser.

Markeeta was tightlipped and followed James into the living room. They both sat down, and she found it hard to give him eye contact because his face was so frightening. It felt rude, like she was staring. The type of disrespect you're taught as a child, and there's someone with a perceived handicap, and your parent says, *"Don't stare!"*

Agent Dough was a hideous sight to Markeeta. Looks that would stop your heart if accosted on a desolate block after sundown. He was a tall, lanky sasquatch. Unavoidable.

He began a litany of questions.

"What made you want to inform on your family, knowing what the outcome would be?"

"Excuse you," she said in an offended tone.

"You heard the question. Answer it."

Markeeta blew out air and considered the statement. What was this? An interview? Interrogation? Could she answer incorrectly and be sent home where she had no home?

Truthfully, she replied, "I didn't care. I don't care what's gonna happen to any of them. All I'm concerned with is me and my son."

"Fuck everyone else?"

"Fuck 'em," she said and shrugged.

James's lips curled slightly. A barely negligible movement that couldn't qualify as a smile. But was. He asked, "Is it fair to say that you would feel nothing if I told you that Lucky was dead?"

"Is she?"

James nodded. He searched Markeeta's eyes, and body language, for any sign of empathy or compassion and saw none. Although the news made her stomach rumble inside, her exterior was stone.

She asked, "Who did it?"

"One of our agents." His tone was cavalier, flat.

Markeeta thought about the sex tape uploaded to the gram and wondered if there was a nexus. She wanted details and had questions but asked nothing. It was better if she didn't concern herself with things that didn't concern her.

"Manny Machiavelli. How did you get him to trust you?"

She shrugged. "I dunno. Manny just did."

"If you learn anything from me, please learn that shit just doesn't happen. There are no coincidences, and opportunities are created. Manny trusted you because you made him trust you. I want to know your methods; what did you do?"

"I fucked him," she began. "Is that the right answer?"

141

"Depends on how good you are in bed."

Markeeta took a moment of silence to revisit the question. "I listened to him 'cause he liked to talk about himself. When I moved into the building, Shirelle, his girl, was probably tired of listening to his war stories. So, I acted interested, followed up with questions, and his mouth kept running."

James nodded knowingly. "Tell me about his girlfriend. Did she know you were fucking her man?"

Markeeta's head shook. "Not at all."

"How are you so sure?"

"Because Shirelle would have fought me over her nigga. She ain't no punk bitch, and neither am I."

"Let's try to stay away from violence, okay?"

"Absolutely," she agreed. Markeeta didn't come here to be fist-fighting anyone. She came to get paid. Markeeta asked, "You mentioned that if I get you what you want, there'd be a payday for me."

James shrugged indifferently when Markeeta wanted absolutes. She pushed further. "How? How am I getting paid?"

"There's a law on the books that few people know about. It says you're legally entitled to a small percentage if you help the government retrieve ill-gotten gains. When dealing with dealers, racketeering or white-collar crimes could be substantial."

"Like a whistleblower?" she asked, and James was impressed.

"Yes, exactly."

"So, this law...the reason the hood ain't heard of it is that the government doesn't extend it to us, right?"

"I don't understand what you mean."

She doubted that. James knew exactly what she was getting at. Markeeta clarified with, "You see wives like Mrs. Madoff whose husband stole billions get to allegedly walk away with millions—no jail time. And then you see these mob wives get reality shows and collect these phat-ass checks—no jail time. And then you see my homies and think, what happened to

Pookie's wife? Feds kicked her out of her home, took all vehicles, jewels…didn't leave her with a fuckin' crumb. Locked her up, the mama up…grandmama's mama up, and treated everyone from A to Z like pieces of shit. Where was her cut? Where was this law? Because as I see it, they're all criminals."

"If Pookie's wife was locked up, it's because she was involved or had criminal knowledge of his enterprise."

"And these white women didn't? They had no clue their husbands were doing shady shit? No fucking clue whatsoever?"

"Evidently, they didn't."

"Nor are these women forced to take the stand and testify against their dudes. Y'all never make these women turn snitch. That's left up to us."

"Look, no one's forcing you to inform. We can part ways now if you feel a way about this setup."

"I'm making conversation," she admonished. "I thought with all that reading material you assigned, you wanted conversationalists."

The two locked eyes and James waited for Markeeta to break the stare first. She didn't. Until then, he had her summed up as a one-dimensional hood rat. And he knew she was that, but could she be a smidge more? He was stumped.

Dough finally asked, "Bo Jangles. You up for the challenge? He has specific tastes and loses interest quickly."

"I can pull any nigga I want. Just make the introduction, and Bo Jangles is mine."

Markeeta stood up and walked to the bar.

"You want a drink?"

His head shook as she poured herself a glass of cognac.

James noticed that she was feeling herself. It was how she was strutting around in the expensive heels, her body movement in the pricey garment. He didn't like it.

"You look a couple months pregnant. Are you?"

Markeeta's face twisted. His question and her inability to respond the way she knew made her uncomfortable. Her usual response would be to lash out, but she kept her composure.

"Last I checked, no."

"Then check again," he snapped and continued, "And your makeup is too light for your complexion. You look clownish right now."

Markeeta's heart sank at the onslaught of insults. She didn't know what prompted his harsh language.

"When I heard about what you did on the Machiavelli case, I thought you were a dime piece. I couldn't wait to get you here." Now it was James's turn to stand up and pour himself a two-finger glass of scotch. Meanwhile, Markeeta was hanging on to his every word.

"Sight unseen, I upgraded your housing from a condo to a townhouse. Put two luxury vehicles in the driveway and stuffed the closets with nearly a million in clothes, handbags, and shoes."

He looked down at Markeeta's feet.

"Speaking of which. You really wear a size nine?" James snorted. "God damn...that's huge. Most women I know your height...what are you? 5'3?"

She nodded.

"Exactly," he admonished. "You should wear a six or seven at the most."

"I don't, though," she snapped, not checking her tone. "But I'll do my best to make this work. Big feet and all."

Markeeta hoped he would change the subject and move on.

"Yeah...yeah...that's what I want to hear."

Apparently, yeah, was appropriate English as long as it was coming from him, she thought. Dryly she asked, "Anything else?"

"Your hair."

"What about it?"

"It's long but thin and stringy. I want sexy, full hair, not what's equivalent to a man's comb-over," he stated. "I have someone, top in the industry, to give you a weave."

Markeeta's head shook rapidly. "I don't want no weave. That's what thinned my hair in the first place! Bitches be pulling out ya edges and popping ya strands on purpose!"

James ignored the profanity and assertive remarks. "This isn't a democracy."

The glass of scotch was finished, and so was their meeting.

Angel only needed to hear Lulu humming along, crooning to Thalia and Vincente Fernández—both Méxican singers before promptly hiring a vocal coach. His daughter barely spoke complete sentences, but to Angel, he was listening to nothing short of greatness.

Marbella got in on the action too. "She's a natural, Angel. A born entertainer. We shouldn't stop at vocals; let's get her dance classes too."

"You don't think that's too much?"

"We can certainly afford it."

"Yes," Angel agreed. "Let's hire only the best choreographers for Lucchese."

It didn't take long for Marbella to be just as obsessed with the child who had known two other mother figures—both not wanting anything to do with her. But Marbella was childless and realized she could finally have it all—man and child.

And Lulu instantly warmed up to her new guardian, wrapping her arms tightly around her neck for hugs and crawling into Marbella's lap for a bedtime story.

At first, Angel was jealous. He didn't want to share. But then that emotion suddenly subsided because Lulu had enough love to go around. She brought nothing but smiles to the faces of her siblings. Even his hired henchmen were clamoring over her.

Angel spent his days trying not to think about Dahlia. He missed her and wished she could have loved his child. Maybe he reacted too harshly. Perhaps he should have given her a couple of sterner warnings. But Angel knew thinking of her was fruitless, and nothing would come of it, so he stopped.

He was surprised when he received the call from America, and once Scott identified himself, Angel remained guarded.

"What is it that you want, Scott?" Angel wondered if Lucky wanted her daughter back. And if she did, then there would be another war.

"I got some bad news that I thought you should know."

"What's happened?"

"It's Lucky. She's missing."

"Missing? You must know more than that?"

"Not much, but it's being handled."

"I know it's difficult knowing what you've been through with your other children," Angel said earnestly. "But my heart isn't really breaking here. And missing isn't dead, sí? Should things turn for the worst, I promise our daughter will know who her birth mother was."

Scott got to his point. "That's not why I'm calling."

"Of course not." The sarcasm in his voice wasn't undetected by Scott. Angel knew the West family wasn't concerned about his daughter's welfare.

"I have my hands full in New York concerning the family business. And I have firsthand knowledge that the remaining sicarios are now my problem. Remember Félix and Pedro? The spicks you hired to go after my children's empire and left everyone dead?"

"So?" His response was cavalier.

"These men are under the thumb of the Garcia cartel, and my wife's life is in danger, which by default means mine too."

"This is not my business," Angel deduced. "You and I shook hands like men. I did the same with Javier, so…I'm…as they say, Switzerland."

Scott knew a closed mouth don't get fed. And right now, he needed a full plate of allies he could forge an alliance with because the impending war would be monumental. The full force of the Garcia cartel, sicarios, their militia, *and* FBI—combined would take him out and his family.

The gangsta was above begging, but as a businessman, he knew how to negotiate.

"You and I know it's only a matter of time before Juárez and Javier Garcia are back at war—"

"I don't run Juárez, Scott. You know this," Angel said. He was walking through his mansion, his cell phone pressed against his ear. Scott's call had stirred conflict and dissension, making him feel alive. He missed picking up the phone and ordering a man's death. Or watching the carnage on the news of murder sprees, he'd orchestrated. But then he thought of Lulu. And said, "I benched myself for the love of my niña, your grandchild."

"You're no less retired than me. We both know Louis will call you to ask how to tie his shoes. If you greenlight this operation, Louis and Juárez will back you."

"What is it that I get out of this? And don't insult me with money."

"You get to play a role in your daughter's grandparents staying above ground. Think five moves ahead, Angel. Should anything happen to you—natural causes or otherwise—you should feel confident knowing someone with resources can pick up where you left off."

Angel chuckled. "The grandparents who wanted my daughter dead?"

"The past, Angel. Let's move forward. Because as I remember correctly, you wanted her just as dead. And if it wasn't for *my* daughter, there would be no Lucchese."

Angel wanted to change the narrative. He didn't like the tale of the father who wanted his innocent child killed. Scott made a good point, though. *What if something were to happen to him?*

Still, he said, "Switzerland."

And disconnected the call.

Lacey's Soul Food Restaurant was a popular eatery on 135th Street, on the west side of Harlem. It was known to have some of the best soul food in the city, from its tasty ribs, fried fish, and cheesy macaroni to its peach cobbler and sweet potato pie. It was frequented by locals and tourists, but today it would be Bugsy's place for business. Their parents had benched Meyer. He had only recently kicked his addiction to an opioid, so they weren't ready to trust him to have a sit down with potential undercover agents.

Bugsy walked into Lacey's well-dressed and sat at the back of the restaurant where he could watch the comings and goings of everybody. He sat alone, but he wasn't alone. Standing outside was two armed men, covertly carrying holstered pistols and watching the area like two hawks perched on a ledge. And inside, his men unassumingly mingled with other patrons.

Ten minutes later, Pablo and Diablo arrived. The two men stood out like Klans men at a Muslim Mosque. People looked their way and were somewhat taken aback by their presence. One man was suited sharply in a three-piece suit, and the next was wearing crocodile boots, cowboy hat, and a bolo tie.

The location didn't bother the two men. They wanted Bugsy

to trust them. They walked into the establishment unbothered—cocky and confident, consumed with a swagger you couldn't fake and approached Bugsy in the back. Bugsy didn't take his eyes off them; finally, seeing these two men face-to-face was interesting. There was no denying that the two had a presence.

Bugsy chose Lacey's because he knew the restaurant's owner, the place wouldn't be bugged, and it was in public. The aged woman, Lacey, was close with the family and had been for years.

Pablo and Diablo came to the table, ready to sit down and talk business. However, before they did that, Bugsy slightly nodded to an individual seated in the restaurant. Mason removed himself from a table and came their way. He locked eyes with Diablo and then Pablo. Mason quietly said, "Before Bugsy talks about anything, y'all muthafuckas need to be searched."

They relented. One by one, Mason escorted them into the restroom and thoroughly patted them down—no weapons, no wires. But Pablo or Diablo hadn't expected their cell phones to be confiscated.

It was cool, though. Pablo and Diablo didn't need to wear a wire, which being undercover agents afforded them. Their testimony alone had held up in each case they were involved in.

Satisfied, they were allowed to join Bugsy at the table in the back. They sat across from him. Bugsy immediately sized them up, one dressed opposite of the other, contradictory. He studied their movements and features; he wanted to read their minds to see what they were about.

Diablo was the first to speak. "Are we waiting on your brother before we start?"

"He won't be joining us."

Scott had drilled into Bugsy's head to not say *anything* incriminating. And unbeknownst to Bugsy, the restaurant was already crawling with several agents posing as customers, Black and Latino. They were there for backup in case Pablo and Diablo's meeting went south. Outside of Lacey's, were two federal vans parked on opposite ends of the place, one block north and one block south. And agents in non-descript vehicles were ready to react if something went terribly wrong inside. Everyone knew the young Wests were at war with Juárez and their parents with the Garcia cartel. They didn't want their men caught in the crossfire. It was a tense moment for everyone.

Before they got things started, Bugsy ordered a large plate of soul food: fried whiting fish, potato salad, and a side of collard greens and cornbread. Diablo and Pablo simply ordered coffee.

"Y'all not hungry?" Bugsy asked them.

"We're okay," Pablo replied and then added. "Now give me a plate of tamales or bandeja paisa, and I'll close down the kitchen." He patted his belly, lighting up the tense moment.

Bugsy smiled slightly.

He started to eat as Pablo began to speak. In a low tone, leaning closer to Bugsy, he said, "We want your accounts."

"My accounts...?" Bugsy replied incredulously. "I have many accounts. I'm a businessman."

"Accounts, business...," Diablo chimed. "You understand, no?"

"I do."

Diablo said, "Good. First, we can guarantee shipment from Texas to our warehouse in New Jersey. Our coke is ninety—"

Bugsy interrupted him with, "Just logistics. References and numbers."

Diablo understood. The kingpin didn't want him saying unnecessary shit like kilos, cocaine, coke, or yayo...anything that could be used against him in a court of law. Bugsy wanted to know how the operation worked, names of other organizations that could vouch that they weren't feds, and the price per kilogram.

They continued to speak about their operation in detail,

which seemed legit and well-organized. They claimed to have scaled distribution from South America to the North in just a few short years.

"We've contracted with the Perez organization in Miami, Kenneth Haynes in D.C., in Atlanta we've done business with the Santo brothers, and in Baltimore the Richmond Hill gang."

Pablo said, "We haven't made inroads in New York other than Larry."

"And why is that?" Bugsy asked.

Pablo shrugged. "Well, it's simple. Competition."

Bugsy wanted to hear more. "Expound."

"Our competitors are Kiqué Helguero, Caesar Mingo, and the Méxicans."

Diablo and Pablo were providing Bugsy with names and services. Both men looked like they'd buried a million people collectively. They looked shady and murderous, and something sinister and ominous was in their eyes. Bugsy had seen that look in many men's eyes—killers. They looked like the real deal, and they spoke it too.

Bugsy wondered if he had made a mistake about them. But he trusted his gut. They were law enforcement. Had to be. As Kiqué and Caesar explained to Scott, no American distributor on their level would fuck with the West family. It was a one-way ticket to prison. Once the streets knew the feds had claws in your organization, it was a wrap. That's why Scott had to go and mend fences with Angel and Juárez. And although they beat their federal cases, there was a high probability that the West organization was still targeted by the government. Because the government didn't give up until they had their man or men. Usually, it was a domino effect, one goes down, and it brings the others with it.

Pablo and Diablo continued to speak candidly, and Bugsy continued to stuff his face and nod. He was doing what his father suggested, talk little, listen—don't make incriminating statements.

Bugsy finally asked a question. "Larry?"

"What about him?"

"A man like him connected to people like y'all. Make that make sense." The last piece of cornbread went into Bugsy's mouth.

"We needed help to expand our blueprint in New York," Pablo said. "And my cousin, Gino, vouched for him."

After spending less than twenty minutes with them, Bugsy had heard enough. Dismissively, he said, "We're done here. Someone will be in touch with you."

Pablo and Diablo both nodded their heads. It was time to leave. Pablo smiled, and he acted like everything was all good. But inside, he wanted to smash Bugsy's smug face onto the table and shove that plate down his throat. They stood up, shook hands like men, and left the restaurant.

Bugsy remained, ready to order dessert.

CHAPTER 12

Gregory's two-bed, two-bathroom apartment in Harlem was in a three-story building. He was located on the first floor, and the block was quiet, treelined, with homes with character.

The fireplace wasn't functioning inside, but the mantel was a beautiful, reclaimed wood. Unlit candles were below, and an antique brass screen enclosed it. The home's hues were warm browns, merlots, and black. The smell of sage was throughout, with a hint of vanilla and cinnamon.

"This is your room back here," he said, leading the way to a small but well-appointed guest bedroom. Her bathroom was directly across, with towels, washcloths, new toothbrushes, and toiletries. "Let me know if you need anything."

"Thank you, I will." Maxine looked around. "Gregory?"

He stopped in his tracks. "Yes?"

"Thank you. This is more than generous of you...to open your home to me."

"No need to thank me, Maxine. I'm sure you'd do the same in my position."

Would I? she thought. Maxine hardly knew herself anymore. At her core, was she Maxine, an aspiring law student? Or Max, child killer?

Maxine knew better, but she did it anyway. She had packed the smoking .45 she knew had bodies on it with her to Gregory's and tucked it under the mattress. Looking around— the carpeted floor, clean sheets, comforter, and plush pillows— she didn't want to touch a thing. Her grubby hands and dirty fingernails would only make his nice things filthy.

"Greg," she called out. "Could you bring me a trash bag if you have one?"

A few moments later, he came to her room with a Hefty. "What's this for?"

"My things. Maybe, we could find a laundromat to wash them before I leave?"

"Sure. We have one in the basement."

She nodded.

"I could loan you a sweatshirt and pants to walk around in tonight, and I have some pajamas if you'd like."

"That sounds great."

Maxine sat in a hot bath until her fingers and toes were pruning, and the water was dark and murky. Layers of dirt had soaked off, yet Maxine was far from clean. She drained the tub, scrubbed it with bleach, and ran another bath. Maxine would rinse and repeat this four times before she stood to shower.

She washed and conditioned her hair, but it was a lost cause. Her locks had locked. Maxine's hair had matted beyond salvaging; she would need an expert and had no money. Using the scissors under the sink, her dreads were clipped into a small afro, and the clippers did the rest. Maxine ran her hands over her newly shaved head and felt renewed. That small gesture was akin to carving years of bad energy off her aura. She felt lighter and more optimistic. Maybe it had something to do with Gregory's sage burning throughout his home; maybe not.

Although she could still use a manicure and pedicure for her calloused heels, hangnails, and peeling cuticles. And some mandatory waxing. She looked into her eyes and got a glimpse of someone she used to be—a good person was still there.

It took nearly three hours for her bathroom door to swing open. Maxine had on Greg's pajamas, oversized and warm. She could smell that he was cooking a meal and heard a television in low tones turned to Jeopardy.

"What is Mount Rushmore," she heard him say. When he saw her, he smiled, "I thought I was going to have to hire a search party."

"It is massive in here."

He looked at his clothing. "Good. They fit."

She looked down too. "Just, barely."

Maxine noticed that he didn't mention how she came out of his bathroom bald. He was too polite for that. So, she broke the ice, "New beginnings?" And pointed toward her scalp.

He nodded. "I like it."

"You do?"

"Yeah, you look like that British actress from *Queen & Slim*."

"What's that?" she wanted to know.

"You didn't see that movie with Daniel Kaluuya?"

Her head shook.

"Cool. I have it. Let's watch it after dinner."

"Let's."

That night, James's words replayed in Markeeta's head, causing her to toss and turn. His words felt familiar. She was really taking what he had to say to heart, and then her mind remembered who she was. Markeeta never had a problem getting any nigga she wanted—cute, ugly, big, or lil' dick niggas were on rotation. She thought about Brian, her ASAP Rocky lookalike with good dick. He had that chocolate skin that looked airbrushed, a Colgate white smile, and some coins in his pockets.

Brian didn't criticize her hair, feet, or body. All he wanted to do was party and bullshit, smoke weed, and fuck. A secure dude will *never* tear a woman down to build himself up.

And then there was Otis. She only fucked with him because the streets said he was tricking his paper on girls and loved to spend hours on his knees pleasuring chicks. His ugly ass always had something slick to say, too. Always criticizing 24/7.

Markeeta knew in the kitchen, she could burn. Still, he'd eat a plate of her food, scrape that plate cleaner than a dishwasher, and then complain it was too salty or unflavored—anything to avoid a compliment. Otis criticized her when she didn't shave her legs in the winter; remarked if her panties didn't match her bra. Otis also pointed out that her hair was too thin, and her feet were too big for his standards. He was a miserable muthafucka and didn't last long in her bed.

Markeeta shook off her self-doubt. Ugly, broken niggas, even ones in high positions, used criticism as a weapon. They weaponized insecurity and low self-esteem; it was psychological warfare to get subjects to submit. She knew she had to watch Agent Dough. He had shown his hand tonight, and Markeeta wasn't ready to fold.

As the late hour ticked by, Markeeta felt a chill that turned into damn near frostbite. She jumped out of bed, realizing that there wasn't any heat. At the same time, Ralph had come upstairs to her room, noticing the same thing.

She clicked the light switch and nothing.

Walking downstairs with the outside streetlights filtering through her window treatments, she went to the kitchen. She tried the stove, and the gas burner clicked several times—no ignition.

It was evident that the electricity and gas had been turned off. Undoubtedly by her new handler. For Markeeta, it foreshadowed what was to come with Dough and mirrored what had already transpired with Tannery.

"These fuckin' men are boys," she murmured.

Still new to the house, Markeeta had no idea where a candle or flashlight was. Or if the home had either.

"You didn't pay the light bill?" Ralph asked.

"Something like that," Markeeta snapped, leading her son to the living room. "Stay here."

At this point, her fingers and toes were stiff as the chill of the home intensified. The last remnants of heat had evaporated, and she was certain, in daylight, she could see her breath.

Markeeta grabbed several comforters and pillows and made her way back to the living room, where she started a fire. She and Ralph bundled up and fell into an unpeaceful sleep.

To help acclimatize back into society, Maxine would walk around the nearby park for fresh air and meet the locals. She was learning to smile more, engage in small talk, and let go of her fear of being recognized by the West family and their affiliates. Usually, she would make it back to the apartment before Greg returned home from work, but time escaped her this Friday.

Maxine walked into a quiet apartment; Gregory was sitting on his sofa—the .45 nestled indiscreetly on his lap. She saw the judgment in his eyes before he spoke. Or was it disappointment?

"Why do you have a loaded weapon in my home?"

"I can explain."

"My home," he repeated. "A weapon?" Greg stood up, palming the weighty object, and carefully placed it on his table, hoping it wouldn't go off. He'd never handled a gun before and was sure he would never again. "Who are you, Maxine?"

She now heard the disappointment in his voice.

"I never believed you were the woman they said you were. A heartless, jealous woman who murdered someone over her lover's infidelities. But here we are. In my home, where I slept oblivious of your habits, your proclivity for violence. You could have killed me in my sleep."

Maxine was ashamed to maintain eye contact with him.

"You're not who I hoped you were." He dug deep into his pocket and pulled out a couple hundred dollars. "I'm going to need you to leave here. Tonight."

Maxine searched for words and then burst into tears. She wanted to defend herself, convince him she wasn't a thug, grab ahold of his waist, and beg him to allow her to stay. But she couldn't move, speak, flee, or bolt from his apartment. Maxine's whole body shook violently as she collapsed in despair. She was spent.

Greg allowed her to get her emotions out before his sensitive side kicked in, and he found himself on his knees, cradling her.

"Shhh," he crooned. "It's not the end of the world. We can drop the weapon off at the precinct and start over. They have a program where you can turn in weapons, no questions asked. You wanna do that?"

Maxine nodded. Her sobs were now a whimper. They moved from the floor to the sofa, and she decided to open up and start from the beginning.

"Layla convinced me to go to Cypress projects that fateful day," she began.

"Your friend, Layla?" He asked, remembering the loud-mouthed female Maxine had begun hanging out with. The papers never mentioned an accomplice.

"Friend is overly generous and utterly inaccurate," Maxine said dryly. "We went to Sandy's house to confront her about whether she was pregnant or not by Scott. In my gut, I knew this was wrong. I didn't want to go, yet I did."

Maxine wiped away tears only to have to wipe her face again. She unpacked her past, unfolding the layers of trust and betrayal, love and hatred, foe and fool. She continued, "Layla beat that girl to death with her bare hands...murdered her unborn child in what seemed like a few seconds."

Gregory wasn't shocked. The whole neighborhood knew Layla was what men like him would call a hood rat; brawling, bullying, and terrorizing those she felt were prey. Greg never understood when Maxine began hanging out with her. She was a bad influence, and the pair was an odd couple.

He asked, "But why?"

Maxine wiped away more tears. "Isn't it obvious?"

"Layla was sleeping with Scott?"

"Yup!" Maxine snorted and then managed a sarcastic chuckle. "I was clueless. A motherfucking fool to not have seen even a hint—however small, that they were having an affair. I could rewind until my tape popped, and I could never pinpoint when they started sleeping together. Whether she came before me...or Scott sought her out because I wasn't enough."

Greg's heart sank. She looked pitiful, eyes puffy, voice cracking through humiliation and vulnerability. She was wounded; decades later, she was no closer to closure.

"Surely, you must know that their affair isn't on you. A woman can't stop a cheater from cheating no more than a man can."

Maxine shrugged almost irritably. That advice was practically a mantra. *It isn't your fault,* said the wise man. Meanwhile, they're thinking about how society doesn't suffer fools.

Gregory continued, "I'm assuming you told the police and your lawyer about Layla and weren't believed?"

Maxine lifted her eyes and made contact with his. She needed him to know who she was, on that day, at that moment.

"I had every intention of pleading my innocence and letting the detectives know what happened. And then Scott came to the precinct and told me the golden rule: *don't snitch.* And I didn't. He assured me I would never get convicted because I was innocent."

The rage Greg felt had startled him. It was an unfamiliar emotion for the mild-mannered man. He wanted to go after Scott and kill him with his bare hands. Greg knew he wasn't a killer; he wasn't built for such cruelty. But the thought comforted him as he thought of ways to comfort Maxine.

"Is that why you carry a gun? To protect yourself from predators like Scott and Layla?"

Maxine decided to come clean. Well, the cleanest version of Max that she could part with. She told Greg about getting paroled and the affair with Scott under Layla's nose. The fed raid that had landed her face in the papers for a second time. The subsequent affair with Bugsy, Scott's son. And the assassination of her son, Dillinger. But his mouth opened when she explained she had plans to murder father and son for a huge insurance payout.

"There," she said. "Now you know everything! I'm not the good girl you keep replaying in your head. I've done terrible things, and I'm considered a horrible person. A felon."

Maxine conveniently left out that she had three young children murdered for the sins of their parents. That information would put her back behind bars for life. And there wasn't any coming back from, *I'm a kid killer*. There is no redemption. But she shared what she felt ready to purge.

"You don't need to do that insurance scam," said Greg. "You're better than this guilt you've been living with. Scott isn't worth you potentially spending another day of your life behind bars because murdering him and his son for insurance money is exactly where you'd end up."

Maxine exhaled. He was correct on all levels.

"If you allow me, I'd take care of you. It wouldn't be as lavish or the danger-inducing excitement you got with Scott. But I'd love you...*only* you. If that's something you'd consider."

And she would consider it. She was ready.

James didn't spend time looking in his own mirror to see the monster he was. Where was the fun in that? Instead, he used any chance he got to tear a woman down. It irked him when a woman felt cute and liberated, singing Beyoncé lyrics. James would always use his arsenal of tricks to knock her off her high horse; always. It was one of his many methods for complete dominance. He called this the *Humiliation Clause* and inserted it with *all* women.

If you had a morsel of self-respect, self-esteem, or self-awareness by the time James and his team were through, you'd be calling the suicide hotline. He didn't want independent thinkers. Agent Dough's stable of informants was akin to the movie, *The Stepford Wives*. They all spoke alike, thought alike, looked alike. Under his tutelage, it was all about conformity. And his standards were specific. He only recruited light skin Black women, but you didn't get in his rotation if you only had fair skin. You had to be under 5'4"; he hated tall women. You couldn't have a pudgy or wide nose; long hair was required, and soft-spoken. He was attracted to African American women who didn't look it. They needed to look exotic or be biracial to offset his perceived view of his lack of beauty.

Tight bodies, dainty hands, and feet were also high on his list, and he made no apologies.

Markeeta's body, voice, diction, and unrefined nature were all fixable. However, the men he sent her after would eventually resent her enormous feet, masculine hands, and thinning hair. Men with money and power wanted perfection. They pursued it just as aggressively as the almighty dollar. And unless Markeeta had that bomb snatch, he'd cut her loose.

James slept with *every* snitch he employed, and if he didn't, then someone on his team did—that testing the merchandise that most bosses' believed in. But only one had held his heart, and that was Karen Williams.

Markeeta was the exception. A couple shades darker than he usually enlisted, she didn't fit his mold. It wasn't because she was uneducated and ghetto—only women with those traits could be persuaded to join his regime. And the fun part was the brainwashing—complete mind domination. James could make sister turn against sister, mother disown her child, and lover turn against their lover. He was that good with his bullshit. He chose Markeeta because she was Bo Jangles's type. One of Dough's mistakes was forcing Karen down his throat. He knew the rapper loved cinnamon to chocolate brown complexioned curvy women, hood exterior, and shiesty.

Along with his many duties, he was also a matchmaker. When his informants aged out of the desirability construct of the criminals and were looking forward to having children and marriage, he oversaw that. He coupled these women with men who had helped his side hustle. These men were primarily retired military—mid-forties, early fifties looking for someone to treat them like kings. And this is precisely how the informants were trained by James since they were recruited at fifteen.

The men were all unattractive, like Dough, who wanted dime pieces on their arms. James would send them beautiful, mature women who, under any other circumstance, wouldn't look twice at these unappealing men with average salaries. They were used to fucking kingpins and celebrities, but now in their mid-thirties, those days were over. They had to settle and find love, marriage, and stability wherever it bloomed.

These former snitches knew how to cook award-winning recipes, satisfy any man in the bedroom, and had decent paying employment thanks to Dough.

They catered to these men too. James taught them to get on their knees and give his colleagues pedicures. Scrub their crusty feet while they sat back and enjoyed what they felt they deserved.

Karen gave Dough pedicures too. His large foot would be propped up on her knee as she applied clear polish, blowing the liquid dry with her full, sexy mouth. His wife would never do such things, but Karen did. They all did.

And so would Markeeta.

The social club in Howard Beach, Queens, had seen better days. In the late eighties, this place was filled to capacity with high ranking made men of the Gambino crime family. Scott had often come through an invitation from Santino Costello, the great-grandson of Vincente Costello.

Santino had dreams of being an enforcer when he and Scott met and had slowly made it up the ranks of the organization.

By the mid-nineties, Rudy Guiliani and the federal government had decimated the New York mob with the fall of John Gotti—statements from Sammy the Bull burying the mob boss.

Now, in his mid-forties like Scott, Santino's comfy lifestyle had dwindled to just getting by.

Scott was low-key. He chose to drive himself to his old stomping grounds in Queens rather than show up with Mason and a dozen of his armed henchmen despite Javier Garcia having a price on his head. And any day, moment, or second, someone would come to collect.

The large room had a jukebox playing old Sinatra tunes while an aged bartender wiped the bar with a dirty dish towel. A few patrons were scattered throughout, and the familiar smell of homemade tomato sauce permeated the air. Scott scanned the room, and his eyes met Santino, who waved him over.

Santino sat on a chair, legs spread wide, protruding belly spilling out of his shirt. His silk shirt was unbuttoned just enough to show his gold chain with St. Augustine, patron saint of two opposing forces, and his slacks hugged his chunky thighs. Santino wore his good clothes to this meeting with someone he still considered a friend. His thick, jet-black hair had remained black from his monthly dye jobs, his mustache and beard shaved, but his five-o clock shadow showed salt and pepper stubble. There was a black leather jacket draped over the back of a chair. He had put on weight, lots of it.

Santino stood and embraced Scott in a bear hug. Both men smiled warmly before sitting down to discuss the purpose of the meeting. Santino knew of Scott's rise in the drug game; the media had aired his dirty laundry as they did with Gotti. But unlike the mob legend, Scott had avoided life behind bars because the jury didn't believe the rat in his camp, Whistler Hussain.

Before they could discuss business, the bartender came to their table with massive plates of spaghetti and meatballs, garlic bread, and red wine. This was the Italian way. You ate great food while ordering hits against your enemies.

Scott dug in quickly. And after devouring most of his meal, he began with, "I got a situation with someone that used to be employed with my sons' organization. This individual is possibly working with the feds as an informant."

Santino nodded. "Yous want me to make 'im dead for yous?"

"It's not an easy kill, Santino, or I'd do it myself. I'm coming to you because I don't want my sons, Bugsy or Meyer, involved."

"How are my godsons?" he asked and felt a sting of animosity surge through his body before quickly checking that emotion. Santino's father gave Scott the names of his twin boys when Scott asked Santino to be their godfather. Scott's sons were Christened in the Cathedral of Saint John the Devine with half the Gambino crime family in attendance. This was rare because few Italians especially made men, allowed Black people in their circle.

The two grew apart as Santino expanded as an enforcer, and Scott branched out with the Méxican cartel. Scott had more children, and Santino did as well. And the two, once as tight as brothers, didn't circle back around to each other until now.

"They could be better," Scott answered truthfully. "Bugsy has a case in federal court for a gun, and Meyer was hooked on codeine." Scott drank from his wine glass and continued, "They can't get their hands dirty. It'll fall back on them. None of us can."

Santino understood the order. What Sammy the Bull had done to the Italian community still haunted most, and that was thirty years ago. It was a polarizing move, one that many would learn from.

"Who's the rat?"

"His name is Larry Jenkins from Harlem. I'll give you all the specifics, but if I'm going to outsource this hit, I have to be assured that the Santino Costello I knew in '88 is taking the job."

"Scott, we're all good at something, and since yous known me, yous known that the only thing I'm good at is sending rats to their Maker." Santino lifted his shirt to reveal a revolver. He was old school henchman. Santino never used Glocks, fancy guns, or automatic weapons. He kept it simple. Revolvers don't jam, are lightweight, easy to conceal—efficient murder weapons.

"The contract is for a million for his head. If you trace him back to his federal handlers, I got ten million per pig."

Santino whistled. He hadn't had this much action since 2001 and could use the money. However, he said, "I'll take the contract for no monies; you heard me, Scott. I'll put that rat in the grave for free! May my mother turnover in her grave if I took money for killing the scum of the earth. But the feds, I'll have to charge you for that." He grinned. "But not ten million per body. What am I? An extortionist? Are we not friends? I'll kill those pigs for, let's say, half that."

The gesture was generous. And to Scott, they were friends. But this was business.

Scott stood up. Business was concluded. He held out his hand, and Santino shook it. Scott said, "One million for Larry and ten million per fed. That's the deal, Santino. You can take the business deal, or I'll find someone else."

Santino understood. "Yous got it, Scott. I won't let yous down."

CHAPTER 13

Whistler committed several more home invasions leaving dead bodies and unsolved murders piling up. Detectives investigating these open cases hardly put in work. Not when the victims weren't victims. They were men the city wouldn't miss, men with dozens of arrests on their jackets, menaces to any society.

Getting back into the drug game was like pulling a trigger—child's play. Before long, he found a connect in Baltimore, Maryland, and began his distro business in Delaware. Whistler moved out of the foreclosed home and bought a modest house away from prying eyes and foot traffic. A used Corolla got him around, and he bookended his organization between henchmen and corner boys.

Whistler's profits were reinvested in triggermen. He needed an army to go against Scott and Layla, and soon he'd have that.

"Guess who I ran into today?" Bugsy said as the siblings stepped into the boxing ring to spar.

Meyer shrugged. "Bee, we ain't got time for guessing games. Shit is thick out here."

Bugsy nodded. "You're right, my bad. I ran into Yvette."

"From Queens?"

"Exactly. Yvette was looking cute as shit, flirting with a nigga like I was the last man left standing."

"You always had a crush on her, right?" Meyer asked.

"Yeah. That's why she's the perfect snitch," Bugsy deduced.

Meyer smirked. "Yvette? Snitch? You buggin'. That bitch got murders under her belt. Didn't she body the Jackson sisters over in Crown Heights, Brooklyn? That shit is still an unsolved homicide. It was over some stolen jewels, right?"

Bugsy tightened his gloves and jabbed at the air a few times, warming up. "Nah, it was over some petty shit. I think an argument."

Meyer said, "And she was fuckin' some out-of-town nigga named Abdul. Streets said they robbed a local bodega, and he didn't wanna give her her cut."

"That's right. He was an undercover crackhead." Bugsy thought for a second. "They found him in a dumpster."

"The feds gotta be desperate if they're using her to inform. That bitch got bodies on her résumé. Where's the justice," Meyer joked. "She's never been convicted or even arrested."

Bugsy through a combination of punches as Meyer ducked and weaved past each one. "She's fed affiliated...she's gotta be. No way the feds don't know what's common street knowledge. If they've given her a *get-out-of-jail-free* card, it's because she's valuable."

"Watch her, Bugsy." Meyer hit his brother with an uppercut and attacked his ribs before Bugsy tossed him into the ropes. "Why would they send her to you and not me? She's more my speed." Meyer wanted to know.

Bugsy thought for a second. "I had a crush on her, and I'm newly single. They think my current situation will make me vulnerable, an easier target than you. Also, no disrespect, brother, but her life could be compromised should you suspect you were being played."

Meyer said, "No disrespect taken. I would blow a fuckin' hole in that bitches' head…boy fuck with me!"

Kimberly Cooper had been benched. As she suspected, clashing with Franklin had cost her the opportunity to participate in career-making cases. She was ignored daily. Kimberly's days at work could have been spent surfing the internet or swiping right on Tinder. Her work hours were empty. She only showed up to collect a paycheck.

And then Lucky West went missing, and Franklin Garrett was relocated to Illinois. Nefarious things had been brewing, and everyone attached to the West case had been classified—above her pay grade.

But she had her ways to backdoor information. Now she spent long days at her desk, forgoing lunch stockpiling facts. Kimberly sifted through decades of allegations by drug distributors, king and queenpins, and informants about Agent Garrett. It was always alleged that he had stolen millions from drug profits. He'd target dealers before ultimately putting them behind bars for long stretches of no less than 25 years. Football numbers.

Her subsequent inquiry was on the man who had requested Garrett, Agent Dough. Information on him was harder to retrieve. He was elusive, ghostlike, mysterious in an ominous way. The more doors that closed on Dough, the more intrigued she got. Now, Kimberly was bringing her work home, working into the wee hours of the morning and on all weekends.

When she reached a dead end on James Dough, a new identity began with a different name, Lamont Dough. And then George, Jayson, Malcolm, Odell, and Donovan. Kimberly realized these were aliases, all the same man who had apparently done some terrible, reprehensible things.

Her investigation outlined the similarities and contrasts between Garrett and Dough. Franklin did his own dirty work. He was a hands-on predator. Dealers were robbed, and women dealers were pursued, but Garrett played his cards close to his chest. Of course, he had a team, but they were his colleagues, men he could trust—other agents.

Special Agent James Dough had a network. Kimberly found herself reading a report taken in the early '90s that had been buried. The retired snitch claimed that Agent George Dough had recruited her to set up Kingsley the Kingpin, one of the largest narcotics dealers on the east coast. He groomed her to catch his eye, chauffeured her to parties where the kingpin would be, and ultimately, she got his attention.

The woman said she slept with Kingsley for two years and earned his trust. She told Dough when large shipments went out, who was Kingsley's connect, and where the locations of large sums of money were hidden.

Kimberly gleaned that the young woman came forward because she didn't receive her cut from the monies confiscated from the headlining bust on Kingsley. The snitch swore in the report that Dough took $6 million, and she was promised 10%. Ultimately, he gave her $10,000 and another assignment with a new dealer in the Midwest.

The report outlined that Dough's network of retired military helped him with surveillance. He hired a gaggle of rejected applicants who applied for the FBI or DEA to cover his illegal wiretaps. And he groomed a harem of young girls to be his informants, who joined his network at fifteen and completed the trinity.

Kimberly logged into her database and looked up the woman's name. She wanted to interview her in hopes of exposing these rogue agents. Her heart sank when she read that the young woman died of a drug overdose shortly after she'd made this report.

Report after report spanning four decades, Kimberly noticed that the women, Dough's informants, all had similar qualities. All were light skin, African American women, petite in height and weight, with petty criminal records. This could mean nothing, but she knew that it meant something. Was Dough attracted to them? Was this *his* standard of beauty? If so, Kimberly didn't fit the mold.

And then she stumbled upon several reports that confirmed her suspicion. A treasure trove of reports was filed against the agent with many first names. Some were letters written anonymously to the bureau, buried, never acted upon, disregarded. These letters were from people who had crossed paths with Dough. They alleged that they or family members were stalked, indirectly threatened, poisoned, shaken down, or murdered.

One mother wrote that her daughters were denied education. One pistol-whipped and sexually assaulted. Another was exposed to highly addictive narcotics and blocked from gainful employment. The last was infected with an incurable disease. To anyone reading her complaint, it read like pulp fiction—too unbelievable to ever be true. The rants of a delusional, bitter woman. But as a seasoned agent, Kimberly knew the resources at their fingertips. How any of these things is as simple as making a phone call, emailing someone, or buying a colleague a drink.

Each allegation outlined a history of violence and utter depravity on Dough's end, yet nothing materialized.

Kimberly compared the two agents: Garrett versus Dough. Garrett, a devout Catholic, used religion to justify his actions, most likely finding justification in the Old Testament.

But Dough had no religious affiliations whatsoever.

Kimberly riffled through several reports—hard copy and electronic. Her fingers rapidly shuffled pages, eyes speed reading with acute accuracy. Most reports said Agent Dough required his women informants to be faith-based, practicing believers. But why? And then there were the active gym memberships and mandatory readership. She combined those details with the glaring fact that these women all favored each other, which seemed very cultist. Mind control.

Dough kept himself once removed from the action, unlike Garrett. James was more akin to The Wiz—he could destroy those he deemed a threat in anonymity. While if you played for his team and joined his cult, you were granted your heart's desires as you traveled down the yellow brick road.

Kimberly shuttered. A chill traveled down her spine as she remembered something her grandmother would say. *Satan comes to steal, kill, and destroy.*

Kimberly Cooper was investigating evil.

Special Agent Randall hung up the phone and sighed. He leaned over, pushed his intercom, and Devonsky picked up.

"What's up?"

Randall said, "Meet me in my office."

A few minutes later, Devonsky came in and took a seat. He looked like a mirror image of his superior—weathered and sleep-deprived. The shit hit the fan after Laurence Warren and Gwyneth Sullivan were murdered in Dubai. Pile on Franklin

Garrett not only recording a porno with Lucky West but *posting* it! And then, finally, the queenpin's disappearance and presumed murder. The whole bureau was buzzing with salacious gossip—an undercurrent of whispers greeted him each morning when he arrived and shoved him out the door as he departed.

"I just got off the phone with Yvette. She couldn't get Bugsy to take her bait."

Sourly, Devonsky replied, "Yeah, well, we can thank Garrett for that."

Randall shrugged. "Or Laurence. Or Gwyneth. We don't know who exposed our operation."

Devonsky grimaced. He was a hardnosed, in-your-face, alpha male and always fake mad about something. Pointing fingers and placing blame at others' feet was in his DNA; this month, it was Garrett. Never mind that Randall and Devonsky greenlit most of what Garrett did. They indulged his insanity and watched with gleeful eyes as their subordinate crafted various ways to violate the West's human and legal rights. They all participated in breaking the law, but with selective memories, events tended to get fuzzy.

Devonsky asked, "You don't think we should send her back in? Have her show up randomly, maybe at Bugsy's gym or residence? The intel says he's wanted to bed her for years."

"That'll get her killed."

"We got two dead agents," Devonsky snorted. "Do we really care?"

Randall really had to ponder the question. He took a moment to look at the big picture and replied, "Yes. Another dead person attached to this case, and we're done. Both our careers are DOA. I don't want that, and neither do you."

Devonsky blew out air. "So, what's next?"

"I was hoping to pick your brain. Garrett is working with Chicago, and we know he thinks outside the box. There's no way we'll let Illinois close the case we started. You hear me?"

Randall gritted his teeth, his face turning beet red. "No fucking way!"

"We've tried surveillance, wiretaps, undercover agents, informants, bullying, and subterfuge," Devonsky assessed and lowered his voice. "Let's not forget about the apartments...and missing...West woman. What more can we do to make them break?"

Randall snapped, "I'm asking you!"

Both agents were spent. They were operating on thread-thin patience and under enormous pressure. Turning against each other was fruitless, so they agreed to roll up their sleeves and brainstorm.

Randall asked, "What would Garrett do?"

Devonsky replied, "Pit them against each other and burn the whole house down from within!"

"Baker, you have a visitor," Correction Officer Katz said. "Come on, let's go."

Riley was in her cell, lying down on her cot. She didn't feel well. A usual occurrence for her nowadays. Somehow, she mustered the strength to rise, thinking it was most likely her court-appointed counsel. And then a random thought popped into her head. What if it was Meyer?

A surge of energy flowed throughout her, and her steps quickened.

"Do I have time to wash my face and comb my hair?"

CO Katz stopped dead in her tracks. She smirked, "Are you serious? You think you're in a college dorm? Come now or don't. I got shit to do today!"

Riley didn't say another word. She obediently followed, wondering what she'd do if Meyer was on the other side of the metal door. When the door opened, she saw Agent Garrett.

"No fucking thank you!" Riley spat and tried to leave. Only CO Katz had shut and locked the door.

Franklin looked at Riley and assumed she had seen better days. She was a football field distance away from the strikingly beautiful woman he had met at Momma Luigi's. Their tactics had worn her down. He was there to see if they'd broken her.

His voice was upbeat. "Change your mind yet?"

Her eyes rolled, and her lips twisted. "I already answered that."

"You did. But that was so long ago. You still want to do life behind bars for this guy?"

"Who said I'm doing life?" she wanted to know. "And don't think I don't know this is illegal. How's the judge gonna set no bail until trial?"

Franklin shrugged. "And yet that's exactly what he did."

"I fucking hate you!" Riley screamed. Her outburst startled Franklin because it wasn't expected. "Get the fuck outta here and don't come back! I already told you I'm taking this bullshit to a jury."

"You'll lose."

"So be it!" she roared. "It's my life to lose, isn't it?"

In a mocking tone, he said, "You may not think so, but I care about you, Riley. And you're forcing my hand, kid."

"You make me sick. Stay away from me. Stay out of my business. And find other things to do with your free time than harass my Black ass. I'm done talking."

Riley returned to the door and began banging—she had never taken a seat. She didn't look back to see Agent Garrett, but she felt his energy suck the air out of the room. He was angry, and she didn't want to think about what his wrath would look like.

"How far do we want to go with this?" Franklin asked. He was back at headquarters discussing his brief meeting with Riley. "I told you both that these ghetto girls need other methods to break them."

James had something on his mind, but his punishment was something he would have done to her whether she cooperated or not. Riley had crossed over to his bad side, and once you made his list, there wasn't a reprieve. He didn't like her. She thought she was too cute for him to ever be comfortable, allowing her to walk away Scott free. But he wanted to know how far Franklin could go. James knew Franklin could go as far as murder, and James would split hairs on that subject.

James had no problem murdering drug dealers throughout the years. Once he was done pilfering all their illegal gains, he'd have them knocked off if he didn't send them to jail for life. Some murders James did; most he didn't. Murder was a job for his support staff, so he only got his hands dirty if he took something personally.

But and however, in four decades of crime, he'd never killed a *woman*. He slept with them, exploited them, controlled, and bullied them. Most notably, he toted a fine line between life and death with them for the past two decades. James had a few women—exactly three, infected with HIV. Murder, nah! All three women were still alive, taking medication that left them undetected.

So, to James, Franklin was the monster in the mirror. The agent was willing to go further than anyone in the room.

Terrence looked to James to see what he'd say. James said, "What do you have in mind? We're open to suggestions and remember, we're willing to do anything to close this case."

Franklin nodded. He sensed that they were three like-minded individuals who served the same god: power.

"I say we break her down from the inside out. The H. Pylori and shingles were both creative, but how about we go that much," Franklin spread an inch between his thumb and index finger. "Further by adding arsenic to her beverages."

"Arsenic?" Terrence asked. "Is only going that much further?" Terrence also held out his thumb and index finger an inch.

Franklin shrugged. "Arsenic given in small doses isn't a death sentence. But in small enough dosages, she'll notice things like her hair shedding, coming out in clumps. Her teeth will yellow, and her throat will burn. Her small and large intestines will slowly be eaten away. Riley will want out of jail if only to find adequate healthcare." Franklin took a beat to read the room and continued with, "A Black woman's hair is her crown. I'm telling you this will work."

James grinned wide. This Garrett nigga was cut from the same cloth.

"I'll make the call," James said, backing the devilish plot. "And have Elane start implementing small doses."

Agent Kimberly Cooper sat atop the hood of the flashy car. It would take three years of her gross salary to afford something so exquisite, yet she had no qualms about sitting her wide ass on something that didn't belong to her. Kim wore a hoodie, jeans, sneakers, and a goose-feathered jacket that concealed her government-issued firearm and badge. Her hair was pulled into a tight ponytail, baseball cap—hoop earrings, lip gloss. She didn't know what to expect, but she would shoot her shot.

With the wind at his back, Bugsy bent the corner and paused briefly. He stared at the woman using the hood of his Bentley as a lounge chair and continued his stride until he stood inches from her face.

"I take it you don't have a warrant?" he said coolly.

Agent Cooper said, "Even dressed like this, I look like a cop?"

Bugsy shrugged. "It's not just a look. It's a stench...and you got both."

She chuckled. "You're correct...well, sort of. I'm a federal agent." Kimberly whipped out her badge, and Bugsy read her credentials.

"Fed or not, get your ass off my muthafuckin' ride. I have places I need to be."

Kim stared at the infamous twin, one member of the dynasty that she was trying to take down, and couldn't help but notice how fine he was, more so in person than in pictures. Her training taught her not to be affected by such trivial things as personality or looks, but it was hard not to stare. She was human.

"No, you don't," she challenged.

"Excuse me?"

"You're going one of five destinations. None of which are more important than what I have to discuss."

"Which is what?"

"Lucky."

His interest was piqued. "Okay. So, tell me. Where do I have to be?"

Finally, she slid off his hood. Standing five inches below the gangster, she looked up and said, "I've always wanted to ride in one of these. How about you drive us to grab a coffee."

Bugsy looked around, his eyes scanning his perimeter, looking for her colleagues. Kimberly noticed and said, "It's just me."

He snorted his surprise. "You must be gunning for a promotion...the ambitious type, are we?"

She grinned. "I got dreams."

Bugsy didn't drive far. In fact, they could have walked to

Joe's Java, a coffee bar he frequented a few times a week. Almost every female barista wanted the young thug and would flirt unceremoniously when he came in with his sleepy eyes and large tips. But he would never ask anyone out on a date. So, the café lit up with chatter when he walked in with a woman who looked—basic.

Seeing their crush walk in with his tailored suit, cufflinks, and hard bottom shoes, and then their eyes rolled over to see the round-faced woman, sporty, plain—had them all vexed.

"She must suck a good dick," one worker whispered to her peers.

"As do I," quipped her coworker, subsequently rolling her eyes.

Bugsy rattled off their orders, and they found a seat toward the back at the window. Both took a few sips of their lattes and a couple bites of their muffins before he said, "My sister. Where is she?"

"I met her briefly. She and your brother were looking for a man named Ragnar Benjamin at Borough Park Towers. What do you know about him?"

Bugsy was quickly angered. A vein bulged and creased his forehead connecting to the bridge of his nose. Something that happened only when he was this irate. He said, "I didn't come here to provide information. That's not what I do! I came to find out what happened to my muthafuckin' sister!"

Kimberly swallowed hard. Not out of fear but because the sheer look on his face outlined why he was America's Most Wanted. There was a shadier side to the mild-mannered killer, and it would serve her well to keep that information at the forefront of her mind. She had chosen to speak with him over his brother because he was supposed to be levelheaded. However, his reaction—which she understood when dealing with issues of the heart, caused her to pivot; rethink her strategy.

"That's what I'm investigating," she began slowly, "Lucky

and I spoke on the night a porn tape hit the web. She believed Ragnar Benjamin posted the vile clip to humiliate and embarrass her."

"Is Lucky working with the feds?"

Kimberly heard the hurt and disappointment in his voice. Her badge told her to lie, but that's not who she was. Lucky West was exposed in the most disgusting way possible, and Kim also knew she was murdered by a man who had sworn an oath. There was no way that she would sully her name further.

"No," she answered truthfully. "I was at the building investigating a ghost named Ragnar Benjamin, and your sister showed up. She was livid, thirsting for revenge. And I most likely prevented her from spending the rest of her life behind bars."

Bugsy nodded. "So, Ragnar. A colleague?"

It didn't go over her head how casually he asked that question. Kim's instinct told her to answer wisely. She said, "No. That's why I'm here. I was looking for him and hoped you knew something through Lucky."

Bugsy thought for a moment. "Why not ask Lucky?"

Clever man, she surmised. Asking the same question in different ways was a tactic law enforcement used. Especially a question that has been asked and answered. She realized that he didn't trust her. And why should he? Feds were his enemy, so why did she think he'd feel otherwise? Why was she really here? With him?

"I told you she's not working with us," Kimberly stated. "And I know she's missing because your parents' attorneys said so. It's all over the bureau."

She could see his shoulders relax. He took a couple more sips of his latte, and his face softened. Bugsy nodded, "Yeah, she's missing. And the only person who benefits from her disappearance is Ragnar."

"How so?"

"She was pregnant by him." Bugsy couldn't believe he was spilling family secrets. "And had decided to keep the child."

That news nearly leveled her. *What a tangled web Franklin weaved,* she thought. Bugsy noticed her silence. She knew things that she wasn't sharing.

He asked, "Ragnar. He's fed, isn't he?"

"Absolutely not!" Kimberly insisted. "We don't have men like Ragnar employed at our administration. I can assure you that Ragnar Benjamin is a man of interest in your sister's disappearance. That's all!"

"Ragnar Benjamin is clearly an alias." Bugsy pursued, "What's his government?"

Again, she lied. "I don't know. That's why I'm here."

"Here's what I do know. This Ragnar Benjamin is a field agent trying to build a case against my family and me. Somehow this nigga thought it was okay to use subterfuge and gain his way into my sister's bed. He met Lucky, slept with her, and when he couldn't control her, he humiliated her and then killed her. Your agency knows all of this...that your agent went rogue, and that's why you're here. Wondering if the infamous family has pieced this shit together. And if so, then your man's life is at stake." He added, "Allegedly."

"That's not true!" she protested. "Ragnar Benjamin isn't an agent because if he was, why would I be here? The bureau protects our own, but we wouldn't tolerate someone who has done what Mr. Benjamin has done to get an arrest. I'm only here to see if you have any information to help us pursue him. He needs to speak to your sister's whereabouts to get your father's lawyers to back off the agency."

"Our lawyers aren't backing off shit. My sister took a noninvasive paternity test which should expose this muthafuckin' coverup," he lied. Bugsy then stood up, hoovering over the table. "We're done. And thanks for the information."

"I didn't tell you anything."

"Oh, but you did."

Bugsy walked off, leaving her to ponder the last ten minutes.

CHAPTER 14

Everyone was at home when Bugsy arrived. Scott was in his den having a spirited conversation with Christopher Azul, one of his lawyers, about the person Bugsy wanted to discuss. Bugsy whistled and caught his father's attention. Scott nodded, webbed his fingers, and mouthed, "Five minutes."

Bugsy then gathered his mother and brother, and everyone met in the kitchen around the breakfast bar—their new meeting spot.

When Scott joined them, Bugsy said, "I got accosted today by a female FBI agent. She wanted to talk about Lucky's disappearance."

"Yo, why the fuck is everyone runnin' up on you?" Meyer wanted to know. "And who is *this* broad?"

Layla asked, "What did she say about your sister?"

"And why is this bitch comfortable enough to be making introductions?" Scott added.

All members were highly annoyed.

Bugsy placed his hands in his suit pants pockets just as his father does when discussing crucial matters. He said, "She does have balls, I can say that. But our encounter was brief, and she was on a fishing expedition, trying to find out what I knew about Ragnar Benjamin and Lucky."

"And? Why come to you? She's the fed?" said Meyer.

"Here's what our conversation told me. It says that Lucky was correct; it's not just theory. Ragnar is a federal agent—"

"Tell us something we don't know, nigga!" Layla snapped impatiently, waiting for her son to get to the good part of having a meeting with the enemy.

"Ma, Lucky suspected it, and we rode with it because we did too. But after meeting with the agent, it's not a supposition. It's all facts. Ragnar is FBI, and he went off script."

"Ya think?" Layla sarcastically remarked.

"You sure about this?" Scott wanted to know.

"Exactly," Bugsy replied. "You know a hit hog will holler."

"So that bitch was hollering, huh?" Meyer asked.

"Nothing but ear-piercing denials."

The room fell quiet for a beat. And then Scott said, "This fed. What's her name?"

"Kimberly Cooper," Bugsy retorted. "What you thinking, Pops?"

Layla replied, "He's thinking that we find and torture this bitch because she's the only one who can definitively identify Red Negro other than Lucky."

"She's the answer to this riddle Lucky left us with. Who's Black, and red, and fed?"

"Bingo!" Meyer replied. "They done fucked up now."

It was a vast case; nearly 15% of New York City's DEA agents worked on the task force. They had over a dozen agents surveilling Scott, Layla, Bugsy, and Meyer—subtly and meticulously following their movements. The agents snapped many pictures of the crime family doing their daily activities. They had surveillance footage of their comings and goings. But so far, nothing was indicative of illegal activity. It appeared that everyone's movements were limited, at least when they wanted to be seen. Resourceful, they had ways to make it appear they were inside their home when they were doing nefarious things. The family had a hunch that the government would trail them, especially after Understanding and Jackie were murdered. Scott wanted everyone to be extra careful and not keep routines.

Several agents snapped rapid pictures of Bugsy leaving Lacey's restaurant in Harlem. They observed him climb into the backseat of his Escalade, and it drove off, traveling south to lower Manhattan. The problem that the agents were having was that everyone they were trailing had many cars and many properties, and they were sneaky.

While traveling, Bugsy removed his burner phone from his suit jacket pocket and called Scott to give him the 411 about his meeting with Diablo and Pablo. Scott answered, "How did it go?"

"It went as planned. They seemed legit, Pops."

Scott was disappointed. "Is that what you think? That they're legit?"

"Nah, not at all. They're just good with their shit…feds are pulling out their grade-A agents on us."

Scott knew exactly what his son was saying. He, too, had been fooled in Dubai. "Okay. I'll get it handled," was Scott's only reply, and their call ended.

Covertly, the agents followed Bugsy from the restaurant to his parent's home. They watched him exit the vehicle and go into the swanky Manhattan building. Half an hour later, he emerged and returned to the SUV. The agents followed Bugsy to his barbershop. They sat parked in the distance and watched him in the barber's chair, snapping dozens and dozens of pictures. It appeared that Bugsy was unaware that he was being watched at first, but then he suddenly turned and looked their way and waved. The agents halted their picture-taking briefly and gawked his way. Bugsy appeared to smirk like he had something up his sleeve.

"I wonder what the fuck he finds so amusing?" said one of the agents.

"Don't worry, we'll wipe that fucking smirk off his face once we slap the handcuffs on him," said his partner.

Meanwhile, unbeknownst to Pablo and Diablo, Scott had his team doing counter-surveillance. The feds watched and followed Bugsy. Santino and his men—his two cousins, Vinnie and Paulie, watched and observed them right back. Scott had been in the game too long to know how and how not to move.

The crew added a GPS tracker to Pablo and Diablo's vehicles at the restaurant. It took the team 93 hours to bypass the government's firewall and security until they received the locations of where the government had them staying until the case would ultimately close. Santino had to find where they were most vulnerable. Both agents were staying in different locations in Jersey City, New Jersey. Diablo had lovers coming in and out, and Pablo loved busty blondes with huge breast implants. But in their actual reality—when they weren't undercover—they were *happily* married with children. One of Pablo's daughters would be heading off to Harvard soon.

Santino sat parked outside the New Jersey home near Newark Bay. It was after eight; the area was quiet and tranquil. Santino and his cousins sat in the stolen SUV parked near his target's home. Every night, per stakeout, they tried to get the perfect timing to ambush the agent.

Surveillance on Pablo revealed that his only vulnerability was takeout. He ordered food from different eateries each night. Santino had to assume that the apartment had an alarm and surveillance system, thus the high bounty on a federal agent's head.

His team was ready to strike. Santino had taken as many precautions as he could foresee to execute the pig and get away with it. Everyone was dressed in black, faces covered, hands gloved up. And then, a vehicle arrived with the food Pablo ordered through Grubhub.

The driver exited the vehicle with two bags of piping hot food, none the wiser that this would be his last delivery. Santino approached the driver from behind, wrapped a wire around his neck, and pulled. Paulie punched the victim several times in his gut while Santino's herculean strength nearly snapped the guy's head off.

The driver's body went limp before he succumbed to the strangulation. He was quickly yet quietly tossed into the trunk of his vehicle.

Pablo was inside his government-expensed palace, enjoying a thick line of grade-A cocaine and a nice bottle of Chianti. His mouth was salivating for the Asian food from Nobu's. He didn't bother to look through the peephole when his bell rang. With a gush of energy, he swung his front door open, and his eyes nearly crossed as he stared down the barrel of Santino's revolver.

Bak! Bak!

Two to the head. Simple yet effective.

The agent's body dropped, but they weren't out of the woods. The front door was closed, and with precision, Pablo was wrapped in plastic and added to the trunk of the delivery sedan. Vinnie hopped in the driver's seat and followed behind Santino and Paulie to their next location.

Diablo's home was next. Other than a steady stream of sex workers on random nights at random times, the agent was consistently inconsistent. Therefore, they couldn't use the same tactic they had used with Diablo. Also, his murder had to be tonight. Come morning, once Pablo didn't check in, all hell would break loose.

Getting to Diablo was brazen. Santino literally had to kick open the front door waving his revolver. The alarm blared throughout, and they reasoned they had less than two minutes to make a clean getaway.

Diablo evidently was a heavy sleeper. He didn't even stir at the obnoxious sound. His death was peaceful—two bullets to the back of his head. And then body transport.

Just like that, both men would disappear into the night and never be heard from or found.

Scott hired the best, and he got the best.

Riley had written numerous letters to her peoples—friends, past lovers, and most importantly, her mother telling them about her predicament. It was her only way to communicate because she realized she never got through to anyone using the federally monitored phones. All her calls went to voicemail, so Riley eventually gave up. She knew that any one of her homegirls would have flown to Chicago with the quickness. So, the fact that no one sat across the table from her for a visit summed up her future.

And then she gave up wanting to see a judge, speaking to her court-appointed lawyer, and finally, Meyer West. Suddenly, Riley was only concerned with getting through each day without being stricken with another ailment. Visibly she was a shell of her former self, thin and weak. Riley operated on low energy and kept to herself, obeying the jail's rules.

Dashing quickly into chow, she grabbed an apple, banana,

milk, and a fruit cocktail cup. Riley knew she couldn't live off this sustenance for much longer but couldn't focus on tomorrow. Not when today was so painful. Heading to her cell, she heard, "Look at this bird bitch."

Riley kept walking.

"Cluck...cluck...cluck...chickenhead!" And then someone laid hands on her, pushing her forward with a hard shove. Riley swung around and, with a closed hand, bashed the girl in her nose—blood squirted down her lips—eyes welled up with tears. Stunned, the girl hollered, clutching her face.

The second assailant started swinging, landing a few blows before Riley began fighting back. The two women went pound for pound, Riley quickly becoming the aggressor. Even in her weakened state, she made time for this ass-whipping, noting that the girls were the same ones from the infirmary.

Riley had beat the girl down to the ground. And was now sitting on her stomach, bashing her head into the tile floor, before being yanked roughly off by a correction officer.

"Get the fuck off me!" Riley hollered, still swinging.

Another CO joined the melee and placed Riley in a headlock while the other twisted her wrist so far back she could feel it was seconds away from snapping.

"Okay," Riley yelled. "I'm not resisting! You gonna break my wrist—" And it did. "Oww!"

The pain was excruciating as she let out an ear-piercing scream. Riley was almost in hysterics as the COs continued restraining her using unnecessary force. Flex cuffs were applied to her wrists. She was subsequently taken to the infirmary but not before receiving a couple shots on her record.

CO Katz informed her, "When you're done in medical, you're going straight to the hole, inmate!"

Riley didn't care. In fact, she stopped caring about many things, including today's event.

Doctor Middleton placed Riley on a 24-hour medical hold so

that she could run some more tests.

"You don't look well, Riley. Have you been eating?"

Riley was tired of this bitch. She pretended she wanted the best for her, but Riley knew otherwise.

Assertively, Riley replied, "I'm good."

"You sure?" Middleton pressed. "I can have a dinner tray brought up for you. Get some meat on these bones."

The more the doctor spoke, the angrier Riley got. She just wanted to be left alone.

Riley snapped. "I said I'm fuckin' good. What part don't you understand?"

Riley's eyes said she was less than good and that Elane Middleton would do well to stay off her bad side.

"Okay, great," Doctor Middleton said. "We'll get your wrist in a cast and run some tests. Only one person is admitted, so you should have a good night's sleep. And I'll see you in the morning."

More needles, a cast, and finally, peace and quiet. Riley slept soundly in the hospital bed and was awoken by a somber-looking doctor the next day.

"Riley, darling, I have some bad news. Your tests came back, and you have trichomoniasis vaginalis."

"Trigger what?"

"Trichomoniasis. It's a venereal disease."

"Are you fuckin' dumb?" Riley hollered. "Who am I fuckin' in here?"

"That's your business," Elane said curtly. "And I'm not here to judge. I'm here to help."

Riley's eyes took in the whole scene. Mind blown; she couldn't believe the doctor would go this far. There was an undercurrent of jubilee in the doctor's eyes. It was an expression that said she could do whatever she wanted to Riley, and there wasn't anything she could do about it.

Elane took Riley's silence as submission. It didn't matter that

Elane was a general practitioner, not a gynecologist, nor that Riley hadn't undergone a GYN exam. The sillier the diagnosis, the more powerful all involved felt. That's how James operated his network. He could and did have Riley injected with shingles, Trichomoniasis, fat injections, arsenic, and next up was HIV.

It never bothered James that his uncle was 1 in nearly 400 men injected with syphilis by the Tuskegee Institute, which performed a study on 600 African American men from 1932-1972. Injecting 399 with the venereal disease. These men participated in the experiment to receive free health care.

James was knee-high when he'd listen to his relatives speak of the depravity done to his uncle. James's father spoke with such hatred and disdain that this went on for nearly four decades, using his brother and others as lab rats.

And instead of becoming a man and reversing the method used to oppress his people, he chose to use the same barbaric practice on another African American person. And he gave no fucks. Her life meant nothing. He valued a piece of paper with his signature more than Riley.

Doctor Elane Middleton was feeling too warm and fuzzy inside as she explained to Riley the cocktail of medication she would need to take. Elane should have noticed that she'd grabbed a ballpoint pen and, with great force, plunged the inconspicuous weapon four inches into her carotid artery and twisted.

Blood squirted, saturating Riley's good hand before she let go and watched. Doctor Middleton's eyes widened before her own hand removed the object. Gushing blood that supplies blood to the brain was pouring out of the open wound like someone had uncorked a wine bottle and poured it.

The good doctor knew what she should do: remain calm and stop the bleeding. But what she did was panic, stumbling around the small area, knocking over tray tables. It was abundantly clear by the amount of blood that she wouldn't make it.

Now it was Riley who had the undercurrent of jubilee in her eyes. She sat still as the medical staff ran around, grabbing a gauze, clamps, needles, and thread trying to stop what had already been done.

Riley stood still, chest heaving, eyes drinking in her handiwork. And then she heard his name. Meyer West. The television was on Icon Hollywood. The story said it was rumored that Meyer West, a notorious New York businessman, was dating an up-and-coming actress. Riley looked and saw her nemesis, Abigail, who dances at her club. Not only was she shocked that Meyer would go for a ho like Abigail, but also, when did she start acting?

Riley's heart swelled, and she felt faint. This couldn't be happening.

The correctional staff came next; that was the last thing she remembered. Everything went black.

It takes a lot, more than the latest sensational headline, to shock James. The Oklahoma bombing, the double attacks on the World Trade Center, and the attempted assassination of Reagan—nothing surprised him. But getting the call about Riley murdering Doctor Middleton with a pen had him motherfucking shell-shocked.

He hadn't even pushed her as far as he'd planned, yet she snapped? Already? All he had asked Riley to do was participate in a bit of subterfuge, set up her ex, and move on with her life. Why did the young woman take it so personally?

James always had a full psychological report drafted on all his subjects—perp *and* snitch. And nowhere in the hundreds of pages did it ever say she was capable of murder. Mostly because

Riley never followed up on what she started—she was a quitter. And she had empathy, was naturally an empath, and if pushed or challenged, she would fold rather than lean into conflict. That's how they knew Terrence, aka Elliott, would get Riley to drive that fateful night. All Elliott had to do was keep pushing his agenda.

So, how does any of that explain what was done?

James couldn't even place blame at his feet. He didn't feel he pushed, let alone *shoved* Riley into this position. James could only admit to a few taps—gentle nudges to get her where he wanted her. It had to be Elane. She did have an annoying voice, one that got under his skin the few times they spoke.

The rainbow at the end of this storm is that Riley was authentically facing life behind bars on a murder one rap. Perhaps now she would be ready to see things his way. If not, HIV was in her future.

While Garrett was cozying up to the Caucasians in the Chicago office, James and Terrence were looking for that motherfucking five million. Other than running his wife to Walmart and Target or taking his son to indoor golf or bowling—his two stops were home and the office. There was always someone in his home, and although Franklin was devoutly religious, he went to mass each day from work, not for Sunday mass.

Those actions told Dough that that's where the money was hidden.

It took weeks before James and Terrence gained entry to Franklin's rental. Because his wife homeschooled their son, the residence wasn't vacated for long periods. And there was also the surveillance system to get past. The alarm *and* cameras had to be deactivated for the home invasion and reactivated covertly—a feat that was extremely delicate when dealing with someone with the same training.

The opportunity came when James found out that Franklin and his family had accepted an invitation to the masquerade-themed wedding of one of the agents. James and Terrence were invited—both declined because they knew the invitation was out of etiquette, not earnest. It also irked James that Franklin didn't utter a word about the wedding, most likely assuming they hadn't made the list.

"You see him?" James asked Terrence. "You know this brother doesn't think he's Black."

Terrence nodded. Both men watched Franklin daily hobnobbing with white coworkers, chitchatting, cackling with a huge grin, his voice bellowing with hearty laughs.

"How many times we asked him out for drinks or lunch?"

"Countless," Terrence answered, his face stone cold.

With arms folded across their chest, both leaned against a long desk, just taking in the scene. The more Franklin floated from one pale face to the next, the angrier James became.

James said, "This nigga doesn't leave Chicago alive."

James and Terrence watched the day of the wedding as Franklin and his family backed out of the two-car garage in his SUV. Franklin had on a leather plague doctor's mask, which had a huge beak, his wife a Venetian peacock mask, and Junior wore an eighteen-century jester's mask.

James broke through Franklin's firewall within minutes, deactivated his security system, and went to work. His fingers moved lightning-quick on his laptop as he searched for a backup trigger, a failsafe mechanism that skilled hackers implemented. James found the backdoor and deactivated that.

His laptop slapped shut. "Let's go!"

The agents went to the back of the home; the glass double doors were hardly challenging. Terrence easily picked the lock, and the moment they stepped inside the modest-sized house, it was on. They were almost salivating at their mouths as they took off in separate directions.

"I'll cover the upper level; you take the main," James ordered as he took two steps at a time, heading toward the master bedroom.

There wasn't an inch of the home that wasn't opened, kicked, pulled, or tapped looking for secret passages. Three hours later, they found nothing.

Back in his sedan, James peeled out. He asked, "Where would he keep that amount of cash? If I'm him, I don't leave that in New York."

"Nah," Terrence began. "No way would I take that chance."

"Safe deposit box?"

"Nope! He's dirty. And if he's ever indicted, that's the first place law enforcement looks."

"He buried it," James concluded as he spun his sedan around dramatically, making a wide U-turn. "We didn't check the yard."

Terrence tapped his watch. "Time, Dough. It's not on our side."

James smiled wickedly. "Sure, it is. And should the family come home while we're looking for *our* money—"

"Then we lullaby them. Point blank..."

James finished with, "Period."

CHAPTER 15

Three key men sat at one corner of a large rectangular table: James, Terrence, and Franklin discussing Riley Baker.

James said, "I'm taking Riley to Detroit for a few weeks to recuperate before we throw her out into the field. She looks like shit."

Franklin's stomach did somersaults. This wasn't what he had in mind. Franklin's plans for Riley didn't involve her leaving the state without him. It seemed he was her handler and had made all the follow-up contacts since Terrence was still undercover as Elliott. James's identity was seemingly top-tier classified. Why would James break protocol and step from behind his mask as Steve? Franklin had to tread carefully; any question was the wrong one. He wanted to ask, "Is that wise?" Or announce that he'd be happy to take Riley to Michigan but knew either question would open the door to the Lucky fiasco.

Franklin thought about Riley's juicy booty and how he imagined it jiggling as he slapped it repeatedly and couldn't help himself. He said, "Listen, James. You've given me the reigns with Riley thus far; she and I have an understanding. If she's introduced to another handler, it will take much longer to cajole her into who we want her to be. She doesn't trust me—I'm fed. But she will listen to me." Franklin's eyes bounced from James to Terrence with confidence. He continued, "My wife and son are settled, so I don't mind flying to Michigan to stay with Riley for a few weeks."

Terrence mused. It was like watching two dogs fight over a bone. A bone that he already ate. Terrence had eaten that steak bone and damn nearly sucked all its marrow out. But he wasn't intelligent enough to realize that he had Riley, but she'd never *given* herself to him—not entirely. Not as a woman does with the man she loves, not as she's given herself to Meyer.

James seethed. His nostrils flared wide as he inhaled and exhaled short breaths to prevent himself from smashing a lamp over Franklin's head. Each day James met with Franklin was one day too many. Terrence knew the look well, but Franklin was unbothered. James was old, past his prime, and still used archaic means. Even his computer skills were rusty. Only an arrogant fool would have walked into the trap Franklin had left for them. When James and Terrence disconnected his alarm system and bypassed the trap door. Essentially, they activated a ghost system manned 24 hours/7 days a week by his buddies back in New York. Franklin saw it all. Pathetic, really. James and Terrence, on a Jack Sparrow mission, ran throughout his house looking for treasures that were snug as a bug in a rug at his in-laws.

James said, "He who learns but doesn't think is lost; he who thinks but doesn't learn is in great danger."

Lucky. The conversation always began and ended with Lucky so much that Franklin was now immune. Franklin replied, "Give a man a mask, and he will show you his true face."

It was an Oscar Wilde quote, and James wasn't sure how it was germane. What the fuck did it have to do with the price of tea in China? And then he thought, mask? Was that a setup?

James didn't have to think long. After watching Franklin fiddle with his phone, James's phone tinged.

"You wanna get that?" Franklin asked. "I think you should get that."

James opened the file, and it was a video of him and Terrence running throughout Franklin's home on the day of the masquerade-themed wedding. The footage was so clear you could see sweat trickling down James's face.

If this nigga was one thing, he was consistent, James thought. *He loved video cameras.*

James growled, "So! What's next?!" And handed his phone to Terrence to review.

"Next, I go to lunch with my peers and then home to pack for my trip to Michigan."

James and Terrence watched as Franklin casually walked into the hallway and was embraced by a sea of white faces—smiles and an overabundance of love were exchanged.

Terrence said, "Houston, we got a problem."

Markeeta wasn't thrilled when James called to inform her she'd have a guest for the next few weeks.

She complained, "All the shit I got on my plate, and now I gotta babysit a whole grown woman?" Markeeta sucked her teeth and continued with, "Who is this bitch?"

James had it on his bucket list to officially indoctrinate Riley into his team by bedding the sexy vixen before she was shipped back to New York. He wanted to know that he fucked the girl that took down Meyer West; see what she offered that had the kingpin losing his mind. Of course, James could have just asked his colleague, Terrence, but he felt that that would be lazy. As James pondered why he despised Markeeta, he settled upon her directness. He had quickly gotten over her basic looks, large feet, ghetto tendencies, and unambitious nature. But he couldn't get past her unfiltered mouth and random outbursts. It was too soon for her to not fear him. What was it about this new generation of informants—Markeeta and Riley—that he had to practically play a game of Russian Roulette to make them see he wasn't fucking around.

He replied, "You know what? Pack your shit!"

"Wait. What?"

"Pack your shit. I'll be there in a few hours," James said, then clarified, "And I mean *only* your shit. What you and your son came with."

"Come on now, you bugging!" Markeeta hollered. "You actin' real childish right now…a bitch can't ask questions?"

Dough pressed END.

A few hours later, James used his key to enter the residence. Markeeta and Ralph were in the kitchen making tacos. Shredded lettuce, tomatoes, and cheddar cheese were plated on the kitchen's island. Turkey ground and seasoning were grilling in the skillet, and Markeeta was drinking a three-finger glass of cognac. She hoped this nigga wasn't coming to kick her and her son out like Tannery had done, but with these feds, anything was possible. They discarded informants like trash, and stupidly she thought he was different. Markeeta had the game fucked up. She had no job security.

Markeeta looked at two figures—James and a weathered-looking female. Her long hair was in two cornrows braided down past her shoulders, dark circles punctuated swollen eyes, and a cast supported her wrist. She looked joyless, defeated, like a shelter dog that needed a hug. But and however, she was

James's type—a fact that didn't escape Markeeta.

So, this the bitch that's supposed to take my place? She thought. *Bo Jangles won't like her fragile-looking ass. She's too prissy, and he likes us hood.*

Markeeta said, "Good. Just in time for dinner. I'm making tacos." Her eyes went to the woman. "Do you want anything to drink?"

Markeeta was on her best behavior, using her corporate voice. She wanted James to know that whatever ticked her off was water under the bridge. She was raising the white flag.

The woman's head quickly shook at the question. And then James said, "I told you to be ready. Come on, let's go."

She stalled, "Wait. I gotta feed my son first!"

"Bitch, please," James chuckled, amused. "Oh, you're a mom now?"

"I'm not going to dignify that with a response," Markeeta said. She had read that line in one of the books she was reading, and it felt appropriate.

Even James was impressed because there was a pregnant pause, his eyebrow raised. Finally, "Markeeta, get your shit and stop fucking with me!"

Markeeta's pride wouldn't allow her to grovel, not in front of this new bitch. She yelled to Ralph, "Come on!" and he followed.

James looked at Riley, "I'll be back in a couple of hours. Make yourself at home. And for my sake, eat something."

Markeeta was relieved that she and Ralph weren't carted off to the airport, but the destination was less than desirable. James pulled up in front of a two-bedroom, one-bathroom, 650-square-foot home in a crime-riddled area near Eight Mile. With few streetlights, the darkened, gloomy block had an eerie feeling. Hooligans were huddled at the corner. Loud music blared from more than one home, making it feel like a block party was going on, and a few blocks over, she heard a succession of gunshots.

Markeeta was Brooklyn born and bred, had fucked more than a gaggle of murderers, and had been at the epicenter of dozens of shootouts. Yet, when it's not your hood, it hits different. She was shook.

James said, "Take these keys and get comfortable. You act right, learn how to control your vile mouth, and I'll be back to get you, and we'll pick up where we left off."

Markeeta kept her eyes straight ahead, staring up the block and observing her surroundings. Her head nodded.

"I'm not going to give you another warning, Markeeta. This is it. You fuck up again, and I promise you that your last station in life will make this house feel like Buckingham Palace. Understood?"

She nodded.

"Open your fucking mouth and answer me," James growled.

Markeeta turned to face her bully. Her face softened, "Yes. No problem. I'll see you soon…come on, Ralph."

The George Floyd murder reverberated throughout the world. As more and more footage leaked, Maxine sat sobbing her eyes out on her sofa. This was the second time she had watched a human life being snuffed out at the hands of another. That up close and personal slaying of someone using only their hands as a weapon. George's murder triggered the helplessness she felt when Layla killed Sandy.

When Gregory arrived home, he was just as upset. As a Black man, it felt like him lying face down on the pavement, knee to neck, violating all human and civil rights.

"I have to do something," Maxine cried out. "I can't sit here and allow this officer to get away with this."

"We will," Greg agreed. "I've wanted to run for City Council for my Harlem district, and I have influential backers who say I could win. I can start there, climb up the ladder, and make a difference for our communities. Laws must be enacted to ensure this doesn't keep happening."

"I wanna help you," she blurted out. "How can I help?"

"You can start by coming with me to a dinner to discuss my campaign and logistics hosted by Reverend Lionel Carmichael and a couple civil rights attorneys in Harlem."

"Okay, I can do that," she agreed. "But that's long term…I want to do something specifically on behalf of George Floyd. Something immediate." Maxine's face crumbled into an unrecognizable ball of grief. She had that ugly cry going on, and Gregory had to gather his emotions, or he'd join her. He pulled Maxine close and wrapped his arms tightly around her, her head snuggly resting on his chest. Greg didn't want her to see the tears streaming down his cheeks but knew she would.

He said, "We'll march. We'll march as our ancestors did, and our voices will be heard. Would you like that?"

She nodded.

And then he thought about her earlier dream of being a lawyer and remembered his friend, Zion Jones. Greg asked, "I have a good friend, a civil rights attorney in lower Manhattan. He specializes in these cases, wrongful convictions, and police brutality. If I called him, I'm sure he'd have a position for you, entry-level. But you'd be around what was once your passion and help fight for the underdog. Would you like that?"

Maxine looked up. She was nearly a foot shorter than him, so she had to get on her tippy toes to meet his lips with a succulent kiss. This was the most intimate they'd been since she moved in. "I would," she agreed.

Riley had to admit that the home was impressive, not because she had spent the last few months incarcerated. She had no idea that the federal government had access to such lavish dwellings, but at this point, she realized that nothing was off-limits to them. She wondered who the woman and her son were, but it wasn't her business. Something was going on with the agent formerly known as Steve and the female with the strange name.

Riley walked around the impressive home before circling back to the kitchen. She ate around six tacos before making a glass of tea and falling asleep on the sofa. She awoke to James stroking her cheek. Riley slapped his hand away and sat up, startled. She glared at her oppressor and realized he had her fucked up.

"Don't touch me," she commanded. "Ever again!"

James nodded. Her disdain for him was a challenge. He wanted to turn that frown upside down. He said, "Understood. Listen, I want you to stay here for a few weeks, get your weight up, and heal. Whatever's in the closet you want, it's yours to take to New York. Use the gym, steam shower, all the amenities. I'll have my top hair stylist give you deep conditioning treatments, clip your ends, and get your hair bouncing and behaving again."

Riley remained silent. She was irritated by how casually he spoke to her, knowing he was one of the men who had placed her in this predicament.

James asked, "That's all your hair, correct? No weave?"

"Yes."

"It's beautiful...your hair...as are you."

Riley diverted her eyes and stared toward the exit.

James felt her uncomfortable energy and didn't care. He continued, "And I have a Korean woman who gives the best manicures and pedicures. Her small, strong hands will massage any stress you have in your body away. Would you like that?"

His voice was intentionally soft, monotone.

"I can do my own nails for now. And hair. I just want to be alone for the next few weeks to decompress and process everything that's gone on. It's a lot...a lot has happened, and I need to heal before I go back to New York and lie to the man I love."

"You think you have choices?" James's voice deepened without a proper transition. "You think this is a holiday...that you're on vacation? You're working...you work for me!"

"I know that!" she snapped back.

"Do you? Because right now, you've lost at least thirty pounds," James stood up and began doing what he does best. "Your hair has thinned; your ass looks flat...and if you saw the new lady that Meyer has in his life, you wouldn't be refusing shit. On your best day, you couldn't keep his attention. What do you think will happen when he sees you now? He's going to friend zone you; ignore your calls. And I repeat, you don't get what I need from him, and you're doing life for the murder of Elane Middleton! I won't even have to charge you with drug distribution. But I will."

Riley's eyes welled up. How many times can you smash a broken glass? There weren't many more parts to break, but that didn't stop his tenacity.

"You're right. Anything you suggest is good with me. But can I have at least a day or two alone?"

James waited a beat and then replied, "That's my girl. All you have to do is ask me for what you want."

The tone he used sounded creepy. Riley didn't like it. She didn't like him. Nor did she like looking at his face. She also wondered why Steve, aka Agent Dough, had taken over where Malcolm, aka Agent Garrett, had left off.

"I thought Agent Garrett was supposed to fly me out here?"

"He was. But got called away last minute to consult on another case."

Riley had more questions. Lots of them. But knew the more

she talked, the longer he'd stay. She said, "Thank you, Agent Dough. For everything. I think I'm going to call it a night."

With that, she headed to the top floor's bedroom and locked herself in. And hoped in the morning that Agent Dough would be gone.

Whistler Hussain felt nostalgic as he spoke to a handful of henchmen, all on his payroll, reliving his glory days as second-in-command to the Scott West empire. They were in a trap house—well, an apartment, in a housing project near Prospect Heights. Whistler had successfully flipped the three ki's he'd murdered Isaiah and A-God for. He was now moving nine kilograms of cocaine a week.

The apartment belonged to a nineteen-year-old female with five kids, all under six. It was a typical unit with three bedrooms, dingy walls, and roaches. The sinks—kitchen, and bathroom had rust stains, broken ceramic tiles, and window bars. The mother was relocated by Whistler to a townhouse rental in a better neighborhood with a competitive school district. He didn't do this out of the kindness of his heart. The arrangement was a business decision. The cocaine moved quicker in that prime location, and his men took fewer risks transporting the drugs to their clientele. In the projects, the dealers came to them, and local law enforcement didn't view the consistent foot traffic.

There were a few caveats. The wolves were always watching; someone would try to test Whistler's crew sooner or later, hoping for a quick come-up. And then there was always a goon lying in the cut, quiet-hating because their dreams of becoming a kingpin never materialized. Hence, they run to the cops and start snitching. Finally, his safety was a concern. There was only one way in, one out. So, if something popped off, Whistler would have to shoot his way to safety.

"I got some beef with an organization in New York," he began. "If I structure this jux right, it could be a big score."

"Beef?" Cappo said. "With who?"

"Scott West," he explained. "He's one of the biggest suppliers on the east coast, and I know where he lays his head at night. We go in, murder him, his wife, and two sons. But let me make myself very clear, nobody touches his daughter! She's mine!"

Cappo snapped his fingers repeatedly. "Scott West...Scott West...Scott West...I know that name from somewhere...."

Whistler eyed him suspiciously.

Cappo continued, "I think I read something...."

"You always tryin' to act educated nigga!" one goon commented. "Readin' and shit."

"Nah, I'm fo' real. Feds thought they had him and his wife dead to rights. They had a snitch who worked for the organization, and that nigga still walked." He looked at his boss. "How are you affiliated with him?"

It was a simple question. Should have been answered in the same vein. So, everyone's eyes widened when Whistler pulled out his pistol and knocked Cappo upside his head with the barrel of his gun. Stunned to immobility, Cappo couldn't defend himself. Whistler didn't stop with one blow. The weapon's force pounded until a dent grew into a gap and expanded several inches in diameter. Cappo's body jerked pound after pound, blood coating Whistler's hand.

Cappo's head ultimately caved in due to blunt force trauma.

The lifeless body toppled over on the secondhand sofa that now absorbed his AB-positive blood. And although Cappo had grown up with everyone in the room, had a cousin who was a few feet away from his dead body, and the hooligans clearly outnumbered their boss. Not one man made a move against the one-eyed monster. They all sat stupefied, not willing to avenge shit.

Whistler tucked his murder weapon back in his waist and continued where he had left off. "Her name's Lucky, and she will fight for her life. But I repeat. Don't muthafuckin' as much as break a fingernail on her. When we go in, subdue her, and bring her to me. I'll be focused on Scott. Am I clear?"

"Yeah," Wise said dryly. He was Cappo's cousin. "We hear you."

"Good. Now get this shit cleaned up!"

Whistler came strolling out of the building, unaffected by the bloody carnage he'd left behind. Oblivious that the predator had now become prey.

Scott and Mason sat a few cars behind his. When Whistler pulled out, they followed.

CHAPTER 16

It was a chilly night and a full moon. Meyer sat on the terrace bundled in a comforter, smoking a Newport, wishing it was Kush. Since detoxing, he'd given up all forms of narcotics—alcohol, weed, and codeine. Alcohol and weed were gateway drugs to something more potent, and it seemed that he had an addictive gene, so he had to go all in, leaving no room for temptation. Now nicotine was his only vice.

Near his reach was a loaded Ruger SR9C. Where he went, his guns went too. Meyer's brain was now clearer than crystal, which was good because he'd almost lost his life if not by Rakim then by Whistler's hand.

His phone rang, and it was from an unknown number. He answered cautiously, and it was a voice he recognized, saying to him, "She's back in town."

When he heard *"she,"* Meyer knew the caller was talking about Lollipop. He had paid someone to watch her place 24/7. He wanted to know the moment she returned to her uptown apartment.

"How long has she been back?"

"About a day now."

"A'ight. Good looking out. I got you," he said.

"Thanks, Meyer, anytime."

Hearing about Lollipop being back in New York felt good. She had been gone for so long, leaving unexpectedly with some random fiancé. Meyer did feel a way about her not running back into his arms after he told her about Lucky. And her voice sounded cold when she told him not to call her again. But he understood. He wasn't ever good to her. The disrespect she endured just to be in his presence was a testament to how she felt about a nigga.

It took her to fall back for him to crawl back. Meyer was ready to fight for his—give her a moment to choose. But if she chose incorrectly, well, then, he would dead her new friend. And be a shoulder for her to lean on. This new nigga in her life was in the way, and Meyer wasn't about to lose Lollipop so quickly as he'd lost Zoe.

The following afternoon, he was climbing out of the black Chevrolet Suburban on 121st Street. His three-armed goons lingered outside, watching the block, cars, and every fucking thing moving. Since Javier Garcia declared war on his mother, each man was vigilant. What operated yesterday changed today, and tomorrow they will switch it up again.

He knocked on her door, anticipation bubbling inside the gangsta. So far, no answer. He knocked again—a bit harder. Meyer heard movement on the other side and knew she was glancing at him through the peephole. She didn't open the door. Instead, she said, "Why are you here, Meyer?"

"Just open the door, Lollipop. We need to talk."

"We did talk," she said. "But you won't listen."

Meyer wanted to lose his temper and demand to be let in like

209

he owned her. As if she was a possession that you controlled. The months apart, his sister's disappearance and fleeting drug dependency had taught him that you don't treat the people you love as he had treated her. Meyer hadn't known he loved Lollipop. He hadn't gotten that analytical about his thug love life. But now he had *growed* up.

"You gonna let me in?" he asked.

To his astonishment, he heard chatter, a man's voice, a discussion. Meyer was going to kill dude, put him six feet under without provocation. *This had to be the fiancé*, Meyer thought. He was ready to act a fool, but then a calming feeling swept over him. Meyer thought about how his father or Bugsy would handle this situation, and cooler heads would always prevail. If he was going to kill dude, it wasn't wise to broadcast it. Not with the feds on their asses.

Meyer knocked again. And this time, he heard the click-clack of locks unlocking. The door swung open, and before him was Lollipop and a dude. Meyer didn't know what he expected to see once he found her fiancé, but this wasn't it. The African American male was plain, like vanilla ice cream—no flavor. He had the face of a menacing goon and the swag of an educated nerd. The nigga tried to dress it up with a suit and some jewels, but Meyer would place him in the *hell fucking no* column.

Lollipop had a sour look on her face. Meyer knew it well; she was pissed. She said, "Meyer, this is Elliot. Elliot, Meyer."

Elliot was intentional. Firmly, he shook Meyer's hand, kissed Lollipop on her cheek, and said he'd see her soon. Confidently, he left his fiancée with her former lover and headed out.

Meyer was confused and incensed. Was he really that secure? Did he know how good Meyer used to fuck Lollipop? Was Elliot aware that standing before him was Meyer West? One of the most sought-after bachelors since Michael B. Jordan?

Meyer was speechless.

Lollipop said, "Come in, Meyer."

He stepped inside and noticed the massive rock on her finger. Meyer felt he'd entered the boxing ring and had already lost the fight. The urgency in his voice was unmistakable. He gushed, "Lollipop, how you gonna do me like this?"

"It's Riley, now. Call me by my government."

He challenged, "I got so much on my mind right now, and you want me to remember some new name too?"

"I can't concern myself with your worries, Meyer," she spat. "It's *always* about you. Only *you*. Or your family...never about me or what I wanted!"

He could tell she was in a mood. Meyer felt anger and accusation in her words. He was a piece of shit, and he knew it. But he hadn't come here to argue over a name.

"Riley, I see you've moved on, but I can't just give up on us without a fight—"

"He's not like that, Meyer!" she barked. "Elliot isn't on that bullshit you're on."

Meyer blew out air. He knew this wouldn't be easy. Calmly he said, "I meant to fight for you, not *over* you. I came here to say a few things"— Meyer looked around— "Can we sit down...and talk. I promise I'll leave when you tell me to. No drama, no bullshit."

Meyer followed Riley. She led him from her doorway to her modest living room. He noticed that she'd lost a lot of weight and her sparkle. And there was an ACE bandage around her dominant wrist. She was still beautiful, his heart, but something about her seemed different. While she was all boo'd up, she had stopped caring for herself. As if that nigga had drained her.

Meyer sat down on her sofa while Riley towered over him. He said, "Why you treatin' me like some random dude...like we don't have history?"

"I'm not."

Meyer shrugged. "I'm gonna keep it one hundred. I've been sick without you. And not because you've moved on and found

211

someone else. It's not about dude. It's about *you!*"

Riley shifted her weight from one foot to the other before sitting beside him. Meyer continued at eye level, "I never told you how I felt about you because a nigga didn't know it was this deep. I was a young nigga when we hooked up," Meyer chuckled. "I'm still a young nigga. But I thought I displayed my love by pistol-whipping niggas over you, controlling your movements, and hitting you off with paper spoke for me."

Riley's nostrils flared wide, and she released an uninterested exhale of wind.

He continued, "Within *The First 48*, your fiancé was gonna be dead."

"Meyer!" she yelled.

"Listen," he said. "That ain't gonna happen. Not by my hands."

"Good. Because that wouldn't bring me back to you."

"I see that," he replied. Meyer glanced at her exquisite diamond and thought it was something he would have picked out—flawless and flashy. The nigga got good taste. The emerald cut weighed down her finger, practically shouting, yelling in Meyer's ear that he blew it. "Tell me you love this man, and I'll believe you."

Riley hesitated momentarily and then replied, "I do."

Meyer nodded.

He stood to leave, and Riley stopped him with, "Wait, Meyer. Don't leave...not yet. You're right. We do have history. The last time we spoke, you mentioned Lucky being missing. Please, sit back down. Tell me what's up."

Riley offered to pour him a three-finger glass of cognac, but he refused.

"I cut all that shit out. I don't drink or smoke no more."

Her eyes widened. "Why? I mean...that's good and all. But I hope you won't judge that I still need to get fucked up."

"Do you, ma. You know a nigga like me is the last to judge."

Riley made herself a drink and then made a homemade pizza, extra cheesy with sausage and peppers, as Meyer liked. During dinner, he told her of the nightmare he and his siblings had gone through until Lucky's disappearance.

Her eyes were popped open wide, mouth agape for most of his story. The harassment, frozen assets, police shakedown, vermin infestation, vandalized apartments, porn video, federal agent impregnating Lucky, and Lucky's presumed disappearance was frightening. Yet she believed every word. She had just escaped her own nightmare, and it wasn't over.

"You think she's dead?"

Tears welled up in the gangsta's eyes, and Riley went and embraced him. She rubbed his back soothingly as he released half a year of emotions. Meyer couldn't lose his sister, not Lucky. He missed their bickering, getting under her skin. Their competitive nature and the bond they had. He loved her style, the way she dressed and wore her clothes, her bravado, quick wit, and courage. His heart told him she was gone; his mind wouldn't allow that to sink in.

Finally, he took the back of his hand and wiped his tears away. "Nah. She just missing. We gonna get her back."

Riley nodded. "I know you will."

This time when Meyer stood to leave, she didn't stop him. He asked, "Could I still call you from time to time...check in...or is that crossing a boundary?"

There was a pregnant pause, and then, "That would be okay."

Riley walked him to the door and asked one last departing question. "Hey, did you ever get a message from me when I was in Chicago?"

Meyer's head shook. "A message? Nah. What did it say?"

She shrugged. "Nothing important."

James's jaw tightened at the astonishing news he'd just received. He thought momentarily before walking across the hall to Franklin's office. Walking in without as much as a tap on the door to announce himself, James barged in, slamming the door behind him.

Franklin looked up—a little jumpy after receiving his own bad news from the New York bureau. To his chagrin, the West family wasn't backing down on the accusation that their daughter's disappearance was connected to an FBI agent. And that would be him.

Franklin said, "You don't knock?"

James sat down, legs spread wide, informally reclined like he was watching the Super Bowl halftime show at home. He said, "Tell me about Kimberly Cooper and why she's in my motherfucking business?"

Hearing Kim's name soured his stomach, but he didn't show it. In addition, Franklin was tired of being on the receiving end of James's disrespect. Passive aggressive tactics were in both their playbooks, but usually, unsuspecting civilians experienced their wrath. Agent against agent wasn't new territory, but male agent against him was a dance he wasn't used to. Franklin was emboldened battling the Kimberly's and Lucky's of the world— James Dough was delicate.

Franklin shrugged. "Ask her."

"I'm asking you!" Dough growled, his body now stiffening. "This bitch is investigating people attached to my old cases, and I would wager it's because of you!"

"What do you want me to say?" Franklin casually said. "Although, I would like to ask how investigating your old cases has anything to do with me? I'm not attached."

Franklin waited a beat and then continued, "I would warn those who have anything to hide, though. Kimberly Cooper is like a bloodhound. Once she gets a scent of any improprieties…she stays the course. But, um, I'm sure you have nothing to worry about."

"I don't!" James snapped.

Franklin deliberately hit him with a pregnant pause, eyeing his enemy. And then said— "Of course, you don't," —his voice dripping with sarcasm.

James took that remark as his cue to leave, not forgetting to slam the door upon his exit.

Franklin called after him, "Good talk."

Whistler was sound asleep in his full-size bed just inches off the floor. The home was sparsely furnished with just the necessities—bed, chair, kitchen table, utensils, television, and sofa. The aged hardwood flooring, splintered, was original to the Victorian-styled home built in 1915. The electrical needed updating, the roof had a tarp covering a leak, and the basement resembled an English dungeon. However, it was cheap, secluded, and the perfect location to spot unwelcome guests— police or predator.

So, he was quite shocked when he was woken up by a pot of icy water on his face. Instinctually, Whistler reached under his pillow for his Glock and grasped air. His eye adjusted quickly, and standing before him was Scott West and what he considered an army. Over two dozen goons had squeezed into his modest room. Their eyes spoke loudly—he had fucked up. Whistler had gotten cocky with it, and now he wouldn't get a second chance to make the same mistake.

The home's stale air—a mixture of dead mice in the attic and rodent droppings—nearly strangled the elite bunch of killers as the sparse oxygen quickly thinned out due to overcapacity.

Whistler's face creased in anger as he glared at the nigga he once had love and respect for. The two enemies went way back, predating Scott's wife and kids. His nemesis stood erect, overcoat opened, two guns snug in Scott's shoulder holster. Whistler's eye next focused on Mason. Their friendship was a distant memory as lines were drawn in the sand, Mason choosing to land on a winning team. His eye next hopped on Meyer West. He was posted up against the bedroom wall, one knee bent against the grimy drywall for support, arms folded across his chest. The knucklehead was dressed in army fatigues like he was going to Kuwait or Afghanistan rather than a shabby bungalow in a rural area of Delaware.

Bugsy was next to hold Whistler's unflinching gaze. The oldest twin was suited up, hard bottoms, cufflinks, there wasn't any love lost between men. And then she spoke; his eye quickly pulled to the woman who demanded his attention.

"You can't make this shit up, right nigga?" Layla joked. "I bet when your head hit that pillow, you never dreamed shit like this was possible."

"So, you just gonna skip over the fact that y'all were invited." Whistler slid out of bed, naked, toned body on full display. His flaccid penis making more than a few killers uncomfortable. "I practically drove y'all here."

"We're here," Scott casually replied. "Now what?"

"May I?" Whistler asked before making any sudden movement. He pointed toward his boxers on the floor; Scott nodded. The gangsta quickly stepped into his undergarment and continued with, "Now we kick it. There's a lot that you and Layla don't know."

Layla snorted. "Like how someone with your pedigree turned snitch?"

Whistler seized the moment. "Exactly. Feds had me dead to rights. They applied pressure, and I knew the whole case rested on my shoulders. If I'm credible, then you and Scott blow trial."

Scott said, "So what you saying?"

"I'm saying that what you and the jury saw on the stand was my way of squashing our beef over Lucky and Deuce." Whistler's eye scanned the room again, looking for his former lover, Lucky. He desperately wanted to see her again but realized she didn't feel the same way. Or else she would be there. He continued, "Look and listen to me. Am I even remotely the man y'all saw on that stand...forgetful, stumbling over my words, easily rattled?"

"I shot you point blank in your face, took your eye out, and you want me to believe you sat on that stand, placed your hand on the Bible so you could get my Black ass acquitted?" Layla was tickled. "You can't be serious right now."

Whistler looked to Scott. He was lying to live, and the only person he felt he needed to convince was the head nigga in charge.

"Scott, you know me," Whistler protested. "You know I hate those pigs and would never turn snitch. True, Layla caught me slipping. You know we charge shit like that to the game. No way do I get up on the stand and send my brother up north for life. Why you think they cut me loose?"

The whole room was uncomfortable over this man's groveling. Everyone came to put their murder game down. Whistler's procrastination interrupted the natural order of things, dragging out the inevitable. The goons thought the legendary gangsta would be more gangster and go out like an O.G.

Scott's silence unnerved his wife. Layla hoisted her skirt and pulled out her .22 holstered around her thigh. There wasn't any way she drove three hours to not leave with Whistler's blood on her hands. She said, "Your nine lives are up, rat. We trusted you around our daughter, and you fucked her. We trusted you to kill our enemies, and you partnered with them. We trusted you with our business, and you hopped up on that stand. You're done!

You hear me, bitch?"

Ignoring Layla, Whistler turned toward Scott. He pleaded, "You know I'm keepin' it one hundred. I never wanted to do you or your family harm. In fact, I saved your son's life. If I hadn't been there, Meyer would be—"

The bullet whizzed past Whistler's left ear and lodged into the flimsy wall causing him to duck.

"I missed on purpose," Layla spat. "Disrespect me again and speak to Scott, and I'ma blind you nigga. You still got your ears, so I know you hear me!"

Whistler was tired of groveling. There were too many cooks in the kitchen that he'd have to convince. And even if saving Meyer's life had garnered him favor from Scott and his sons, there wasn't any way he'd win over Layla.

His original plan resurfaced. Whistler couldn't go to his grave without knowing who was more formidable—him or Scott. Whistler challenged, "Y'all brought all this gunpower for a nigga like me? I'm not worthy, am I?"

Whistler's voice deepened, the friendly mask dissipating. The switch was flipped, and his dark side emerged. "Niggas go after cartels this deep...kingpins...niggas they fear!"

Scott chuckled. He had come through so deep for the X factor. Last he checked, Whistler was working for the feds. He and his henchmen were prepared to go to war if this was a trap.

Whistler continued, "Y'all niggas better do your homework on Whistler Hussain." His one eye scanned Scott's goons so there'd be no ambiguity. He was speaking directly to them. "I know y'all niggas feel me. Why roll so deep for one man?"

Scott had promised his wife that Whistler could die by her hands, but with this reckless sermon, he would need to make a concession. Scott locked eyes with his wife, and she nodded. Layla was ready for her husband to skin Whistler alive, chop his balls off with a butter knife while their subordinates watched Scott's handiwork.

Whistler knew torture was in his future, but he had other plans. "Let's do this old skool, playah. Mono y mono until the death...show these youngins' how we used to get down in the '80s." Each second he spoke was a second he lived, so Whistler kept yapping. "You win, you win. But if I win, I still don't leave here alive. The mission will still be accomplished unless you're scared. Of me."

Whistler gritted his teeth, flared his nostrils, and crumbled his face. He was everyone's nightmare and knew how to use his newly acquired look. He had just given Scott an offer he couldn't refuse without looking weak.

Bugsy said, "Pops, I got this," prepared to go toe to toe with a man he once considered family. His father was nice with his hands; Bugsy knew this because he challenged him to a similar situation not too long ago. Bugsy felt stronger, younger, more agile. Scott glared at his son, so Bugsy cleaned up his statement. "I handle all your lightwork."

Scott slid off his overcoat, not wanting to do much chitchatting. He pushed through the crowd and stopped in the more spacious living room. As Scott began lightening his load by stripping down the unnecessaries—his coat, pistols, dress shirt, and suit jacket were handed to his family. Whistler sat on his sofa, pulling on joggers and lacing a pair of Puma track shoes. He thought Scott was a muthafuckin' fool to be baited into this fight, which he had trained so hard for. Whistler's mind and body were weapons; he no longer felt pain.

Whistler stood up from his sofa; his lean, bare chest had an eight-pack, his arms rippled with muscles, and his thighs strong and sturdy, ready for battle. His opponent, Scott, was no less in shape. His body wasn't as lean. Scott had at least thirty pounds on his adversary. And although under his t-shirt, Scott didn't have an eight-pack, his frequent visits to the gym sculptured his stomach into the quintessential six-pack. Scott's shoulders were strong, his arms like boulders, and his mind razor-sharp.

Meyer wanted to offer his father his combat boots, nervous Scott's hard bottoms would put him at a disadvantage. But after Bugsy's offer of assistance failed, Meyer remained mute.

Whistler did that thing where boxers hop in place, tilting their head left then right, loosening up their limbs. And Scott threw a few combination punches with lightning speed to let niggas know what he was working with before the rivals locked in battle.

Layla said, "Buss his ass, Scott. Fuck this nigga up!"

Those words set it off.

A swift, solid fist rammed into Scott's ribs; the force moved him a few inches causing him to slip, nearly folding over from the blow. Before Scott could rebound, Whistler leveled an uppercut to his jaw, dropping Scott to one knee. Whistler was going to teach this arrogant negro some manners. He stood over his former boss and shouted, "I'm the real King of New York! You wouldn't be shit without me!"

Scott realized that his hard bottoms could be a liability. He quickly found his footing and attacked Whistler with a hard right, followed by a quick left to his jaw. Whistler's face stung from impact, but the blows wouldn't stop his momentum. He focused on his opponent's ribs and chest cavity, hoping to break something. Two solid blows in rapid succession smashed into Scott's side, nearly lifting the patriarch off his feet.

Bugsy winced in pain, feeling each blow that Whistler landed against his father. He wanted to tap in and take over because he was playing Monday night quarterback. Bugsy knew Whistler was trying to break his father's ribs, and Scott was doing a piss poor job at protecting them.

Eventually, Scott dropped his left arm low, a defensive move to guard his ribcage while his right fist smashed into Whistler's good eye. The blow pushed Whistler back a few steps, his eye swelling instantaneously. The retreat emboldened Scott, and he moved forward with two-and three-piece combinations backing

Whistler farther into a corner.

Feeling trapped, Whistler swung wildly, connecting with Scott's flesh, each man's hit landing. Fists slapped flesh rapidly, and everyone in attendance marveled at the skill and tenacity of the enemies as they weaved, ducked, and landed blows. They both went pound for pound—both men were skilled brawlers.

Swollen knuckles, bruised faces, and a black eye later, both men were breathing hard, sweating freely, refusing to fall by the other's hands. Both refused to be beaten, looking to fight to the death.

Scott was poised in a boxing stance, his ribs protected, glaring at his foe. The arrogance Whistler had to challenge him in front of his wife, sons, and subordinates. The ego Whistler had to fuck his underage daughter and toss her away when he was done. And the gumption Whistler possessed to get on the stand and testify against him had culminated into an irrepressible rage. Scott just snapped.

His fist rapidly smashed into Whistler's face, his neck snapping back repeatedly—it seemed his head would dislodge from his shoulders. Multiple punches to his face and body made Whistler's knees buckle; he crumbled to the floor.

Scott towered over his fallen foe, and he berated him.

"You thought you could walk in my shoes, nigga!" he shouted. Scott lifted his Christian Louboutin hard bottom shoe and smashed his heel into Whistler's mouth, knocking out several teeth. "You fuckin' rat!"

Choking on teeth and blood, Whistler struggled to breathe. Helplessly he scrambled on the floor, his arms unable to shield him from Scott's wrath.

That same shoe continually crashed into Whistler's face, blow by blow, his skull crunched under the volley of violent kicks. Scott was irate. "I'll kill you, you ungrateful muthafucka!"

It was evident that Whistler had stopped resisting. The force and friction from Scott's heel had sliced into Whistler's face opening it up to the white meat. Blood oozed, splattered, and sprayed, yet Scott wouldn't chill. Whistler's face had ballooned to an unrecognizable creature that most in the room had quickly sickened at the hideous sight.

Even Layla had seen enough.

"Scott, baby...he's gone," she softly said, touching her husband's arm. "Let's go home."

Scott wouldn't acquiesce. He continued to pummel the one hundred and seventy-five pounds of dead flesh. Sweat rolled down Scott's back, his armpits dampened, and his saltiness stung his eyes.

Layla gathered the men, including her sons, and sent everyone home. Only she and Mason remained with her husband. When they reentered the house, Scott was sitting on the sofa. His breathing was labored—short, rapid exhales, and he was in deep thought.

Layla and Mason stood in silence, allowing Scott to process the situation.

"I loved this nigga," he eventually said. "On any occasion, I would have laid down my life for his."

Scott choked up and had to dig deep to hold back his emotions. He continued, "I was good to him, respected him...and his betrayal...he was my brother."

Layla wondered why this kill was affecting her husband in this way. He wasn't that broken up about Delores; she *was* his sister. That bromance runs deep for men, their bro code superseding bloodlines. She wouldn't pretend to understand.

"So, um, we need to go, Scott," Layla said. "Get this shit cleaned up, buried. Let me remind you that this piece of shit works for the feds and what all that means."

Scott nodded. His grieving process was over. He cleared his throat several times and remarked, "You're right. And I see that he's wired the property with video surveillance. Mason, we gonna need all of that erased."

Everyone had a part to play. Mason got busy deleting the surveillance footage. Layla disinfected the home with bleach, ensuring her husband's DNA from blood droplets was untraceable. And Scott buried his longtime former friend in an unmarked grave.

CHAPTER 17

Markeeta was none the wiser that her mother was dead and buried, murdered by her uncle for the part Markeeta played in his daughter's demise. Family members and friends were trying to locate her, searching damn near the whole borough of Brooklyn for her whereabouts. Meanwhile, she was living her best life. The type of life you post on Instagram and Facebook. When Markeeta finally did call her mother to check in, Delores's cell phone was disconnected. Markeeta assumed her mother had changed her number because she didn't want to be bothered by her.

Back home from her recent exile, she spent hours exercising in her home gym. Once she got started and saw results, she got addicted. James also saw the results and hired a personal trainer to take her to the next level.

Markeeta noticed her ass lift and firm up. She was achieving that coffee table ass you could rest a cup on, which wasn't from a BBL. A hula hoop coupled with a waist trainer had cinched in her sides, giving her a more pronounced hourglass figure. Markeeta could see the outline of a six-pack, and her upper arms had slimmed down and were toned.

Parading around naked felt mandatory to her, admiring her shape in each mirror as she passed by. Markeeta spent hours lotioning her body with shea butter and coconut oils, sugar waxing, pruning, and plucking. And James was correct. The woman who did her hair weave did an exceptional job. The more she liked what she saw in the mirror, the more her ego ballooned—the narcissism oozing out with each switch of her hips.

She listened to two or more audiobooks daily, practiced cooking gourmet meals, and worked with a voice and diction coach provided by James.

When she arrived, she was angry, broke, and sharp around her edges. Markeeta had blossomed into a gorgeous woman that any man would feel privileged to have on his arm.

Agent Dough explained that she was ready to be placed in proximity to catch Bo Jangles's attention. First, she would meet with Chanel Dior, and they'd take it from there. He was coming over tonight to go over the details.

The heels, expensive garments, and bravado weren't entertained when James arrived. Markeeta had learned her lesson and wouldn't repeat that mistake. Always good at reading people, it wasn't a stretch to glean she needed to appear unworthy of him, his network, and the perks he showered upon her. To James, this wasn't a two-way street. He failed to see that he couldn't get any of what he'd gotten if it weren't for women like Markeeta.

So, she'd play meek—he loved meek. Markeeta couldn't show her inner strength, she couldn't fight back if only during an argument, and she certainly couldn't defend herself against his onslaught of insults. Because if she did, she would be disciplined.

Markeeta never mentioned this to James or asked if he was behind the mishaps. But the first night they'd met, several things happened after he left. The gas and electricity were shut off. And then the alarm would blare throughout the night. And when the cable went out, Ralph had a fit. It was adjacent to what Tannery had done to her, so she kept her cool and rode it out.

On their visits, no matter how degrading he was to her or how many harsh remarks he would hit her with, Markeeta would nod, agree, and promise to do better. Soon, she had him wrapped around her finger.

He likes his women subservient, Markeeta thought. Using her new word of the day, she had learned. And a *subservient* bitch wasn't in her DNA unless it came with a price.

Markeeta had prepared a lovely meal; seared rack of lamb, baby potatoes, and sauteed spinach. And after dinner, James went over the particulars.

"You've shown great improvement," he began. "But the real test comes once you're with Bo Jangles. I need him to trust you enough to sign with my nephew as his new management team."

Markeeta nodded. She knew the assignment; it had been drilled into her head for weeks. James continued to talk, and Markeeta wondered why they were having this meeting. Everything he was saying had already been said. And then she heard, "The last thing we need to do is see how good you are in bed."

Markeeta couldn't front. She heard exactly what he said but prayed the sentence meant he wanted a verbal portrayal, not a physical one.

She replied with, "I can't speak of my highlights, but I'm certain I've left all satisfied. No complaints."

James stood assertively. No time to play coy, woo her with seduction or engage her with wordplay. She was his subordinate, his property, like cattle. And just like Tannery did, she could be traded. Markeeta would sleep with anyone he told her to, including himself.

"Let's go," he said sharply. "And I want you to give me all you got. Don't hold back because you won't get a second shot at the title with Bo Jangles."

There was a dizzying reaction to his words. Markeeta felt faint like she was losing oxygen. Sure, she'd fucked more than her share of niggas for one reason or another. More precisely, she'd fucked a few frogs. Low-life pieces of shit who were fortunate enough to taste her nectar. But James? He was thrice her age! And a monster! Markeeta literally felt her boots shaking.

For some reason, the movie *Sparkle* flashed before her. She imagined James pounding her in the face and telling her to *crawl.*

With a false sense of sanity, she stood to her feet and, in an automated fashion, made her way to the bedroom that was glaringly on loan.

A dark blue Chevy Impala stopped in front of the New Jersey home, and the engine shut off. It was a federal vehicle, and three DEA agents climbed out of the sedan and stared at the home of one of their own. So far, everything looked copasetic but looks could be deceiving. They approached the front door cautiously and entered the house using a key.

"Pablo," one agent called out. "DEA doing a welfare check!"

Looking down at the red stain was unmistakable. With Glocks, the agents cleared each room, yelling, "Clear!"

They thoroughly went through the house, checking each room, which was completely empty. There were no signs of a disturbance except a small amount of blood in the home's foyer. Besides a pile of cocaine on a coffee table and an opened bottle of wine, nothing looked out of place. The locks were attached, the windows were closed, and the home was neatly furnished, nothing disturbed.

Diablo's alarm going off a couple hours ago prompted the DEA to do a welfare check on his partner. Diablo's front door had been kicked open, and blood was found on the mattress in the master bedroom. He wasn't there, and there were no signs of a scuffle. The quantity of blood left at each residence wasn't enough for a coroner to declare homicide. Still, the administration was operating on the assumption they were missing and presumed dead.

Tannery and Brown wanted a complete analysis of each place. He wanted to collect fingerprints, all surveillance footage from highways, gas stations, neighbors—the whole gamut. DNA samples would be taken, and trace evidence—anything that would deduce what happened.

Within *The First 48*, it became a manhunt for the missing agents. Over two dozen men hit the streets to shake the branches of many trees to see what would fall from them. They rattled felons and informants and raided primary locations that the Wests' organization owned to disturb the natural order of things. Tannery and Brown wanted answers, and they were willing to fuck shit up by any means necessary. Tannery especially wanted to show these crooks, the criminal organization, that you don't kidnap two DEA agents and think the ground won't shake underneath your feet.

But it was clear to Tannery that Pablo and Diablo had been made somehow. The West organization saw through the agents' covers. *But how?* Was it during the meeting at the soul food restaurant? Where did they go wrong? He knew that the two agents were most likely dead, and then he finally thought about Larry. What happened when Larry's phone was tossed at that meeting with Bugsy and Meyer? Tannery only had Larry's word for what took place. For all he knew, Larry could have given the

228

agents up to save himself. Snitching worked both ways.

Operation MAFIOSO had come to a full stop. The project was dead until the higher-ups gave the green light again.

Tannery and Brown were alone at the Williamsburg location, and both men were livid. They were back at ground zero—square one. They'd put a lot of work into the investigation. For it to suddenly crumble—with no arrests and no results—and two presumed dead was a clusterfuck. He and Brown walked into his office, and Tannery closed the door. He then pivoted and looked at Brown, saying, "What's said in this office stays between you and me."

Brown nodded. "What's on your mind?"

"I'm willing to do something drastic to finally bring these motherfuckers down."

Brown looked befuddled by the comment and replied, "What are you talking about?"

"We should set up these lowlifes, give them a taste of their own medicine."

Taken aback by the comment, Brown asked, "What? What are you saying?"

"Obviously, doing things by the book is getting us nowhere. We have two undercover agents missing...fuck! Not missing, they're dead, and we both know it. And the people above our pay grade want to stop Operation MAFIOSO. I want to steal the drugs we have in evidence and plant them on a few organization members. We get them on a serious drug charge, and that will get the cookie crumbling."

"Are you fucking serious?" Brown exclaimed. "You're insane, Tannery!"

"They come after us; we go after them."

"We're not them! We're federal agents, and we do things the right way, or we don't do it at all," Brown countered.

Tannery wasn't trying to hear it. The right way just wasn't cutting it for him anymore. He was on a war path. All his years in law enforcement, this moment he faced was his lowest. Tannery always got his man. He could hear the West family yelling *checkmate*, a seething feeling.

"What if they try to come for us next?" said Tannery. "They've killed those FBI field agents, and now us! They've come after the DEA, too? Well, not on my watch! These thugs are emboldened because they've barely received a slap on the wrist."

"Listen, what you're proposing is unwise. We took an oath, Tannery, which means something to me. It means that no matter what happens, we will always separate ourselves from them because justice will always prevail. We continue doing this by the book, or we don't work this case at all."

It looked like Brown had brought Tannery back down to reality. Tannery nodded and replied, "Maybe I'm getting too old for this shit."

"We're going to get them. We just have to look over our evidence more thoroughly and rethink our strategy," Brown said.

Dough sat in the woven silk chair in Markeeta's bedroom as she tried on numerous outfits. Tonight, she would be introduced to Bo Jangles through Chanel, and she had to make a lasting first impression. Men like Bo were surrounded by beautiful women—video shoots, nightclubs, private parties, and mutual affiliation. As he scrolled through social media, women slid into his DMs and vice versa.

James had chosen Karen after doing cursory research on the elite rapper. Initially, Karen was selected because she had skills with men of Bo Jangles caliber. But his mistake was that the connection was superficial. James was attracted to Karen, and foolishly, by default, he assumed Bo Jangles would be too. And he was. Karen could get any man she wanted; the conundrum wasn't getting a man but *keeping* him. So, Dough dug deeper. He realized that before the fame, glitz, and glamour—before this man had made it to celebrity status, his girlfriends and two baby mamas had one thing in common. And that X factor was that they were all raw.

Dough realized that if he could mix that refinement he had created with Karen with that hood element Bo was attracted to, he'd create a woman that had Bo Jangles eating out of the palm of her hands. And that woman was the new and improved Markeeta.

Markeeta's backstory was that she had a profitable makeup line overseas in three countries and was working on bringing her business to the United States. Her social media pages were already set up; verified. She had a combined four million followers. Dough's team worked around the clock to flood her pages with two years of content, comments, and reels for authenticity. A while back, Markeeta and Dough's team shot numerous videos of her looking flawless, promoting her fake product. They knew that once Bo Jangles showed an interest in Markeeta, he would head to her pages and needed to like what he saw.

Markeeta had begun to perspire as she pulled off the Prada blouse and skirt in her closet. It was the fifteenth outfit she had tried on, Dough disliking them all.

He called out, "You need to be business and sexy. His curiosity needs to be piqued about what you do for a living. And his dick needs to peak too. You understand?"

She rolled her eyes. It wasn't that serious for her. An outfit was an outfit. The nigga was either gonna like what he saw or not. But she hollered back, "Yeah," and didn't correct herself.

And then, she found an outfit similar to the one Lucky wore

when she was supposedly going to meet with Meyer. A deep green Fendi dress hugged her ass, cinched in her waist, and outlined her cleavage. It was classy and sexy, and the color against her skin made everything pop. Markeeta would use green eyeshadow, mink lashes, and nude lipstick. The Fendi heels and matching clutch completed the look. She made up her mind that whether Dough agreed or not, she was wearing this.

When she walked out of the closet, his grin said everything.

He nodded and said, "That's it."

With her outfit settled upon, strategy was discussed next. James said, "He smokes blunts. You don't! You hear that? If he asks do you smoke, you say no. You don't smoke weed, none of that brown juice—"

"Hennessey?"

"All that rapper shit—in the studio dropping bars—you're not down with. He offers you cheap cognac, and you order Macallan. He offers you—"

"I got it!" Markeeta snapped. "You keep telling me the same shit every day like I'm dumb."

Dough chuckled, amused.

"Anyway, I picked this up for you." James handed Markeeta a tiny earpiece and a transmitter. "Place the transmitter in your bag, and when you meet Bo, I'll be able to tell you exactly what to say through your earpiece."

She was perplexed. "I don't understand what you mean?"

"I'll listen to what he's saying and tell you what you should say. I know this kid, studied him. If you follow my lead, he'll be in your bed by the end of the week."

Markeeta finally responded with a sour, "I won't need your help. I got this. Let me do me."

James knew there was too much at stake. And he wasn't about to put millions in potential profits from his nephew signing on as Bo Jangles' manager in Markeeta's hands. Dough said, "I micromanage this whole setup from you swallowing his seeds to holding his burner should the heat roll up on him. If I tell you to jump in front of a speeding bullet to save his Black ass, I don't want to hear you ain't superwoman! You got me, bitch?"

"You not gonna keep calling me outside my name!" Markeeta hollered, heated. He was threatening her every week, and she was over it. "You can send my son and me home asap. Fuck outta here with all that."

She was smarter than she looked. Markeeta realized that early on, his threats were valid; he would send her home. But now she was this far along in the game that he'd be a fool to scrap her. And start with a new chick. But Special Agent James Dough didn't get this far without having an Ace up his sleeve. He said, "Home? Where's that because you can't go to your mother's."

He purposely held back the facts.

"I said I didn't *want* to return to my mom's house, not that I *couldn't*. Me and my son will always have a roof over our heads!"

James gave a wicked chuckle. "I thought you knew?"

Dough savored the moment. He watched as a now nervous Markeeta's face showed concern. She knew something life-changing was about to be said, and her body language—wide eyes, trembling lips, tense posture said she didn't want to hear it.

"Knew what?"

"Your mother was murdered in her own bed. Shot several times in the face by an unknown assailant. Apparently, she was moving large quantities of cocaine out of her apartment—"

"No-ooo!" Markeeta hollered, breaking down uncontrollably in front of the unsympathetic agent. Tears streamed down her naked face. "That's a lie! That's a fuckin' lie!"

James shrugged. "My sources tell me that your uncle is likely behind it, with you being the intended target."

"Mommy!" Markeeta screamed. "Mommy...."

Dough continued to taunt the slick-mouthed informant. "I can't imagine how it must feel to know that your mother was brutally slain…shot in the face…over your life choices."

Markeeta took a few steps before her knees buckled. She collapsed face down on her carpeted flooring and sobbed, her chest heaving up and down, trying to make sense of a brother murdering his sister.

"I can put you and Ralph on a flight tonight to JFK, and we'll part ways," James said. "Or you can dry those crocodile tears, get your funky ass in the shower, and go fetch that nigga for me."

Mason was waiting curbside in the Range when he saw a gaggle of blue flight jackets. He had to adjust his vision and blink a few times to ensure his eyes weren't deceiving him. The moment he confirmed they were feds, he called Scott. Scott and Layla were on their way downstairs so Mason could drive them to the cemetery to visit their children, Capone, Bonnie, and Clyde. They went on the same day each year.

The phone went to voicemail, and Mason deduced they must be in the elevator. He stepped out of the SUV, walked around to the passenger's side door, folded his arms, and leaned his back against the vehicle. Mason glared at the feds, but none looked his way. He was irrelevant.

Seconds later, Scott and Layla came walking out. When timed perfectly, a tall white male in a blue flight jacket with the letters: FBI etched on it bumped into Scott.

"Pardon me," the fed thundered. "We're just out here protecting these good citizens from drug dealers, ain't that right?"

Another fed called out. "That's right. All drug dealers will be prosecuted to the fullest extent of the law."

"Life!" Another called out. "All dealers are doing life!"

Scott paused his conversation with his wife and stood still. He observed the spectacle and resumed his steps. He loaded his wife in the car, got in, and Mason peeled out.

"What's that about?" Mason asked.

"Some bullshit. Your question is exactly what they want us to do. Sit and think about the meaning behind nothing." Scott asked, "Layla, what do we know?"

"We know that when shit gets thick, they'll be no warnings. That's not how goons move—feds or otherwise."

"Tsu Zu said it best. When your enemy is at rest. Exhaust them," Mason replied.

CHAPTER 18

Markeeta's Bentley glided effortlessly in and out of traffic as she made her way to her destination. The navigational system spewed out left and righthand turns as she concentrated on the road. It was hard to suppress her emotions and not fall apart, having received the devastating news about her mother only hours earlier. And the way James dropped something as monumental as that, making her pull the information out of him, withholding something as vile as it was, and then weaponizing that information was beyond baffling. When she told herself Dough was a good guy, he showed her he wasn't. His delivery was cavalier, then giddy, and concluded with nothing short of barbaric.

She hated that muthafucka with every ounce of who she was. As she drove, she wondered if things went well with Bo Jangles, and she got the nigga to love her—would he kill for her? At that moment, she was thinking crazy. Killing an agent? Could it be done?

Markeeta pulled up to a mega-mansion that Bo Jangles had rented through Airbnb for two nights for his daughter's ninth birthday. It had heated indoor and outdoor pools, a bowling alley, a nightclub, an indoor basketball court, a wine cellar, and many other baller amenities.

Markeeta was met at the wrought iron gate by armed security. She rolled her window down, and the crisp, frigid air clashed against her car's interior warmth.

"Markeeta Toussaint." Toussaint was a part of her fictional identity. Her parents were Canadian French, thus her makeup line in countries other than America. Dough felt that minor detail would set her apart from other women. He knew that anything out of the ordinary always brought forth intrigue.

Security scanned the list, found her name, and buzzed the gate.

"You in?" she heard Dough ask through her earpiece, which irked her nerves. He could clearly see and listen to what was happening through the car's video footage but chose to remind her early on that he was running the show.

She replied, "I am."

Markeeta could see a handful of men outside smoking what appeared to be blunts. It was confirmed when she stepped out of her vehicle. Desperately, she wanted to take a hit but knew she couldn't. Not now. Not today.

The Fendi mink coat flowed freely as Markeeta approached the crowd. Clutched in her hand was a makeup case stuffed with samples from her line. Only the real creators were M·A·C, Fenty Beauty, Kylie Cosmetics, and Victoria Beckham's new line. Dough had his team remove the original branding and replace the packaging with Toussaint Cosmetics.

Everyone stared at a woman they didn't recognize but wanted to get to know. She was pushing a six-figure whip, bundled in exotic fur, and had a mean switch they wanted to meet on a personal level.

Markeeta stood before the small crowd, gave direct eye contact to the nigga with the most jewels on, and asked, "Is Chanel here?"

"Yeah, she's upstairs toward the back. You here for her?" Dude asked the obvious, then realized how dumb that sounded. But it was too late.

Markeeta said, "Evidently."

He looked at his crew. "Let me walk this pretty lady to Chanel. I'll be back."

He held the door open, and Markeeta glided through. Everyone caught the backdraft from her perfume and was heated that Rumi had pushed up first.

They walked through a large foyer. Snaked past tables of catered food and dodged support staff running amuck, putting the finishing touches on the party, Rumi decided to shoot his shot.

"My names Rumi."

"Markeeta."

"What business you got with Chanel. I have never seen you before and never forget a pretty face."

Markeeta heard— "Get rid of this guy!"—from Dough. But said, "We go way back, and I'm glad to see her progress. She's an amazing makeup artist and stylist."

She hadn't answered his question, but he seemed satisfied. Rumi led her to an elevator at the back of the property, and they rode up one floor. Rumi said, "So, Markeeta, you gonna let me get your number...I'll holler at you later. Maybe we hook up, grab something to eat when I'm done here."

He pulled out his cell and palmed it in an anticipatory move, flossing his iced-out watch and rings. When Markeeta didn't give him a quick reply, he added, "I manage Bo Jangles, so my time is limited—"

"Oh, isn't that cute," she said. "You're management."

Rumi was highly insulted. Usually, his jewelry did the talking for him. His position with Bo Jangles always sealed the deal if he needed backup. But this bitch said he was management like bougie bitches said you're the help.

When the elevator doors opened, Markeeta quickly scanned the room and strutted toward Chanel, who grinned. She didn't even look over her shoulder as a last departing gesture because if she had, she would have seen Rumi's angered expression.

The two women embraced like longtime friends do before Chanel made the introductions.

"Markeeta, this is Stephanie. She's the mother of the birthday girl, Bo Jessie James Jackson. She's nine today."

Markeeta smiled at Bo Jangles's baby mother and daughter. She said, "Happy birthday!"

"Stephanie, this is the woman I was telling you about. Her makeup line is in all the top retailers in Canada, France, and Japan...Sephora...Ulta Beauty...Nordstroms, and Sally Beauty. Wait until you see your results."

Mother and daughter sat in makeup chairs, and Chanel had a buffet of makeup brushes on a table. To the right were three garment racks of women's and young girls' clothing in preparation for the photoshoot that would take place to be featured in Ebony and Vibe online. After the photo session, Bo Jessie James would enjoy two nights with twenty of her closest friends. Her guests didn't include her father's other child. Her half-sister.

Markeeta slid her coat off her shoulders and tossed it over an empty chair. She handed the makeup case to Chanel, who opened it to many oohs and ahhs. As Markeeta moved around, helping Chanel unload the makeup, she saw Stephanie staring at her through the mirror.

Stephanie knew her ex-man, and although they broke up while pregnant with his daughter, she still loved him. Felt she would love him until she died. Stephanie also knew his type, and when Markeeta removed her mink, and she saw her sexy shape, the story practically wrote itself.

Makeup artists and hairstylists are known to be chatty, and Chanel didn't disappoint. As she applied Stephanie's makeup, she and Markeeta pretended to catch up on events. Markeeta discussed fake mergers, meetings, and brand elevation, while Chanel was her biggest cheerleader. Meanwhile, Stepanie's ears were burning. She kept moving, which would cause Chanel to pause midsentence or create a conversation with her daughter, who was more interested in her iPhone than her mother's questions.

Markeeta felt his presence before he approached. And then she heard, "Daddy!"

Bo Jessie James jumped from her chair and ran into her father's arms. He swung her around before placing her back on her feet. Bo Jangles then walked over, gave Stephanie a lackluster peck on her cheek, and said, "Y'all good?"

"Yeah, I've picked out our outfits for the shoot. They're in the bedroom."

"A'ight, cool."

"You not gonna see what we're wearing?" Stephanie asked, hoping to lure him away from the business-savvy female.

"Chanel's in charge. I know y'all straight," he replied. The whole time Markeeta's back was to him.

Chanel said, "Bo. This is my homegirl, Markeeta. I forgot to tell you about her, but we're using her makeup tonight for the shoot."

Markeeta swung around and was met with glares from all men. The whole entourage. Rumi had filled his man in on the disrespect he felt he received, and Bo was determined to put Markeeta in her place. He promised Rumi he'd get it when he asked for her number. And not use it.

Bo said, "Nah. I hope you not using some no-frills generic shit on my daughter!"

Markeeta heard Dough say, "Tell him that your makeup is

3rd party, quality tested in major labs."

Instead, she pulled out her cell and handed him her profile. Her generation spoke tech; a quick Instagram scroll could tell him more than her yapping gums. Bo saw her distributors, brand affiliates, and followers and changed his tune; quickly.

She extended her hand, "Markeeta Toussaint."

"Bo Jangles." The grin was hardly subtle.

Chanel's hands were still moving, turning the plain jane Stephanie into a beautiful swan. She said, "Now you know I don't fuck with less than perfection. I would never jeopardize the name I worked this hard for on some lower-tier makeup brand."

"You right," Bo said. "I feel you."

Markeeta felt like she had given what she wanted him to seek out, which was her profile, so it was time to go. She grabbed her coat and gave salutations. "Nice meeting everyone."

Chanel said, "You leaving? I thought you'd stay for the shoot."

Dough screamed, "You better not walk out that door, Markeeta, without exchanging numbers with Bo!"

"I have to go. Just make sure my company gets brand credit with Ebony and Vibe."

"Most definitely, we gonna do that." Bo pulled out his cell phone and continued with, "Let me get your contact information so I can holler at you and let you know how the shoot went."

"Chanel will keep me posted," Markeeta said. "Bye, everyone."

Dough was hollering and screaming in her ear, but she'd said what she'd said. And Markeeta would swear that she saw relieved smiles on Rumi and Stephanie's faces.

She hoped her gamble paid off. If not, she and Ralph would likely end up in a Brooklyn women's shelter.

Bo Jangles was slighted at his daughter's party when Markeeta didn't exchange numbers. At his level, he wanted what he wanted and always got it. Initially, he thought he'd play her on the strength of his man, who had described her as some bird bitch; a groupie who disrespected support staff because they wanted to fuck the boss. But then he met her, and she was uninterested in him, his A-list status, or platinum plaques.

Bo said, "Yo, what's up with your homegirl?"

Chanel had pulled several outfits for Bo Jangles's upcoming concert in Atlanta. He was coheadlining with Jeezy and Chris Brown. Balenciaga, Gucci, Prada, and an up-and-coming Black designer named Diesel Savoy were on her rack. Scanning the garments, she took a moment to shrug and said, "Who?"

"The one with the cosmetics line."

"Oh, Markeeta?" she casually replied. "Nothing. Why? What's up?"

"She wasn't givin' me no rhythm. She got a man?"

Chanel's head shook as she grabbed a Gucci jacket and handed it to him to try on. "No. But she's not looking for one, either. Especially not a rapper."

"What you mean by that?" Bo asked, offended. "A nigga not good enough for her?"

"Not like that," Chanel explained. "It's just she's about her business and had gotten distracted once before by another artist, and you didn't hear this from me, but he broke her heart."

His interest was piqued.

"Who?" he asked, his voice rushed. "Who was she fuckin' with?"

Chanel exhaled. "That's not my business to tell, but he's in everybody's top five."

Bo's mind quickly scanned his top five; of course, he was on his own list. And then another gaggle of five rappers floated through his mind, and then another. Everybody's top five depended on the rap era they were born into. He didn't know who this nigga was, but he knew that whoever he was, to be in the top five category meant that her last dude was a top-tier entertainer. Suddenly, her ambivalence toward him made sense. She was used to dating A-list celebrities, possibly a legend.

"Yo, hook a brother up with shorty."

"I don't want to get involved," Chanel said. "You know I don't play matchmaker. Besides, she and I got business, and the moment you do you—"

"What that mean?"

"The moment you start your womanizing shit with all your groupies, you fuckin' up my bag."

"It won't even be like that with her," he pleaded, sounding thirstier than he wanted to.

"You don't even know her."

"She different," he explained. "I can tell shorty got a vibe."

"Then shoot your shot, Bo. Do what you need to do to get her attention."

"I did," Bo said. "I sent her mad DMs."

"Well, I don't know what to tell you."

Bo felt like Chanel was quiet-hating and could do more to hook a brother up. Her uselessness only made him aggressively pursue Markeeta.

For days he stalked her social media pages, and when she told her followers that she would check out the latest film, *Birds of Prey*, at AMC, he was more than up for the challenge.

Maxine found herself blossoming under the caring and loving nature of Gregory. She was mentally stimulated doing her outreach and volunteer work but was ready for sexual stimulation. Impatiently she waited for Greg—the consummate gentleman to make a move. He didn't. She was dropping clues so vivid, in 3D, that a blind man could see she wanted intimacy, but apparently, they were too subtle.

Late one night, they'd stayed up drinking red wine and cuddling on the couch, laughing at the silliness of a movie. Gregory kissed Maxine on the forehead and said, "I'm going to turn in. I have an early morning meeting."

She didn't want to hear that but smiled and said, "Good night."

In the spare bedroom, Maxine tried to sleep. She'd even dosed off several times before her eyes peeled open shortly after three a.m. She stared at the ceiling for over an hour before summoning the courage to make a move.

Maxine crawled into Greg's bed and climbed on top of him, parting his lips with her tongue. He instantly responded with deep, sensual kisses, cupping her tiny face into his large hands. Maxine reached under the covers and released his manhood that came tumbling out of his boxers. She wanted him to take charge, and he did. Easing Maxine onto her back, Gregory pulled his t-shirt over his head and slid off his boxer briefs. He'd quickly undressed but would take his time with her.

His pajama shirt—hers now was slowly opened, button by button, to reveal her dark chocolate skin and ample breasts. Her chocolatey areolas outlined her dime size nipples stood erect the moment he began to suck them to life. Her panties were removed, sidled down her thighs until she was naked underneath him. He buried his head into Maxine's neatly shaved pussy, biting licks and circling her vulva as she squirmed, rocking her hips to his rhythm. Her swollen clit was almost too sensitive to be touched. Greg was nibbling and sucking on her ecstasy button with a hunger only Maxine could satiate. There was manna between her thighs, and he wanted to siphon it, selfishly take it all for himself.

"Open for me...wider...wider...." Maxine didn't lose eye contact with Greg as he took two fingers, placed them into his mouth, and inserted them into her deep cave. "You're so wet," he breathed.

His fingers twirled, opening her up while kneading her clitoris with his thumb. The sensation aroused her, and Maxine wanted more.

"Fuck me," she purred, almost begging him to please her because it had been so long.

Greg grabbed a condom and rolled it back on his penis before applying stern, steady pressure. Her throbbing pussy was dripping wet and ready to be explored as he entered. He grabbed her hips and slid in easily, exploring her cave and hitting all her sensitive areas. Waves of pleasure enveloped her body, and the intensity was magnified by suppressing her verbiage.

Maxine's pussy muscles contracted around his stiff penis as she pushed back against Greg's pelvis. They were both peaking, bodies responding in pleasurable ways before orgasming—a sweet release of satisfaction nearly wiped them out.

Finally, Gregory said, "Good morning."

Maxine moved permanently into the primary bedroom, and Greg finally got the relationship with his first love that he'd waited over twenty years for.

Incensed doesn't describe how James felt when Markeeta ignored his direct order and left the party shortly after arriving. Her assignment was to drop the cosmetics to Chanel, catch Bo Jangles's attention, and exchange numbers.

"You think you're the only female with a fat ass pushing a Bentley!" James hollered. "You thought he was supposed to fall to his knees and beg you for your time!"

They were conversing through the car's Bluetooth as she drove home. James's outrage was palpable that she had to lower the volume so her eardrums didn't burst.

"You're not drop-dead gorgeous, bitch!" Dough continued calling her outside her name. "There are layers to getting and keeping his attention. And strutting your Black ass in there wasn't enough!"

"Are you done?" Markeeta asked.

"Hell, motherfucking no, I ain't done!" James became more enraged at how cavalier she sounded. "You're basic, Markeeta. Do you hear me? Basic! With your average looks, thin hair, menial personality, and limited education. Don't you ever forget that I made you! You will never get into the type of rooms I just placed you in on your own accord, so if I give you a direct order, you better follow it down to the letter of the law or so help me, you're going to have problems!"

Markeeta's eyes rolled, but she didn't voice her discontent.

James continued his onslaught of insults. "And if I hear you ask me about a fucking dollar...even a dime of money...for your cut of proceeds, you're done! You hear me, you broke bitch! You should be paying me for my services."

There wasn't any way she would let that slide. Why was she here if she wasn't going to get paid? To do all the work as she did in Tannery's case and then get tossed out on the street, broke.

"Whatchu mean I should be paying you!"

"I bet that ass heard that, didn't you?" he asked but didn't wait for a response. James continued with, "Did you read Genesis yet?"

"You know I didn't."

"Well, had you read it, you would know that Joseph's brothers sold him into slavery, and he was ultimately falsely imprisoned."

"Okay, and?"

"And years later, he was able to assist a Pharaoh by deciphering a dream. The king then placed Joseph in charge of the palace, and in this new position, he could help those same brothers who had him enslaved."

"I don't get it."

"Had his brothers not enslaved him, he would have never reached his full potential. So instead of resenting a person for their betrayal, you should pay them for helping you reach greatness."

Markeeta let that sink in. And then asked, "Did you see Dreamgirls with Eddie Murphy and Jennifer Hudson?"

"Your point?"

"The math ain't mathing to me. Reminds me of Dream Girls, where one word, *think*, smashes your whole theory. Beyoncé starts out brainwashed by her manager, thanking *him* for *her* voice, and as the song builds, she sings that she found the voice he *thinks* he gave her. It's all about perspective. I wish I would pay a nigga for fucking up my shit after I hustled to put it back together. Ain't no way." Markeeta then sang the verse so there wouldn't be any ambiguity.

Again, Dough was taken aback because his little snitch could also sing. Another thing that surprised him about her. His palm began itching, so he knew that meant money. He couldn't continue to argue what he felt was a moot point. James said, "I'll salvage the damage you did with Bo Jangles once I speak with Chanel. In the meantime, once y'all hook up, I want you to make it a point to sing in front of him."

"Why? Is that part of my cover story?"

"I want him to ask you to sing a hook on one of his tracks."

She couldn't resist. "Am I going to get paid for my vocals, or did you give me my voice too?"

Dough disconnected the call.

CHAPTER 19

The gym was how Scott released his stress. Usually, there were no hiccups. But today, the feds had time. Exiting the elevator, he saw sweaty bodies jogging on treadmills, elevating on the elliptical machine, and weight training. Scott would do a quick warmup before heading to bench press some free weights.

A few steps in, and he is accosted. "Clyde?" the unidentified Black male asked.

"Excuse me?"

"Clyde, right? From Brooklyn. You don't remember me, man? We went to school together."

"I'm not your muthafuckin', Clyde," said Scott. His voice was leveled, casually checking the irritant.

The male's hands went up in surrender. "My bad."

Scott walked to a treadmill, grabbed paper towels and disinfectant, and began to clean off the surfaces that the last patron had touched. Tossing the used items in the trash, he ambled back to his treadmill when he heard, "Capone Williams? Is that you?"

Scott's eyes scanned the man, then his perimeter. Instantly he saw all the unknowns that didn't belong. The gym was overstuffed with federal agents. All waiting on him. Hoping he'd glance their way, give them a morsel of attention, show respect or disrespect—it didn't matter.

It didn't go over Scott's head, from the first encounter, that the men reminded him of his dead sons just in case he'd forgotten.

Scott ignored the white male and got on the treadmill to finish what he'd started. As he ran six miles at a moderate pace, a different pair of men thought it practical to stand a couple feet away from him and talk about a young woman who turned up missing. Her parents had no clue whether she was alive or dead.

Scott's Nikes kept pounding the track as he inched closer to his goal. Once done, he headed to a bench, repeated his cleaning duties, and straddled the bench.

He heard, "Do you need me to spot you?"

Scott ignored the voice.

The voice repeated, "Excuse me, sir. Do you need someone to spot you?"

Scott laid back, firmly planted his hands on each side of the weight bar, and bench-pressed two hundred pounds, easily. As he repeated his reps, another group of men inched over and began to speak loudly about phantom errands they'd made that day. Each stop they'd mentioned was exactly how Scott's day had unfolded.

Scott smirked. He found these little skits amusing but refused to chuckle. It wasn't that type of party because both parties had declared war.

Later that night, Scott thought it wise to warn his wife about the feds' latest play. He didn't want their harsh words to jangle any composure Layla had on reserve.

"I would have smacked holy hell out of each of them," Layla barked. "Fuck outta here with all those childish antics. I'm a grown fuckin' woman, Scott."

Scott exhaled. "No, you wouldn't have. You would have peeped exactly what I did and acted accordingly."

Layla responded, "The punch didn't land if you didn't make a sound."

Markeeta was able to read the room when she was in the presence of Bo Jangles and his entourage. When he asked for her number, she knew that if she gave it to him, she would play herself. Dough wasn't there, so he wouldn't understand that she peeped his body language, voice cadence, and eye contact. The smirk on Rumi's face, the cocksure attitude Bo had, and the glares directed toward her spoke loudly. Hence, she had to make an executive decision.

Living in crowded tenement buildings in different boroughs of Brooklyn, you learn that your instinct means everything. She could never say this out loud, but informing was second nature, skills you had or didn't have.

It was her idea to ignore his DMs. Also, her idea to upload a reel to Instagram telling her millions of fake followers that she would see the seven-p.m. screening of *Birds of Prey.*

Markeeta bundled up in a white Moncler goose down, tight jeans, and UGG boots. She grabbed her Louis Vuitton knapsack and stuffed it with Doritos, ginger beers, Twizzlers, BonTon Popcorn, and a couple candy bars.

"What are you doing?" Dough asked.

"It's called authenticity."

Dough was getting a little pissed with her expanded vocabulary. He knew it was his requirement, but her delivery got under his skin. Mostly because he expected her transformation to take longer, like his other girls. Markeeta was picking up what he was putting down too quick. She was a sponge.

He said, "Say what now?"

"This is me. This is what I do when going to the movies with my homegirls. We don't pay for shit in the movies cause their prices are too damn high. You said Bo is from the hood and loves a hood chick."

"I also said he's graduated to elegant women."

"Hood is hood. You can buy your way out and bury it deep inside you but trust that shit is in reserve. The real you will always resurface. You remember when Barack Obama got his second term, and the news reported that he put his swag back into his walk, that little bop that men his age used to do?"

James surprised himself when he grinned at the memory. "I remember."

"Right. So, we all know that Barack's highly educated, a Harvard man. And up until then, the media wanted his white side to take all the credit. They glamourized and glorified that he was half-white. And then that second term rolled around, and folks were none too pleased with our first Black president, and the media reduced him. No more half-white references. He was Black Barack Obama with his African father, angry Black wife, and wild, unruly Black kids."

Dough found himself nodding.

Markeeta continued, "I'm sure our president peeped that shit. When he got reelected, he went in one door as Clark Kent and emerged as Superman. The one thing he couldn't keep contained was his swagger, the flavor he got from his Black side, and the culture. It was bound to make an appearance."

Dough nodded again. He found himself trusting her

judgment and enjoying her point of view in conversations. It wasn't deep or profound, but she did have a perspective on things, and he began to respect that.

"I promise you; It'll be the same with Bo. Trust me."

Markeeta made her way to AMC and parked. She strolled past numerous vehicles until she reached the AMC Theatre and bought her ticket. She lingered in the area by the ticket booth expecting to see Bo Jangles so she could *accidentally* run into him, but he wasn't there. Dough, giving her distance, would wait five minutes after Markeeta went inside before he purchased a ticket.

He wanted to see what she was doing right or wrong with his own eyes.

Markeeta gave her ticket to the young man, eyes still scanning her perimeter. She noticed no patrons at the concession stand, most likely due to the exorbitant pricing. The aroma of buttered popcorn was always enticing, but she kept it moving. She stopped dead in her tracks when she pushed open the swinging double doors. Bo Jangles was posted up against the aisle, leaning against the wall. He wore a red, green, and white Gucci hoodie, Balenciaga jeans, and sneakers. Layers of platinum and diamond chains, iced-out watch, and diamond pinky ring. A wool Gucci hat was pulled low, covering his tightly braided corn rows.

He smiled, "A nigga gotta rent out a whole theatre just to spend time with you."

"Or you could have just called." Markeeta grinned and walked closer to her mark. "Or, rent out a whole theatre."

Bo laughed warmly. "So, your cosmetic line is used in this joint, huh?"

"Yes. It's not product placement, but the actors did use my foundations and new lip stain," she explained. "I know it's silly because only I know this, but it still feels good. You know?"

"I feel you, ma," he said. "And all milestones need to be celebrated."

Bo grabbed Markeeta's hand and led her up the aisle to the seats. A beautiful bouquet of exquisite flowers was there. He said, "That's why giving people their flowers is important." Bo handed her the bundle.

"Thank you."

"You're welcome," he said. "Pick anywhere you wanna sit. We got this whole joint for the night."

Markeeta walked up a few rows and chose seats directly in the center. When they sat down, he asked, "I got my chef preparing us a meal. I hope you like it."

"You didn't have to go through all this for me."

"Why I didn't?" he asked. "I know a successful woman like yourself is used to this and then some."

Bo had deduced that her ex-man had to be Drake. Markeeta was a cross between Rihanna and Megan.

"This is sweet...I can't say thank you enough."

He nodded. "What do you want from the concession stand?"

Markeeta smiled sheepishly and said, "I'm old skool."

"What you mean? Just popcorn?"

"Don't judge...," she said, opening her knapsack and showing him her goods.

"Oh, dip," he said and chuckled. "That's what's up, ma. Let me see what you working with."

Bo Jangles peered inside her bag and pulled out the beers. He opened one, handed it to Markeeta, and then opened one for himself.

"To my future wife," he said, clinking their bottles together.

"Okay, husband," Markeeta replied. "Can I know your full name before I'm taken off the market?"

"Bo Kenneth Jackson."

The two sat back, and he waved his hand. Within seconds the movie came on, and the newly minted couple munched on snacks from Markeeta's goodie bag.

"What type of exotic beer is this?" Bo asked. "This some Canadian shit?"

"It's ginger beer. You like it?"

"I do," he said and stared at her lips. "I know this is forward, but your lips are so sexy. I wanna kiss them, and that ain't even me."

Markeeta leaned in and snaked her tongue inside his mouth. In slow, rhythmic movements, they explored each other with a sensual kiss that Bo wanted to transition into more. But she pulled back.

Midway into the movie, Bo placed his arm around Markeeta's shoulder, and she snuggled against him, smelling his expensive cologne.

After the movie, Bo's chef brought them a five-course meal and a bottle of Dom Perignon champagne. A round table, white linen tablecloth, crystal glasses, and chairs were set up for them.

"What were you like as a child?"

Markeeta said, "My parents would say precocious. I'd say bad as fuck, a brawler. And I didn't listen. I was inquisitive, but that helped me do well in school."

"How far did you go?"

"All the way. Master's Degree in Business."

His smile was wide, his pearly whites on full display. "I've been thinking about returning to school to get my high school diploma to show my daughter's daddy did it."

"You should do it. I could tutor you for your GED if you want. You could have your diploma in ninety days."

Markeeta was overstepping her own boundaries. She didn't even have her GED. How the fuck was she going to pull this off?

He nodded.

"Rap. How did you get started?"

"My uncle produced beats out of a condemned home in

Detroit. The house was scheduled to be torn down for years. That whole block was. But he went in and repaired holes in walls, and flooring, rewired the electrical, and connected the house to the city's power lines. That man could fix anything with his hands."

"What's his name?"

"Jim Jangles," Bo said solemnly, and she knew there was more to the story. He continued, "I was over his house four, five times a week, and he'd say, 'lil' man. Let me see what you can do with this beat.'"

Bo smiled, recalling the memory. He then got animated and began using his hands to help tell his story. "I'd sit down and write my lyrics, and he'd produce beats. Jim started shopping his beats around, and they were selling like hotcakes because he was practically giving them away."

"How much?"

Bo blew out air. "A hundred a track."

Markeeta sipped on her champagne and replied, "Get the fuck outta here."

Bo nodded.

"His name started circulating throughout the industry. And Detroit rappers wanted to get on and rep for our hood like the east or west coast, and it was said that Jim Jangles had them fire tracks. My uncle upped his price to one large, and Ducati bought a track and laid down the lyrics to Snow."

Markeeta was thoroughly impressed. Snow was on repeat in her hood and household. That was Ducati's only hit, and so long ago.

"Jimmy should have moved out of that house, but he said living there kept him hungry. He charged fifty large for a beat, and niggas wanted a come-up. A couple goons went in and left him slumped. I found him the next day. He was tortured and then shot once—execution style."

This wasn't exactly a date night conversation, but Markeeta

had asked the question. The morbid conversation invoked feelings of her murdered mother; before she could stop them, tears streamed down her cheeks. Bo gently wiped her tears away, thinking they were for his family. He also noted that he had told the same story to his baby mamas and every serious relationship he had entered and never got that response.

"I'm sorry," she said.

"Nah, don't be. I should be the one apologizing. If you don't hit a nigga back when I call your joint, I'll know why."

She smiled, warmly. "You went on to finish what Jim started."

"Added Jangles to my name and throw deuces in the sky for him at all my concerts."

"And you single-handedly put Detroit on the map."

He grinned and shrugged modestly.

The silence allowed them to take large bites of the delicious ribeye steak and potatoes the chef had prepared. Markeeta also took a large fork full of the buttered lobster tail before asking, "Name a book that changed your life."

He thought quickly. "A book? Nah, I can't think of one. What about you?"

Bo pushed back in his chair and attentively waited for her response. Just as she and Dough had rehearsed, Markeeta replied, "The New Jim Crow by Michelle Alexander."

"Maybe I should read that," he said. "Damn, ma. You got a nigga wanting to continue his education, read books...by the time this dinner is done, will I be running for president?"

"I can't take credit for your drive and ambition. That's not what I do."

"It's all good," he said. "I like your vibe."

It didn't take long for Markeeta to have Bo laughing at her jokes. He was drawn to her and didn't want the night to end. He said, "How'd you get here?"

"I drove. I'm parked in P2."

"Let my man follow us in my ride, and I'll drive you home. Cops out here on some other shit, pulling over peoples for no reason, and I see you a little drunk right now."

Markeeta was as far removed from drunk as possible. Still, she played along, handing him her key fob. Bo called Quincy, his road manager, and ran down his instruction. When they got to her car, he asked, "This you?"

"Yeah. Why?"

"Damn, baby girl, you stuntin' on a nigga. Weren't you pushing a Phantom the other day?"

Markeeta nodded meekly.

Bo said, "Let me find out you're the Black Kylie Jenner."

Bo hopped in the driver's seat but not before opening the door for Markeeta, which she appreciated. No man had ever done that for her, and that simple act wouldn't go unappreciated. Markeeta programmed her address in the navigational system, and Bo peeled out, with Quincy following.

In between chitchat, her cell phone tinged. Bo assumed it was a nigga. Who else was hitting her up this late? He had no right to feel territorial or jealous, but he felt both.

Markeeta was going to ignore it because she knew who it was. But then realized it could be her son and she hadn't seen him in days.

The text read: IF HE WANTS TO FUCK. FUCK HIM.

It was Dough.

Markeeta snorted and tossed her cell back in her bag but not before shutting it down.

She didn't care about her image for the first time, even if that meant she seemed desperate because Kim knew she wasn't.

There weren't any misguided romantical fantasies twirling around inside her head. There was, in fact, a real connection she felt for this man. She was drawn to him. Wanted to be in his presence. Kimberly Cooper wanted his friendship as ridiculous as that sounded.

She called, "Hey, it's me again."

"I can see that."

"You wanna grab lunch? I'm about to get off work soon, earlier than planned."

"Trouble in paradise?" Bugsy asked.

Kim gave a nervous chuckle. "Absolutely not."

"All right," he agreed. "You pick the place this time. Show me who you are."

That last line panicked her, and then she relaxed. "Cool. I love this Asian place on Bleeker Street. It's—"

"I know it. I'll meet you there in an hour."

He hung up.

That was precisely why she wanted to connect with him. Bugsy was cocksure, confident, decisive, and spontaneous and didn't shy away from danger. Who could resist those qualities?

At lunch, they laughed a lot, she giggled at his funnier side, and both understood they had interested parties who would disapprove of this budding friendship. It was taboo on both their ends. Kimberly knew that Bugsy wasn't attracted to her if only because she was a fed, a predator, and he and his family were prey. But the more forbidden their alliance was, the more alluring it became.

She was pleasantly surprised when her phone rang, and it was Bugsy calling to hangout, unprovoked. They began spending a couple days a week together. He would take her to places, corners of New York City she didn't even know existed. Bugsy knew everything about anything. He was educated and could hold a conversation that rivaled her Columbia University education. He was well-versed in wine, spirits, art, history, and science. Of course, he was a scholar in drug distribution and money laundering. There was that, too.

Kim didn't know why she asked. Maybe it was the wine. Maybe because he made her feel so comfortable. "Are we friends?"

"Us?"

"Yeah," she said, tilting her head sideways to better gauge his response.

Bugsy shrugged and blew out air. "It's a good question because I've been asking myself what the fuck we're doing. Wondering what's your agenda other than the obvious."

"I don't have one. And without risking my position, I can only say that I'm not personally investigating you or your family. I've been benched."

"Sounds like an agenda."

"Oh no," she gushed. "That's not why I keep calling...hoping to get you to spill family secrets."

"Then why do you call?"

"I like you." There. She'd said it. "As a friend, a buddy."

"A fuck buddy?" he slyly asked.

Kimberly blushed but kept her composure. "A sibling I never had. I know how it sounds. Like I'm a lonely fuck who needs to find a girl squad, but it's the truth."

He shrugged. "I can be that. No judgment."

Bo didn't have to do much arm-twisting to get an invitation inside. Quincy was promptly sent home with instructions to pick him up in the morning. Bo Jangles soon realized that everything about this woman he'd met on the humble was surprising, including her lavish home.

"This all you?"

"It is," she said and walked farther into the foyer. Markeeta allowed her coat to slide down her shoulders while her back was facing him. She wanted him to look at her ass in her jeans. "Come in. Let's sit in the living room."

Bo's eyes darted around the home, and everywhere they landed spelled wealth, and he knew because he was wealthy.

Markeeta went into hostess mode, took his jacket and hat, and asked, "You want something to drink?"

He looked at the well-stocked bar. "Whatchu got?"

"Everything."

"I'll take a glass of Henny."

"How about a glass of Macallan."

He smiled. She was scoring major points. Bo nodded his approval and then pulled out a blunt. "You mind if I smoke?"

Markeeta handed him a three-finger glass of cognac and replied, "Why would I mind?"

"You smoke?"

She nodded and then said, "Why are you grinning? What's funny?"

"You got a nigga ready to put a ring on it, and we ain't even fuck yet."

Markeeta looked at her iced-out watch. "It's still early."

Layla knew the feeling well. It's something you can't predict, time, or outmaneuver. She could, however, manage it through meditation, medication, and alcohol. And those remedies were temporary, less effective, and harder to rely on. Lately, Layla was leaning into the pain and grief, opting to not numb her feelings. She went through each unhealthy emotion just as she had gone through childbirth.

The doctor said she was situationally depressed as opposed to clinically depressed. Layla understood that to mean that she could beat this. The heavy cloud that woke her up in the morning hovered throughout her day and wouldn't let her sleep peacefully through the night. Her depression didn't manifest into heavy sobs or emotional outbreaks. There wasn't a somber look on her face, so no one was asking her what was wrong.

There were signs, though. Layla would miss a hair appointment, have no interest in getting her nails done, and has begun to shower less frequently. Her feelings were bottled up so tight that she feared she would snap if she ever lost control.

That's where her husband came in and helped her put her pieces back together. Scott noticed that her morning and nightly showers were now every other day. He heard her on the phone canceling her weekly hair appointments, and he saw her chipped polish and jagged nails. Now in the mornings, he'd ask his wife to join him in the shower. At night, he'd run her a bath and add salts and oils. Scott couldn't polish her nails a color, but he'd remove the old enamel, buff, and paint using a clear. He also gave his wife deep body massages, including her scalp. He did everything for Layla that she couldn't do for herself.

For Scott, it wasn't about vanity. He understood a portion of what she was going through. He was battling dark demons too. Lucky, Bonnie, Clyde, and Capone were equally his children. But it would take a woman, a mother, to fully understand the void felt when you lose a child you carried, nurtured, and developed in your womb. And to such violence. It was unfathomable. Yet, it happened.

Layla lay in the dark wondering how she could be so exhausted yet couldn't maintain a healthy number of sleep hours. She couldn't remember the last time she'd made love to her husband and noted that she had no desire to. Layla wanted her child. She wanted Lucky back—the good, bad, funny, sassy, sneaky, conniving, sweet, intelligent, and witty elements that made her daughter who she was.

But life didn't give back what it took. The universe doesn't function that way. And all she could do was close her eyes and tell herself that tomorrow she would beat this, but today was okay to not feel okay.

CHAPTER 20

The cognac and weed had Markeeta and Bo feeling nice. She allowed him to initiate the intimacy with deep, sensual kisses that escalated to Bo on his knees, between her legs, performing cunnilingus. Markeeta was completely naked, a contrast to the fully dressed Bo Jangles. With the fire crackling and the lights dimmed low, he had removed each article of her clothing.

Bo's head was buried deep between her legs, her thighs wrapped haphazardly around his neck. He gripped her waist. His tongue rapidly flickered her clitoris, and then he'd slow it down and suck her sweet nectar. Markeeta's hips twirled in rhythmic bliss as deep waves cascaded through her body. The biting licks circling her vulva, Bo sucked and nibbled on her ecstasy button until she squirmed beneath him.

"Fuck!" she called out. "Fuck me."

His head shook.

"Come for me," he murmured. "I want you to come in my mouth."

Markeeta couldn't resist, nor did she want to. Her swollen clit had her fully aroused. She gave into the pleasurable feeling until she came.

"Shittt." She released satisfactorily.

Bo stood up, pulled his Gucci sweater over his head, and tossed it. His white T, jeans, and sneakers were still on. "Where's your bedroom?"

"Upstairs."

He reached for Markeeta, threw her over his shoulder caveman style, and carried her up the stairs as she giggled. Bo tossed her on her bed, the bed she had just fucked Dough on, and he began to undress.

Bo slid under the covers, and Markeeta pushed him on his back, body propped against her goose-down pillows. The lovers began exploring each other with their tongues, familiarizing themselves with their body canvases. Hungrily they explored until Markeeta had fully engulfed his engorged penis. His thick, mushroom tip swirled around her warm, wet mouth as one hand massaged his girth and the other fondled his balls.

The trifecta had Bo fully stimulated until he released a steady stream of his juices in her mouth. Markeeta swallowed, planting juicy kisses on his belly until he pulled her to meet his lips. Bo couldn't get enough of how she kissed him and how familiar her body felt in his arms.

But he wanted more.

"Let's fuck," he whispered in her ear. His voice had deepened, a combination of lust and passion, a throaty murmur. Wedging himself between her legs, Markeeta stiffened her body in an anticipatory entry. Bo applied pressure. His tip opened her deep cave inch by inch until he sank low and couldn't go deeper.

Markeeta was wet, dripping wet, her pussy expanding wider with each thrust. Bo's manhood was hitting all her sensitive areas as his hips circled, slamming into her again and again with unbridled pressure, sensational waves cascading throughout her body. Bo fully pulled out and then pushed into her again, causing Markeeta to shudder.

"Oh, shit, Bo…" she cried out.

Bo moaned loudly. His voice was choppy, hoarse —"Fuck me back!" Thrusting so deeply, so wildly, that Markeeta was overcome with mind-blowing pleasure spiraling throughout her body, swirling around her stomach, moving toward a gratifying orgasm.

Markeeta contracted her pussy, gripping his dick and releasing her Kegel's muscle—it drove him crazy.

"Oh, shit…" Bo groaned. "Do that shit, ma," he encouraged.

Deep waves of pleasure were brewing; Markeeta purred, "I'm about to come!"

Bo sunk deeper, lower, entirely into her and began a slow grind that drove Markeeta crazy. Her thighs curved around his backside as she kneaded her fingernails into Bo's muscular, masculine ass.

Bo's voice was low, gritty, and controlling. "This pussy is mine—you hear me!" His strokes hit her walls, punctuating his point.

"Fuck, oh…nigga," Markeeta whispered almost inaudibly. "And fuck…me, shit…"

Bo's hands dug into Markeeta's weave and twisted. He fisted her hair, gripped tight, increasing his rhythm: hardy, vigorous, strong, unrelenting strokes drove her crazy. Bo wasn't playing fair. He demanded, "Tell me you're mine!"

Markeeta wasn't about to say shit; she wasn't that bitch. She switched positions and climbed on top, rocking her hips against his pelvis. Leaning forward, she sucked on Bo's bottom lip, her hair falling into his face, caressing his cheeks. The couple moved in sync until both simultaneously reached an orgasm.

Spent, Markeeta collapsed on Bo's chest, and the pair fell into a deep, peaceful sleep.

The lovers were clueless that a third party was present. Special Agent James Dough had seen *and* recorded it all. Furious because she didn't fuck him the same way.

James began making more trips to Markeeta's than necessary. He was just as surprised as she was. But nonetheless, there he sat, reclined, feet soaking in a spa—eucalyptus and Epson salt detoxing his toes.

Markeeta was on her knees, a towel in her lap and a pedicure kit by her side. She reached into the lukewarm water, grabbed one large foot, and centered it between her legs. Markeeta used the callous scraper to remove his dead skin, attacking his heel, then the ball of his foot, and smoothing out his corns. James's eyes closed shut the moment she started massaging. Her strong fingers kneaded his arch and stretched out his toes. It wasn't until she began to polish his toenails with a clear coat that he began small talk.

"I'm going to make you rich," he said. "I see you got Bo Jangles's ear about my nephew, Curtis. Once that deal goes through, you're set for life."

Markeeta nodded, glad he brought the subject up, leaving the door open to get shit off her chest.

"What about the money from the burglary? I know the nigga had a few hundred thousand."

Markeeta had spent the night with Bo at Quincy's house, his road manager. While there, she saw Quincy putting stacks of cash into a safe after he collected profits from a show. It was Quincy's cut, not Bo's, so she figured it wouldn't come back on her. Plus, the whole house thought she was passed out drunk upstairs.

James sent his men in and cleared over a half million. Markeeta knew this because she was there when Quincy came through and told Bo that his house was hit. He was hollering and crying real tears. Apparently, that was all the money he had in the world. Eighteen months of income working for the prolific rapper.

Bo felt bad; gave him $5000 to get on his feet, but he wasn't coming up off of more than that. If the nigga didn't trust banks, that was his bad.

James said, "The bureau went in and seized the cash. Once we arrest the whole team, it'll be used as evidence."

"So, in other words, I don't get shit?"

Markeeta clearly had an attitude.

"What I told you about thinking small?" he asked. "I told you I gotchu. Fuck with me for a minute longer, and I'll get you that bag."

She noticed that he would slip into one of his other personas occasionally. Right now, he was trying to sound like a hustler hitting her off with bundles of cash. When all he was hitting her off with was dick. And she didn't want that. Markeeta wanted to get paid, not laid. But it is what it is. She did have a roof over her head.

Markeeta had finished polishing one foot and was now blowing his toes dry. Something about how she puckered her lips had him going crazy. James wanted to speed this up so he could take her to her room and get his fuck on.

Initially, he didn't find her attractive. Nothing about Markeeta was his type. But he couldn't deny that she stayed on his mind more than most. And he no longer cringed at her foul mouth and ghetto ways. She was funny as hell, raunchy, and insatiable.

Markeeta had him watching films like *Norbit*, *Don't be a Menace to South Central While Drinking your Juice in the Hood*, and *I'm Gonna Git you Sucker*.

Films he would have never watched. And then he brought over his mandatory classic movie. The film he required all his women to watch.

"What's this?" she asked.

"The Mack."

"What's it about?" she wanted to know.

"You've never heard of this?" he was incredulous. "Your generation needs to do your research, read more, preserve the culture."

Markeeta shrugged.

James continued his lesson. "In my day, this was considered a blaxploitation film. Folks thought Max Julien was doing an injustice to all the working Black actors. He was counteracting what Sidney Poitier did. But me," he waited a beat and continued, "I feel this film is full of jewels."

Markeeta was down to watch this. Anything to delay having to fuck James. A few minutes in, she was annoyed. By the end of the movie, she was muthafuckin' livid. Her stomach recoiled as James quoted lines from the pimp, Goldie, and realized where urban communities and rap icons got, "Your bitch chose me."

Dough quoted half a dozen lines, but even after the credits rolled, he repeated, "Your bitch chose me." He smiled broadly. "What did you think of the movie?"

"Well, you know I like silly movies. Comedies," Markeeta started slowly, gauging how candid she could be. "But this movie did help me understand you more."

"Me?" Dough asked the question as he tried to keep his voice leveled. "How so?"

Markeeta shrugged. She detected hostility. "I just meant that it's your era. Not mine. No big deal. And please don't go on some revenge trip against me 'cause I'm not feeling that seventies show!"

Dough nodded. "You think you know me?"

"I know you're highly sensitive."

Markeeta wanted to add: controlling, exhausting, immature, a man-child, hypercritical, vindictive, and emotional. But she didn't. She just braced herself for his wrath because she knew it was coming.

"You got me all wrong," he said jovially. "And I'm going to prove it to you. One way or another."

James stood and reached for his coat. "I'm going to call it a night. I'll be in touch."

Gustave had to do many unsavory things in his long life to stay alive. Betraying someone as close as a brother wouldn't raise his blood pressure. It's *just business,* as tyrants, hoodlums, and crooks love to spew.

With his thick mustache, high cheekbones, and neatly coiffed hair, the handsome gentleman was immaculately groomed, as were his counterparts.

Three men sat at this exclusive meeting—all partaking with cloak and dagger means to converge on the undisclosed location, all lives on the line.

"You requested that I attend this meeting, sí?" said Angel. "Even though you know that I am retired. That my cousin, Louis, is head of Juárez. Why?"

Gustave nodded. "When you were head of Juárez, and Louis was second-in-command, we all shook hands like men and agreed to a truce."

"I remember because it cost my brother, Alejandro, his life. So, can Juárez no longer consider the Garcia cartel an ally? Is there no longer a treaty?"

"We're enemies as we speak," Gustave replied. "As we sit here, Javier Garcia is plotting war against Juárez."

Louis finally spoke as head of the cartel. "We've done

nothing to dishonor our agreement, so you should weigh your next words carefully."

Before he set out to betray Javier, Gustave knew his life would be on the line. But he was willing to gamble his years for the greater good of the cartel. Many men and women relied on the cartel operating as a corporation; it fed many Méxican families. War brought forth death and dissension. A *senseless* war could mean a slaughter—annihilating the two cartels with a stronghold in México.

"Javier is at war with the American, Scott—"

Angel snapped dismissively. "Yes, I know. Scott West! What does that have to do with my cousin, Louis, and Juárez."

"Tranquillo, Angel. Listen with the two ears God gave you," Gustave quipped. "You may be right, sí? This has nothing to do with Louis or Juárez and everything to do with you. I extended my invitation to your cousin, hoping he would rally to your defense and bring the full force of Juárez with him. But if you don't want Louis at this meeting...fine...we meet with just us."

Angel and Louis were exasperated, picking up the breadcrumbs Gustave was dropping down. Angel said, "Am I a pigeon, Gustave?"

"A pigeon? No."

"Then why do you feed me like one? You come here, to our territory, skulking in the shadows like a little rata with riddles and rhymes fit for a child. You tell us why Javier Garcia has declared war against Juárez, or we'll bury your body and send your head to your boss."

Gustave didn't like to be threatened but was used to threats. He said, "I think you'll be interested to hear that Javier knows that Scott's granddaughter lives in México and that you, Angel, are her father."

Angel and Louis let *that* sink in.

Gustave continued. The silence of the men fueled him. "Your daughter, Lucchese West Morales, is also the daughter of parents who murdered Javier Garcia's nephew in cold blood. A nephew that wasn't in our line of work. A civilian."

Angel cringed hearing Lulu's whole government. But still, silence.

"This baby is the personification of revenge for a man like Javier. And you brought her to México gift wrapped, a 50-pound present for his long-suffering wife."

Angel finally exploded. "I'll kill him! You hear me! He dies if he so much as looks at my daughter!"

"You and what army?" Gustave's sharp tongue was always in attendance. "Tell me again how I will be buried in the backyard?"

"Not now, Gustave," Angel snapped. He looked at his cousin and couldn't read him. "Louis, please, you can't sanction this!"

"You don't tell me what I can or can't do, Angel. I run, Juárez! Not you!"

Angel's guts twisted in knots as he replayed his fateful decision to have Hector Garcia murdered. He would take out as many soldiers as he could, should anyone come for Lucchese—that included Louis. Knowing that his baby would die if he didn't have the backing of Juárez, he gave Louis the respect he now demanded.

"Sí, Louis. I would never disrespect my cartel leader and will respect any decision you make," Angel lied.

Louis nodded, finally feeling like the head honcho that he was. Both men eagerly waited for him to speak—both had their lives on the line.

Louis said, "I don't want a war, Angel."

"Then we sit down with Javier...come to an understanding," Angel suggested.

Gustave spoke up. Any sit down equated to his unequivocal demise. He'd be murdered moments after Javier got word that he betrayed him. He said, "Angel, you're speaking like a woman with hopes and dreams for your child, no? Put yourself in

271

Javier's shoes and ask yourself what understanding you would accept for the murder of someone you held dear to you?"

Angel shouted, "This is my daughter, Gustave! I will fight for her. She's just an innocent baby."

Louis knew what Gustave said was true even if Angel wouldn't admit it. The only understanding Javier would take was a life for a life. And as far as Louis heard, Angel hadn't offered that. However, he knew how much his cousin loved that little girl. In fact, he did too. It was something about her that said she was special. You don't kill souls destined for greatness. You protected them. Louis asked, "Gustave, you came all this way. You must have a solution."

"I do," he began. "I have a way to avoid war and take Javier out of the picture. But we're going to need help from the Americans."

"What the fuck, what the fuck!" Larry shouted as he smoked his cigarette and continuously gazed out his window. It was all over the news, two DEA agents went missing from their homes a few days ago, and Larry knew he was in deep trouble. Pablo and Diablo's pictures were circulated on every channel. Top federal officers gave limited details on the operation the agents were working on at the press conference.

Larry had called Tannery several times, and it went straight to voicemail.

"Tannery, come on man, hit a nigga back. I'm watching the news. Your men are dead, and that shit ain't on me!" Larry thought for a second and then added, "Shouldn't y'all come to swoop a nigga up? Put me in protective custody...some shit like that? If not, I'm a dead man!"

When he didn't have more to say, he hung up.

After a week of waiting for the DEA to save the day, Larry dowsed his cigarette against the wall and scurried around the room, putting clothes into a duffel bag and armed himself with a .45 with real bullets. His heartbeat was fast, and his hands were clammy. He continued looking out the window to see if any threats were looming, but so far, there were none that he could see. He stuffed the DEA's cash—pocket change they gave him to floss with and clothing into the duffel. He lit another cigarette because it was needed. His nerves were so bad that it felt like he was about to come apart.

It was dark, late. Larry knew he couldn't stick around for another moment. His McLaren was parked across the street. He tucked the .45 into his waistband, threw on his jacket, and bounced. Outside, Larry pulled the gun from his waistband and held it tightly. He couldn't get ready. He needed to stay ready just in case something popped off. Although he wasn't a killer or a hardcore gangster, with his life on the line, he would shoot the first thing that came his way.

Larry took several steps toward his car and then felt the hairs on the back of his neck stand up like they were ready to take off. Some ominous figure or figures speedily moved from the shadows and charged his way. Larry desperately pivoted to try and take aim, but they were too quick. Nervously, he got one shot off, but to no avail. Larry was quickly subdued, gun taken from his hand.

Three assailants had ambushed Larry, and he found himself riding in the back seat of a vehicle sandwiched between two Italian males. He knew they weren't feds but was taken aback that they were white goons—mafiosos. And since he didn't have beef with anyone except the West dynasty, he knew they were on some other shit.

An hour later, Larry would have all his questions answered. Santino and his men had beaten him within an inch of his life. Standing, he had a noose around his neck, hands duct-taped behind his back, and his pleas for mercy went unanswered.

He had expected to see Bugsy and Meyer. Instead, Scott and Layla West walked in. The very sight of them made Larry piss himself. A warm, fluid stream slid down his leg and puddled at his feet. The two overdressed for such an occasion—Scott in a cashmere trench coat, navy-blue Tom Ford suit, crisp shirt, silk tie, and 18-karat gold cufflinks. And Layla's luxurious fur coat swept the cement floor as she walked. She wore nearly a million dollars in jewels, a Valentino dress, and stilettos. Under any other circumstance, Larry would have complimented the gorgeous couple; but being they were there to murder him, he didn't utter a fucking word.

Scott opened his suit jacket, placed his hands in his pants pockets, and stood inches away from Larry's face.

"So, my sons call you Unlucky Larry," Scott said. "Why is that?"

Larry gushed, "Mr. West, I promise you this is a mistake."

His words were breathy, rushed. He sounded pitiful like a child trying to convince his parents it wasn't his hand they just caught in the cookie jar.

Scott stared at the disfigured man—eyes ballooned almost shut, jaw twisted, teeth broken, lips split—and it was just a regular Tuesday night for him. His victim could cry, plead, offer money for his life, and he wouldn't be spared.

Scott said, "Larry, listen. Today is your unlucky day—"

"In fact, today is your last day, nigga!" Layla chimed in.

"You're not walking out of here alive," Scott continued. "I know that. And you know that."

The sobs and wails of a grown man facing death are something you can't unhear. Anyone with a heart and compassion would feel something stir in the pit of their stomach, empathy.

Yet all you had to do was read the room, and there wasn't anyone—man or woman, who felt anything other than disdain and pure hatred for the rat that stood before them.

"Why y'all doin' me...like this, Mr. West? I've...always been a good soldier for...your sons' organization."

"Stop...stop..." Scott said, amused. "Let's not waste what little time you have left. Now, Lucky. What the fuck happened to my daughter. You give me straight answers, tell me what feds you work for, what they got on us, and I'll make sure your death is quick; clean. No more pain."

Larry whimpered some more. He said, "I don't know anything about her...I swear."

Santino walked over, his fat fingers strangled by brass knuckles. With great force, he gave a solid punch to Larry's ribs. You saw Larry's body shift, his ribs easily breaking like a chicken's wishbone.

"Ahhh," Larry hollered. "Please! Please make it stop!"

"I told you that if you answer my questions, you won't ever feel pain again, Larry." Scott looked at Santino and placed his hand up, pausing his movements. "I'm going to give you a second to think through your options...get your mind right."

Larry's chest expanded as he filled his lungs with air, and then he released all his fight with his exhale. He thought over his options, and the kingpin kept it real. Larry knew he wasn't walking out of there alive. He was also certain the feds weren't kicking in any doors for him. They couldn't even keep their own alive, so why would they care about a piece of shit like him?

Larry said, "You promise I won't feel no more pain?"

Layla growled, "It's less than what you deserve, but if my husband gave you his word, that's what it is!"

"Okay, y'all right," Larry began. "The feds got me on some bullshit...forced me to inform on your sons. But I swear, I don't know anything about Lucky...other than the streets sayin' they ain't seen her around."

Scott was so vexed that he bit his cheek, tasting his blood. "What they got on us?"

"Nothing. Not that I didn't try," Larry said honestly. He didn't want more abuse to come. "But they wanted Meyer *and* Bugsy. But Bugsy was locked up. All I had to do was make the introduction to Pablo and Diablo. I did, and then y'all came through, murked them, and now I'm here."

Larry was coming to terms with his reality. He was a dead man and wasn't taking any secrets to his grave. He continued with, "But there's more agents, not just the two DEA agents y'all murdered."

"DEA?" said, Scott. "Not FBI?"

"Nah, they DEA. But the bosses runnin' things are agents Tannery and Brown."

Larry gave up all the locations he would meet them.

"What about an agent named Ragnar?" Scott asked.

Larry's head shook. "Never heard of him, and I would remember a name like that."

Scott reached into his suit chest pocket and retrieved the sketch Lucky had drawn up. He held it in front of Larry's face.

"He looks familiar? Is this Tannery or Brown?"

"No, Mr. West. They're both white."

Layla said, "Where's your phone! We want numbers."

"Meyer tossed my phone, and I left the replacement at my crib so they couldn't track me."

Scott looked at Santino and said, "Make sure you go back and get his cell."

"Y'all don't need to. I was instructed to memorize the numbers." Larry added, "Besides, I don't think going back there is a good idea. Ya, feel me?"

Larry knew he was a dead man, but he wanted death certificates to be passed around. He wanted to die knowing Tannery and Brown would meet him on the other side. He rattled off their numbers and hoped the West organization would put that information to use.

Larry had given them much more than they had, but it still

wasn't shit.

Layla asked, "What about a girl informant. Markeeta? You met her? Did they ever mention anyone else they had working against us?"

Larry reiterated what he kept trying to convey. He'd only met with four agents. No one else was involved.

Satisfied, Scott said, "Make an example of this fucking snitch!"

CHAPTER 21

Meyer sat in a chair smoking a cigarette. Riley's cell phone had been ringing during his visit, and she ignored it. Elliot was blowing up her phone, back-to-back, yearning to hear from her again. It had only been a few days since she called off the engagement, and he wasn't taking the rejection well. The incessant ringing didn't go unnoticed by Meyer. After the umpteenth ring in three hours, Riley knew she couldn't ignore his calls anymore, and it looked like Meyer wasn't leaving anytime soon. She looked at Meyer and said, "Excuse me, I need to take this."

Riley walked away from Meyer, fading from his view by entering the kitchen. Meyer's ears perked up. He knew who she was talking to and wanted to give her space to handle her business. Meyer sat there quietly for a moment but couldn't remain that way. Sneakily he crept toward the kitchen. Meyer could hear Riley speaking softly—a soft, sexy tone that he didn't like. The perceived happiness and flirtation with her ex-nigga made Meyer angry—he became emotional. Abruptly, he marched into the kitchen, startling Riley. Her eyes widened. He heatedly snatched the cell phone from her hand and shouted, "Yo nigga, stay the fuck away from Riley before I body you!"

Riley desperately tried to snatch the phone back from his hand, but Meyer held her away. He was too strong for her. She cried out, "Meyer, don't! Please!"

He wasn't done speaking yet. "You still there, muthafucka? I'm warning you, don't die over my bitch," Meyer added.

It was reckless. But Meyer's rage got the best of him.

Silence. The person on the other end suddenly hung up. Riley fumed. "Why did you do that? I was handling it."

"Fuck that nigga," Meyer hollered. "You don't need him! You with me now."

"You can't come into my life and tell me who I can't and can speak to. You don't fuckin' own me, Meyer. This is my life!" she heatedly cried out. "Elliot and I were engaged! He's still trying to process that it's over."

"Stop saying that," Meyer said. "Engaged. Each time I hear it coming from your mouth, I wanna go on a murder spree."

"It's the truth!"

"You ain't gotta face that nigga anymore. Fuck him! I got you, Lollipop," he screamed. "I meant Riley."

She chuckled. "You got me?"

"I ain't joking. I'm for real with this shit. I got you, and I don't want you with nobody else but me." Meyer moved closer to his woman. "Fuck that...marry me."

"Wait...? What?" Now she was utterly flabbergasted. "You want me to do what?"

"I said, marry me, Riley."

She was left speechless. Was she hearing things? Did Meyer just ask her to marry him—this murderous and womanizing thug? *What changed?* She thought. *Another man?*

Meyer locked his eyes onto hers, and his intense stare made

Riley stand there in silence, heart pounding in her chest. Under different circumstances, her life would have been complete. Under different circumstances, the thought of being Mrs. West would have made all her dreams come true. But under this circumstance, there would be no wedding. Under this circumstance, she was helping to put the man she loved, her soon-to-be fiancé, in jail—for life.

Riley began sobbing her heart out. Foolishly, Meyer thought it was happy tears. He said to her firmly, "Next time you ever see that nigga, it's gonna be as my wife!"

The small, glass vial with that pure white was discreetly hidden in her Prada. Markeeta excused herself from the table, leaving Bo Jangles, Chanel Dior, Quincy, Rumi, and a couple bodyguards. She practically bolted into the stall, her back leaning against the flimsy door.

She immediately pulled out the powder, sprinkled a round bump on the back of her hand, and inhaled. The cocaine flew up her nostril like it was a Dyson. She repeated the action up the other nostril and tilted her head back for a few seconds before turning to sit on the toilet.

Her eyes glassed over, her heart rate accelerated, a rush of energy swept over her, and her mood picked up.

Delores had told Markeeta when she was young that if she saw someone addicted to drugs, look one degree over. Because usually, it was a friend, family member, or lover who turned them out—giving them a taste. That person was Chanel Dior.

Tannery went berserk when he got the disgusting news. It wasn't because he felt sympathy or empathy for the young punk. Because Larry didn't deliver the twins and the DEA had spearheaded a piss-poor operation, Tannery had left him to die. The optics of the situation had him vexed.

Larry Jenkins, aka Unlucky Larry, was found in his DEA-issued McLaren, parked in an alley next to a few commercial trash bins with a rat stuffed in his mouth. The message was crystal clear: *We ain't afraid.* Signed by the whole West organization.

Angel stood in the doorway of the large room he had converted into a dance and recording studio equipped with a stage, musical instruments, microphone, and ballet bar. He watched his little baby in her pink tutu, tights, and ballet slippers learn the salsa footwork. *Las Cafeteras's* music blared throughout, and Lulu moved on and offbeat, feeling the music with her instructor.

Marbella couldn't resist joining in. Her feet doing six steps to an eight-beat count, hips swinging one way, arms the other. Chicano music was in her blood. Movements were a part of Marbella's DNA as she swayed to the music.

Angel left his youngest child in good hands. But not unprotected. After hearing Javier's plan for her fate, he upped his armed security. His most trusted team guarded his children's rooms while they slept, chairs on each side of the doors, assault rifles, and Uzi's gripped tight.

Angel walked out onto the cultured marble balcony overlooking the saltwater infinity pool and several acres of lush grounds and called.

"I've thought about your ask and made my decision."

"I don't have time for this," Scott snapped. He was heavily entrenched in the blood of his enemies and wasn't sure if he needed to add Angel to his list. "You must have me fucked up...I ain't begging for shit."

Angel explained the new revelations from his meeting with Gustave. Scott chose to not focus on the blaring fact that when he called in a favor to Angel, he was rebuffed. That Switzerland shit was on repeat. Now Angel needed him, which meant they needed each other to go against an enemy they shared.

"Gustave has gotten Javier to arrange to have Félix and Pedro head your way to assassinate your wife and bring you back to México. He's declared, *The Rules of Genocidio War* on my daughter." Angel explained what that meant.

"And you're going to give me their locale?"

"Yes. Sí. I will. We know that this kill is personal to you."

Scott said, "At this point, it's all personal."

Angel agreed. "The next parts to Gustave's plan aren't as easy as executing two sicarios, Scott. Do we agree?"

"We do. Just guarantee my safety in México and leave the rest to me."

Angel said, "You have that."

Markeeta had been seeing Bo Jangles for a minute. She knew he was open because he spent numerous nights at her house, their bodies entwined, locked in all sorts of sexual positions. If he wasn't over at her place, it was vice versa. Or, they were up in the club, bottle service galore, and he was showing her off to his friends.

She loved the limelight. And was overwhelmed by Bo's attention, not wanting this ride to stop. But she did need a break. These nonstop rendezvous, back-to-back partying left her little time with her son and even less me time. She needed time to recuperate between fucks, after the club, and accompanying Bo Jangles on press tours, concerts, and studio sessions.

Being the new girl to a man on his level meant there was no time to get ready—she had to stay ready. And that wasn't an easy feat. Her gel mani and pedi had to be done every five days, her makeup needed to be flawless, her weave tight. Markeeta's kitty kat had to stay Massengill fresh, and her head game had to have his eyes rolling in the back of his head.

If she got caught slipping, if only once, she could be replaced. And under all this pressure, she had James not only in her ear about getting him to switch management, but he, too, was coming over for weekly fucks.

Markeeta was drained. And the only thing that kept her head above water was the steady line of cocaine she snorted to get her through her days.

Rushing to meet Bo at another event, she ran out of the house without her car key. The rage she felt after walking down the flight of steps in five-inch heels only to have to walk back up to retrieve her key fob had her muthafuckin' livid.

Ralph was downstairs yapping away to some unknown stranger playing a random video game that kept him out of her face for a long time.

Markeeta was originally going to drive the Bentley. However, she now decided to push the Porshe. It was fast, sleek, and worked best with her outfit.

She got in, and it never got old listening to the engine purr and roar as she sped through her neighborhood approaching the highway. As she neared the intersection, she pushed on her brakes, and her foot went straight to the floor. Her heart sank. She tried again, and her foot touched the ground as the car accelerated.

Panic-stricken, she tried to find a soft place to crash land, or it would be adios amigo. She steered the wheel to an embankment and skidded along the wall before coming to a hard thud against the railing.

Markeeta was able to immediately get out to inspect the damage. So thankful to be alive. She did not understand why a new luxury vehicle would have brake issues. As she sat waiting for a tow, she did have to consider her handler was behind the incident. She would be a fool not to. Markeeta's mind had to go over each conversation and interaction she had had with James in the past week. Had she upset him? Did she insult him? Any perceived disrespect and the man-child she knew as James Dough would lash out in a childish tantrum and then claim innocence.

She was about to call him when her phone jangled in her purse. It was Dough.

"What the fuck just happened?"

"You tell me," she sourly replied.

James detected her attitude and understood the implication. He ignored the remark and got down to business. "Hurry up and get that situation handled. Take the Bentley to meet with Bo. And use the crash to your advantage."

"Meet with Bo?" she hollered. "I was almost killed! The last thing I wanna do is get behind the wheel of another car and go out to a social event."

"You have to be the stupidest person I've ever encountered," James said. "Do I have to beat you into submission? Is that how you take direction? I've already explained this isn't a democracy. I own you like cattle until you are no longer needed, and I will discard you. Bitches choose me because they shine under my tutelage."

James quoted The Mack. Again!

Markeeta understood the nexus. She slept with who Dough sought out, including himself. James took all the profits she helped bring in. And finally, he controlled what she ate, what she wore, and when she worked. He placed a roof over her head like the pimp Goldie in the movie did for his stable of women. And James deprived her of the one thing that could give her her independence—money.

She didn't realize tears were streaming down her cheeks until her vision blurred.

Her mind reverted to the unceremoniously hostile meeting with DEA agents Tannery and Brown. She now wished that things could be different. That she had gone to Lucky and became an ally, not an enemy. Maybe they would have taken her under their wing and protected her. There's also a chance that Lucky and her mother would still be alive. Each time that thought entered her head, she pushed it out. But right now, on the shoulder of an active highway, Markeeta allowed the truth to sink in. She absorbed every ounce of guilt until she was sobbing uncontrollably.

She heard Dough yelling obscenities but could no longer tolerate his bullshit. Markeeta powered down her phone, left the Porsche on the side of the road, and walked back to her temporary dwelling. Tonight, she would not be meeting with Bo—no popping bottles or devouring overpriced food.

Tonight, she wasn't for rent.

Tannery didn't expect his phone to ring, but it did. And he knew exactly who was on the other line.

"Tannery."

Without salutations, he jumped right to the point. James said, "I thought we had an understanding?"

"Oh yeah?" Tannery's voice was upbeat, jovial. "And what's that?"

"That I would be using your informant for my operation."

"And?"

"And why are you fucking with her?"

"Because I can," he said, matter of fact. "And I told you I would...not that I needed your permission!"

"Fuck with her, Tannery," James spat. "Not try to kill her."

Tannery chuckled. "If I wanted her dead, she would be. Make no mistakes about who I am. We do things differently in the northeast region. You don't come on a man's playground and take his toys."

Tannery was livid when he learned about Markeeta's new position, living arrangement, and quality of life. Especially when she was only a few days into her exile from him. He had just begun to drag her when James came through and upgraded her. Tannery was also amused that Dough had no clue that he had Chanel Dior playing double agent. Tannery asked the young influencer to turn Markeeta out on drugs, and she did. He wanted Markeeta's life to mirror her mother's down to the letter.

Markeeta would be strung out on drugs. She would do unquestionable things to maintain her habit. And most importantly, she would crash land into a pine box.

To James, there was no ambiguity that he was being challenged and disrespected. These New York agents felt they were the only ones with guns.

"I had the kill switch removed from the brakes on both cars," James said. "Leave my motherfucking informant alone until my case is concluded. You may think you know how far I'll go to secure a conviction. Trust me, you don't. New York agents may get their hands dirty. In Chicago—our hands get bloody!"

Kimberly had been making her rounds interviewing women who had met the elusive Agent Dough, and each story sounded the same. They were petty hustlers, dabbling in larceny, battery, and some had breaking and entering closed cases. The girls were recruited at fifteen and worked for Dough until their late thirties. Each female had housing and vehicles financed by him. He cleverly arranged for the government—taxpayers, to foot the bills. And when it was time to settle down, Dough arranged that too.

He was a Svengali, Kimberly assessed. Lording over these women for his personal gain, and in return, he gave them what? Kim needed to ask. She was interviewing Deidre Turner, one of the women who had gone to authorities to report Dough nearly thirty years ago.

"Why work for him and do all these things?"

"What choice did I have back then?" she explained. "George contacted me and offered me a way out of my environment, making it sound so glamorous and lawful. You must remember that I was young, uneducated, and poor. My family and I were living in squalor. I had been hustling to feed and clothe myself for years, and then Satan appeared disguised as Santa Claus."

"Satan?" Kimberly wanted her to expound on why she chose that word. "Did I hear you correctly?"

"You did." Deidre's eyes were insightful, like a woman who had done and seen more than her share of evil. "And I don't use that word lightly."

"For religious reasons, correct? You're a born-again Christian?" Kim knew that James insisted on all his followers choosing religion and hoped that Deidre wasn't about to go off on a *praise the Lord* tangent.

Deidre nodded, then clarified. "Agent George Dough lured me in with his *we're catching bad guys* spiel. He spewed I had a chance to redeem myself for all the wrong I had put out into the world with my theft and uncontrollable temper. I was a product of my environment. With no resources, role models, or infrastructure, I was pliable in his hands."

Kim nodded and added— "Um-hmm,"—to keep the story flowing.

"He had all the right answers before I even asked a question," Deidre continued. "Dough explained why I should sleep with the lowlifes in my neighborhood for free when he could help me catch a kingpin. The thought of hooking someone on the caliber of the infamous men he mentioned at my age had blown my mind. You have to realize that it was a different time back then...the eighties...very different from today."

"Yes, of course." And then Kimberly added, "So these men, you slept with them?"

"And then some...including him. To be frank, I was a prostitute for the federal government. Nothing more. Nothing less."

"Prostitute?"

"He's obsessed with sex workers. Dough makes all his girls watch the movie The Mack fancying himself akin to a federal pimp. The parallels for him were the same; we did the work, and he reaped the rewards."

"So why go along with it for so long? Why not go straight to the authorities early on?"

"Who would believe me?" Deidre snorted. "Besides, when you go from eating a can of ravioli every three days to sitting at the best restaurants. And dining on lobster with men as well known in the drug trade as Frank Lucas and Bumpy Johnson, you learn to take the good with the bad. And there was a lot of bad."

"Tell me about that."

"George wasn't as masterful at manipulation as he thought he was," she said. "But I had to go along to get along...afraid that if I opened my mouth, I would be permanently silenced. You know, instinctively, what you can and can't do. The streets have always been the greatest teacher...shit you can't learn in school."

Kimberly nodded like her education wasn't from Columbia University.

Deidre continued, "George would call with these outlandish stories, long sermons of bullshit, shit a ten-year-old in my hood wouldn't believe and want me to dive in headfirst. So, I did. We all did, and he loved it...high off how stupid he thought we all were. He thought he could sell the Brooklyn Bridge to anyone he encountered."

"Dough made millions off that Bridge, didn't he?" Kimberly asked.

"He did," Deidre said truthfully. "And we didn't."

"Therein lies the conundrum."

"Exactly," she admonished. "A few years after being a hustler's wifey had worn off, and my days of faking orgasms had dissipated, I began questioning my finances. George was the only one seeing real wealth. Generational wealth. I mean, at this point in my life, I had aged out of pulling hustlers or rap icons. I wasn't refined enough for him to send me after the investment banker or geeky enough to land the head of a startup. Soon I realized that I had been benched with no severance package."

"So you began sending letters to local authorities, politicians, and civic leaders trying to expose him."

"And I didn't receive so much as a *go fuck yourself* reply."

"You think Dough got to them?"

Deidre's eyes rolled. "What do you think? Most likely, half of them letters never reached their intended destinations...usurped by him."

"Well, some landed. How do you think I found you?"

"How many decades later?"

"But I'm here."

Deidre shrugged.

She hoped the young woman would help her get justice but on what?

Kimberly circled back. "I want to follow up on the Satan

comment."

"Oh yeah," she said. "That part. You'd be surprised what a quiet mind and prayer will reveal. I wasn't making the world better by sleeping with these men to help George steal their drug money. Nor were we doing the Lord's work after he took all their funds, locked them up for life sentences during the day, and came to fuck me at night. He received promotions for my hard work and huge payouts! And me? I got a job working for the city, a rent-stabilized apartment in midtown, and some investment tips."

"Satan?" Kimberly asked for the umpteenth time.

"Satan is also an angel...."

And Kimberly got it.

"You ask Dough, and he did everything for me."

"Is that what he said?"

"Indirectly," she explained. "Dough never came out to say anything...he's a coward. So, what he'd do is talk in riddles."

"Riddles? Like the Riddler in Batman?"

Again, Deidre's eyes rolled. "No, not like that. He'd use passive-aggressive tactics. Talk disrespectfully about one of his other informants, but what he's really describing is you, his words as sharp as knives. And you know it's you and what he's doing, but again, he's the smart one. And your position is to play stupid, so you do. And when he asks what's your take on the fake situation, you give it to him. You laugh at the woman you know is you, and he hangs up feeling warm and fuzzy inside."

"My goodness. How could you take it?"

"I thought I had to. I was all in."

"How did you part ways?"

"As I said, I got old. And then, unexpectedly, this man shows up, trying to get to know me. He's saying all the right words. Too right. You understand?"

"You think Dough sent him?"

"I know he did," she definitively replied. "When I continued to rebuff him, he showed his hand."

"How so?"

"He began that passive-aggressive shit, speaking about me but pretending to be speaking of someone else, saying shit he shouldn't know about me but did. A page right out of Dough's playbook."

"Did you know from the outset that Dough had sent him?"

"I suspected but didn't know know."

"So why push him away? Were you involved in a relationship...?" Kim let the last word drag out for clarification.

"I wasn't. But he wasn't my type."

"How so?"

"I know looks aren't everything, so let's just say he had a face only his momma could love."

Kimberly felt judgy for just a second. Deidre was beautiful in her youth. And she still was pretty. But was all this from an egotistical woman with a grudge?

"And that turned you off."

"Maybe," she admitted. "But more so, it pissed me off. It was rumored long before I came on board that Dough was an uncredited matchmaker. His favorite hobby was redeeming the unattractive male species. The uglier the male, the prettier the wife he received. If you don't believe me, do your homework. It's the quintessential, *look at me now*, vendetta that all outcasts want to receive. The ugly man, nerd, the geek all want payback, and Dough was their vindicator."

A week later, she was back at it. This time Kim was sitting across from Luca Linn, and she had worked under the tutelage of Lamont Dough. Luca wasn't the mirror image of Deidre, but they were from the same tribe. Luca had pale skin, high cheekbones, thick, long hair, and was petite but shapely. Recruited at fifteen, she, too, wasn't happy with how her relationship with Dough ended.

"I watched with my own two eyes Lamont confiscate millions of drug money from the safe of the trafficker I was sleeping with," Luca said. Her eyes widened as if reliving the moment. "I couldn't believe it. He was shoveling bundles of drug profits into several duffel bags, and he was feeling good."

Kimberly nodded.

"But when it was my turn to get some of that, he said he was taking it to the bureau, tossed me $5000 in cash, and advised me to lay low for a few days. Lamont said that this was a career-making case and for me to watch the news."

"Who was arrested?"

"Carlos Perez. I watched him get perp-walked through a sea of cameras. Then the FBI stood at the podium announcing his apprehension," Luca said. "You can guess what was missing?"

Kimberly knew the case well. "Lamont Dough and Carlos's millions."

"Exactly!" she retorted. "And when I pressed Dough for my cut, he threatened me."

"He threatened you?" Kimberly's voice rose.

Luca nodded. "But indirectly."

"Please, explain."

"Well, weird things began happening immediately, like the next day after I cussed him out for my money. I woke up, and my front door was wide open, and I didn't leave it that way. Anyone could have walked in while I was asleep and did...you know...I could have been killed. And then I'd search all over for my house keys, open the front door, and there they were, dangling in the lock. I didn't live in some security-laden high rise; even if I did, that's still dangerous. Agent Dough had me in a rent-stabilized apartment in Boston. It wasn't a high crime neighborhood, but it wasn't Mayberry either."

"That's more than frightening," Kimberly said. "Was there more?"

"Nonstop," she affirmed. "I shut on my television. It would be cued to the original movie Psycho at the horrific shower scene of the woman being stabbed. At first, I didn't think anything of it until I tried to change the channel, and it wouldn't. Eventually, each time I shut on my TV, the same movie would be playing...and I mean each time...hundreds of times!"

Luca was exasperated and slightly startled, reliving the highlights of Lamont Dough.

"Were there more threats?"

"Absolutely. But too many for me to rattle off. And, frankly, I don't want to. That motherfucker got my nerves so bad that I take a cocktail of medication just to get through each day."

Kimberly looked down and saw the ring and a red string around her wrist.

"You're married?"

Luca nodded. "Going on twelve years now."

"Congratulations. Any kids?"

"One. We have an eight-year-old boy named Dillon."

Kimberly took a shot. "Any pictures?"

Luca pulled out her phone, pulled up a family photo, and passed it to her. Kimberly looked at the husband and knew what Luca apparently didn't. She was still under the control of Agent Dough. He was keeping tabs on his retired informant. Luca's husband most likely had an affiliation with him. That's the main reason for his matchmaking; championing the rights of the ugly man was secondary.

"What a beautiful family," Kim said.

Luca grinned. "Thank you. They're everything to me."

Kim asked, "Kabala? Do you study it?"

"I do. And not because of Madonna," she said and smiled.

"I understand."

There was a pregnant pause, and things got uncomfortable.

Luca said, hoping to end this, "You know...if you want to

know who Lamont Dough is, you should look up a woman named Karen Williams. I didn't know her personally and heard she's worked with him for a long time. Other girls have said she's one of his favorites."

"Meaning?"

"Well, meaning, she got the good shit. The best amenities, top-of-the-line cars, premium housing, clothes, jewels, and large sums of cash."

"Karen Williams?" Kim asked for clarification.

Luca nodded.

Kim gathered more information and felt like this needed to be said, "Luca, maybe we should just keep our meeting between us girls, okay?"

Luca looked skeptical and then let out a breathy, "Sure...of course. I won't say a word."

Riley suspected that she and Meyer connected on this deeper level because of trauma bonding. He was still broken up about Lucky's disappearance; for her, it was the ordeal the FBI was putting her through. Meyer was spending more time at her apartment, wrapped between her legs as she massaged his scalp. He had bought her a huge engagement ring from Tiffany's, and they spent hours making love as the newly minted husband and wife-to-be. Guilt from what she had signed on to do was like cancer that had metastasized, taking over every inch of her body.

It wasn't said. Not much was, but Riley suspected her apartment was wired for video and sound. The feds were watching her, watching them in their most intimate moments. She often wanted to come clean and tell her nigga what was happening; she knew she couldn't. But then she found a way.

Riley took a shower and grabbed her lipstick. She wrote on her stomach and came out, typically wrapped in her terry cloth robe. Meyer was lying on his back, arm prompted under his head, the other hand scrolling through his phone. Riley slowly climbed on top of him.

"You got that look, ma," Meyer said.

She ground her hips into his and said, "Oh yeah...what look is that."

"Like you wanna go a few rounds again."

Riley bent over, her hair falling into his face, and whispered, "Don't react. Just read what I wrote, and then fuck me."

Meyer froze; momentarily.

Riley allowed her robe to fall open, exposing the red-laden words. It read *FBIs on me to entrap you. Apt wired. Help me. Need to talk in a safe place.*

Meyer nodded.

Riley had gotten dressed and texted Agent Garrett.

HE WANTS TO TAKE ME TO MEET HIS PARENTS TO DISCUSS OUR ENGAGEMENT. I DON'T WANNA GO. FAMILY SHADY AS FUCK.

She knew what his response would be.

GO! KEEP YOUR PHONE ON AND GET SOME PROSECUTABLE INFO. OR ELSE!

Franklin watched Riley roll her eyes and toss her cell in her pocketbook in real-time. He'd also sat stewing for the couple hours it took Meyer and Riley to finish their lovemaking marathon. How she moved, swayed her hips, and sucked Meyer's manhood had Garrett in his feelings. Franklin went after the flat-booty white women when he was a young man.

Post Kim Kardashian, he wanted his turn to palm his pound of flesh, and Riley's backside had him going crazy.

He wanted her. He wanted his turn. Franklin wanted to control and exploit her for his sexual pleasure, but currently, all he could do was watch.

Running a militia group out of México City had placed Félix in power. Having an army at his fingertips, vatos whose thirst for unmitigated violence propelled him to the top of all kingpins' call lists. Leading the militia group was his day job; being a sicario was his side hustle. It took great skill to ascend to the level of a top assassin, and he was all that. Félix loved to murder with his bare hands because the kill took much longer, his victim squirming, struggling, fighting for survival. Decades in the business garnered him a lot of powerful allies, namely, the Garcia and Juárez cartels.

Pedro, a federalés in Tijuana, México, spent his days terrorizing his jurisdiction's good and bad citizens. His position allowed him to shake down young punks, rip off drug mules carrying cocá, and extort tráficantes for cash. His work in law enforcement kept his bills paid in full; his status as a top sicario afforded him everything else.

The two hitmen boarded Javier Garcia's private jet to Teterboro airport in New Jersey. The cream-colored, plush bucket seats were soft like butter against their heavily starched clothing and rough skin. An entire staff was on deck to be at the men's beck and call—no expense was spared.

The assignment was simple; capture and kill. The sicarios were to murder Layla West in front of Scott. And then smuggle the businessman out of the country to their native land, México, where they would torture Scott and update the kingpin of his granddaughter's fate.

Casamigos tequila was poured with a heavy hand throughout the flight as the two friends commiserated about the untimely demise of Arturo and Raffa.

"There had to be an ambush, Pedro...somehow Scott must have known they had entered Australia...I don't see how he could have gotten the drop on them."

"Australian customs...those ratas must have been on the take," Pedro nodded. "Or the policía."

"Of courseee," Félix sang out. "They make the call, take the dinero, and Arturo and Raffa walk into a trap!"

"Fucking putas!" Pedro spat.

The irony was lost on the two killers. Who was seemingly upset over the possibility of law enforcement being on the take, resulting in two friends being murdered.

The flight attendant brought Javier's guests a tray of expensive Cuban cigars. Félix grabbed one and passed it to Pedro before selecting one for himself. Félix took the straight cigar cutter, clipped the tip, and sparked the flame from his monogrammed lighter. With a few quick pulls and the expensive tobacco sizzling an orangey hue, Pedro repeated this action.

Both men sat back, legs crossed, and spoke distastefully about America and Americans.

"They know nothing of Genocídio War or how deeply entrenched we are in our culture," Félix spat. "Americans only know how to enslave!"

"They treat our people as slaves," Pedro returned. "Want Méxicans to do all the hard labor and pay us peanuts!"

"Pendajos!" Said Félix. "Americans say they don't want us there and will build a wall to keep us out that we'll pay for! Our présidente, Enrique Pena Nieto, told America what to do with their fucking wall."

The men shared a laugh. And discussed assassinating several American presidents.

"CIA, please," Pedro spat. "They couldn't last one week in México! You know why? We don't want them there."

The conversation about politics and assassinations continued for hours as the men felt untouchable until the jet landed at Teterboro.

As the plane taxied to its designated runway, Félix's satellite phone rang.

"Holá?"

"It's a trap. Scott West knows you're in America."

"Que? Who is this?" Félix said. "Dígame!"

The phone went dead.

Back at the bureau, Kimberly's search for Karen Williams came to an unfortunate end. She read the report of the woman, slain in Detroit, Michigan—a bullet to her head, in the driver's seat of her vehicle. No leads, no suspects.

"Fuck," she muttered, highly annoyed. It would have been germane to her case to find out what women received who were in James's good graces.

Kim leaned back in her chair and tapped her fingers on her desk in a repeated rhythm. She looked at her computer monitor with Agent Dough's federal identification photo. His eyes were cocksure, sinister. She wondered if money was the only motivation for going down this path in life after swearing an oath. Kim hadn't ever stumbled upon anyone like Dough—not even Garrett. Sure, in movies, you always came across the federal agent selling government secrets to the Russians for a big payday. But this?

She'd uncovered so much. James's reign was widespread,

extensive, spanning from drug pushers to production companies. Dough had more than a few murders under his belt—she couldn't prove that...not yet. But she would. And she had to be careful. A man like him wouldn't go down quietly.

And then there was Agent Franklin Garrett, the catalyst that started the Dough investigation. Garrett was personal. He had her career benched and was the only suspect in the disappearance and suspected murder of Lucky West.

Kim wondered, *what happens when two men like these two cross paths?*

Markeeta parked her Bentley in the assigned spot that belonged to Chanel. She owned a three-bedroom, three-bathroom lakefront condominium priced just under two million. It was a beautiful property in a well-appointed building.

As Markeeta made her way through the lobby toward the lift, she ruminated on her past life. A year ago, none of this was possible. Her son was in juvie, she was a single mother struggling to make ends meet and constantly faced food insecurity.

Her eyes scanned the building's residents. She drank in wealth, lux, and prestige and didn't want this ride to end. Quickly she made her way to Chanel's apartment. When the door flung open, her host enveloped her in a bear hug.

"You look gorgeous, sweetheart," Chanel said, scanning Markeeta from head to toe. "Bitch! I can't with you!" Chanel snatched the ostrich, peach-colored Hermès Birkin bag that Lucky had gifted Markeeta and squeezed it as one would a child. She asked, "Bo Jangles?"

"Nah, I bought it," Markeeta lied.

"Ohh...kay, baller," Chanel said. "Come in."

Chanel's apartment was modern—clean lines, functional,

expensive. It was primarily decorated in creams and whites with chrome nickel fixtures, hardwood floors, and wide, costly rugs. The bedrooms were large, with high ceilings and an open-concept design.

Chanel led her into the kitchen, and Markeeta sat on a barstool at the huge Carrara marble island. Without asking, Chanel poured her guest a creamy-colored drink while she continued preparing dinner for them.

Markeeta took a sip.

"This is good," she said. "Real good. What is it?"

"The Chanel."

Markeeta swallowed another gulp. "Damn, I'm gonna need this recipe. I know Bo would love this. He's always drinkin' some new shit."

Chanel didn't want to say that Bo had already tasted her drinks and other things. Her juices lined his lips on more than one occasion. That would be rude. Instead, she replied, "I don't give out my recipes," as she diced a mixture of herbs.

"For a fuckin' cocktail?" Markeeta was incensed. "I ain't never heard no shit like that."

"Why am I not surprised."

"What do you mean by that?!"

"Well, just that it seems you don't get out much," Chanel casually declared. She sidestepped, reached low, slid out the kitchen drawer holding her pans, and grabbed the cast iron. Chanel placed the skillet over the open fire. She continued prepping for their meal, oblivious that Markeeta was glaring at her. Chanel continued, "If you were in more refined settings, you would know proper etiquette, and that's you don't ask a host for their recipes. But you're with James, so you'll learn."

Markeeta hated bitches like Chanel. The Lucky's of the world thought because they were pretty, they could talk recklessly and not be checked. Markeeta thought, *she's in a three bedroom, I'm in four. She pushes one whip—I got two. I'm fuckin'*

Bo Jangles; she works for him. Chanel got shit twisted.

With her drink, Markeeta stood up, walked around the island, and invaded Chanel's personal space. Chanel tossed diced peppers, red onions, minced garlic, and herbs in avocado oil, pot sizzling, the aroma permeating throughout.

Markeeta said, "I like you, Chanel. I do. But if you ever try to drag me like I'm some dumb, bum bitch, I won't be able to control my hands. Now since I drove all the way over here, I wanna eat and get fucked up, so I'ma disregard all that fly shit you just said on the strength that Dough vouched for you. But my mercy has limits. Understand, ho?"

The icy-cold glare told Chanel to not defend her good name. Apparently, her guest was sensitive and wasn't partial to free speech. Chanel spoke condescendingly to women like this all the time. What was the big deal? And if Markeeta wanted to make it in her world, she'd better grow thicker skin. Chanel smiled warmly. "I do. And I meant nothing by my remark."

Markeeta's eyes rolled, but she was satisfied with the half-assed apology.

Chanel was being secretive about the drink because it was a cocktail of liquors. Tannery had called and explained that Markeeta might have an addictive gene, and if so, he wanted it triggered. Before Markeeta's arrival, Tannery had Chanel purchase Vodka, Scotch, Bourbon, Tequila, and Gin, which she mixed with amaretto and milk to mask the blend. So far, her guest loved it.

Between the cocaine and buffet of alcohols, Tannery's assessment was that Markeeta's demise was approaching.

After dinner and four glasses of *The Chanel* later, Chanel brought out a plate of premium pure white. The white powder was on a crystal saucer and placed before Markeeta.

"Nah, I'm good," Markeeta said. "I gotta drive home."

"That's why you take a hit. It'll keep you alert so you can

safely make it home to your son. All that alcohol you drank," Chanel explained. "And out here, they keep roadblocks looking for people driving under the influence of liquor."

It was killing Markeeta to refuse the cocaine. Her lips were saying no, but her body felt otherwise. She stared at the small mound of that grade-A, uncut block of feel-good and threw in the towel. Markeeta said, "Just a little bump...enough to wake me up enough to drive home, right?"

"That's right," Chanel agreed. "And this that good shit too."

"For real?" Markeeta was already reaching for the sharp razor and began dicing, breaking down the mound resembling a cheese block into tiny granules. She leaned forward, moved her obstructing hair out of her way, and inhaled. The substance burned her nostril, which flared as her eyes watered. Markeeta pinched her nose and sat back. A moment later, she repeated the action as Chanel just watched.

The narcotic completely took over, and Markeeta suddenly felt giddy. Because she had alcohol in her system, she wasn't bouncing off the walls like a hyper fool. She was upbeat but not erratic. Markeeta slid the plate toward her host.

"I can't," Chanel said. "I'm styling Doja Cat in the morning, and if I hit that, I'll be up all night."

Markeeta understood. She now felt like she had energy for days and wanted to call Bo and hook up, but he was in Memphis for a show.

"I should go," Markeeta finally said. "Get home to my son."

Chanel nodded. "You can take that with you. I got more."

The grin was so broad Chanel thought Markeeta would split her cheeks.

"Thank you," she said. "And I'm sorry about earlier...you know how I get sometimes."

Chanel didn't know much about Markeeta. But said, "Don't mention it. And drive safely."

"I will."

CHAPTER 22

Scott handed a random teenage Hispanic boy a crisp hundred-dollar bill at a bodega. The teenager was given a cell phone and said, "It's a trap. Scott West knows you're in America," in his thick accent. Scott didn't have to make the call—he wanted to. He felt like being petty. Scott knew that information would enrage and embolden the sicarios, making the capture and kill taste sweeter.

While Scott was in midtown Manhattan, Mason, and several henchmen had successfully walked onto Javier's jet and forcefully kidnapped the killers.

Scott and Layla walked into the long island warehouse to silence when they expected screams. "Mason?" Scott called out quickly, pulling his 9mm from its shoulder holster.

"Yeah, we're in here."

The scene was as it should be. Félix and Pedro were strung up by their wrists, stripped down to their boxers, and the torture had begun. Fingers and toes were removed, Félix had his ear sliced off, and Pedro was anally violated with a broomstick. Yet, neither man uttered a fucking word. Not a moan, plea, or scream escaped their mouths.

Scott grabbed a wooden chair and placed it mid-center in front of his captives. He said, "You were going to do what to whom?" Scott opened his trench coat and sat down. "Let me hear all your threats!"

Silence.

Scott looked at Mason, who shrugged before smashing Félix's ribs with brass knuckles. Félix winced but remained mute.

"Oh, this what we doing?" Scott said. He walked over to the table of torture devices and grabbed a blow torch and sparked it up. The reddish-orange flames shot out six inches and hissed. Scott stood before Félix; the weighty torch gripped tight and dragged the fire from his chin to his naval.

Félix winced in pain, gritting his teeth, and maintained eye contact with his torturer.

"What type of shit is this?" Scott asked out loud.

"It's like they don't feel pain," one henchman commented.

"Cut their balls off!" Layla snapped.

After their testicles were removed and Scott and Layla didn't hear the sweet sounds of their victims hollering in pain, they quickly lost interest.

Scott had to give respect where respect was due. Showing a rare display of benevolence, Scott asked in Spanish if they had one last request.

Finally, after hours of torture, Félix replied, "México." He wanted to be buried in his native land. Scott said to Mason. "Wrap this up and place them back on the jet."

Kimberly's desk was piled high with photographs, witness statements, and redacted privileged information. She was spending a small fortune on lattes from Cocoa Beans on the lower level and was surviving off little sustenance.

"What are you two up to?" she asked as she stared at competing photos of agents Dough and Garrett. Why would James request to relocate Franklin to the Chicago bureau if they weren't colluding on something big? There has to be money involved and a woman who'll potentially help them. Or who'll potentially fall victim to them? Perhaps both. Kimberly wasn't sure.

No matter how hard she tried not to go for *his* picture, she couldn't resist. Kim had several images of Bugsy, but one stood out. It was a close-up of him staring directly into a camera; she's sure he doesn't know is there. His smooth, unblemished skin looked baby-soft, glowing under the summer sun. Bugsy's full lips were soft, extra thick eyebrows framed his naturally sleepy eyes, and his curly afro was tastefully tapered. This man was fine.

There were also pictures of his twin, Meyer. He looked rugged, worn around the edges like her favorite sneakers. In the photo, he had sleeve tattoos, diamond earrings, and layers of diamond chains. Meyer, too, was fine. The quintessential *bad boy* would tear a woman down only to have his brother, Bugsy, piece her back together.

It was a shame, though, really. Because if Kim collected RICO evidence against either of these individuals, she wouldn't hesitate to proceed with prosecution.

Yet, she couldn't help herself. Kim grabbed her cell phone and dialed him.

"Hello?"

"Bugsy?"

"Yeah."

"How about we try a new restaurant tonight," Kimberly suggested. "I have some things to run by you." This was a ruse. She simply wanted to see him and noticed that he had started to avoid her calls.

"Why do I feel like my civil rights are being violated," Bugsy said.

"Really? How so?" Kim's voice was soft and casual.

"My right to privacy," he continued. "I'm assuming this is Agent Cooper, and I know I didn't give you this business line. You had to have looked it up."

"Well, it is listed," she said and was sure he knew she was smiling. She thought they were past the formalities and wasn't sure why he said Agent Cooper, not Kim.

He chuckled. "You did some digging because this line isn't on the internet. I don't move like that."

"Fair enough," she agreed. "But we both know this isn't your bat line, so no harm, no foul, right?"

"You're right."

There were a few seconds of silence before she asked again. "So, can we meet?"

"Sure. I have personal time allotted that I could donate to a fed."

"Fed," she repeated. "Ooh, that sounds nasty." And as soon as she said that, she wanted to crawl under a rock and die. She came off as desperate, like a cougar, and they were only four years apart.

The pregnant pause felt like a gap as wide as the Grand Canyon. Kimberly didn't know what to do, so she had to ride out the silence.

Bugsy knew all about Jacqueline St. James and how his father said she begged, continually, to get fucked by him. And then there was Lucky and Ragnar. Bugsy knew his brother wouldn't hesitate to bed this agent. But he wasn't his brother.

"Nasty, huh?" Bugsy said. "I know racketeering cases are harder to prosecute nowadays, but you didn't strike me as a woman who'd allow the bureau to pimp her out for a conviction."

Kimberly felt a hot flash ride throughout her body. Her cheeks were a beet red hue, embarrassed by his direct response.

"I didn't mean it like that," she began, the words falling out her mouth like vomit. "I was trying to be wittier and less nerdy, and it came off as desperation. I can promise you that I wasn't flirting...I don't know how."

"Tonight. Lacey's. Eight p.m." Kim detected underlining irritation. He seemed different. She thought they were friends or friendly, but his icy reception said otherwise.

"Lacey's? Where's it located?"

"There's only one," he said and disconnected the line.

Kimberly didn't allow feelings to get in her way. She had embarrassed herself and felt a sting of hypocrisy while doing so. Kim had skewered Franklin for his inappropriate relationship with Lucky, yet Kim found herself thinking about Bugsy. Professional boundaries were crossed, but she was far from her former colleague's abhorrent behavior and vile antics.

She was going to this meeting. And was obsessing over what she should wear. It was a restaurant *and* during dinner time. Does she come in with work clothes, a badge, and a gun on her hip? Or should she put on something she would wear to meet with friends?

She was stumped as she sat on the edge of her bed, exhausted. Piles of outfits she had tried on were now on her floor, taking up precious real estate in the compact room. This was her conundrum. Had Bugsy returned her flirtation, she would wear her sexiest dress and sit across from him on her best behavior. But he didn't. He had called her out on it, and she cowered, lied, and apologized.

Kim settled on riding boots, jeans, and a silk blouse. She styled her hair in a messy, top-knot bun and did her make-up—lashes, scarlet lipstick, and eyeshadow. Kim looked pretty, casual, and effortless. Taking a last look in the mirror, she was glad she hadn't settled upon a fitted dress and heels.

Kimberly arrived at the restaurant fifteen minutes early, and Bugsy was already there. Her FBI-issued pistol was in her pocketbook as she'd again come to meet with the kingpin without any backup. As soon as they locked eyes, a surge of excitement burst through her body, and she wanted to quicken her steps.

Calm down, girl, she told herself. *He's not feeling you.*

Kimberly made her way to his table, and Bugsy stood up to greet her, walking around to help her remove her overcoat. Kim smelled his cologne as his strong hands maneuvered her coat from her shoulders and slid down her arms. Her wool coat was handed to the wait staff, and Bugsy pulled out her chair and she glided in.

Always a gentleman, she thought. *Always!*

Bugsy sat across from her in a charcoal grey suit, silver silk tie, platinum cufflinks, and no jewels. He was clean-shaven, well-rested, and curious about why she wanted to meet. Again.

"Wine?" he asked.

She shrugged, giving herself time to think about optics. Kim wasn't on duty but wondered what he'd think if she said yes after his awkward exchange earlier. And then she was angry at herself for caring what this man thought about her.

As Kimberly struggled with a response, Bugsy looked at the waiter and ordered an expensive bottle of red.

She liked that. Bugsy taking charge. Exhaling, Kim relaxed somewhat and opened a dialogue. She asked, "I've never been here before, to Lacey's. Do you come here for the food or own it?"

"You must not live in Harlem," he said. "Either that, or I'm revoking your Black card because everyone in the five boroughs knows about Lacey's."

"Not me."

He said, "You look nice."

Kimberly blushed and thanked him but noted that he never answered her question. He would do well working at the bureau.

"You must be wondering why I wanted to meet again."

"You're going to ask me more questions about Ragnar, swear you don't know who he is, and then toss in a couple questions about my missing sister."

The sommelier came with a 2010 Château Lafite Rothschild and did his routine. With the linen napkin wrapped tightly around the fourteen-hundred-dollar bottle of wine, he poured a taster into Bugsy's glass. Bugsy smelled the grapes, swirled the wine around in his glass, took a sip, and nodded. Both glasses were filled, the bottle was left in the bucket, and the sommelier excused himself.

Momentarily distracted, Kimberly was now ready to address Bugsy's comment. He made this meeting seem forced, unnecessary, and inconsequential. Then why did he come?

"That's not—"

Kim was interrupted when Bugsy stood. She looked up and was sure she had turned pale. There, standing before her, was Scott and Layla West. Kimberly felt fucked.

"Kimberly, I'd like you to meet my parents, Scott and Layla. You don't mind them joining us, do you?"

"Not at all," she said and stood. Kimberly extended her hand, and they exchanged pleasantries. The party of four sat down, and Kim thought, *awkward!*

Bugsy poured his parents glasses of wine, and Kimberly could have slapped her own face for not noticing the extra plate settings at the table.

"Now," Bugsy began. "You were about to tell me why you wanted to meet."

The tingly feelings of romance she had felt for this man quickly dissipated. Bugsy had ambushed her, and she didn't like it. Instantly, she reverted into fed mode.

"I've been tasked with investigating your sister's disappearance," she lied. "And given your parents' strained, contemptuous relationship with the bureau, they thought it would be best if I met with you in a more relaxed environment. Because we all have the same goal."

Layla smirked. "And what goal is that?"

"I just told you. To get Lucky back."

Despite how angered she'd become, Kimberly sat through dinner and asked and answered various questions.

And then Scott said, "I'm a straight shooter; we all are. And we know that your interest in Bugsy has nothing to do with locating his sister—"

Kimberly tried to interject and was silenced by Scott holding up his hand.

Scott continued, "Let's let our attorneys handle Lucky's disappearance. Stop using our child as leverage, as a pawn, because it's disrespectful. And I'm a man who doesn't tolerate disrespect."

Did he just threaten me? She wondered. *Do they know where she lived?*

Her hand went toward her purse, and Layla said, "Bitch, please. What you gonna do with that?"

"Ma, don't," Bugsy said. "We stated our position on Lucky, and I'm sure Agent Cooper can appreciate our honesty. I don't think she should be called outside her name."

Kim stood.

"Sit back down," Scott demanded.

"Or what!" she snapped.

"You will walk out on an opportunity to advance your federal career to boss bitch," Layla returned.

Kimberly's interest was piqued.

An agreement was met by all parties, who then parted ways. Kimberly will never know how close she had come to being kidnapped, tortured, and murdered for the whereabouts of her colleague, Ragnar Benjamin.

When Meyer walked into his apartment with Riley, all heads turned. Layla said, "I already told ya ass this ain't no hotel."

"Come on, Ma," Meyer said. "Chill."

Scott, always more diplomatic than his better half, said, "Introduce me to your company, son."

Riley finally laid eyes on the matriarch and patriarch of Meyer's family. She wished it were under better circumstances, but it is what it is.

"This is my fiancée, Riley Baker."

Bugsy was taken aback. No way had his brother put a ring on it. He said, "It's Riley now?"

She nodded.

Scott gave the petite, pretty young woman a warm embrace. She nearly disappeared into his arms. Scott announced, "This calls for a celebration."

Layla snorted her discontent. "You're too young to get married, Meyer. You don't have my nor your father's blessings."

"I'll make a good wife for your son, Mrs. West," Riley said meekly.

"Girl, bye," Layla retorted dismissively. "You can't tell me shit about my son. I know what he needs, and it ain't you!"

"Layla!" Scott admonished. "Be nice."

Meyer would have interjected to defend his fiancée, but he was too busy scribbling a note on the notepad for his family to read.

FEDS LISTENING. FOLLOW MY LEAD.

Meyer hollered, "I'ma grown-ass man, Ma. And shorty done held her nigga down on more than one occasion. I love this girl, and we will get married!"

"Calm the fuck down, nigga!" Layla spat. "You always actin' like a hooligan."

Bugsy said, "Look, Riley's been around and outlasted everyone. She's loyal, and I trust her, so I'm there for you if you need a best man."

"That's what's up," Meyer said.

"So?" Scott said. "Celebration. Let's pop some champagne."

Every member of the West clan was angered beyond measure, but you wouldn't know it with tone; they sounded upbeat. The champagne was poured, and Meyer opted for sparkling apple cider. The family drank, chitchatted with Riley about herself, looked at her magnificent ring, and then Scott put some steaks on the grill.

Downstairs in a Ford Transit sat two agents: James and Terrence, listening via Riley's cell phone. This was the closest the FBI had to bugging the West's apartment. They salivated at the thought of overhearing something incriminating. But felt the margins were slim. It would be doubtful that a family of their caliber would be making statements about the family business in front of an outsider. Riley was the side chick who had only recently graduated to Meyer's main woman.

As James listened in, he eavesdropped on the family bickering and heard as they went through several bottles of wine.

And had a large meal before settling in to watch an advanced movie copy of Black Adam. When the movie came on, James and Terrence were beat.

James said, "Next time she goes in, we'll have her plant a few bugs."

"She can't," Terrence objected. "They find them, and she'll be killed."

"How will they know it was her?"

"Come on now, Dough. Don't play stupid," Terrence said. "We know they sweep the place continually. It's in all the files."

"Don't tell me you caught feelings," James accused. "I say we have her plant the devices, and if they suspect her and she's killed, then we get them on first-degree murder."

"We're not the first-degree murder police," Terrence said. "You're thinking small, short-sided. I'm in this for RICO convictions, splashy headlines, promotions, and an uptick in pay."

James grunted, annoyed.

Riley's purse with the hot device was left in the living room, television blaring on the movie. At the same time, the family converged in the kitchen area. Before anyone spoke, Scott swept his home again and then patted down Riley.

Layla growled, "Why you got this snitch bitch in my home!"

"Calm down, Ma," Meyer said. "There's a lot I don't know either. So, let's allow her to speak. And before y'all start disrespecting her, know that I love this woman, and if I'm forced to choose sides, I will choose her."

Meyer stared at his mother so there wouldn't be any ambiguity.

"That's how it should be because I'm going to always ride with your mother; first. But she's my wife! So, I'm going to keep it one hundred. If I feel Riley isn't forthcoming, if my Spidey senses tell me there's deception, she isn't walking out of here alive. Take that however you want to take it, and note that I don't give a fuck," Scott explained.

Riley didn't have any intention of not being transparent. She was ready for full disclosure. But the immediate threat from Scott and all the glares didn't make what she had to say any easier. And when Layla said, "Speak, bitch!" She did.

Riley began at the beginning. She outlined how she met Elliott, the whirlwind relationship, and ultimately the trip to Chicago.

"When Chicago P.D. pulled me over, found a weapon and a trunk full of drugs, I lost it."

Bugsy asked, "What's his name?"

"Elliott McDonald. But then the feds told me that he's one of the biggest drug distributors from the Midwest to the east coast—"

"Hell fucking no!" Scott interrupted. "Feds did the same shit with Uriel and Jacqueline. Top drug distributors are a small community. Anonymity doesn't come with the position."

Riley was confused. "It's true. They said they didn't need me to testify against him for making me a drug mule, but they wanted me to go after Meyer."

"He's not a kingpin, Riley. He's fed."

"And I met dude, too," Meyer explained. "Ain't no way that nigga pushing weight."

"So, they lied to me?" she asked.

Meyer said, "That's what they do."

"You was gonna testify against my son?" Layla asked, her eyes letting Riley know precisely what she thought of her.

Riley diverted her eyes from Layla and looked at her fiancé. She saw hurt. "Initially, no."

Riley explained the torture she endured while incarcerated, contacting Meyer, family, and friends for help, and ultimately murdering the doctor. At this point, she was in tears, reliving her ordeal.

"I had murdered the doctor in cold blood, and they came around again and offered me a get out of jail free card. And I'm ashamed to say I took it."

Everyone, including Layla, felt empathy for her. It wasn't her fault that she had fallen for Meyer West, nor that the federal government was determined to imprison the whole family. Meyer enveloped her, his arms tightly wrapped around her waist. Riley buried her head in his chest and began sobbing again.

"I can't do it," Riley admitted. "I'll do life before I hurt you!"

The family was quiet, giving the couple a few moments of bonding.

Scott said, "We string them along...feed Riley information that won't pan out."

"How long will that last before they remand her?" Meyer asked. "That ain't good enough."

"Then what is?" Layla asked. "Now I love that she has your back. It reminds me of a young me. But I won't do a bid, not even a small one, for Riley. You got me, Meyer? We're not feeding her no actionable intel."

"Nah, that's not what I'm saying," Meyer began. "I feel like I don't have a choice here. We gonna go on the run."

"Wait. What?" Bugsy asked.

"Y'all heard me. I can't love this lady if she's behind bars."

"Meyer," Riley said. "You can't...you can't choose me over your family. You'd never be able to see them again."

"I already told you and them that if I gotta make a choice, then I'm choosing you!" Meyer made known. "And I know my mother would have done the same for my Pops!"

Layla had murdered a woman and her unborn child over Scott, so she couldn't argue otherwise. Still, she wasn't going to lose her favorite son.

"Be smart, nigga. Think!" Layla said and tapped the side of her temple. "How long are you going to last alone without us? Without your father and me looking out for you?"

Bugsy said, "How about we focus on supporting my brother so that he has a successful run. If there's ever a reason to break away from this life, love is a great one. We all know that the FBI and DEA are on us; they won't stop until we're dead or in jail. There's no greater example than coming to terms with what they did to Lucky. She's gone. We all know that."

Scott thought for a few seconds, always willing to listen to his son's advice. Scott spoke up, "I'll have Mason get you and Riley several fake identifications—"

"Scott, no!" Layla screamed, unwilling to lose another child, especially not her favorite one. "You can't let him go! We've lost enough."

"Layla, he's gone. With or without our help."

Abruptly, Layla rushed from the kitchen and locked herself in her bedroom, crying her eyes out.

Scott continued, "I've had an evacuation plan in place since the early nineties that I've never updated. Fifteen million in small, unmarked bills is buried in multiple locations throughout the United States on property owned by several LLCs. A Jewish hippie chick from Rhode Island automatically pays and manages the taxes. No paper trail leads back to me."

"I've never heard you mention that?" Bugsy said, slightly peeved that he was omitted. "Does Ma know?"

"Nah, I never mentioned it to your mother either. I set it up for all of us but felt the fewer people that knew, the better our chances. And again, I never updated the stash. This family can't allude the feds on fifteen million. No fucking way."

"Thanks, Pops," Meyer said.

Scott nodded. "Sit down."

Riley and Meyer sat at the bar stools surrounding the breakfast bar. She was still wiping her tears away but experiencing a myriad of emotions.

"If Riley is your rib, she must also be your third eye."

"Like Ma?"

"Exactly. I can put together another couple mill in small bills, but if I start to move more than that, I can attract some heat."

Meyer nodded.

"You'll need to consider your life expectancy, inflation, children, and the unknowns. For you and your family, less than twenty million must last through five decades or more."

Again, Meyer nodded.

Bugsy said, "You understand what Pops is saying, right?"

"Yeah, keep my expenses down."

"And stay under the radar," Scott advised. "You have those sleeve tattoos. That's the first thing the feds will send to all local and federal agencies. When you walk out your front door in spring and summer, you wear a cheap suit or whatever long-sleeved shirts millennials wear in the summer to work. Your outfit needs to fit your narrative. Should you have any neighbors who ask too many questions, don't wait around to see if they're harmless. You wipe down all fingerprints in your home and move to another destination. Have acquaintances but no friends…don't ever get behind the wheel of your vehicle without checking your signals and lights."

Bugsy added his two cents. "Not only should you be spending less than six figures a year—"

"Come on, Bee. That's lunch money for me," Meyer joked.

"This ain't funny," Bugsy replied. "You can have a comfortable life on that, but I was about to say that you and Riley need to get jobs to blend in with your neighbors. They see niggas ain't working and bills getting paid, jealousy seeps in.

They start going to websites looking for wanted criminals to get a quick come up or calling tip hotlines."

Riley said, "Always appear to be struggling, right?"

"Or do life in prison," Scott said flatly.

That line sobered a sober Meyer up. Riley wasn't doing another day in jail. Not on his watch. He said, "Have Mason buy me a Ford work truck, not fully loaded. The parts are American and cheap. I think it's best that I don't tell y'all where we're heading. Shit, I don't even know. But I will stay away from small towns and predominantly white areas. Look for a bustling city where we can blend in."

"And that huge rock on your finger," Scott said. "Riley, you can't keep it...Meyer find her something with diamond chips, that Pitkin Avenue, Nassau Coliseum type of jewelry that won't catch envious eyes."

Riley dreaded giving up her ring but focused on Meyer, who was giving up his family.

"Sure, I'll leave it here."

"No, not yet. Right now, you're still working for the feds until I can put all the pieces in place for my son to have a successful run. He takes off with you at the minimum, he's aiding and abetting a fugitive. If they find y'all, my son ain't walking out of prison. So, we got to do this the right way."

"We understand," Meyer affirmed. But clarified. "If they find us, I ain't going to prison. That's on my buried brothers and sister."

Scott momentarily thought about the unlimited number of informants the feds sent their way, the bottomless amount of resources they possessed, and their dogged tenacity and remembered a quote.

He said, "Machiavelli said it is better to be feared than loved if you cannot be both." Everyone allowed those words to sink in. "I used to believe that and ruled with an iron fist. Riley has shown me that fear can be overcome, but love... transcends all understanding. Love can have a woman lifting a two-ton car off her son, a medically dead person's heart to pump again, or a single Black female facing life behind bars to choose her nigga and ride it out. And on that foundation of love, that infrastructure is where your mother and I built the House of West. Our love—your mother and I is what kept us together. Meyer, I hope you and Riley have that."

CHAPTER 23

The torrential rain hammered onto the pavement. The gusty wind shrieked, pushing Kimberly forward as she power-walked to her building. Her umbrella was on its last three ribs as she desperately clutched the broken canopy inches from her now-soaking wet head of hair. Exiting the subway, she had six blocks of walking to her apartment, and each time she stepped into a puddle or thought about the new leather heels she had on, she cursed. The meteorologist said nothing about rain, so the cheap, flimsy umbrella was purchased for ten bucks outside her job. The vendor was making a fortune for the one-use items.

Arriving at her building, she tossed the umbrella in a trash bin and entered her lobby. Kim didn't live in a building with a doorman, concierge, or many high-end amenities like the people she investigated. Yet, she still paid a fortune in midtown Manhattan rent. Her building was large—high and wide, and this helped her keep her anonymity. Other than the customary morning or evening greeting, which neighbors exchanged to be polite, she enjoyed not participating in chitchat.

All Kim could think about was stripping naked, taking a hot shower, and eating a piping hot cup of Ramen. Just feet from the lift, she heard, "Ms. Cooper. You got a minute?"

The voice was unmistakable. Kim turned toward the irritant, and there stood Franklin Garrett. *Arch Enemy Number One.* Her nemesis. The man who made her blood boil from the slightest smirk or head gesture.

To ask how he'd gotten her address would be rhetorical, so she said, "Nope," and kept it moving. Kimberly had taken a few steps before he was on her, saddling up against her, his FBI-issued firearm pressing aggressively against her lower back.

"Don't be rude, Kim," he chided. "Not after I've come all this way."

Kim's heel dug deeply into Franklin's Gucci loafer, the soft Italian leather unable to withstand such an assault. He, too, hadn't dressed for the inclement weather. The sharp heel slid across his big toe and nicked his index before his body jerked in pain, yelping loudly. Kim spun around to face him.

"You got five minutes!"

There wasn't any way she'd invite him into her home. Her sacred space was where she sipped tea, burned sage candles, and did daily meditation.

The lobby had a quaint seating area that few tenants used because sitting there made one feel like fish in a fishbowl. In front of the massive floor-to-ceiling window were a sofa, several chairs, a coffee table with magazines, and two end tables. Franklin followed behind, trying not to limp, but his toes were in excruciating pain. The two sat on the couch facing one another. Kim placed her pocketbook in her lap, her hand gripping her pistol. She felt this was a power move, but Franklin viewed it as fear.

"Why are you here? Shouldn't you be in Chicago running from the scene of your last crime?"

He couldn't believe this bitch wouldn't play dumb like most people did when they didn't have enough evidence to support their claim. Kim went straight for his jugular.

If she wouldn't play along, he would. The first thing you're taught is to deny, deny, deny. Franklin said, "And what crime is that?"

"Oh, I don't know. There's so many." Kim exhaled, letting out a breathy sigh. "Maybe the ones that involve you fucking the perp, brilliantly put it on YouTube, and ultimately robbing and killing her. Maybe those crimes aren't aging that well for you, huh?"

"You're crazy," he said and smiled broadly. "Cuckoo…cuckoo…"

Franklin did that thing where you twirl your finger around in circles to emphasize his point. He appeared to be amused, but Kim felt otherwise. If he was unbothered, then why show up?

"You came all the way here to tell me I'm crazy?" she chuckled. "Okay. Anything else?"

Franklin envisioned smashing her teeth down her throat, ripping out large chunks of her hair as the butt of his gun pounded into her flesh. Before emptying the clip into her round, pie face. But, today, he was on a fact-finding mission.

"Listen, Kim. Despite what you think about me, I came here to set the record straight. The allegations made by the West family are false. I had nothing to do with any of it." Franklin gave his most earnest face he could muster, a look he had perfected throughout the years, something women couldn't resist. His eyes manifested sincerity and strength, vulnerability mixed with valor. He needed her to know that she was wrong about him. And using his looks—he was eye candy to all women—his fiery red hair, freckles, copper-colored skin, and full pink lips. You didn't see men that looked like him each day. Kimberly Cooper was an agent, but she was still a woman. He continued, "I'm a married man who has never cheated on my wife, and my faith would never allow me to do what I've been accused of. You got me all wrong, Kim. I just need you to see that. I'm one of the good guys."

Kimberly snorted, amused. "Even Satan is an angel."

Boom. She'd dropped the Deidre line about Dough.

The theological reference didn't go over Franklin's head. He was motherfucking furious that he couldn't win her over. He said, "There's a joke. A racist, a misogynist, and a coon are sitting at a bar. Bartender asks, 'who's a maid, chef, chauffeur, doormat, irrelevant, inconsequential, parasite, punching bag, scapegoat, and has three holes you can fuck?"

"Franklin Garrett?"

He paused, not expecting that response. Franklin glared but continued, "The misogynist answers, 'a woman?' While the racist and coon simultaneously shout, 'a Black woman!'"

Franklin forced hysterical laughter holding his belly and heaving up and down. He looked stupid until Kim's deadpan expression halted his side show.

"I don't get the joke, but I take it you do from your belly rolls. You are the racist, misogynist, and coon, correct?"

Garrett snapped, "Look bitch! Keep my name out of your fucking mouth and find some business and stay the fuck out of mine. I won't ask you again."

"Or what?"

Franklin had assumed initially that Kim was gripping a pistol. But what if she were recording this just as he had done with Lucky West and countless others. He was on the verge of threatening her, saying something so heinous that she would be afraid to sleep tonight. Kim had made him so emotional on the inside, but outside, he was stone. You couldn't even tell his teeth were clenched.

"Or my feelings will be hurt because, as I said, I'm innocent of the allegations. I know it, and the bureau knows it...and I did consider us friends."

His repeated denials were expected, but the Franklin she knew loved to toss a threat or two and then walk it back. That was his foreplay.

"We were never friends, Franklin. We were colleagues. And speaking of colleagues, how's your new one? Special Agent James Dough. Or is it, George?" Kim snapped her fingers a few times for recollection. "Or Donovan...yeah, that's it, right? Lamont Dough?"

Franklin stood up and stretched out his body. It would be her funeral. He said, "Good talk."

He proceeded to leave, but Kimberly wasn't done. Not after he accosted her on her territory and had gotten her riled up. She called out, "She was pregnant, you know...Lucky West. And was smart enough to get a noninvasive paternity test performed on the baby before she was murdered. All I'll need is a matching DNA donor."

That leveled him. Franklin's legs nearly buckled underneath him. He couldn't even turn around to face someone who, up until two seconds ago, he thought he had outfoxed. Franklin needed air. Quickly he scurried off. But he wasn't quick enough because he heard, "You're right, Franklin. Good talk."

Agents Randall and Devonsky were abducted, hogged-tied, blindfolded, and transported to Culiacan, México by the Juárez cartel on orders from Louis. Scott made the case that these feds were bad for business, interfering in the distribution of Juárez's cocaína into the United States.

Their abduction and murders would be high profile, international news. They would bring a lot of heat on Méxican cartels. Still, México operated under its own flag, not American. And always went against the grain. The last American federal agent kidnapped, tortured, and killed was in 1985—DEA Agent Kiki Camarena.

The men were thrown into the back of a dark-colored Hummer and driven to Newark, New Jersey. The vehicle was torched, and the agents were loaded into another SUV and taken to Teterboro Airport, where a private plane awaited their arrival.

The abductors only spoke Spanish. Devonsky understood a word or two, but that was his extent of the language. It didn't matter. He didn't need a translator to tell him they were fucked. More bluntly, dead.

Early on, both men shouted threats and obscenities— "Do you know who we are?! The FBI will fucking bury you all for this!"—But now, hours later, they leaned into their fate.

Neither said much to the other during the flight they assumed would land in México. Both are lost in their thoughts of their parents, wife, and children. It's an ominous feeling having time to accept your death, to come to terms with your life choices.

Other than the effort it took to subdue them, the cartel members hadn't done any bodily harm to Randall and Devonsky. So against common sense, logic, and reason, it gave the agents a small window of hope.

Sitting to his right, Devonsky could feel his partner. He said, "Randall, what do you think this is about?"

"Does it matter?"

"I just want to know why I'm being murdered."

Randall blew out air, perturbed. "You'll know. We both will."

That was the last conversation both men would have with each other.

Her eyes shot open, and she stared at a dark figure. She could make out an outline; tall, lanky, gloved hands, mask. A .44 with a silencer dangled from his left hand. Agent Dough? The warm liquid expelled from her body and puddled beneath her buttocks before seeping into her Stearns & Foster mattress. Her body shook violently as one would with seizures—aggressive jerks popping her limbs up and down. Her skin tingled, sending warning signals to her brain to get the fuck up out of there.

But it was too late. She was fucked.

"Kimberly Cooper."

"Agent Dough," she squeezed out. "It's James now, isn't it? Is it still James?"

Even under these conditions, she couldn't stop herself. This man was in her home, with a firearm gripped in his hand, she had just pissed herself, yet she couldn't acquiesce.

"You can call me God if you like."

"What do you want?"

"To not kill you," he said. "But I will."

They both let that sink in.

Kimberly sat up and leaned against her headboard. The warm urine had instantly cooled, and the liquid against her skin, coupled with her wet pajamas, was a combination she wished she didn't have to experience.

"No one makes a man like yourself do anything. Am I correct?"

He nodded and then shrugged. "But I'm no different than most. We like to blame our shortcomings on others, our failures. And take sole credit for our victories. Bluntly, I kill you—it's all your fault."

"That's how you sleep at night?"

"I sleep counting dollar signs. Period," he explained. "Things that most people are tethered to. Beliefs, good versus evil, God, gods, the spiritual realm, purgatory, the unknown—all the spiritual acumen that keeps people in line don't apply to me.

When I leave here, that's it. No judgment. No reincarnation. No heaven. No hell. I fade to black."

"So, you do whatever's necessary to make sure you and your family are provided for in this life—"

"Because there won't be another one."

"No matter who you hurt?"

"People...feelings...don't affect me."

Kim asked, "Are you a sociopath?"

"Absolutely."

"Psychopath?"

"Perhaps."

"Why the different names? What's that about?"

"You shuffle the deck so many times, and people can't remember the last card you played."

"I thought your various names connected to the Rendition program."

"Rendition? Where the CIA illegally tortures people for information?"

She nodded.

"I'm FBI, Kim. Not CIA. You know that. If there's one thing you believe I say tonight, it should be that I've never participated in Rendition."

"I believe that," she said, gaining her courage. Her need for a morsel of the truth was more significant than her common sense. She forged on. "What about Charlie Brown?"

"Where are you going with this?"

"But there is a program, correct? The Charlie Brown Program. You've heard of it. Allegedly founded by Hoover, the bureau experiments with Black Americans, using the data collected for the government to make informed decisions. I've heard whispers that the intel we receive is from unsuspecting individuals placed in abhorrent situations just to see how they'll handle each one. Some Black Americans were injected with infectious or venereal diseases via vaccination shots."

"Like Tuskegee Institute?"

"Like that but so much more." Kimberly couldn't see his eyes so she couldn't read him but the fact that she wasn't dead yet and he kept listening told her that she had something. She said, "You know that minorities will soon out-populate Caucasians making us the majority in another generation or two. If my research serves me right, this lottery began in the sixties. It's run by a secret faction of the Federal Bureau of Investigations."

"Let me stop you right there," James said. "I didn't come here to kill you. But as I said, I will. Stay on the shallow end of your pool before you drown. Go after the toddlers and leave the deep end as unchartered territory."

"Is Franklin Garrett on the shallow side?"

"He doesn't concern me."

"I would like to ask you one more question, please." Kim felt it necessary to ask a man like himself for permission.

"Go ahead."

"Religion? Why is it in your wheelhouse if you're an atheist?" she asked. "I mean, I have an idea…supposition but would like to hear it straight, no chaser. It's control, isn't it?"

"Religion does all the heavy lifting for a man like me because most people are born into one. Their beliefs are inherent, and all I have to do is say a word or phrase, and instantly they let their guard down, and then I sweep in and plant the seed, any seed," Dough explained. And then said, "Hallelujah, sister."

"Praise the Lord," Kim replied without thought. Then nodded.

"It's practically Pavlovian. The brainwashing is ingrained. So, I studied the Bible, Quran, Kabala, Hinduism, and Buddhists. It made my work feel like less work. For instance, you take a passage from the Bible and use it out of context. I'll keep it elementary." James decided to pull up her accent chair and sat down. He got comfortable before continuing. "I want to justify why an informant must help me set up someone to get murdered, allegedly. So I'll say, The Bible says an eye for an eye. This perp has killed people, so their death is Biblical." He laughed. "They eat that shit up."

Kim shrugged her disapproval.

Dough continued, "You read through the pages of the Bible, and there's justification for everything. I want numerous women in my life, a wife, mistresses...baby mamas. The Bible will justify that too. Most people won't state that there's a nexus between all these books, saying the same message differently. You agree?"

"I do not."

"Sure, you do. But you'd rather play the outlier."

Dough was done. The weapon was tucked in the assailant's waistband before he backpedaled toward the exit. He said, "Don't bother reaching for your Glock. I took it. As collateral. And to reiterate. Keep my name and affairs off your motherfucking to-do list. Or the next time you see me will be the last time you're seen alive!"

"Rápido, rápido!" someone shouted as the agents were shoved off the plane into a waiting Humvee military vehicle. The terrain was unpaved, rocky, and unsteady as the agents' heads bobbled up and down, dust filtering into their throats and nasal passageways, causing them to cough violently.

Randall and Devonsky listened to endless Spanish—fast speech coupled with lots of laughter, and both felt ill. This wasn't how the period should end their sentences.

Finally, they were stationary. Bolted to chairs with chains fastened around their waists, ankles, and wrists. When the blindfolds were removed, eyes were adjusted. Through the low filtering light, they recognized the two prominent men that stood before them: Louis and Angel Morales.

Angel said, "I ask you only once, and then take a body part. Ragnar. Name and location."

"Listen, if we give up something, we're going to want some assurances in return," Special Agent Randall said, negotiating the terms.

Angel nodded. But not to Randall.

Two men came behind the hostages and tied their mouths with black and white bandanas. The agents tried to resist the bondage; struggled somewhat. And then the growling sputter of the chainsaw's motor cranked up, and Randall and Devonsky's eyes widened in horror. The rickety blades sliced through Randall's wrist, whose muffled cries were akin to a wounded bear. Powerful and pitiful. Devonsky received the same treatment before Angel spoke again.

"Ragnar. Name and location."

Devonsky rattled off Ragnar Benjamin's whole government, Chicago address, and whatever information he thought would help send him to the other side with the least pain.

"Lucky West. Dead or alive?"

Randall spoke, "Most likely dead...but we truly don't know. It's Franklin...it was all him...I swear!" Blood-infused saliva drooled out of his mouth down a cheek on a face frozen in fear—almost unrecognizable.

Their cooperation didn't lessen the torture. It did move things along, though.

Angel said, "You Americans, do you get it?"

"Get what?"

"You finally understand, sí?"

"Understand what?" Randall asked earnestly.

"You don't fuck with Juárez!"

Kim was unable to go back to sleep after Dough left her apartment. He had managed to get past her locks and security system with ease. And there was her missing Glock that she had to report to the bureau. She was sure she'd be assigned desk duty—which wasn't different from how she was already spending her days. And an investigation would be opened into her stolen firearm.

Back at her desk, she couldn't stop investigating James Dough. He'd moved himself up in pecking order from the second chair to the first. Garrett would have to take a backseat.

Since joining the bureau, she'd heard whispers, rumors, and unfounded claims that J. Edgar Hoover had started a highly classified program, The Charlie Brown Program. Enacted in 1961 and was designed to control the success of the Black community. It took weeks of digging, but she found classified, redacted, highly prejudicial, and above her paygrade documents.

It's alleged that Hoover was no fan of Lincoln, who had signed the Emancipation Proclamation freeing the slaves in 1863. Hoover knew he couldn't go back and undo what had been done but could play his part moving forward. J. Edgar noted that slaves with nothing more than scraps their masters had given them to eat had created meals Caucasians wanted to eat. These meals would later be coined Soul Food until the Caucasians stole the recipes and renamed them Southern food cuisine.

Hoover noted that his counterparts stole Black American music—Blues and Rhythm & Blues and named it Rock N' Roll. No other race could be beaten, stripped down to their bare bones, starved, maimed, disenfranchised, killed in cold blood, and still come up humming hymns and creating recipes out of cornmeal, sugar cane, and water.

Hoover feared the worst. If he didn't stop this race, then one day, someone would be bold enough to run for President of the United States. And he couldn't allow that. Hoover knew that when banks refused to do business with Black people, they opened their own. When realtors refused to allow Blacks into their neighborhoods—they built their own community—Black Wall Street. He was there in real time for Martin Luther King's speeches and the insightful, prophetic teachings of Malcolm X.

The strength, tenacity, and culture could take over America if left alone to grow and expand. And there wasn't any way he'd allow that to happen. Not on his watch.

J. Edgar didn't have to look far for assistance. If you find what works, work with that. And since it's widely known that Africans participated in capturing other Africans in the 1619 Slave Trade, he would use Black Americans in the same vein.

Unsuspecting individuals were entered into this lottery system by enemies, friends, and family members. And once the government had you on their list, the only way out was death—natural or unnatural.

The system wasn't that sophisticated. A studious, Black American's name, social security number, and date of birth were entered into the program. The Charlie Brown Program and the proverbial rug would get pulled out from under them.

Kimberly read until her eyes were blurry. She needed to connect the program of 1961 to her present day. How was Dough connected? Furthermore, she couldn't mention this to anyone because it technically didn't exist. And what about Dough's threat?

She had to ask herself. Was there still a program today designed to keep educated Black Americans from reaching their full potential for the white race to maintain a stronghold over minorities?

She wasn't sure. But something was indeed amiss.

CHAPTER 24

Meyer woke up that morning with an adrenaline rush. He was back—drug and alcohol-free, and his body and mind were cooperating. His parents trusted him again and assigned him, Bugsy, and Mason to go to Chicago and kill the pig, Franklin Garrett.

Scott opted to stay behind with his wife. Layla had fallen back into depression, and he needed to be there for her.

The arrangements were preplanned down to the last detail to ensure a successful capture and kill. Meyer told his partner in crime, Riley that he was heading down to México to handle some business. And would be back in a couple weeks—buying himself time and hopefully sending the feds on a fruitless mission.

She played along. "I'm worried, Meyer. What's in México?"

"Business."

"I know. But you never discuss your business with me, and if I'm going to be your wife, you'll have to start trusting me."

Meyer paused for dramatic effect. And then said, "You right, wifey. And I promise I'll keep it one hundred as soon as I return."

"We shouldn't keep secrets."

"I just said a nigga gonna come clean when I get back. And check this...I got something big planned. One last transaction coming up in a few weeks, and I might retire."

Riley gave Meyer a sultry kiss and warm embrace, and both hoped this was enough to keep her handlers from yanking her off the case. With Meyer missing for days up to weeks, her freedom was in jeopardy. But he couldn't worry about that. Meyer had to trust the process.

Mason had arranged through Scott's affiliates to have a vehicle waiting per state—clean registration, insurance, and excellent driving condition. It was arduous and would add a day to their trip. But Agent Garrett couldn't get wind that the twins were headed his way. Scott had also arranged a full arsenal of weapons for his sons once they entered Illinois.

"Don't linger, y'all hear me," Scott advised. "Snatch him up and apply pressure about your sister's whereabouts. He doesn't talk"—Scott tapped his temple— "Two shots to his dome and y'all bounce."

They nodded.

"Feds find out he's missing, they could shut down the whole state, do a dragnet. Prolonged torture is too risky. I won't trade y'all lives for Lucky. She wouldn't want that either."

It wasn't what either brother wanted to hear, but they understood their orders. The twins would love to be drenched elbow-deep in Franklin's blood, torturing that fed. Have him singing Mariah Carey high notes, but as Scott had once said, *dead is dead.*

Día De Muertos, Day of the Dead, came around again with added meaning. The pedestrians marched down crowded streets in colorful, festive costumes holding bright banners, signs, and posters. Two American federal agents dangled from the overpass, chains looped around their broken necks, all limbs missing. The stark reminder was evident. This was México. And no one fucks with Juárez!

The sign read: *Adios Bendajos!*

There were nine African Americans in Kim's unit. She most respected Roderick Calloway, a newer agent—intelligent, ambitious, honest, and assertive in any case he's working. Kim called him into her office, and he took a seat.

"What's going on?" he asked.

"I'm working on some things in my spare time that could materialize into a case. I wanted to pick your brain on a few things."

"Shoot."

"You ever heard of The Charlie Brown Program?"

"I have," he said. "It's supposed to be bullshit."

"Yeah, I know. But humor me."

Roderick pushed back in his seat and crossed his legs. Like a politician, he placed his hands in the prayer position. He thought for a few seconds piecing together tidbits of hearsay that had circulated throughout the bureau.

"Hoover allegedly put together a program that targeted Black Americans on the trajectory to success. I heard it started small, with just ten individuals. He wanted to see how easy it was to break someone's will using the power of suggestion."

"So, if someone is in medical school, he would place people around them to suggest trying a narcotic to get them through the day?"

"Indeed. And not just any somebody; it had to be someone the person trusted."

She nodded. "My grandmother used to say you want your spouse dead, have their child give them the poison."

"Exactly. And Hoover knew this. He took a page from our history and used Black Americans to destroy Black Americans. When this program was enacted in the sixties, no fucking way are our ancestors trusting white folks."

"But why, though? Why do this?" she asked.

Roderick frowned.

"You can't be serious with that question," he said. "You know why. Hoover was in the thick of it. He was now watching a race of people fighting back. Martin gave our people hopes and dreams; Malcolm gave us pride and power. What started small for Hoover had expanded... extermination, if you will. And if brainwashing and subterfuge don't work, he had a backup plan. Flood the community with drugs and liquor stores. One on every corner."

"Keep our people handcuffed and allow White Supremacy to flourish."

"It's all in cycles," Roderick said. "You see what they did in the eighties long after Hoover. Again, flooding our communities with drugs."

"And what about STDs like the Tuskegee Institute. Any truth to that?"

"Not just venereal diseases, Kim. This is the bureau we're discussing. Our people—" Roderick looked over his shoulder to ensure they were still alone. Then continued, "Our people were infected with anything scientists had hatched in that petri dish."

"Like, HIV?"

"Possibly."

"Cancer?"

"Absolutely." Roderick shrugged and cleared his throat. "Ebola, West Nile, Encephalitis. It's all just a needle prick away."

"Okay," Kim said. "You've heard what I have. The bureau started small. Targeting brilliant Black Americans who had sidestepped pitfalls, forged on despite poverty and violence in their neighborhoods, and had tunnel vision of being on the path to success. Those people were deceived by the ones they most trusted?"

"But there were levels to it. The original ten were placed in situations where they would advance one step, and the bureau would yank them back three...over and over again until they ultimately snapped."

"Therein lies the name. The Charlie Brown Program because Chuck would go to kick that football, and right before he punted the ball, Lucy would yank it away—"

"And he'd fall flat on his back."

"That's done to you enough times," Roderick said. "Well, what would you do?"

Kim chuckled. "Fold like a cheap suit."

"I suspect I would have, too," he admitted. "The resources we have, the bureau...these people never stood a chance. We have psychologists, sociologists, doctors, lawyers—a person in every field with the same goal: to knock these people off one by one."

"And yet, this doesn't exist."

"If you say it aloud, you'll be branded a fool." Roderick stood up to leave. "Your case, this is what you're working on? A phantom program that no one will own up to?"

"That sounds about right," Kimberly acknowledged. "I'm trying to figure out if this person has ties to the program and is working for a classified faction of our government. Or has he heard the whispers we've all heard and is using the foundation, the program's blueprint, for his own gain?"

"Is this person an agent?"

"He is."

Roderick exhaled. "Be careful, Kim."

"I always am."

Kim didn't want to say that she had blown through careful. She was as far removed from careful as possible because she knew she couldn't stop.

On the day of the Chicago trip, Meyer and Bugsy lookalikes headed out in Meyer's SUV just before dawn. It would take the feds on a journey into México, where the lookalikes would disappear with Angel's help until Scott gave them the word to resurface.

During the drive, Bugsy and Mason munched on fresh fruit, protein shakes, and Red Bull while Meyer chomped on Chick-O Sticks, Funyuns, Twinkies, and Snicker Bars. Since kicking his habit, all he did was crave sweets and nicotine. Bugsy and Mason recognized the pattern but knew this was the least of their worries.

The trio made four stops which included an overnight stay in Indiana. Well rested, they arrived at Franklin's block in three different vehicles. Bugsy had the closest eyes on the residence.

And now we wait, he mumbled to himself.

Riley had no idea that the man her fiancé went to murder was standing in her living room questioning her about México.

"Get him on the phone," he demanded. "And find out where the fuck he's at!"

"I'm trying," Riley shouted. "He said he wouldn't answer his phone when he's down there."

Franklin said more to himself, "The surveillance team lost him once he entered México."

"How is that my fault?" she asked.

Franklin snorted. "When he gets back, you better get us some actionable intelligence or—"

"I know! Back to jail with no bail."

Franklin chuckled. "That part."

Riley glared at Agent Garrett and impatiently waited for him to leave. He stalled and then said, "Fix me something to eat!" When she didn't move, he spat, "Now, bitch. Isn't that how your fiancé speaks to you? Isn't that what you like? Huh, bitch? You ghetto girls are all the same."

Riley was incredulous. She hollered, "Get the fuck out!"

Franklin snickered. "I don't think I will." He took a few steps forward, invading her personal space. Garrett had waited for this moment since the morning he'd interviewed her. He despised strong-willed Black women. Hated ghetto, gum-chewing, neck-popping females who thought their slick mouth was a match for him.

Riley roared, "Get the fuck out or take me back to jail!"

She bluffed. She had to. Franklin had this crazy look in his eyes, and she didn't know what to expect. It was like he went to the dark side without provocation. Suddenly her apartment felt small, confined, claustrophobic—nowhere to run.

Franklin fingered his Glock on his waist and repeated, "I said fix me something to eat!"

"I won't do it—"

Riley was slapped silent. Stunned, she held her face and glared. Franklin grabbed her by her neck and pushed her toward the kitchen.

"Get in there and fix me a four," he paused for dramatic effect. "No five-course meal!"

Downstairs in the undercover surveillance van, James and Terrence were stupefied. Franklin had no clue that they were tailing him and had followed him to Riley's.

"What the fuck is he doing?" Terrence asked as they listened, horrified.

"He's compromising my motherfucking case!" James spat.

They bolted out of the van when they heard Riley scream and beelined straight to her apartment. James opened the door, and he and Terrence tumbled in, nearly tripping over their feet. Riley was in the fetal position on her living room floor, Franklin towering over her, raining down a litany of punches. Terrence tackled Franklin to the ground, and James helped Riley.

"Get the fuck off me," Franklin yelled, trying to shake loose of Terrence. But he couldn't. Terrence's hold was vice grip tight, too firm for the thin-framed agent to overcome.

"Are you crazy!" Terrence shouted. "What are you doing!"

At this moment, Riley realized what the West family had already assessed: Elliot McDonald wasn't trafficking drugs. He, too, was a federal agent. But she said nothing to her former lover. Instead, clutching her eye, she focused her rage on her abuser.

"Meyer will kill you for this!" she threatened. "You hear me, bitch! You're fuckin' dead if I tell him, you punk bitch!"

She was losing it. Her body trembling uncontrollably.

James said, "Terrence. Get him the fuck out of here."

Terrence nodded and practically dragged Franklin from Riley's residence.

Alone, James allowed Riley's sobs to turn to sniffles as she spewed more threats of Agent Garrett's demise. James picked up a couple of knocked-over chairs and a broken vase and straightened some lopsided pictures on her wall. He was now ready to talk.

"Come, sit down."

Riley's scowl on her face was epic. James wanted to crack up laughing, but he had to contain the emotion. She folded her arms and spat, "I'll stand."

James got serious. "You threatened my agent. And under normal circumstances, I would have your ass back in Chicago, and you will only leave that place in a pine box."

Riley glared his way.

"I like you, Riley. I do," James said and then barreled her way. Without hesitation, he removed his Glock and placed it at her temple. "But if you compromise my case and utter a fucking word of what happened in here tonight, I will blow a cannon size hole in this pretty face of yours. Understand?"

James had a handful of her hair, the same hair he told her he loved. His grip was so tight that she couldn't maneuver her neck and nod. Riley said, "I do."

She was released.

"Make up some shit about what happened to your face, and it better be believable." The Glock was placed back in his waist. "Notice how we got here in time to save you. That's because I got eyes and ears everywhere. I own you. Your life is mine. I own your mouth, pussy, personality, disposition…I even own your thoughts. If you even *think* about telling Meyer that he's under investigation—I'll know!"

I already did, she said to herself. *Did you know that?*

Maxine spent her days at *The Law Office of Jones & Jones*. It was unpaid volunteer work, but Gregory said he didn't need her to contribute to the household's overall expenses.

"I'm just glad you're doing something you love," he had said.

And she was. Working on cases where Black and Brown people's rights were violated by law enforcement was redeeming. She also volunteered with a nonprofit organization that did a lot for the homeless community. It allowed her to keep her eyes on Wendy and hook up with her friends.

Early Saturday and Sunday mornings, she hit the streets weekly in the company's minivan, stocked with donations and items bought through federal grants.

Her first stop was always Wendy.

"You got this for me?" Wendy asked as she tried on a new puffer coat.

"You know I did," Maxine said. "An anonymous donor gifted us twenty, and my boss gave me five to give out."

"She stole the rest, didn't she?"

Maxine laughed. "No, she's not like that. The other coats went to other volunteers in different boroughs."

"Ain't I a mess?" Wendy asked. "Thinking the worst of folks."

"Me too," Maxine admonished. "But not anymore. Not since I met this new community. They're helping me change my outlook on people. There are good humans in this world who want to give and not take. You know?"

Maxine was beaming, which made Wendy glow too. She was happy for her friend.

"What else you got?"

"Lots."

Maxine handed Wendy a few gift cards valued at $15 each to Dunkin Donuts, Subway, and McDonald's. And then dug in the van for packages of clean socks and toiletries before heading out.

"I'm going to midtown to hook up our peoples," Maxine said.

"You better not give shit to Slick Willy Pete!"

"Yes, Slick Willy Pete gets some of these things too."

Wendy smiled. "Okay. But not the good shit."

The two friends embraced.

"I'll see you next week. Take care of yourself in the meantime," Maxine called out as she circled around to the driver's seat and hopped in.

Before pulling out, she and Wendy exchanged huge grins. Maxine thought about how far she'd come with Wendy's help. The night Bugsy had almost beat her to death with his bare hands, jumping off the Brooklyn Bridge, breaking her ankle, and being nursed back to health by a nurse.

Despite everything she had gone through, Maxine felt like she was the lucky one. She rolled down the passenger's window.

"I love you," she called out.

"Huh? What's that?"

"I said, I love you."

Wendy beamed. "I know. And I love you too."

The trio returned back to New York after nine days in Chicago. They weren't sure if the intel from Randall and Devonsky was legit, but there was a white woman and a light skin teenage boy living in the home. Scott hired a crew out of Illinois to keep sporadic eyes on the house and report back if they saw anyone resembling the agent.

When Meyer walked in to see Riley's face, he nearly went ape shit. Her eye had almost swollen closed and was a deep purple, almost black. His beautiful lady had endured so much just from his affiliation, which didn't sit well with him.

She didn't have to say a word; he knew. Meyer knew that fed had laid hands on her. He assumed it was Elliott.

"Who did this to you!" he roared. "And it better not be your ex because I'ma kill that nigga. On my fuckin' mom's, he's a dead man!"

Riley's look pulled Meyer back down to reality. She couldn't speak the truth about the situation because they were in a crisis. Riley utters the wrong words, and her freedom is jeopardized.

"I went by the club, and me and Abigail got into it."

Riley studied Meyer's face for any hint of guilt or awareness by mentioning the woman the television show Icon Hollywood said he was seeing.

There wasn't anything to see. Meyer showed no recollection when he said, "Why are you exchanging blows with her? You know she isn't on your level."

"Her mouth is too reckless," Riley explained.

"Damn. You let shorty do this to you?" Meyer replied, going along with the lie. "I thought you were nice with your hands."

"I don't wanna talk about it."

"Then what do you wanna talk about?"

"Your work. México. What's going on, Meyer?"

"I got something big planned for next month that could be huge with one of my father's ex-business partners. He's coming to New York in a few weeks, and if all goes well, then I'm gonna be set for life."

"You mean us? Correct?"

"You already know."

"And who is this individual?"

"Javier Garcia."

"Who's that?"

"Most likely the richest man in México."

James and his team listened to this exchange salivating at the information. This was the Greeks pushing the trojan horse into Troy.

"She's a natural," James commented to his team. "She's going to walk him into a life sentence."

"I told you she could do it," Terrence said, wanting credit where none was due.

"*The New York Times* better spell my name right when they cover the West and Garcia cartel takedowns," Franklin said. He knew his colleagues had been giving him the cold shoulder. He was practically ignored each day since the incident with him and Riley. Franklin felt emboldened in his hometown, so he said, "What name are you going to use, James? I think you should keep it simple and stay with James Dough. But I have to ask. Why not John Dough? Isn't that All-American? Or is that too obvious, considering how complex you are?"

There was deadpan silence.

"I'm joking," Franklin said. "Too soon?"

It took Markeeta weeks to realize that Dough hadn't made his regular visits to her home for booty calls. He did call for progress updates, but those calls were less frequent. She summarized that someone or something else was occupying his time. Markeeta hoped Dough had loosened the reigns because she had made inroads into Bo's camp and had gotten Bo to sign Dough's nephew as his new manager. Still, no compensation. She decided to call.

"Hey," she said when he picked up. "I haven't seen you in a while. I hope I'm not being replaced by the woman you had in my home a few months back."

James's voice was casual. "It's not your home."

"Yes," Markeeta said, using her corporate voice. "About that. It's not my home, but I would like one. And you promised that when Bo signed your nephew, I'd see a big payday."

"You will. I'm going to hit you off soon—"

"You can hit me off now," Markeeta said assertively.

There was a pregnant pause, and then Dough said, "Markeeta, you don't have to worry. I'm in New York, and you'll be taken care of as soon as I get back."

Markeeta tried to detect any anger in his voice, but there was none. She felt relieved that he would actually honor his words.

"Oh, I didn't know you were out of town."

"Why should you?"

Markeeta also didn't know that James didn't live in Michigan. She didn't have a clue that she wouldn't see a dime from any transactions she helped facilitate.

"You're right. I shouldn't," she replied. "I should go."

The call ended, and Markeeta turned back over to sleep. She awoke hours later, fiending for a hit. Stepping out of bed, she avoided mounds of clothing on her bedroom floor. Shoes, purses, hats, and undergarments were tossed untidily around— she hadn't cleaned up in days. Her bathroom, gym room—all a mess. When she made her way to the lower level, the stench from the kitchen flared her nostrils. Plates of uneaten food were molded; takeout bags were littered from the kitchen to the living room. The sink and dishwasher were overloaded with dirty dishes. The place was a hot mess. Still, she had no intention of cleaning. Not today. And especially now, knowing Dough was out of town and wouldn't be doing a drive-by.

Markeeta opened the refrigerator and took a swig of Tropicana. The ice-cold, orangey flavor quenched her thirst. She swallowed a couple more gulps before returning the carton to the mostly empty shelf; food shopping was another thing she should do. But she didn't want to. Her new lifestyle consisted of dining out with her man and friends or ordering meals and having them delivered. Markeeta no longer had time for menial things. She felt she was practically on tour, accompanying Bo to most of his concerts.

Markeeta scribbled on a post-it note: MAID. To remind herself to request James hire one for her. It was unrealistic for him to think she could continue to clean a four-story home. Oversee her son, fuck and deceive Bo Jangles, fuck and please James, study his required reading, and have a little Me Time.

It was nearing seven in the evening, and she was hungry. The old Markeeta would have fixed herself a greasy bacon, egg, and cheese sandwich with mayo and ketchup on white bread. But this new and improved bitch would settle for an egg white omelet with tofu crumbles and mushrooms.

Her cell phone rang. It was Bo.

"Hey, you," she said sweetly.

"Hey," he began. "Listen. You coming through?"

"Where?"

"I'm at the studio and want you to lay down some vocals."

She beamed. "You serious?"

"You know it."

"I'm on my way."

Food was placed on the back burner. Markeeta found her coke supply on the fireplace's mantle and did a couple lines before texting James.

BO FINALLY ASKED ME TO LAY DOWN SOME VOCALS. U WERE RIGHT. BTW, I WANNA GET FUCKIN' PAID. NO MORE LIES, DOUGH.

CHAPTER 25

James was sitting on the sofa of his luxury suite at the Soho hotel when he got the call from his nephew.

"Did you see the news?"

"What news?"

"Bo Jangles. He was murdered last night as he drove through a Popeyes chicken drive-thru. It's all over the news out here."

"Got damn!" James spat. "How the fuck that happened?"

"They said niggas set him up. We were in the studio last night, and he was beefin' over some beats with a producer and an engineer for Markeeta. Your girl was there too."

"Markeeta got hit last night?"

"No," Curtis explained. "But she was in the car. They said niggas sprayed only the driver's side. When bullets started flying, Bo turned his back toward the window and covered Markeeta with his body. I'm told cops spoke with her at the scene but let her go home. That's why I was sure you knew before I did."

James was slipping. This New York case had him so wrapped up that his attention in Detroit had waned. Had he known that Bo had beef with anyone and heard any threats on the rapper from wiretaps, he would have had a team of agents covering this man. But as Curtis explained, it seemed the incident transpired that night. Could he have prevented it?

James scolded his forty-year-old nephew like he was a child. "The moment shit jumped off in the studio, you should have called me to have someone watch his back! I've been carrying your Black ass your whole life, just handing shit to you on a fucking platter! And you didn't think to protect the merchandise? I've got to think for you too?"

"I'm sorry, Unc," he said earnestly. "It won't happen again."

"Tell that to Bo Jangles!"

With his moneymaker murdered, he no longer needed Markeeta. All his years of planning had evaporated in one night. He called Tannery.

"Listen, I'm done with Markeeta."

"I know. I heard. Bo Jangles got murdered last night."

James's jaw tightened. "Yeah, shit happens."

He disconnected the call.

The murder of her mother had started Markeeta on her benders. The assassination of Bo Jangles and her near-death experience had pushed her over the edge. She was an addict. Markeeta woke up mid-afternoon to brown juice and cocaine, flying through the highways and byways coked up, amazed she wasn't pulled over. She usually ended up at Chanel's house, where she was treated to *The Chanel* drink and more cocaine. Markeeta would head home and smoke a couple blunts laced with coke.

And after being awake for days, she would fall out, face down in her bed.

Only to wake up and repeat.

Chanel Dior reported this behavior to Tannery, who, again, was amazed that Dough was none the wiser. He *hoped* James would call him again, acting all aggressive.

Meyer and Riley hopped in the F-150 with nothing but the clothes on their backs and a few million in small bills gathered by his father. Neither knew where they were headed, but the fact they'd be together made this journey something to look forward to.

"Where are we headed?" Riley asked.

"I'm thinking Las Vegas or Los Angeles."

"Really?" she said. "You don't think that's too flashy?"

"Nah. No way are we headed south. No North or South Carolinas, Atlanta, Alabama, or any other southern state. And I think we should avoid cold, predominately white cities like Boston or Rhode Island. The Midwest is also off-limits. I just left there, and I don't like the vibe."

"Oh, yeah. The job you and your brother did when you said you were going to México."

Meyer nodded.

"What was that about. We never got the chance to speak about it."

Meyer gave her the side eye. "You sure you ain't wired?"

Playfully, she smacked him upside his head.

"I'm just fucking with you," he said. Meyer got serious. "You know Lucky is missing, but before we couldn't locate her, she explained that she had been seeing a man she believed was an undercover agent."

A hot flash cascaded down Riley's back. She knew it would be a while before she wasn't triggered by this type of conversation.

Meyer continued with, "Lucky only knew the man's name as Ragnar Benjamin. And my Pops and his legal team were stonewalled by the feds who denied any affiliation to this man."

"Y'all think they lied?"

Meyer nodded. "Hell, yeah, they lied. That's what they do. But when my niece's father got involved, he kidnapped the two federal agents and forced them to give up the information on that pig. His government is Franklin Garrett, and he lives in Chicago, Illinois."

"Franklin Garrett?"

"Yeah. Why?"

"Well, there was an Agent Garrett attached to my Chicago case. He was supposed to relocate me to Detroit, but Agent—"

"Those niggas move around," Meyer said, amped. "How does he look?"

Riley described Franklin down to his freckled face.

Meyer hit the steering wheel with his fist and then gripped it so tightly you could see the veins bulging in his hands.

"That's him!" Meyer growled. "So he's in Detroit? You got an address on him."

"Meyer. Franklin Garrett is in New York. He's the one who did this to my face."

Meyer felt like he got the wind knocked out of him. He was on the expressway and had to look for the nearest exit to pull over. His SUV rounded the exit ramp to a local street, and Meyer parked behind a sedan. He placed his truck in idle.

"Riley, walk me through this. I thought you were locked up in Chicago. Where does Detroit enter the picture? Because right now, shit ain't adding up. A nigga didn't wanna harp on this, but why are you now just mentioning you were relocated to Detroit!"

Meyer's face distorted with rage. And then he looked into his baby's eyes and knew he had hurt her. "I'm sorry, ma, listen. You know a nigga is still fucked up over his sister. And I trust you, I do. I wouldn't give up those I love and head west in this basic vehicle. But please make this make sense."

Riley understood. The optics looked suspect, and she had been through too much to sweat the small stuff. She explained, "I was in Chicago. But once I agreed to help them, I was chartered off to Detroit to heal from all the injury that was done to me. For a few weeks, the feds placed me in a mini-mansion with another girl and her son. The girl lived there, but they kicked her out so I could have the place to myself."

"Another snitch?"

Riley shrugged. "I assume so. And she wasn't pleased with being removed. She had one of those names that make you think her mother combined the parents' name and came up with some foolishness."

Meyer wanted to direct the conversation back to Franklin, but Riley kept snapping her fingers for recall. She said, "Mar...Mar...Marwetta...Marweena."

"Markeeta?"

"That's it! Markeeta."

"Please tell me you remember the address."

"I do," Riley replied. "Why?"

"I think the Midwest is calling my muthafuckin' name!"

James hadn't been to the Detroit residence in weeks. But as soon as he entered the home, the unmistakable aroma of death permeated throughout. He pulled out his Glock, eyes scanning the perimeter.

"Markeeta?" he called out.

Dough heard a television upstairs as he went room-to-room clearing for intruders and went to the primary bedroom. James saw a blood trail that led him to the bathroom. There, he found Markeeta—throat slit, fingers broken, face beyond recognizable.

James took another look around and surmised this wasn't a robbery. The home was filthy. It looked like ten vagrants had moved in and got comfy. But it wasn't tossed. No open drawers, unturned furniture, or missing items. This was simply murder. Undoubtedly personal.

He exhaled. This shit was the last thing he needed. Just as he was about to call his associates to help with body disposal, he remembered Markeeta had a son.

Dough did a slow jog down to the basement, and there he was, Ralph, seemingly unaffected. James said, "When was the last time you saw your mother?"

Ralph thought for a moment. He said, "Saturday."

Today was Saturday. And Markeeta, James estimated, had been dead for several days. "Last Saturday?"

"Yeah."

James snorted. This young boy was literally raising himself. He said, "So, your mom's dead. She was murdered. And so was your grandmother. Your father was killed, too, so that makes you an orphan. There isn't any reason I have to go through the trouble of sending you back to New York to be placed in a foster home when I can wrap this up tonight."

James thought about the Michigan taxpayers footing the bill for Markeeta's son's foster care stint and figured he could live with that.

Ralph asked, "My mother's dead?"

"She is indeed."

He waited a beat for the boy to cry. But he didn't. James could tell he wanted to, though. Most likely, he was in shock.

"I'm going to need you to pack your things?"

"What things?"

"Whatever you want. Clothes? Underwear?"

"Last time you kicked us out, you told us we couldn't take anything you gave us."

James stood erect. He did, in fact, say that. "How old are you, Ralph?"

"Thirteen."

"Okay. You can take whatever you want from down here. If you want to take that game, take it."

Ralph hesitantly asked, "You sure? I can take this game? It's expensive."

"Consider it a down payment. In two years, when you're fifteen, you'll see me again. And I'll have some work for you to do for me. You cool with that?"

Ralph nodded.

Before the night ended, Ralph was placed in a placement center by ACS. Markeeta's body was removed, and the residence was scrubbed clean. Agent James Dough would have this unit occupied with a new informant before sunrise.

The scene was reminiscent of Scar Face. Dozens and dozens of armed men violently ascended onto the sprawling property with a thirst for blood. An intense gunfight broke out between hundreds of men. Assault rifles and automatic weapons lit up the night like fireworks. It was War World III against the Garcia cartel. Each man was out for blood. It was a huge payday to capture Javier.

Scott had gotten the intel on Javier's whereabouts from Gustave. Javier had a private compound in Texas, miles from the Méxican border. Underneath this large compound was a tunnel that stretched from México into Texas. The tunnel moved kilos of cocaine and people from one end to another. Now, this location had been compromised, and Javier found himself in an intense firefight between two prominent organizations that wanted to see him dead.

Javier's personal bodyguard hurriedly ushered Javier from room to room. He was armed with a Mack-10 and was ready to protect his boss with his own life. The gunfire was getting closer. They both heard screaming and men dying, not knowing if it was their own or enemies. But Javier didn't plan to stick around to see the outcome. He had to leave the compound immediately. His only option was the tunnel, but the problem was that it was outside where the madness was happening.

Javier was flabbergasted. How did they find him?

"Vamonos! Vamonos!" the bodyguard shouted to a few men.

Javier was pushed into a sealed room, and the door closed behind him. He was left alone while his henchmen fought with their own lives to save him. He was only armed with a 9mm, and compared to the heavy firepower his men were up against, his pistol might as well be a water gun.

Ratatatatatatatatatatatatatatatatat......!

Bratatatatatatatatatatatat!

More men were screaming and dying. The gunfire loomed closer to where Javier was hiding out. They were coming for him.

Rat-a-tat-tat-tat-tat-tat-tat-tat-tat-tat!

He heard yelling and chaos, and then Javier heard his bodyguard trying to protect him by any means necessary. The machine gunfire had reached right outside his door. A few bullets cut through the walls and came inside, where he stood armed and frantic. And then, it got quiet—too quiet. Javier suspected that his men were dead. He was alone. Javier would soon find himself between the teeth of his predators. But he planned on taking as many men as possible out before they came for him.

Abruptly, the door burst open, and two men charged into the room. Javier didn't hesitate, and he opened fire.

Bak! Bak! Bak!

He cut down the men grabbing an automatic weapon tightly in his grip. Javier's heart pounded as he looked left to right and peered out of the massive picture window. There he saw the unmistakable image of Scott West slowly advancing toward his home. Scott was dressed in all black, a knit wool hat pulled low near his eyes. A .44 was strapped to each thigh, 9mms in his shoulder holster, and his massive hands gripped an AR-15. But he was unmistakable.

Javier's men were doing a valiant job protecting their territory. Still, three things placed his army on the losing end of a gun battle—the element of surprise, they were outmanned *and* outgunned.

The east wing of the property was littered with dead bodies—no active shooters. Javier had a small window of time to make it there and access entry to his underground tunnel. Javier sprinted across the vast lawn undetected with the agility and stamina of a man half his age. He made his way to the hidden trap door. Lifting the access panel, Javier descended the steel ladder and took flight. His expensive loafers smacked against the cement flooring of the tunnel as he snaked his way through winding corridors. He jumped into a rail car on tracks, crossing the Méxican border into Laredo, Texas.

Javier drove at full speed for miles before slowing to his destination. Sweat poured off the Méxican drug lord as his head swiveled, looking back for encroaching enemies, 9mm gripped tight. Finally, he reached his destination without incident.

It was a slow climb up the ladder, his knees trembling from fatigue, all his energy zapped out of him. Pushing the trap door open, Javier peered around, looking for threats; he saw none. Feeling confident, he emerged from the tunnel and collapsed on the grassy knoll. Breathing heavily, Javier stared at the now dark sky, searching for the north star to guide him toward his home. Javier knew he had to keep moving but needed a few more minutes to refuel.

When his strength returned, he climbed to his feet and walked through the western area of his property, heading toward the main house. Nothing was more appealing to the drug lord than the vast, empty structure—brick and mortar—a fleeing criminal's dream.

Almost collapsing through the front door, Javier made his way to his oversized leather sofa. Heaving deep breaths, he relieved his unsteady legs, sat down, tilted his head back, and relished the quiet of the moment.

James said, "We all know collectively we have a problem that needs to be stopped."

"And that would be Kimberly Cooper?" Franklin replied.

James nodded. "That bitch doesn't listen! I warned her to stay out of my motherfucking business, or the next time she saw me would be her last. And you know what she does next?"

"It shouldn't matter," Terrence growled. "You gave her a direct order, and she disobeyed you! She needs to be punished."

"Punished?" Franklin was incredulous. "I think we're well past punishment."

No one in this room understood free will, a woman's right to choose, or was down with the feminist movement. They barely saw women as human. You controlled them. Owned them.

Scolded and terrorized them as James did with his blue-eyed, silver Pitbulls, Florence and Weezy.

"Class is no longer in session," James spat. "We roll three deep and put her fucking lights out."

Franklin had wanted Kimberly dead since he'd accosted her at her residence, and she didn't cower before him. At least once a day, he replayed her yelling out that Lucky had the noninvasive paternity test, and all Kim would need was a DNA match. Highly sensitive men like Franklin couldn't take criticism, a challenge, or disrespect. Every action invoked a reaction from him. That's who he was. Since that encounter, Franklin had been working up the nerve to murder his former colleague, but he lacked the courage alone. Kimberly wasn't Lucky. She trained at Quantico, Virginia, just as he did so she wouldn't be an easy victim.

He could order her death through a third party, but she was fed. You don't farm that out. And despite everyone calling him a woman killer, he hadn't murdered Lucky. He felt he lacked the nerve to walk up behind Agent Cooper and blow her brains out. Franklin could lay hands on her. He'd been smacking around women in the bedroom for decades. But this? What James was suggesting was more in line with the West family of hoodlums. However, there weren't any options. And Franklin did his dirt best with a team. Three deep.

How could they lose?

The sound was so slight. So, minute. It was more what Javier felt than heard. His eyelids flipped up, and there stood an unknown assailant. Instinctually, Javier reached for a weapon but had none on his person. He had left his 9mm by his front door.

"No need for that," the man said. "It's not that type of party."

"Who the fuck are you? One of Scott's men?"

"Who me?" the man chuckled. "I'm about as far removed from Scott West's payroll as possible. And you better take that as a Hail Mary."

Javier began to stand but heard, "Sit the fuck back down!" And he did.

The man unbuckled his suit jacket and sat in a nearby club chair. He continued, "I'm Agent Roderick Calloway, and I work for the Federal Bureau of the United States."

Javier shrugged and swatted the intruder away like one would a bug. He said, "I have no interest in you." Javier then stood up, disregarding the earlier command. With his back to Agent Calloway, he opened a nearby drawer looking for a pistol. None was there. He saw an unopened pack of Marlboro cigarettes and lit one. Javier inhaled the carcinogen, allowing the smoke to billow through his parched lips. He wondered if his men or Scott's thugs would come bursting through his front door. Why was an agent in his living room? But mainly, he wondered who the fuck set him up?

When Javier swung back around, he was met with a heavily armed, highly skilled, and expertly trained FBI unit. Glocks, pistols, and AK-47s all pointed toward his chest cavity.

His hands went up in surrender. "Agents. Por favor. Tranquillo."

"Let's try this again." Roderick placed his hand over his heart and continued, "I'm Agent Calloway, and we need to have a discussion at the table. Follow me."

Roderick led the homeowner into the massive dining room. And to Javier's astonishment, his unanswered questions were answered. Their smug faces spoke several words—mostly, fuck you! In the high back chairs were Angel Morales, Luis Morales, and Gustave Calderón. Andrés Enrique Guzmán—the President of México, and Edward Christopher Hansen, whom he would later learn was the Deputy Director of the New York Federal Bureau of Intelligence.

Angel did most of the talking. He said, "You're out, Javier. You no longer run the Garcia cartel."

"Oh, yeah?" Javier retorted. "I've done nothing to relinquish my throne! I've broken no laws and never disrespected my culture."

"You've overplayed your hand," Angel spat, understanding Javier's implication. "You threatened the wrong niña. MY niña!"

"You are nothing, Angel. Your father gave you Juárez. You didn't build it. That's why you couldn't maintain it! I," Javier fisted his chest. "Built Sinaloa, Zacatecas, Toluca, and Guadalajara from the ground up. Territory that belongs to me. Areas that have my surname attached! I am the Garcia cartel."

Roderick knew the men had bad blood, but this meeting wasn't convened to measure who was the better cartel boss. He interjected with, "Javier, you're out. And Gustave is your replacement. Gustave runs the Garcia cartel."

"Gustave couldn't run a marathon!" he bellowed. And it was at that moment he realized that Gustave was stuffing his face with food, unaffected by his recent betrayal. Javier glared at the Popeye's takeout bag and then back to his former friend. A man he had known for over forty years had betrayed him to the Americans. And was now eating American food.

Not missing an opportunity to clap back, Gustave took the paper napkin and daintily wiped the corners of his mouth. He said, "Pardon me, please, I ask. But Javier, this Popeye has come out with a new chicken sandwich—" he kissed his fingers and released it in the air. "And it is unbelievable. Do you know people are killing over this sandwich?"

Javier barreled toward Gustave, desperately wanting to wrap his hands around his neck, but several agents blocked him. Javier was tossed into a seat where he would remain until the meeting ended.

Roderick resumed with his demands. "Javier, you are under arrest for RICO. You will be tried and convicted in a United States courtroom."

"My lawyers will destroy you!"

"It's already been decided. Once you're convicted, you will be secretly transported to Cuba, where your family has already been placed as of an hour ago."

"I'll kill you," Javier threatened, looking at Gustave. And then, he spoke in Spanish to the Méxican president. A man he put in office. "Andrés. You cannot allow the United States to disrespect us like this, our people."

"You are not the people, Javier. You are only one man, and this decision is for México."

Roderick continued, "Javier, whether you see it or not, you're getting a sweet deal. You play along with us with the media. Allow us to parade you through a sea of cameras, place you on trial for the conviction, and then you live out the rest of your life maintaining your wealth—well, most of it. You'll also need to give the US a hefty sum of nine hundred million. In dollars, not pesos, of course."

"Andrés, por favor. Dígame?"

Roderick said, "Some money will be displayed on camera at this home where you'll be apprehended tomorrow evening."

Javier said to no one who cared. "I am Méxican. I should live and die in México! No Cuba!"

"But you will live," Angel snapped. "A better fate than you planned for my daughter!"

CHAPTER 26

The high pursuit chase would end up on the Westside Hwy heading north against traffic. Three SUVs with skilled, defensive drivers were gaining traction against the modest Nissan Maxima. The sedan weaved a few times to avoid colliding head-on with other vehicles while furiously honking the car's horn—headlights nearly blinding her.

Luckily, the road was sparse at this time in the morning but no less dangerous. Kim tried unsuccessfully contacting authorities from her cell phone, but a dozen busy signals later realized they had jammed the cell towers, so there was no reception.

Bugsy sat shotgun, his .45 gripped tight in the palm of his hand, wishing he was behind the wheel. Yet, in such a high-stakes situation, he knew she was probably driving better than he would have.

Agent Kimberly Cooper maneuvered the wheel easily, a tremendous feat under this pressure. Her eyes scanned the lanes for an exit, a detour—an out. Kimberly found an opening as she neared 79th street and slowed down just a smidge. She had to turn the wheel a quarter of an inch while gently tapping on the brakes, or else at that high speed, the car would jack knife or flip over.

Just as she prepared for the turn, she heard what felt and sounded like an explosion. The back glass shattered from what was clearly a gunshot. That action angered the already miffed Bugsy, who pivoted in his seat and returned fire.

His trigger finger let off a barrage of bullets, all hitting their intended moving target. That SUV veered off the road and ultimately stopped, unidentified driver wounded—presumed dead.

"You hit him?" Kimberly asked.

"You muthafuckin' right I did," Bugsy returned.

"Good," she said. "It's them or us."

Kimberly was trying to justify the kill in her fed brain. Even though she believed her colleagues were in those dark-tinted SUVs trying to assassinate her, she still wore a badge. And if she came out alive, she would have to answer to the law—if not, her Maker.

As the second SUV sped up and tapped the left side bumper, doing the PIT maneuver, which caused the vehicle to tailspin, she hollered, "Get him off my ass!"

Bugsy didn't need to be told to save his own life. He had lined up the shot but was waiting for the perfect opening and took it.

Bak! Bak! Bak! Bak!

He could see the outline of a figure slump over the steering wheel before losing control of the car.

They could hear sirens which sounded to be heading their way. Someone must have seen the car chase and reported it to nine-one-one.

"Thank God!" she said. "We just need to hold out until NYPD gets here. I'm sure the last SUV will fall back any second now."

Bugsy wasn't happy at all to hear the calvary. He was out on bail for a gun, had possibly murdered two people, and had a gun with bodies on it on his persons. He wasn't an informant working for Kimberly and wasn't about to become one.

"You gonna have to pull the car over and let me out."

"What?" she asked. "I can't. That's suicide...we'll be killed."

"I'll take my chances against a nigga with a gun or with my fists 24/7."

"You sound crazy!" Kimberly assessed. "I'm doing damn near 100 mph...I can't just let you out."

The two entered an epic argument before the distinct sirens, their saviors, and the calvary grew faint until the sound faded. Kimberly deduced that the last SUV had called them off as it sped up and took over where his coconspirators had failed.

The SUV rammed into her bumper, hitting it repeatedly at the correct angle until she lost control of the Maxima. Her foot slammed too hard on the brakes, and she felt the steering wheel spinning rapidly through her fingertips.

The tailspin was seemingly in slow motion; her neck whipped around, taking in the scenery. The dizzying combination of hearing the screech of tires and the car's rotation had stiffened her body. The Nissan had crossed over two lanes, was hit by another vehicle, and came to a blunt stop. The impact burst open the airbags, and everything went dark.

Momentarily dazed, her eyes opened to a horror show. The car's engine was pushed back, practically on her lap. She could smell gunpowder from the airbags, and smoke rose through the radiator.

Kimberly couldn't feel her legs, but that didn't stop her from trying to push open the door. She needed to escape, get some air. Kim felt claustrophobic. And then she remembered her passenger. Kim looked over, and there he was, breathing shallowly.

"Bugsy?" she called out. "You, okay?"

He said nothing.

The seatbelt had become restrictive. It detained her, kept her imprisoned when all she wanted to do was bolt. The belt buckle pinned her to her seat; she was immobilized. Kim positioned her body catercorner to Bugsy and swiveled her head as much as she could without crying out in pain to face him. He looked okay, unhurt. And then her eyes traveled further down, and she saw that a wrought iron pole had impaled him.

Bugsy didn't know how long he had left but wanted to use it wisely. He knew that New York-Presbyterian wouldn't be able to save the gangsta. Not this time. He had used up all his nine lives. The irony wasn't lost on him. Bugsy West—gifted the name of one of the most legendary gangsters the world had known—born into a crime family that was half mob, half cartel. And yet he didn't go out in a blaze of bullets, wasn't gunned down by sicarios or street thugs.

It appeared that his light would dim from a car accident.

Bugsy's first thought was of his slain son. His little man that he didn't protect. His second thought was of Meyer, his twin. He wanted to see his brother have babies and become a father. And then his parents flooded his mind. It didn't seem fair for them to bury yet another child. That guilt was almost suffocating, even as he struggled to breathe.

He thought of Lucky. For him to die not knowing her fate— was she alive? Kidnapped? Trafficked? Murdered? In Wit-Sec? Would he see her on the other side? Did he believe in such things?

Bugsy wouldn't think of his regrets. What would be the point? Instead, he focused on the good times when they had a house full. All six siblings; him, Meyer, Lucky, Bonnie, Clyde, and Gotti.

Bugsy didn't hear Kimberly repeatedly calling out his name— "Bugsy! Stay with me," —she pleaded. He had already faded into his thoughts. Bugsy could feel his eyes getting heavy, his strength dissipating with each breath. The struggle to cross over his way was the last thing he'd do in this life.

Bugsy West would die—eyes wide open—one final thought on his mind: Dillinger.

Franklin just had to be the head negro in charge, thought James. He jumped into the black Escalade, first and gave chase. Franklin was gaining traction on Kimberly, who became a formidable driver. He did all the tricks taught at the academy, even landing a great shot off and blowing out her back window.

James watched as Bugsy returned fire; Franklin lost control of his vehicle and tapped out. He wasn't sure if he was hit, but he could only assume the worst because Franklin never rejoined the car chase.

Next up was Terrence. He, too, did his best and was ultimately benched by the ruthless gangster who evidently knew how to use a weapon.

Of course, James was the third SUV. He had purposely held back, lagging close enough to see the action yet far enough behind to assess the risk. At sixty, James had nothing to prove. He was long in the tooth, which meant he had the wisdom and experience to let others do his bidding and only intervene when there was no other recourse.

The target was Kimberly. He wanted that bitch dead by any means necessary. And since she wore the same badge, they couldn't farm this out. Besides, James was a man who took most things personally. That would qualify him as sensitive, easily aroused, and annoyed. His switch could get clicked by the slightest infraction.

But he saw things differently. How could gods be emotionally unstable? A man who had amassed a fortune, had people following him *before* Instagram, and managed to stay on top for decades while his colleagues were none the wiser be unbalanced? The answer is he wasn't. A little megalomania never hurt no one. He marinated in it.

Bugsy West wasn't supposed to be on the scene. That oversight would be placed at Franklin's feet. If he's dead, then Terrence's big feet would do. James intended to extort Bugsy until he was coming up for retirement, and then he would prosecute. His mantra was clear: *never kill the cash cow.*

And now this. He had two agents down and would have to clean up this shit show. Marching out of his vehicle, Glock gripped tight, eyes peeled for whatever. James tapped on the glass and startled Kimberly.

"Hey, Kim," he sneered.

Bak!

The first bullet lodged in her forehead.

Bak! Bak!

The second and third hit her square in her chest cavity.

Moving more like a machine, he repeated the same action to Bugsy before ultimately getting on his cell phone and notifying the New York bureau that he'd been ambushed.

"This is Agent James Dough, Chicago bureau. I'm on the Westside Highway. Agents are down. Send immediate help."

James called the incident into the New York bureau. Within minutes, NYPD was on the scene, a police helicopter flying noisily overhead. Within the hour, several high-ranking FBI agents appeared as well.

James was sitting comfy in the back of an ambulance on a stretcher, receiving an IV of fluids. Yet, he wasn't injured. The EMT didn't bother to assist Kimberly Cooper or Bugsy West because Dough assured they had flatlined. NYPD had managed to rope off the scene and took pictures of bullet casings to preserve trace evidence.

The feds and coroners van arrived simultaneously. The brass badges headed directly toward the outsider, the agent in their jurisdiction—the man who didn't announce his arrival.

Kimberly's superior, Special Agent Teller, approached Dough and said, "I guess you should hear this from us. A body was found dead in an SUV two miles back. The man is identified as Agent Terrence Barnes."

Dough's head shook. "Fuck!" he bellowed.

"Now, one of your own is dead. And one of mine. You're going to have to explain what the fuck went on here!"

James noted that Franklin wasn't mentioned. That slippery motherfucker had gotten away. Special Agent James Dough had considered how he would craft this story. And there were two possibilities. He still hadn't settled on one when his eyes diverted to the crew working to remove the bodies from the Nissan.

The blowtorch cut through Kimberly's driver's side, and the metal door was removed. The same was done to the passenger's door. Both victims were cut out of their seatbelt restraints and placed on gurneys in body bags. And then everyone heard, "Oh, shit! She's not dead."

Kimberly rolled off the gurney and fell to her knees, gagging and holding her chest. She ripped off her puffer coat and bulletproof vest. She was struggling to speak.

Dough mumbled, "No fucking way is she alive."

Everyone rushed her. Special Agent Teller pushed medics and men out of his way like bowling pins to get to his agent. Kimberly collapsed in his arms. She whispered, "He shot me...Agent Dough...tried to kill me."

Teller looked over his shoulder, but he was gone. James Dough had fled the scene.

The news of his son's death sent the kingpin into a tailspin. Scott had to clutch the edge of his desk to keep from toppling over. The death notification came from Mason, who had seen the footage on the local news.

"You sure...it's my son?" Scott asked, his voice cracking between words. "You positive it's Bugsy?"

"It's him, boss. He's gone."

Scott wept into the phone. His hand gripped the device tightly, channeling his grief into the inanimate object. After the disappearance and loss of four children, this was the first time Mason heard this amount of emotion come from Scott. The father of six sounded wounded, a pitiful wail that would haunt Mason for decades.

Mason continued, "I'm going to swing by to get you. I'm sure the coroner will need a positive identification."

Scott could still hear the haunting screams of his wife as he rode to the New York City Coroner's Office. He gave Layla a couple of prescribed sedatives she received when Lucky went missing. And placed her in a dark room under a fluffy comforter, head propped under goose-down pillows.

The attending physician respectfully pulled the white sheet that covered Bugsy's face to his neck. However, Scott pulled it down to his son's waist to see the full scope of his injuries. One shot in his head, two gunshot wounds, and a mangled, circular intrusion was also visible.

"What's this?" Scott asked.

"Your son was impaled by a high-velocity pole that entered the vehicle. It's my understanding that this will be the cause of death."

"Not these muthafuckin' bullets lodged in my son's head and chest?"

"Those were postmortem. You see here," the doctor outlined each bullet hole with his latex-gloved hand. "No blood. It means his heart had already stopped."

Scott nodded.

"Give me a moment alone with my son."

Scott West, a looming figure in most circles, was his most vulnerable as he stood towering above his dead son. The father didn't hide his emotions or fight back the tears that flowed freely. It felt like he'd lost a part of himself, his better half.

"Your brother's gone, Bugsy. He got out," Scott said, giving Bugsy some good news. "And don't worry about your mother. She's going to outlive me for sure."

Finally, Mason had to enter the room and escort his boss out. It was unhealthy for him to wallow there. Back in the SUV, Mason offered up. "I had your attorney, Christopher Azul, call the precinct and get information on the incident. A lot of the report is redacted. It says Bugsy was in a vehicle with an unknown party where a shootout ensued. Bugsy killed an unidentified male person when the vehicle he was riding in lost control, and he was subsequently impaled and killed."

"No names?" Scott asked for clarification.

"None."

"And no mention of the bullets in my son's head and chest?"

"Not one sentence."

Scott nodded. He knew which agency loved a redaction. "This was an assassination," Scott concluded. "My son may have died on the humble, some freak accident. But the feds put the death in motion."

The bullet glided across Kim's head like a train on tracks before entering the headrest. The weapon of mass destruction had opened her forehead a half an inch, blood gushing from the open wound. The gooey liquid forced her eyes closed, and then she felt her body jerk—once, twice. She was shot. The sheer pain from the bullets force and the realization of imminent death, she passed out.

Now, Kimberly was home recuperating. Nineteen stitches held her forehead together, and the vodka tonic kept her sanity intact.

She received a call.

"Hey, how are you feeling?"

"Roderick?"

"Yes. I'm calling to check on you."

"I'll be better once I know Dough is in custody."

"Yeah, I understand. So, we're going to need you to come into the office."

"Why? What's this about?"

"I can't discuss it over the phone."

"I'm on my way."

Kimberly knew some bullshit was about to go down when she walked into Roderick's office. Special Agents Teller, Lopez, Harper, and Deputy Director Edward Christopher Hansen, were there too.

She didn't want to be presumptuous, so she allowed the men to take the lead.

Roderick said, "The incident with you and Agent Dough could be a PR nightmare should it get leaked."

"Of course," she said. "I understand. Nor do I intend not to treat this as I would any of my cases. The bureau represents discretion."

Roderick nodded. "So, we've decided that there really isn't much we can do here."

"Meaning?"

Special Agent Teller spoke. His voice was dismissive, cavalier. "Meaning that James Dough out of the Chicago office was never here. To be frank, he doesn't exist."

Kim pointed toward the hideous sight where she used to have a flawless face. "Tell that to my skull, Teller. Dough tried to kill Bugsy West and me."

"About that," Roderick chimed in. "Why were you with him? Bugsy West. Knowing he's under investigation. We spoke with Agent Dough, and he's alleged you were having an affair with him."

"The same agent that doesn't exist?" she snapped.

"Look, Kim," Roderick snapped back. "You're lucky you still have a job and not collecting unemployment after playing cowboys and Indians on the Westside Highway! An agent is dead! And you were with the perp that murdered him!"

Kimberly glared at Roderick. How easily he had become one of them. Had it not been for her benevolence. And Bugsy West and his family handing Javier Garcia to him on a silver platter, he would just be another inconsequential Black man working in government. The night she had met Bugsy for dinner and was ambushed by his parents, they gave her a proposition. Javier Garcia, the infamous drug kingpin, would be lured onto American soil, and she could make the career-changing arrest.

"The Javier Garcia? In America? What's the catch? He hasn't stepped foot here since the eighties. He knows the consequences."

"Let me worry about the details," Scott had said.

But she had refused the generous offer. Even though she was in the doghouse, Kim wanted to climb the ladder on her own. She wouldn't feel good about taking this handout knowing the backstory. Working with a family as notorious as the Wests' was an even graver reality. Kimberly weighed whether her ethics and morals were worth allowing a man like Garcia to remain free. And then she thought of Roderick. A man she felt embodied what their badges represented and presented the situation to him. He leaped at the opportunity and never circled back to offer her a handout, a layup, or an assist. Nothing.

Roderick threatened, "We could easily charge you with second-degree murder. Give this case to NYPD."

"I can make threats too!" Kim reached into a pocketbook, pulled out a hand recorder, and pressed PLAY. The voices were unmistakable. It was her conversation with Roderick about the West family delivering Javier Garcia to him. She tossed the tape on Roderick's desk. "Keep it. I got copies, which could be catastrophic if leaked to the press. A PR nightmare!"

"Are you threaten—"

"You motherfucking right I am!" she spat. "And note that you can't dangle my job above my head because I quit."

Roderick switched gears and tried a diplomatic approach. "Come on, Kim. You're going too far with this. We can't go after James because the Chicago bureau has stonewalled us. They're emphatic that no one by that name works for the bureau. His identity is highly classified."

Kimberly began removing her Glock and badge. She gently placed them on the desk and sighed. "I can't work for an organization that turned a blind eye to Franklin Garrett, who we all know impregnated Lucky West, uploaded a porn video to the internet, and then murdered her. The same organization that allows a man like James Dough to get away with decades of felonious behavior and who also shot me at point-blank range. I'm better than that. I'm better than you all."

Scott sat across from his longtime friend and said, "I'm relinquishing your duties to me."

Mason was confused. "What does that mean?"

"I'm out," Scott said. "I've got to get my wife out of New York."

Mason understood that Layla was barely eating and had hysterical outbursts and anger-filled episodes that were happening more frequently. Bugsy's death had unraveled her, and Layla found new ways to express her grief.

"Here, take this." He handed Mason a check for twenty-five million. "The money's clean. I pulled this through my children's foundation. I know this isn't how you planned our run to end, but you're a man with integrity and have put in work. Plenty of organizations will be lucky to have you on their team."

Scott extended his hand, and Mason pulled him in for a tight embrace. He released Scott and said, "I'm too old to start at the bottom with some other faction. I just don't have it in me. Working with you, Scott, was a privilege, and seeing how far you took us. But, um, you leave the game, and so do I."

Franklin was relieved when he entered his residence, and Martha and Junior weren't there. He had no idea where they were and honestly didn't care. New York was a clusterfuck; he never thought he'd be so happy in The Windy City. When those bullets flew through his windshield, Franklin thought he was hit. He pulled over and frantically checked his person for holes. Franklin didn't know what had possessed him to jump in his

SUV and lead the procession. He could only deduce that he was showing off in front of James and Terrence. Either that or his thirst to finally see Kimberly dead had overtaken his common sense and riding three deep had emboldened him.

But the wildcard was Bugsy West. His presence with Agent Cooper was inexplicable and totally not in her character. Franklin was completely and utterly baffled. Bugsy unloaded his pistol like a sharpshooter, only missing his target by centimeters, even at that high-speed velocity.

Franklin cracked open his refrigerator, grabbed an Artois beer, untwisted the cap, and took a couple of gulps of the cold brew. "Ahh," he said as the beverage coated his throat.

He was ready to put his feet up and watch a few episodes of The Sopranos. Franklin spun around and couldn't believe his lying eyes. He hadn't even felt a presence or heard a noise; there was no motherfucking clue. It felt like déjà vu.

"What are you doing here?"

"You mean after you left me to die on that highway?"

Franklin snorted. "You're a grown man, James. And I'm not my brother's keeper."

"I think Terrence got that memo a day late."

Franklin had gotten the update that Terrence was murdered when the news panned to an unidentified male slumped in the front seat of his vehicle, and he wasn't about to shed a tear. He wasn't broken up about it at all.

Franklin snapped, "What do you want? Why are you here! And how did you get in?"

"I got in this time undetected because your need to expose me exposed that I had missed something when I previously deactivated your alarm," James began. "I'm here to kill you. And what I want is your life. There, all questions answered."

Franklin couldn't glean if this was Dough's attempt at humor. He was sleep deprived and thought the days of him clashing with James were behind them. He felt they bonded over a common enemy. Franklin asked, "Are you serious?"

Bak!

Bullet lodged in Franklin's forehead. His beer crashed to the ground.

Bak! Bak!

Two bullets in his chest cavity before the body dropped.

"Oh my god! Franklin!" Martha yelped.

Bak!

Bak! Bak!

In a robotic movement, James repeated.

Bak!

Bak! Bak!

It was Dough's kill signature.

Mother and son would join Franklin. It wasn't what Dough wanted, but what did he expect?

The irony was that the three individuals who participated in the murder of Lucky West, who stared uncaringly as her body stiffened on the hard tile flooring, would all meet the same fate.

James tucked his smoking pistol into his waist. He leaned over and placed his fingers on Franklin's neck. One couldn't be too careful after the Kimberly fiasco.

He was dead.

Special Agent James Dough bent down and checked Junior's pulse. Also, dead.

He towered over Martha and repeated the step. But before he stood, he saw the pristine, pink diamond earrings sparkling and an equally exquisite Chopard watch. It read: *To baby girl, my luck.*

James removed the watch and flawless diamonds and placed them in his pocket.

"My wife will love these," he said and bounced.

"Wait here," Meyer told Riley. If I don't come right back, if shit gets thick, don't wait for me. I want you to drive out west just as planned and never look back."

"Why are you doing this?" she asked. "We should just go."

"I can't. She's my sister," was his response.

Meyer walked toward all the action. Several blue and whites had Franklin Garrett's block roped off and weren't allowing any cars to drive through. It didn't stop the whole neighborhood from coming out to get an up close and personal look at the bodies being wheeled out in body bags.

Meyer saddled up to a few people, mainly an older woman, and asked, "What's going on?"

The older woman turned to look at the stranger, sizing him up.

"Did you know the family?" she asked suspiciously.

"His son plays with mine." Meyer had thought quickly.

Startling Meyer, she gave him a quick embrace. "I hate to tell you this, but someone came in and murdered the whole family. Franklin Junior was killed."

"No way?" Meyer didn't have to feign shock. He truly was. He also wondered if this was his father and brother's handiwork. It had to be. But he wanted more clarification. "Are you sure that Franklin Garrett is dead too? The father?"

"Yes. They wheeled him out first. I know it's hard for you to accept, but the whole family is dead."

EPILOGUE

James and his wife had just closed on a Montecito, California mansion, and he couldn't wait to get to know his neighbors. Now on the west coast, he wanted to mingle with A-list celebrities such as Ellen, Oprah, Harry, and Meghan—people who went by one name. Speaking of names, his current was Dwayne.

The lavish property, the sprawling estate, was his retirement home. He was finally done with the bureau. And the warm weather had thawed his icy veins. Dwayne was a new man, reformed.

He fielded calls all day with his cell phone pressed tightly to his ear. He had furniture deliveries, an appointment with an interior designer, and his new Lamborghini would be delivered shortly.

Dwayne wore an Adidas tracksuit with matching sneakers, his hair was newly dyed, and he felt half his age.

His line beeped.

"Hold on, let me get that." Dwayne was speaking with his nephew, Curtis, bragging about his home when he clicked over.

"Is this Dwayne Dough?"

"It is."

"This is Sergeant Brown from the North Division precinct of the Long Beach Police. I'm sorry to make this notification over the phone, but, sir, it's about your wife."

Dough began to perspire. "My wife? What's happened? Is she okay?"

"No, sir. I'm sorry she's not. Apparently, there was an incident this morning. Witnesses said a gunman attempted to rob her of her diamond earrings and a costly watch, and she refused to give them up. She was shot once in the chest, and I'm sorry she didn't make it."

Dough's left arm stiffened as he staggard forward. He dropped the phone and clutched his chest gasping for air. He took a couple steps on wobbly knees, crashed into his shallow pool, and died from a heart attack.

Odell, Donovan, Jayson, George, Malcolm, Lamont, James, Dwayne Dough, and his wife expired on February 8th.

The same day as Lucky Luciana West.

Bugsy's death didn't give Maxine the great joy she assumed it would. Instead, she was hit with tremendous sorrow when she heard the news. When she was Max, she had taken out a five-million-dollar insurance policy on him. The plan paid out double indemnity should Bugsy die in an accident. His unfortunate accident had ten million dollars attached, and the check was payable in her name. Wrestling over what she now considered blood money, she waited months before she contacted the insurance company to collect.

In different denominations, Maxine donated the whole sum to several nonprofit organizations supporting Black and Brown children and the homeless community.

Maxine would become one of the most prominent Black activists her community had embraced in half a century. The latter part of her life was dedicated to human and civil rights, working tirelessly to speak for the voiceless. Her husband, Gregory, the Mayor of New York, was running for governor. And together, they set out to make a real change by lobbying politicians.

Their passion project was reparations.

Kimberly Cooper sat on a bench inside a mausoleum that housed a man she wished she had more time with. Each year, on the day of his passing, the former agent would come and place flowers in his urn. The well-maintained resting place didn't need her flowers. But she brought them anyway out of respect for a man that entered her vehicle and exchanged his life for hers.

Unmarried and childless, Kimberly didn't know what pulled her to Bugsy each year. He was the antithesis of what she thought a good man should be. However, she would talk to him for hours about her life goals, her small cupcake business, and her new puppy she named Noodles.

She didn't miss her former life.

Three dear friends sat in the cozy living room in Miami, Florida, watching *The American Music Awards*. It was late for them, but this was a special event.

Scott and Mason drank nonalcoholic beers while Layla had a glass of champagne. In a few moments, the biggest Chicano star since *Selena* was about to hit the stage. There was a grand announcement by an A-list celebrity before the petite woman and her band took over the stage with her crossover hit, *More Love*.

Her shiny locks cascaded down her back in a loose ponytail, and gold leaf eyeshadow outlined her slanted eyes. A cream-colored faux fur hung off her shoulders, fitted sequin leggings, and six-inch custom-heeled cowboy boots. The international superstar moved effortlessly to the beat as she belted out her number-one hit. Lucchese's moniker was her childhood nickname by her mother, *Lulu*. She was one of the rare celebrities that could shoot to stardom with one name. The African American and Méxican communities fully embraced the Afro-Latina, both claiming her as their own.

"Scott, who does she look like?" Layla asked.

Scott took a long moment to respond. He showed signs of dementia, so Layla and Mason usually helped him when he struggled with recall. However, Scott said, "That's Lucky. That's my baby girl."

Layla rolled her eyes. "She looks like me, Scott!"

Mason added, "That's your granddaughter, Lucchese, Scott. Remember? She came last summer and stayed with y'all?"

Scott stared at the television but didn't respond.

The camera panned to the proud faces of Angel and Marbella Morales, grins on their faces as they mouthed the words to Lulu's song.

As Layla aged, it was regrettable that she and Scott had made questionable choices while raising their children. Grooming Bugsy, Meyer, and Lucky to get into the drug game when there was another way. Angel did it. He was a former cartel boss, yet his four children are alive and thriving in legitimate professions, with his youngest a superstar.

Layla tried not to dwell on such things, but sometimes, those thoughts were hard to push away in quiet moments.

The whereabouts of Lucchese's mother, Lucky, is still unknown. After seven years, Scott and Layla legally declared their daughter dead. And had a small memorial in her honor. Their last surviving child, Meyer, was presumed alive. On the tenth anniversary of his departure, a biography was delivered to them. The title, *The Life & Times of Meyer Lansky*.

Layla hadn't seen her favorite son in twenty-two years. She knew he was still surviving and would return to her one day. To bide her time over the years, Layla had put a few hits out on Maxine after she had resurfaced. Each time, Scott thwarted his wife's efforts.

"Stop this shit!" Scott barked. "She's too valuable to our community!"

And Layla finally got it. Maxine was. When Layla sees her former nemesis on television, she only feels respect for who she's become. And has fond memories of a small window of time when they were once friends.

If Meyer had to sum up how he could stay away from his family for decades, he would truthfully say he handled it one day at a time. Throughout the years, he and Riley clung to each other, and her love helped ease his pain on many occasions. A father of four, he owed his and his wife's freedom to a man he once despised.

Successfully being on the run wasn't an easy feat. And when Special Agent James Dough convinced the Federal Bureau of Investigations to add Riley to their *Ten Most Wanted* list, the heat was turned up. Riley Baker was touted as a notorious drug queenpin who had orchestrated several murders, distributed tons of kilos, and was responsible for the death of FBI Agent Terrence Barnes. A million-dollar reward, bounty, was on her head, and folks were looking to collect.

Riley did all she could to camouflage herself. She lightened her hair, cut it, added length, shaved it off—the whole gamut. But that heat was always around the corner, and the now expanding family would continually flee, narrowly escaping capture. The running was taking a toll on the lovebirds, with Riley threatening to turn herself in and be done with the chase.

The pursuit was so fierce that Meyer couldn't take the chance of going to any of the locations his father had outlined with the money drops. It was too risky.

As the money dwindled, the couple found themselves in México. Meyer said it was unintentional, but subconsciously he was led to him. Angel Morales took his enemy under his protection. The men kept that secret from Scott and Layla for nearly thirty years. It was Angel who would tell Meyer about his brother's demise. Meyer openly wept at the saddening news.

The town of Culiacán, México, was where Angel gifted Meyer and Riley a beautiful home on the coastline. They could hear the clear blue ocean crashing against the shore. The sun rises and sets would restore Meyer, who felt broken, and would be the medicine his family needed as his children's toes made imprints on the wet sand.

Culiacán rallied around the strangers under the protection of a man they revered. The Juárez cartel employed more than half the town. No one in Culiacán spoke to the policía unless that person worked for Louis Morales, head of the Juárez cartel.

In México, Meyer was able to watch his niece, Lucky's child, grow into a talented, beautiful woman. Lulu was fully aware of who her family was and understood that she could never risk letting her grandparents know the whereabouts of Uncle Meyer. Meyer would sit in the background while Lulu Facetimed with his parents. He got to hear his parents' voices, get updates on their slow-paced lives, and chuckle at his mother's fowl mouth.

On the 25th anniversary of his departure, Angel notified him that Scott wasn't doing so well. His parents were worth the risk. Angel smuggled Meyer back into America and was delivered to their front door in a refrigerator delivery from Home Depot.

Layla, still spunky as ever, cursed the deliverymen out.

"I said I didn't order no muthafuckin' refrigerator!" she spat.

"Ma'am, I'm sure you're going to want *this* refrigerator."

When the man spoke, he nodded toward the box when he said, *this*. Layla peeped that and replied, "Hold on a minute."

She walked to her study and retrieved her 9mm. With her pistol firmly behind her back, she allowed the men in, and she and Scott received the best shock of their lives.

That was nine years ago. Meyer's appearance was like soup for Scott's soul because the old man held on and was still holding on. When lucid, he'd repeat his lifelong mantra, "It's over when I say it is. I can only die once, and it will be on my terms."

Made in United States
Orlando, FL
19 April 2023

32279235R00231